BOOK OF SCANDAL

SCANDAL

BOOK OF SCANDAL- THE RAMSEY ELDERS
ISBN: 9780615358383

Copyright © 2010 by AlTonya Washington

This is a work of fiction. Characters, names, incidents, organizations and dialogue in this novel are either products of the author's imagination or are used fictitiously.

To the Ramsey readers who've been there since the beginning and the new readers I hear from every day. This is how it all began. Enjoy...

Book of Scandal

~FIRST PROLOGUE~

Seattle, Washington 1958...

"Are there any black people out here, Pop?" Westin Ramsey realized he had been paying relatively little attention during the drive he and his father made from their hotel to the vast expanse of land he now stared at past the windshield.

Quentin Ramsey's contagious laughter bellowed as he stepped from the dark blue Ford Coupe.

Westin shut down the ignition and Little Richard's *Good Golly Miss Molly* silenced in mid-chord. West left the car and then sprinted to catch up with his dad.

"Sure there are," Quentin pulled his eldest son into a hug before spreading a hand out before them. "But the fewer the better- for now anyway," his glinting dark stare glinted anew in the wake of hope.

Book of Scandal

"It'll give us the chance to make a statement and stand out while we're making it."

"But why Seattle, Pop?" Westin stroked his square jaw while skepticism; instead of hope filled his dark eyes.

"Because it's not Savannah. It's far away from Savannah."

Westin let his father walk on ahead before catching up and blocking his path. "Tell me what's wrong, Pop."

Quent stared past his son's broad shoulders to the flat never-ending scope of land which would mark Ramsey Industries' future offices.

"I want you to carry us to that next level, West." Quent clapped the young man's shoulder as they fell in step again. "We're doing fine now but I want us to be more- a force. Not just in Georgia but all over- among black names *and* white." He gave a squeeze to the back of Westin's neck. "You're twenty-four now and soon it'll be time for you to take over completely."

Westin winced. The particular train of conversation never failed to unsettle him. "Pop-"

"It'll be time for you to implement whatever vision you see for Ramsey." Quentin went on before some unreadable emotion shadowed his caramel-toned face. "I apologize son for not doing more to push the company along."

Speechless then, Westin could only watch his father with a mix of incredulous disbelief and awe. "Poppa where would you like me to start? Pushing the company along? Have you forgotten what we are in the steel business? Transportation? What about putting all those black lawyers to work in the legal division?" West laughed shortly while

Book of Scandal

pushing a hand across the natural close cut waves covering his head. "Pop if that's what you call not doing enough to push the company along, then I'll have to work from my grave to surpass you."

Quent's laughter mingled with his son's. "Guess I have done *some* good. The legal division...remember the jaws that dropped over that?"

"You bet I do." West snapped his fingers. "What about the carpentry and remodeling divisions- prime work we've done on homes for black *and* white residents."

"You really know how to make an old man feel proud of himself, boy."

Westin squeezed his father's arm to keep him from walking on. "I don't ever want you to put down where you've taken us, Pop."

"I feel good knowing you'll be here to run things." Quent pulled Westin into a hug. "Then there's Damon once he's old enough."

Westin had to laugh when he and his father broke the hug. "Damon, Pop? The kid's only fourteen and no way is he gonna get his chance before Marc and Houston demand theirs."

"Marcus and Houston will never run Ramsey."

Westin would have laughed again. He dared not upon seeing the dead seriousness shadowing Quentin's face.

"Never." Quentin stressed. "I expect you to uphold that, West."

"Pop...why, Pop?"

"Corrupt." Quentin answered without hesitation in reference to his second and third oldest sons. "Both rotten to the core and I've always known it." He massaged hand

Book of Scandal

over fist and grimaced. "They'll ruin this family one day if I don't make plans to unsettle things a bit."

"Pop?"

Quentin shook his head and began to walk again. "Steel, transportation, carpentry... they're key producing ends for Ramsey but in the future it'll be about brains and power and who's got the smarts to organize and streamline those key producing ends." Pushing hands into the side pockets of his pin-striped trousers, Quentin inhaled the crisp air.

"Black folks have a firm handle on the manual portion of things but we need a mastery of the intellectual side as well." The shadowed look returned to Quent's handsome face. "Your younger brothers know this. They know it all too well. They're two of the smartest men I've ever met. They're also two of the most evil."

"Pop-" West was again interrupted by his father and was starting to feel like a scratched 45 by then.

Quentin however had raised his hand for silence. "They're my sons and I know. A father knows. There's something... dead inside Marcus. It's been there from the time he learned to reason..." Again, Quent shook his head as though regretting such ideas could fester about his own child. "Promise me West; promise to bring your mother, sisters and Damon out here."

"And Houston, Poppa?"

"Lost." Quentin used a handkerchief to mop his brow. "He's weak. Weak enough to be led right along behind Marc."

Book of Scandal

Westin's smile took effort, but he managed one. "Pop, do you hear yourself? You're talkin' about boys-your own sons like they're men already."

"I've got plans for Ramsey, boy." Quent began walking again. "I don't just want to earn money; I want to grow it- to grow wealth, power, privilege, respect..."

"But we've got all that, Pop."

"Among *our* people- yes. I want more." He slid a smug look toward his son. "I want us known- on grand scale and for that to happen it'll take men with values, morals and the ability to stand up under the pressures that'll surely rain down." Quentin extended a hand. "You up to the task, boy?"

Westin's grin illuminated his dark handsome face. He nodded and accepted the hand his father offered before they fell into another hug.

R

~SECOND PROLOGUE~

Savannah, Georgia 1959...

She'd known it was wrong. The first time she stayed she'd known it was wrong. She worked for them- that was as far as it should have gone. It was the promise of all those fine things- the fine dresses. The latest styles from all over the country, all over the world... The Ramsey girls had everything they could possibly want and all they had to do was be born into it.

Others weren't so lucky though. The other maids always talked about it. They'd all have to marry well in order to enjoy half the spoils they'd so far only had the privilege of hanging up or cleaning.

It hadn't taken much for him to lure her. He was after all one of the dreamiest things she'd ever seen. Even at age eleven when he first showed an interest... and he

Book of Scandal

was so persuasive. It started *innocently* enough- her lips were bruised but still she managed a smile over the word. The rubbing across barely there breasts and below... he said it'd prepare her. God if only she'd known what he was preparing her for. Marrying well to rescue her parents from their lives of never-ending work wasn't worth this. Nothing was worth this.

She wouldn't stop running. Even when she made it back to the grand house on the hill. What would she tell her parents? *Would* she tell her parents? They'd surely notice the blood running down her leg in a continuous stream. Her mother would definitely recognize the signs of what she'd been doing. Then what? It would be her word against his. Against his, her word would count for nothing.

Far away from the grand house on the hill, a quaint cottage stood. From the outside, the construction was an appealing oasis amidst the beautiful wooded area that circumferenced the estate. Inside, the cottage was stocked with every necessity making it an exquisite retreat for lovers... and others.

The fireplace blaze burned more ferociously than it should have. The bloody sheets had to be gotten rid of though. He'd wait for the fire to die before he left.

Walking out to the porch, he leaned against one of the banisters aligning the steps leading to the porch. Marcus Ramsey's satisfied smile deepened as he buttoned his shirt.

R

PART ONE
1960-1964

R

~CHAPTER ONE~
Savannah, Georgia~ Summer 1960...

Thirteen year old Carmen Ramsey gave a frustrated tug at the hem of the flowing chiffon skirt of her dress. Jackie Wilson's *"Doggin Around"* had fast become one of her favorites when it was released earlier that summer, but even the song's affective rhythms weren't inducing a positive affect on her mood. If the annual Ramsey cotillion wasn't over soon she truly believed she'd scream.

While her sister Georgia thrived on such festivities, Carmen felt like running for shelter whenever the mention of one was in the air.

Drawing a hand through her wind tangled Shirley Temples; she cast a tired look towards the imposing white brick house in the distance. For a moment, she revered the construction which had been in her family since slavery.

Book of Scandal

She then headed in the opposite direction toward the lush fields where the horses grazed.

Carmen smirked. Horses. What a life her family led. So many people envied what they had- that a black family could boast such trappings.

She shivered delightfully at her quiet use of the word she'd just come across while reading a news article the week before. It was such a fitting word. All the beauty and elegance had certainly trapped her family- some of them more horrifically than others.

Wild laughter caught her ears when she neared one of the stables. Her thoughts on family and trappings cleared as curiosity set in. On softer steps, she ventured nearer towards the sturdy structure.

The laughter was sparse, but never lost its wild intensity. Carmen cast a quick look across her shoulder. Satisfied that she was alone, she took a closer look and gasped at what she saw.

Marcus Ramsey smiled his approval and settled back more comfortably against the tufts of hay lining the stall. To the casual onlooker it would have appeared that he was simply relaxing. But nothing was ever quite what it appeared where Marc was concerned. He smirked and looked down at the young woman draped across his lap. Closing his eyes, he enjoyed her dazzling oral treat and lost his hand in her hair.

He squeezed his fingers in her thick tresses when she would have pulled back for air.

"Stay on it," his voice was soft yet the intent was crude.

Book of Scandal

Rosselle Simon didn't seem to mind and whispered her own sultry taunts while following Marc's orders. Clearly, the couple was involved in the act and; for a time, oblivious to all else. That is, until Marc opened his eyes and looked directly at his younger sister.

Carmen blinked, wanting to look away but unable to. Running was out of the question as well for she couldn't move. Their gazes held. Then, in a purely lurid manner, Marc licked his lips and beckoned her forward with a wave.

Heart lurching to her chest, Carmen jerked away from the stable opening and raced away.

Marcus remained calmed. Instead of panic, Carmen's discovery had sent a rush of sensation through him. The feeling was so intense that he released his need. Rosselle of course took full credit for the reaction even when Marc pushed her aside.

"Run along now before Daniel and Martha start to worry."

"Bastard," Rosselle hissed, lying half naked amidst the hay. Her mouth glistened with tell-tale moisture.

Marc grinned and smoothly fixed his clothes. Thankfully, Rosselle made quick work of leaving and; alone, Marc let his thoughts drift back to his sister watching as he was pleasured.

Carmen was running like the devil was at her back. The chiffon skirts of her dress rivaled the rustling sound the leaves made as she raced back toward the party.

'The devil' however was more of a figurative term just then. After all, she'd bet her brother was still on his

Book of Scandal

back and being treated by the Simon spinster she'd caught him with.

In truth, 'the devil' in that instance referred to the surge of fear Marcus instilled whenever he looked her way. When she saw him moments ago, that fear had been amplified. Carmen was so muddled in her thoughts that she screamed when her running brought her up against a warm, solid wall of flesh.

Jasper Stone smiled, though concern was etched in his deep brown eyes.

"Hey? Carmen? Carmen?" He took her shoulders in a gentle hold noticing the terror on her face when they'd collided. "It's Jasper, you're okay..."

Melting then, Carmen lay against him and took time to catch her breath.

Jasper was bending to look directly into her face. "What is it? What's wrong?"

The soft coaxing tone of his voice only made her shiver more deeply. Her fingers curled like talons into his black dress shirt and she shook her head.

"Alright then, let's get you home."

"No!" She shivered then as though the idea of "home" repulsed her. "Stay with me? Stay with me here?" Without a care for her dress, she sat in the grassy clearing.

As it was a mild Savannah afternoon and full of festivity, Jasper didn't see the harm in spending a few minutes with the youngest Ramsey daughter. It was no surprise though that those 'few minutes' stirred needs that were best left alone.

Carmen Moiselle Ramsey was only thirteen- young but already portioned into the stunning woman she would

Book of Scandal

become. The face of a heart stopping beauty was developing daily. Her soft easy manner mirrored the look in her alluring dark stare. Scores of young suitors had already found their way to her door.

"Do you feel like talkin', Carm?" Jasper asked when the silence sent his thoughts too far in the wrong direction.

"You deserve better that than Ross Simon."

Clearly stunned, Jasper blinked owlishly at Carmen's hissed advice. "Why?" Was all he'd dare ask.

"You're so handsome and sweet. You really care about what a girl says when she opens her mouth- not just whether her mouth could adequately accommodate your cock."

Of course he cared about what a girl had to say. Just then however, Carmen's attempt at flattery simply had him imagining things involving her that he could be killed for.

"We need to head back." He stood and expelled a sigh of relief when she followed suit.

Carmen took Jasper's arm, but squeezed in a warning manner before he could take a step.

"Watch my brother. Don't ever trust him."

Jasper watched her walk on ahead. He didn't need her to clarify which brother for he knew without a doubt that it was Marcus Ramsey.

***

"Thank you, Dora." Marcella Ramsey smiled up at the lovely dark woman who'd placed a glass of iced tea to the woven end table. The cool observation returned to her slate gray stare when the young maid walked off. "Has

Book of Scandal

Westin done anything?" She asked, turning back to watch Sybil Deas.

"Oh no, no Marcella- nothing like that." The woman shook her head. "Westin is a wonderful boy- handsome, smart, mannerly- did I say how handsome he is?"

Laughter resonated between the two friends. It wasn't long though, before concern returned to dull the usual sparkle in Sybil's light hazel eyes.

"The kids are in their twenties Marcy," Sybil began to wring her lace-gloved hands. "Westin's yet to propose and-" she glanced across her shoulder, "and I'm certain the two of them are having relations- sexual relations. Now, Elton may be too nervous to say anything but that's not the case between us, is it?" Sybil straightened a bit while questioning her old friend.

Marcella appeared skeptical. "I'm sure if Elton felt concern he would've said something to Quent by now- they've been friends as long as we have."

"Yes, but Quentin *is* Elton's boss." Sybil cleared her throat. "There's only so much he'd say about something like that and you know how men can be. But you and I-" She reached for her tea glass and tilted it toward Marcella. "We go way back and I don't feel a bit shy about bringing this up. I have to look out for my daughter's future. Having your own daughters, I'm sure you can understand that." Losing her taste for the tea, Sybil set aside the glass and fisted her hands in her lap. "I don't want Bris giving up her goodies with no commitments."

Marcella bristled beneath the fabric of her cream linen dress. She felt no anger towards her friend's

Book of Scandal

perceptions however. Eyes crinkling when she smiled, Marcella leaned over to pat Sybil's clenched hands. "I understand where you're coming from girl, but... from what I've been told by my son, it's Briselle who's shunning commitment in return for her... goodies."

Sybil gasped and then looked around quickly to see whether anyone strolling the wide back porch had heard her outburst. "What are you saying?"

"Sweetie Westin's been proposing for years only to have Briselle turn him down every time."

Stunned, Sybil Deas could only stare open-mouthed at her dearest friend.

At that moment, Briselle Deas was in fact turning down another proposal from her boyfriend of nine years. Lying upon a sea of hay, she stared at the gleaming diamond positioned inside its black velvet box.

"Westin why-"

"Just stop, Bri. Stop. You know what this is and you damn well know why."

Briselle rolled her eyes and tried to sit up. Westin stopped her by smothering her slight form with his lanky, muscular one.

"This isn't going to happen."

She spoke in that soft, breathy tone that never failed to arouse him. Whatever else she was preparing to say was effectively silenced when he thrust his tongue inside her mouth.

Of course, Bri couldn't resist. She'd never been able to resist him and snuggled deeper into their embrace. Boldly, she thrust her tongue eagerly against his. A delicious interlude surfaced and; in seconds, the bodice of

Book of Scandal

her demure white frock was open and his handsome dark face was nestled between her small, full breasts.

Keeping one hand secure about Briselle's wrists, Westin feasted on her firming nipples until he heard her pleading for him to do more. Stopping then, he raised his head.

"Do you really think I'd ever let you go, Bri?"

"Why?" She stiffened and the affect was mirrored on her delicate features. "Why West? Because I'll lift my skirt and drop my panties for you anytime you ask? You could get any girl at this cotillion to do the same."

"But do you really believe I could stand you not being mine?" Softly enraged then, his sleek brows drew close. "Do you think I could function knowing someone else could have you?"

She looked away then as tears pooled her eyes. Covering her face, she quietly willed them away.

"Baby…" West felt on the verge of tears himself.

"Don't," she shook her head and moved to pull her dress together. "We've been going steady nine years West and I've lost two babies already."

"Bri-"

"No. Please West. I've lost *two*." She let him see her wet face. "What does that mean?"

He cupped her chin. "It means we keep trying."

She wrenched her chin from his fingers. "We aren't even married. Now, maybe that's why or maybe it's because it'll never be meant for us to have a child. I can't let you-"

"What? Love you. Love *only* you?"

She sucked her teeth. "You know what I'm saying."

"And what *I'm* saying is I love you and that means more to me than anything- *anything* Bri." He kissed fresh tears from her eyes and tugged her into a crushing embrace.

***

"Daniel!" Quentin Ramsey's voice bellowed above the mingled conversation and laughter energizing the party. He extended hands toward local carpenter Daniel Simon and his wife Martha.

The two men had maintained an easy relationship over the years despite the fact that Daniel had declined Quentin's numerous requests that he dissolve his successful carpentry business and come head his own team at Ramsey.

"Glad you're here and with all these lovelies." Quent teased the dark towering man and then nodded towards Martha and the couple's four daughters.

"Thanks so much for inviting us, Quentin." Martha Simon's honey gaze rivaled the tone of her skin for radiance as she took in the scope of the event and the guests dressed in their finest attire.

Quentin shrugged. "I'll keep trying to win y'all over anyway I can 'til Dan comes to work for Ramsey."

"Precisely why I'll never come over," Daniel's words always carried on a chuckle. "I'd be a fool to give up this kind of bribery!"

As the trio laughed merrily, Marcus Ramsey strolled up to greet his father's guests and their daughters. The girls stood behind their parents and smiled graciously. Like the dutiful and respectful son, Marc greeted the Simons- with special charming attention reserved for the daughters.

Book of Scandal

The three eldest made no secret of their soft spots for the Ramsey's dashing, second eldest son. Rosselle Simon in particular braced back her shoulders and held her head a smidge higher in expectation of a special greeting from Marc. The expectancy in her wide browns dimmed noticeably when he offered no such sweetness in light of the intimacies they'd just shared. Her mood quickly improved though when he spared her a sly wink.

Surprisingly, no one noticed Marc's expression sharpen with intense interest when his dark gaze settled on the caramel-toned beauty that stood a foot shorter than her robust sisters. Marcus moved on before anyone noticed the look he spent on eighteen year old Josephine Simon. Josephine certainly didn't notice, for she'd kept her eyes downcast when the gorgeous Ramsey approached.

***

Boisterous laughter filled the gazebo. The five young women there enjoyed delicious cool cider, the delights of the day and the bawdy yet amusing comments of their often times naughty girlfriend.

Georgia Ramsey made the act of tucking a lock of wavy hair behind an ear; the most seductively glamorous move one could muster without breaking a sweat. Georgia's four friends envied and loved her as much as they feared and disliked her. The girl's allure was intriguing to say the least. She could cut down a friend and build them up in one breath.

It was a difficult thing for one to tell whether Georgia Ramsey was being honest or cruel when she struck out with her words. To Georgia, honesty and cruelty were

Book of Scandal

one in the same as people could rarely accept the truth when it was spoke in reference to them.

"You better keep it down before our mother's get a whiff of what we're discussing." Priscilla Dartmouth scolded her friend.

"Fuck it; they know what we talk about. They talk about it themselves." Georgia inspected her fresh manicure. "My Mama knew the very day I gave it up to Felix. She said I was walkin' different."

The laughter rose to a voluminous roar.

"But that's not so bad Georgia," Greta Weeks was saying before the laughter totally faded. "You and Felix been together for years. Hell, it's almost like you're sleepin' with your husband."

"*Almost*," Georgia appeared to shudder. "And *almost* is all it'll ever be unless that nigga got some money and prospects in his future."

"Well Mr. Q would see to that, right?" Melody Brown asked in reference to Quentin Ramsey.

"I'd hope so," Georgia came down a little. "Felix ain't interested in 'hand me down success'- that's what he calls it. Talkin' 'bout he's tryin' to make it on his own."

"Well that's commendable girl." Denise Orey raved.

Georgia sucked her teeth and focused on her other manicured hand. "Probably," she sighed, "but that still leaves him bein' a broke nigga and I need a man who'll keep me livin' like my daddy meant for me to."

"Well why are you with Felix, then?" Priscilla smoothed a hand across her chignon, hoping to downplay her interest in the matter. "I mean, I know tons of girls who'd love a chance with his fine ass."

"I'm with him because his *fine ass* is *damn good* in bed." Georgia's smile was cool and deadly while adding a sharper loveliness to her pecan brown face. "In light of that, I'll just be keeping him for a while."

The boisterous laughter rose once more.

***

Fifteen year old Catrina Jeffries forgot her station for a moment and indulged in a few moments of fantasizing. She tapped her sneaker shod foot to the Isley Brother's *"Shout"* and imagined she was one of the beautiful girls floating about the grounds of the Ramsey estate in a heart stopping dress of silk and chiffon.

One day, she promised herself. One day she'd be president of Jeffries Catering. By then, her parent's business would have branched out to include conferences and banquets in addition to birthday parties and cotillions. She'd see to it. Then, she'd waltz into a gathering like this- a self made woman. Everyone would whisper that she was the smart, lovely president of the most successful catering company in the whole state.

"Catrina Marie! That tub ain't gone empty itself!"

"'Kay Mama!" Catrina rolled her eyes. Just then, she'd have to accept her current post as fat dumper. She glared distastefully at the vat of fish grease she'd been sent to dispose of.

Casting off her images of grandeur, Catrina took a moment to gather stray tendrils that had fallen loose of her ponytail. She whipped the heavy tresses into a fresh knot and was checking the tightness of her rubber band when she turned to find herself staring at another fantasy.

Book of Scandal

    She studied the boy who studied her. Tall; with deep set eyes dark as night, he was a thing to be swooned over. Catrina found herself celebrating her luck at viewing such a beautiful thing. At the same time she cursed her luck for viewing such a beautiful thing while he viewed her with splatters of fish and chicken fat on her faded pedal pushers and the light blue T-shirt graced with the name JEFFERIES CATERERS in black velvet letters.

    "Catrina Marie! Don't make me come back there, girl! Get them vats emptied and get back up here!"

    Lashes fluttering, Catrina willed her beloved mother be stricken with a momentary bout of laryngitis.

    "Comin' Mama!" She started to turn when she heard him ask if she needed help.

    "Thank you, but no." Catrina celebrated the fact that her voice hadn't deserted her.

    Damon Ramsey nodded and silently ordered himself to stop gawking at the beauty that'd rendered him immobile.

R
~CHAPTER TWO~

"Girl if you don't get in there! After all the money I spent getting' that hair tamed."

Daphne Monfrey glared at the big house beyond the passenger window of the Chevy. "Do I have to go all the way inside, Mama?" She whined.

"Dammit girl," Babydoll Monfrey turned her provocative, full-figured frame on the car seat and pointed a finger at her daughter. "Get on in there. I'll be back for you in an hour or two."

Daphne turned on the seat as well. "Why can't you come with me?"

"You know why." It was Babydoll's turn to glare at the big house in the distance. "Marcella have a fit if she see me steppin' up on her property."

"But I don't know anybody here."

"You work it right, you will."

"Ma-"

Book of Scandal

"Now girl, don't fuss with me. I gotta job."
Babydoll studied her flawless looks through the car's side
mirror. "It'll take 'bout an hour and a half, then I'll be back.
You just tell any boys who come sniffin' 'round who your
Mama is and see what happens." She slanted her daughter a
wink and then waved her out of the car.

Daphne watched her mother speed off with a cloud
of dust blanketing the battered white Chevy. She didn't
need further clarification on the woman's last bit of advice.

At fourteen, she'd already received quite an
education on what being Babydoll Monfrey's daughter
meant. As the local madam, Babydoll had earned an image
not only for herself but for her daughter as well.

Daphne pressed her lips together and resignedly
headed towards the music and laughter. How quickly three
years could fly by, she thought. At the tender age of eleven
she'd discovered exactly what her mother did for a living.
The discovery both sickened and excited her. Of course, the
excitement wore off long before the sickness. The sickness
was still there- festering like an ulcer in her stomach.

The sickness had no chance of abating either once
Daphne realized that her own reputation entwined with her
mother's. Boys flocked her way now having been schooled
by fathers, uncles and older brothers on the delights waiting
between Babydoll Monfrey's sheets. They now expected
the same treats from her daughter.

It didn't help a bit that Daphne stood out as she did.
No playing the role of wallflower for her. She'd once
celebrated her almost white skin and curly blondish brown
ringlets. She loved looking different and how being half-
white made her a girl's envy and a boy's dream.

Book of Scandal

Though it wasn't long before her pride dulled, when she understood *why* the boys dreamed of her. It didn't take long for that pride to dull into shame when she realized one of her mother's white johns had left more than a tip on the nightstand when he slinked from Babydoll's one evening.

Breathing deeply, Daphne discovered her memories had outlasted the trip to the Ramsey gate. She hoped to take a quick walk through the sea of guests and find a quiet hole to hide in until her mother's return.

***

"What's she doin' here Joe?"

"I can't rule over what the woman does, Harry."

"Ha! You was rulin' over it quite nice when you had her in my bed!"

"Dammit Harry-" Joe Cade pulled his wife aside and bore down on her with rage filling his brown eyes. "Don't you do this here."

"Don't *I* do this here?! You son of a bitch. You got your slut here at the Ramsey's and you're tellin' *me* not to do this here?" Harriet Cade spared a moment to cast a pointed look towards a nosy onlooker before glaring back up at her husband.

Felix Cade's intense stare caught on a wince as the argument between his folks gained steam. Conversation, laughter and even the sounds of James Brown's *"That Dood It"* was no match for their raised voices. It was to be expected of course. His parents had been at each other's throats for as long as he'd understood what the phrase meant.

Book of Scandal

Still, he would have been far happier had the older Cades managed to keep things friendly for the Ramsey event. He managed a smirk while tugging at the cuff of his cream shirt. The last thing he needed was for Georgia to start ranting because his parents couldn't act like decent black folk instead of ignorant niggas when they were on her parent's property.

Thoughts of his outspoken girlfriend mellowed only to make room for a new wave of agitation. Jasper Stone was headed his way.

"Where's your Ma at?" Felix asked once he'd shaken hands with his half brother.

"Did she say something?" Jasper was at once on alert. Belleina Stone had never made a secret of how much she wanted Joe Cade to leave his wife.

"Nah, nah she hasn't," Felix winced again. "But my Mama knows she's here, so just keep an eye out, alright? Make sure they don't get too close."

Jasper was already nodding.

"So where're *you* comin' from?" Felix smiled then and studied his brother more closely.

"Lookin' for Rosselle."

Felix's heavy brows rose. "Watch out for that one, man."

"What's that mean?" Jasper's tone was mildly defensive.

Felix only shrugged. "Just don't get in over your head. Sorry man," he patted Jasper's shoulder hoping he hadn't upset him with the statement. "It's just that word is, Daniel and Martha Simon couldn't unload their daughters if they offered a man a million dollars. I'm pretty sure

Book of Scandal

Rosselle is gettin' worried 'bout bein' an old maid. Probably feels puttin' out is a quicker path to the aisle."

Jasper waved a hand. "It's cool, man. Anyway, Carmen pretty much said the same thing."

"'Lil Carm?" Felix grinned and folded arms across his broad chest. "What's a lil thirteen year old know about shit like that?"

"Hmph, are you forgettin' who her family is, bruh?"

Nodding then, Felix's expression sobered. "You still tight with Marc?"

"Yeah, why?"

Again, Felix clapped his brother's back. "Add him to the list of folks you need to watch out for. Nigga scares me."

There was no need to say Jasper was stunned. His expression spoke volumes. Curiously, he observed his brother who stood well over six and a half feet and who Jasper thought could be scared by no one.

"Just look out for yourself, alright?" Felix drew Jasper into a quick hug before they parted ways.

***

"You sure we can trust this fool?"

Near the brook that ran through the Ramsey property, Marcus was huddled in conversation with his long time friend Charlton Browning.

"Yeah, yeah he's cool and down with makin' a lil extra money." Charlton said in reference to the night watchman at the local white high school. "When I hinted at what we had in mind and told him about the benefits- the man was ready to play a part." Charlton shrugged. "'Specially when he found out a Ramsey was in the mix."

Book of Scandal

"Shit Charlt! Why the hell you bringin' my name into it?" Marc's dark features grew fiercer in light of his temper.

"It's cool, it's cool." Charlton waved his hands defensively. "Man said it had to be a prime operation if a Ramsey was involved."

"What kind of dollars we expecting if we pull this off?" Arrogant pride had calmed Marc by then.

"My contacts say it depends on what chemicals we lift from the lab." Charlton passed a list with prices attached.

Marcus let loose a whistle while scanning the list. "We bringin' anybody in on this?"

"More hands on the job mean more hands expectin' money."

"Yeah," Marc worked a hand across his square jaw and grimaced, "but this looks like it could turn into a heavy load easy and I'm out to score as much as possible here, you know?" His trademark wicked grin flashed. "Besides, no body else has to know how much we'll *really* get paid for this stuff, right?"

Grinning just as wickedly, Charlton nodded in agreement with the underhandness. "Who else you got in mind?"

"Jasper…Jeff maybe."

Charlton's grin vanished. "Jeff Carnes? I don't know, man. Nigga's too goody two shoes for me."

"He's loyal." Marc didn't spare Charlton a glance preferring to observe two passing female guests. "Anyway, loyalty's what we need on this."

Book of Scandal

Charlton didn't like it, but eventually nodded to give consent. "We'll need to meet again to discuss the when and other details."

"I saw Jeff a little while ago, but no idea where that fool Jasper is."

"Probably somewhere sniffin' after Rosselle Simon," Charlton saw the cunning look spread like butter across Marc's face. "What?" He listened intently while being filled in on the stable romp with Jasper Stone's supposed girlfriend.

"Be careful, man. Jasper's one of them quiet niggas-never know when they gon' snap."

Marc's shrug was the epitome of cool. "Just doin' my duty, son. I consider it my responsibility to... test drive before my friends waste their time."

"Thanks for the warning!" Charlton burst into laughter while shaking Marc's hand.

***

Eighteen year old Houston Ramsey headed back toward the main house like a man with a purpose. Hands hidden in the pockets of his gray slacks, his mind raced as quickly as his feet. He'd put in three hours at that damn party. His parents should be beyond pleased, he thought. Especially when he preferred to be up in his room enjoying the dry cool of the indoors with his records and skin magazines.

Mama would have a fit if she knew he had the things under her roof, he smirked. Knowledge of that fact was more an aphrodisiac than any of the scandalous photos inside the magazine's glossy pages.

Book of Scandal

Marcus would surely think him a fool for preferring to jerk off to some magazine, instead of helping himself to one of the many ripe lovelies there eager to spread her legs to a Ramsey. Houston knew his limits though and he wasn't at his best with girls. They looked at him like they knew he was faking it- like they knew he was nowhere near the confident leader like West or the suave lover like Marc.

The thought forced him to quicken his steps as the promise of solace in his room filled him with exhilaration. His steps halted suddenly, however when a pair of dainty pink slippers appeared in the line of his downcast gaze.

Daphne Monfrey had raised her hands in anticipation of the contact which never came. Realizing that disaster had been averted, her breathless laughter twittered in the air around them.

"Sorry," Houston muttered, momentarily taken aback by the angelic face looking up into his. He shielded his brown stare quickly then as Daphne continued to smile and giggle.

"'Scuse me," he continued on towards the house.

Daphne's laughter softened. Her gaze narrowed as it followed him.

Houston was almost home free- mere yards away from the back porch steps. It was then that he heard the sharp scream followed by an even sharper curse. Too curious not to investigate, his bland stare turned undoubtedly interested once it landed on a very frustrated, very lovely dark girl.

As if being led by some invisible string, Houston moved closer to where Catrina Jeffries sat on the edge of

Book of Scandal

the wide brick steps leading up to the screened back porch area. She was rubbing her lower calf and wincing when he tentatively inquired whether she was okay.

Catrina looked up sharply but managed a smile in spite of her pain. "I'm fine, thanks. It's my own fault for not being more careful dumping that fish grease."

"Ouch," a playful wince softened Houston's dark caramel-toned face. "You've got a fun job."

Catrina laughed.

Houston took a step closer. "Why exactly are you dumping fish grease?"

Catrina pointed at her T-shirt. "My family's Jeffries Catering and I lucked out on this fine chore, thank you very much."

Her fake haughty tone set Houston into laughter.

"So why are you so interested in my disgusting job?" Catrina asked after they'd talked a while longer. "You're obviously a guest who could be enjoying this great party- unlike me."

"I was invited." The lie rolled so easily off his tongue. He honestly had no idea why he didn't want her to know that *his* family was the reason for the event. "I'm about ready to hit the road, though." He added.

Catrina shook her head. "Nothin' more aggravating than a party you're ready to leave." She rolled her eyes when her mother's voice rose from somewhere in the distance. "I've gotta go." She moaned.

Houston made an awkward move to help her from the steps. He never quiet touched her though and Catrina managed on her own.

Book of Scandal

"Nice meeting you." He waved and watched her until she'd disappeared round the far end of the house.

***

"What's wrong?" Briselle snuggled beneath Westin's shirt but eyed him warily.

"I thought my dad was just talking- speculating before when he talked about relocating." West spoke after several moments of hesitation. "He's serious- wants me to head out to Washington State, establish new family roots in Seattle."

Briselle only absently listened at first. She was far more interested in the way the muscles flexed in her boyfriend's back. Gradually though, she took note of what he was saying.

"I'll be leaving, Bri. I didn't say anything before because... well, I wasn't sure if..."

Her heart lurched.

"This is gonna happen." He kept his back toward her but heard the rustling of the hay and knew she was slowly pushing herself up to sit. "I'd feel a lot better about the whole thing if you were there with me but if you're gonna constantly put yourself down for whatever you *think* is wrong with you, then we can just call the whole thing off right now." He turned his head slightly. Sunlight streaming through the beams of the barn loft outlined a slice of his striking profile. "We can consider this our last time Bri."

"West-" She stopped when he waved instructing her to return his shirt. He tossed over her dress and left her staring after him.

***

Book of Scandal

"Just take the cloths off those tables near the brook, Laney. Folks getting their feet wet and using my tablecloths for towels."

"Marcella!"

Raising an index finger, Marcella turned toward the sound of her name and frowned at the sight of Corinetta Nicols and the young woman she dragged along behind her.

"That's all Laney." Marcella ushered off the maid with a soft smile and then gave her attention to her guest and the girl struggling next to her. "Corin?"

"Look who I found sashayin' around with no invitation."

"I didn't do anything." Daphne hissed, trying frantically to tug free of Corinetta's grip.

"Yet." The woman practically spit the word. "This is Daphne Monfrey- mother's Babydoll Monfrey." Corinetta's brows raised in smug satisfaction when she dropped the tidbit.

Marcella's alluring gray stare did filter with some curiosity. She studied the girl with deeper interest.

"Hmph." Corinetta snorted.

"I didn't do anything wrong."

"Just you being here is wrong," Corinetta's small brown eyes shot disapproving daggers from behind the gauzy white veil of her hat. "You think the Ramseys want associations with the town whore... or her daughter?"

"Corin..."

"Well tell her Marcella."

Nodding once, Marcella managed a weary smile and leaned across to tug Daphne's hand from Corinetta's.

Book of Scandal

"You're right Corin, I don't approve of anything unseemly going on in my own home."

"You want me to throw her out?" Corinetta practically salivated over the possibility.

"I'll take care of it." Marcella drew Daphne closer. "I'd like to have a chat with our uninvited guest first. Thank you so much Corinetta."

The woman looked very pleased, cast a foul look at Daphne and then bustled off.

"She'll be talking about this for weeks." Marcella muttered, knowing the incident would be all the talk by the end of the cotillion. "Settle down girl." She told Daphne who'd tried to jerk from her grasp.

Daphne's face rivaled her teary eyes for redness. "I didn't do anything wrong."

"So you've said- repeatedly." Marcella bent slightly while taking the girl by the shoulders. "And I believe you. Sometimes it's just easier to agree with a jackass so they'll leave you the hell alone and let you get to the real story."

Daphne's lips twitched on an unexpected smile, though she was still rather wary. Subdued and silent, she fell in step with Marcella Ramsey and watched the lovely gracious woman covertly as they headed toward the main house. Marcella tossed out greeting to her guests and instructions to her staff without ever marring the coolness of her expression.

"Now tell me why Miss Corin would think you were doing questionable things at my party?" Marcella asked once they were settled to matching gold armchairs in the parlor off from the foyer.

Book of Scandal

Daphne sucked her teeth. "Because she's a stupid old bat."

"Agreed. Any other reasons?"

"Because... Babydoll Monfrey is my mother."

"Ah..." Marcella re-positioned herself in the chair. "Right and if I'm not mistaken that's a fact you can do nothing about."

Daphne bristled. "Doesn't matter to some."

"That's true- it matters quite a bit to some." Marcella waved over the maid who'd arrived with the tea she'd requested upon arriving in the house. "But it doesn't matter to me."

"Why?" Daphne blinked, still on edge though her voice had taken on a softer tint. "I haven't done anything to earn your trust."

"Well listen to you," Marcella drawled as though impressed. Silently, she took deeper note of the completely adult words coming from the child in her midst and accepted that the girl had leaned far too many *adult* things in her youth.

"Daphne, there are people *many* people in life who offer kindness without ever expecting anything in return." Ice crinkled in the tall glass coolers when Marcella poured the tea. "I admit it may seem hard for you to believe that considering... but it's true." Setting aside the pitcher, she leaned over to cup Daphne's face in her hands. "Remember that."

The two sipped tea and munched lemon crisps for a long while. In Daphne's opinion it was the longest, most wondrous time in her life. The parlor was cool and quiet with the energy of the party shut out past the crystal clear windows lining the plush comfortable room.

It was like a dream, but better because she was awake and thoroughly enjoying the reality of it. She studied her hostess with increasing interest as well.

Marcella Ramsey was; in many ways, the queen of all she surveyed with grace and beauty on top. Even still, the woman was far more than that. She had a generous and understanding soul. She was a lady through and through. This was a lady one should aspire to be like. Even a girl such as herself, Daphne thought.

As with all good things, they inevitably come to an end. Far too soon, one of the housemaids intruded on the parlor solitude to inform the lady of the house that Babydoll Monfrey was at the front gate for her daughter.

Daphne observed the maid. There was no distaste on the woman's face or in her voice when she spoke her mother's name. Daphne realized that it took nothing more than Marcella Ramsey's escorting her inside to grant respect from the servants.

"Thank you, Miss Marcella." Daphne rose from the chair with a sudden grace. She left the room with her head high.

All the while Daphne resigned herself to the thought- to the vow that she would have this life. She'd command respect with the beautiful grace that Marcella Ramsey had shown her that day.

But that day was far off, she acknowledged. If she hoped to greet it, she'd have to use all she'd learned from her present lot in life to acquire it.

***

Book of Scandal

Catrina stood watching her father's male employees load the heavier items into one of the Jeffries Catering work vans. Feeling completely useless and 'girl like' she decided to at least try and offer some assistance. She focused on the big grease tub she'd dumped earlier and decided it couldn't be nearly as heavy now. It was void of all the grease that had settled to the bottom before being dumped and pressure washed at the rear of the Ramsey estate.

She walked over and gave it a tug. No; not as heavy as it had been, but it'd still take a bit of doing for her to get it on the van. Catrina blew at her bangs while straightening to draw her hair into a tighter ponytail. She put her best foot forward only to have her efforts allayed.

Noticing the pair of larger male hands grasping the sides of the tub, Catrina stood prepared to declare her feminine strength. When she looked up, all words flew from her mind.

He was even more gorgeous up close, she discovered recognizing the boy she'd seen watching her earlier. Now within touching distance, she saw that his skin was as rich and flawless as it'd appeared before. His complexion was like molten molasses poured over strong features that would only strengthen and define as he grew older.

His eyes were deep-set, black and unwavering with an intensity that had her swallowing around the lump clogging the way. Catrina tried to clear her throat but only managed to sound like a duck strangling on a pebble. He smiled and her heart leapt in a purely... 'girl like' fashion when she glimpsed the dimples along either side of his

Book of Scandal

mouth. Those attributes combined with the cleft in his chin were the stuff of which the sweetest dreams were made.

"Catrina Marie!"

Catrina's lashes fluttered around mahogany eyes when her mother's voice boomed. Regretfully, she acknowledged her star-gazing had reached its end. She bit her lip, having caught his pitch stare raking her slender form. He then reached for the tub and hoisted it effortlessly onto the back of her father's van.

"Thank you?" her appreciation was given softly, the words left hanging on a question in hopes that he'd give her his name.

"Damon." He obliged with a slow smile.

Her mother's voice loomed once more in the distance with *her* name and something about being fast.

"Thank you Damon." She raced toward the van then. Before stepping in though, she looked around to see if he might be there maybe…watching her.

He was.

$\mathscr{R}$

~CHAPTER THREE~

Briselle never would've believed she'd enjoy helping her mother perform the chores her business required. As the local seamstress and laundress, Sybil Deas; owner of Sybil's Seams, had crafted a well respected name for herself. Black and white clients sought Sybil Deas 'magic' on everything from their daughter's first cotillion or Sweet 16 to their son's wedding or banquet uniforms for their servants. The woman was in high demand and ran her business with a deftness no one could dispute.

Briselle was no exception, but that day her interest in her mother's business simply involved its requirement for manual labor. Working until her muscles ached and her hands cracked from dryness, seemed to be the only thing that would keep her every waking thought off Westin Ramsey.

God, he actually wanted her to pick up and move clear across the country! Not that she didn't want to, but... she loved him, desperately it seemed at times. She wouldn't survive it if he was ever disappointed in her.

Disappointed was exactly what he'd be if they moved away, married and she still couldn't provide him with the child she knew he'd want. Although he said all the right things... 'you're all I want- enough for me...nothing could ever change my love for you...' she knew that was his heart talking and she loved him all the more for it.

Still, he was a Ramsey-the eldest son in a powerful group. West was expected to lead the family into a new era. The same would be expected of his child.

Briselle hissed an oath when she cracked her third nail of the day. Grimacing, she studied the massacred manicure that looked nothing like the dazzling display she showed off during the Ramsey gala almost a week ago. She hadn't heard from Westin since and knew he was waiting on a response to the way they'd left their last conversation.

Yes, was the only response she wanted to give. Silently she cursed again. This time the profanity was directed at herself for putting their relationship in such a state.

The guttural roar of a truck motor drowned everything then, including the thoughts in her head. Her glossy flipped hair bounced about her face which brightened at the sight of her father arriving home for lunch. Leaving the sewing table, Briselle rushed out to meet Elton Deas, savoring the strength and security in his embrace.

Book of Scandal

"Whoa," Elton's deep voice rumbled when his daughter flung herself against his chest. In tune to her mood, he allowed several silent moments of nourishing hugging.

"What is it, sugar?" He finally queried.

"Nothing Daddy.

Elton wasn't surprised. The response was standard whenever he questioned her mood. Still, she did manage to intrigue him when; in a shuddery tone, she asked if she could ride into town with him after lunch.

"That'll be fine, baby." Elton pulled back and kissed Briselle's forehead and then grabbed his hat off the long front seat of the truck. "Where you headin'?"

"Ramsey."

***

Jeffries Catering reigned; not only in providing its customers with the best delicacies for their get togethers, it reigned as one of the best restaurants in Savannah. The establishment drew patrons from every walk and race of life. The place had gone from being a one room lean-to where meals were boxed after being prepared in King and Rosa Jeffries' modest home, to a huge warehouse locale. The dining room could hold almost 80 customers with room for an additional 50 in the add-on King had recently constructed.

It was a place where social clubs held monthly meetings and businessmen met for lunch pow-wows. It was a place where people came to blend in with the crowd-making it the perfect spot for Marcus Ramsey and Charlton Browning to discuss their latest illegal endeavor.

Book of Scandal

"I still don't like him comin' in on the job, man."

"Hell Charlt, you jealous?" Marc teased then laughed when Charlton gave him the finger.

"I just don't like the goody two shoes he always wears- job's too big to be worryin' over whether the cat can handle it."

"It's Jeff's way- always has been." Marc shrugged beneath his navy dress shirt. "What's the real problem, Charlt? We've all done shit together before."

Charlton kicked the toe of his loafer against the leg of the table. "Petty shit, pissin' around. This is big and we all realize that."

Marc smirked. "You really wanna include Jasper in that?"

Laughter rose between the two young men.

"Hell nah," Charlton wiped a laugh tear from his eye. "Not always the smartest tack." He chuckled. "Brainy folk...lots of book sense and not a lick of common."

"And that's why we can trust him." Marc munched on a few more fries. "Plus, he's curious- itchin' to get his hands on all that chemical stuff."

"Which brings us back to your boy, Jeff. This chemical deal is big- lifting shit from a lab. If we get caught-"

"Hey, hey- don't jinx the fuckin' thing already."

"Hell man, you need to understand what's at stake here." Charlton's dark gaze was as focused and as hard as Marcus's. "I know you and Jeff been friends since dirt n' diapers but if he flakes out at the last minute, we'll all do serious time if we get caught." He reclined against the

Book of Scandal

hardback and toyed with the straw in his glass. "I doubt even your last name could save you."

"Well I can't just kick him off the team now." Marc muttered his expression sulky.

"What if he kicks himself off?" Charlton continued to stare at his glass. "Would you bring in another hand?"

Slowly, Marc straightened in his chair, contemplated the possibility and then shook his head. "Jeff's cool."

"Man-"

"Hold it." Marc waved off Charlton's voice like it was an annoying bug. "Now if he backs out. *If*, then I'll take care of it, cool?" He grinned and waved toward the front of the room while Charlton shrugged. "Here comes the rest of the crew now."

***

Georgia arched her back, grinding her hips in a sultry move that sheltered more of Felix's tongue inside her body. Biting her bottom lip, she lost her fingers in his soft, wooly hair and clenched to bring his handsome face deeper between her legs.

Felix raked a massive hand along her toned thighs and grunted his pleasure when he felt her coming against his tongue. He heard her swear as she often did when she climaxed before she was ready. Her fingers ceased massaging his scalp and began to tug- a silent order that he take her fully.

Of course Georgia was used to getting what she wanted and when she wanted it. When Felix didn't respond accordingly, she simply added a bit more forced to her tugs in his hair.

Book of Scandal

Felix thrived in the knowledge of the power he held over the dark lovely in his arms. He knew that refusing to give in just then would only increase her hunger and add more fire in her responses to his touch.

"Son of a bitch," she growled and tried to buck him off her.

Felix met the words and her movement with a harsh slap to the side of her thigh. His heart soared when he heard her throaty laughter. He continued feasting only to have her resume the tugging in his strong hair. Without ceasing the ravishing thrusts of his tongue, he grabbed her wrists, pinning them to her sides upon the makeshift pallet in the middle of the hay-strewn barn loft.

"Son of a bitch," Georgia hissed again then, her words still carrying on amusement. Pushing him away was the farthest thought from her mind as a potent orgasm chasmed through her.

Only then, did Felix back away. His tongue claimed her mouth as his sex claimed hers. Georgia felt seconds away from a third explosion of desire when he imprisoned her hands above her head and added more zest to his strokes...

Much later, Georgia lay sprawled across him, reveling in the tone of his licorice skin, eyes and hair. Her nails raked the chiseled beauty of his torso before her tongue charted the same path.

"I'll kill you if you ever fuck another woman," she promised while her tongue made lazy circles around his nipple.

Book of Scandal

Felix chuckled though silently acknowledge that she was just that passionate (and mean) to do it. "Unless you changed your mind, it's gonna be hard for you to know who I fuck."

Georgia's walnut brown stare was at first blank and then grew sharp as her memory recovered. "I can't believe you're still stuck on that."

"Mama's getting' closer to the end of her rope with Pop." Felix's baritone voice was softer as he scanned the semi-dark expanse of the loft.

Georgia sucked her teeth. "Men stray and women take 'em back- she's gotta live with the consequences of her actions."

Felix laughed despite his mood. "Anybody ever tell you, you're a hard bitch?"

"Who you callin' hard?" She'd taken no offense to the 'bitch' part. Sobering then, she propped her hand to her cheek while bracing weight on her elbow. "Sometimes a woman has to be a bitch if she expects to survive all the bullshit a man can and will take her through."

"Does being a bitch keep a woman from doing stupid things?"

Georgia tugged a tuft of hair from his hair. "Yes- lots of times. It keeps her from sleeping with a man she knows is no good for her, or it allows her to give in and say 'to hell with the consequences'. It allows her control- to say enough is enough and mean it."

"God," Felix held a hand to his forehead and stared up at the ceiling. "I hope Mama reaches that last part and soon."

Book of Scandal

A frown tugged at Georgia's sleek brows and; for the first time, she tuned into the true fear lacing his voice. "Is she in trouble?"

Felix shook his head on the hay. "She hates my dad almost as much as she hates Miss Belle."

"Belleina Stone? Why? Because of Jasper?"

Felix's midnight stare snapped to Georgia's face. "What the hell do you know about Jasper?"

"Well hell boy, everybody knows Jasper is Mr. Joe's son. You really had no clue the whole town knew?" Her gaze was wide with disbelief. Leaning closer, she toyed with his hair. "Anyway, it's obvious y'all are brothers- hair's just different. Jasper's got that silky stuff and your roots are straight from the motherland."

"That a complaint?" He laughed when she tugged his afro.

"No," she sighed while straddling him. "I like it rough."

"Really?"

"Try me." She taunted, seconds before they dissolved into another rapacious love session.

***

Marcella Ramsey slammed the icebox door with such force she knew at least a half dozen of her eggs had cracked. She could've cared less.

"How long you gon' make me deal with the pouting Marcy?"

She bristled at the sound of her husband's voice. "You'll just have to forgive me Quent." Her voice was phony sweetness. "Ain't everyday a wife learns her husband hates one of their children."

Book of Scandal

"God Marcy," Quentin groaned, pushing aside his coffee mug. "I love the boy, it's the trust I have a problem with."

Marcella began to wipe down the counter top. "Can't be one without the other."

"That's when it's between lovers. A parent's love is unconditional."

The natural perfect arch of Marcella's brows raised a notch. "Is that a fact?" She propped a hand to the side of her white pedal pushers. "Is that why you're sending your oldest son off to usher in this damn new Ramsey era while leaving your next eldest to sulk and accept it?"

Quentin didn't bother to tell his wife that their second eldest son would *sulk* wherever he was sent. She'd never seen Marcus for what he really was. Perhaps it was because she'd chosen his name similar to her own. She was completely blind when it came to the boy, Quentin thought. He knew it was killing her to have him at odds with the child.

Walking across the glossy, black and mahogany linoleum flooring, Quent joined his wife at the sink.

"Marcy," he pulled her back against him trailing his nose across her nape bared by her upswept hair. He felt her go pliant against him and smiled cockily in response.

"He's headstrong and clever is all." Marcella tried to keep a firm voice even as she melted against Quentin's tall, massive frame. "You were a lot like him at that age..." she turned in his arms, fixing him with knowing eyes. "Need I remind you of all those trips to secluded fields where that old T-Model would always *just happen* to break down?" She noticed his onyx stare falter and shook her

Book of Scandal

head. "Funny how it always started right up once you were done with me."

"You could've screamed." His nose trailed the curve of her jaw.

She tugged at his thin tie. "I did."

"Ah yes, yes you did…and often…"

Marcella's dark chocolate face burned a deep shade.

"How about I give him some small jobs at the business?" He patted her hip absently but no less possessively. "I'll feel him out a little, see where he fits in."

"Quen? You mean it?" Her fingers curled tight into the crisp sleeves of his dark suit coat.

He nodded, chuckling as she covered his face in kisses before they hugged. Quentin's expression dimmed while he held onto his happy wife. Silently, he prayed he'd not regret his decision, though in his heart he knew that he would.

***

Carmen's steps slowed when she saw Jasper Stone disappear behind the doors of Jeffries Café. She'd followed him since catching sight of his tall frame past the library windows. She often spent her summer afternoons holed up in the elegant, spacious building. After spotting Jasper that day she was no longer interested in losing herself amidst scores of books. She wanted to talk with him. She so loved talking with him but this time; for some reason, she hadn't a clue what she'd say.

Something had changed since the cotillion. She had the distinct feeling something more was dwelling in his bottomless stare than he dared admit. Was he… attracted to

Book of Scandal

her? Did he want to do with her the things she'd seen her brothers do with so many other girls?

Twirling the end of her ponytail braid about her finger, Carmen lost herself on the thought. Drifting into a daydream state, she never noticed the car approaching the narrow intersection as she crossed...

"Dammit!" The curse sounded loud to her ears and Catrina turned to see whether her mother had picked up her swear with her keen sense of hearing.

Sighing relief, Catrina resumed her daily task of scraping hardened grease from one of the eight roasting pans she'd been commissioned to clean until they sparkled. If only...*Damon* could see her now, she thought. Smiling a little, she warmed as his image came to mind.

In spite of her insurmountable tasks during the event, she'd wished the Ramsey party would have gone on forever. She could have stood there forever with him, not talking only...absorbing the quiet power in his dark eyes.

Suddenly, scrubbing the pan overheated her just a bit too much and Catrina stepped back to wipe sweat from her brow. It was then she noticed the girl attempting to cross the street.

"Hey!" Bolting toward the curb, Catrina waved her arms frantically. "Wait! Wait!" She closed her eyes, relieved when the girl jerked to a halt mere seconds before stepping into the path of an approaching car.

"Are you okay?" Catrina's tone was breathless as was the rest of her when she met the girl in the middle of the street.

Book of Scandal

Carmen took a moment to answer- breathless as well.

"Come on." Catrina curved an arm about her bare shoulders and guided her to the lot behind the restaurant.

Carmen was shaking terribly, rubbing arms bared by the calico sundress she sported. She was sitting on a tin barrel by the time she finally managed to nod that she was alright.

Catrina filled a silver can/cup with water from a spicket on the side of the building. "Here," she urged, holding the can lest it topple to the ground between the girls' shaking hands.

"Thank you." Carmen sipped and then took a deep breath. "I'm alright, really."

Catrina accepted the can and took a sip as well. Smoothing hands across her denim shorts she shook her head. "What made you walk out there like that?"

Carmen shrugged. "Daydreaming."

Catrina smiled. "Understood."

***

Kollette David smiled toward the timid looking young woman wiggling her knee and wringing her hands. "Would you like a glass of tea, darlin'?"

Briselle could scarcely shake her head no.

"Want me to check on West again?" Kollette watched Briselle give a nervous tug to her burnt orange slim skirt.

"I don't want to rush him."

Kollette's heart went out to the girl who looked completely out of her wits in the grand executive floor of

Book of Scandal

the lobby. Leaving her desk, Kollette took a seat next to Briselle on the gray leather sofa and patted her hand.

"We'll just wait for him together." Kollette bumped Briselle's shoulder and managed to draw a smile.

"Now you can go back to focusing on what's really on your mind."

Westin was just finishing up a meeting with warehouse supervisor Bradley Justice. Brad's words sent the absent look from his face and replaced it with surprise.

"Obvious you're a million miles away son." Brad folded hands over his protruding belly and grinned.

"Damn Brad, why are women so tough to figure out?"

Bradley's grin broadened. He'd wondered how long it'd take for the younger man to snap. He shrugged. "Makes 'em more interesting."

"And that's supposed to be a *good* thing?"

"If she's *the* one- then I suppose so, yeah."

Westin was quiet for a long time. "Yeah," he agreed finally.

The phone buzzed in West's office, but Brad took it upon himself to answer.

"Are y'all 'bout done in there?" It was Kollette whispering through the line. "West's girl is out here and she'll probably lose her nerve and leave if he isn't free soon."

"He'll be out in a second Koll," Brad set down the phone and snapped fingers at West. "*The* one's waiting for you outside." Brad's laughter rumbled as West practically ran from the office.

Book of Scandal

As Kollette had predicted, Briselle had decided to turn tail and run. She was on her way to Kollette's desk with intentions on leaving a message when she saw Westin rush out into the maple paneled lobby.

"I swear I don't want to lose you," she whispered when the distance closed between them. "I just can't disappoint you."

"I want to promise you things'll always be just right between us." West rubbed his thumb across the belt around her skirt. "I can't be that arrogant though. Well...I *could* but..."

"I swear I love you," he said when their laughter cooled. "Baby or no baby, going to Seattle's a scary thought. Going without you, it'll be terrifying. Please say you'll come with me."

Briselle reached for the hand he tentatively extended. "On one condition," she tugged on the rolled sleeve of his shirt. "I go as Mrs. Westin Ramsey."

West expelled the breath he was holding and helped himself to her kiss.

R

~CHAPTER FOUR~

"Why you so interested, man?" Charlton snapped when the chemistry lab 'crew' was seated around a back square table in Jeffries Café. Jeff Carnes had voiced his unease about the job Marcus had just laid out.

"Why's it have to be a chem lab's all I wanna know." Jeff briefly waved a hand before setting it back wearily against his forehead.

"Jeff man, the shit in that lab's worth a bundle." Marc softly tried to explain to his oldest friend.

"I don't like it." Jeff rolled his eyes. "Shit like this... somebody could get hurt."

"So what? With all the dough we'll make, so what?"

Book of Scandal

"This is big." Jeff didn't bother to look Charlton's way. "A chemistry lab. If we get caught-"

"Do we get to keep any of the stuff we lift from the lab?"

The three arguing friends quieted. They all looked towards Jasper, not quite sure what he meant.

Jasper chewed away on his cheeseburger like he hadn't said anything out of the ordinary. "I been wantin' to get a closer look at the place since we took that field trip junior year in high school."

"What the hell for?" Jeff asked.

Jasper only raised his brows, not wanting to discuss how fascinating he found chemistry. The discoveries, the possibilities, the power…

"Anyway, are we doin' this or not?" Charlton challenged.

"You in or out man?" Marc asked Jeff. "You with us J? Are you with *me*?"

Jeff held Marc's gaze for several heavy moments. At last he shook his head. "I love you like a brother man, but this…it's too big for me. The chances of us getting caught," he leaned back in his chair folding arms over his shirt. "What happens if we get caught is too scary for me. I plan on havin' a life after all this pissin' around and lookin' over my shoulder for the rest of it ain't in the plan."

"Bullshit, bullshit, bullshit," Charlton drawled, his wide mouth curved into what could easily pass for a snarl. "Take yo' sorry ass on somewhere, man."

Jeff stood without argument. "Sorry Marc," he said while leaving the table.

Book of Scandal

"So you got another idea or we goin' in three deep?" Charlton posed.

"I got it covered." Marcus spoke without hesitation.

***

Carmen laughed when a glop of bubbly water dashed in her face. Catrina only shook her head.

"Never thought I'd see the day," she sighed.

"What?" Carmen dried her face on a cloth lying nearby.

"That I'd meet another living soul who actually liked cleaning grimy pots."

Carmen laughed wildly and shrugged. "It's not that I like it so much, but it *does* help pass the time. Keeps my mind off stuff I'm better off not thinking about."

Catrina let her hands rest in the sudsy water. "How old are you Carmen?"

"Thirteen."

"Hmph," Catrina was mildly surprised. "You sound older."

"I get a lot of that." Carmen strolled back to the wash bin.

"So I'm guessing it's a guy you were daydreaming about?"

Carmen would only nod.

"Does he know you like him?" Catrina shook water and soap from the pot she'd just cleaned.

"He's friends with my brothers." Carmen chose another pot to wash. "Even if he knew how I felt, he'd never let on or give in."

"So your brothers are the over protective types?"

Book of Scandal

"Only two," Carmen smiled thinking of Westin and Damon. Then her hands slowed. "The other two could care less. You have any brothers?"

"I'm an only child." Catrina smirked. "My parents got buckets of brothers and sisters though, so I grew up with tons of cousins." She wiped the back of her hand across sweaty bangs then.

"Sounds nice."

"Yeah, thank God for them- otherwise I'd be stuck cleanin' every pot my daddy owns."

Carmen's onyx stare brightened with recognition. She realized she hadn't at first put it together that Catrina was a Jeffries.

"Yes, my sweet, you're looking at the heiress to all this you see!" She waved toward the restaurant.

"I should've guess with all the work you're doing."

"I know." Catrina felt around in the deep tub for another pot. "I should be laid up on my ass like a *real* spoiled selfish heiress."

"Yeah… that pretty much describes us, doesn't it?"

"Huh?" Catrina stopped rooting around in the wash tub and watched her new friend extend a hand.

"Carmen Ramsey."

"Ouch." Catrina winced and straightened from the tub. "I'm sorry girl."

"Please don't." Carmen's lashes fluttered. "You just gave a perfect description of my big sister Georgia."

The girls shared a hearty roar of laughter.

Catrina Marie! There's pots pilin'!" Rosa Jeffries' voice drifted out some time later.

Book of Scandal

"My mama lives for that." Catrina groaned and then squinted up at the softening but still potent sunlight. "But it helps with the daydreaming, right?"

For a time, the girls focused on toiling away with the grimy pots and platters.

"So who had *you* dazed and confused?" Carmen asked when she'd triumphed over a grease-caked roaster.

Catrina washed and began to describe the dreamboat she'd met during the Ramsey cotillion. Carmen's movements slowed as the description sounded all too familiar.

"Wow…he does sound dreamy." Carmen fiddled with the edge of her braid. "What was his name?"

"Damon…" Catrina's expression was sheepish when she shrugged. "He never gave me his last name."

Carmen turned back toward the tub, effectively hiding her smile. If her brother wanted to remain anonymous, who was she to ruin it?

***

Josephine Simon made a mock attempt at dusting the framed portrait of her grandparents, while more avidly attempting to overhear her sisters' whispering in the sitting room. Thankfully, Rosselle ceased her sweeping which allowed her conversation with Clea to drift in more clearly.

The topic of conversation was of course Marcus Ramsey- as it had been since the Ramsey gala weeks earlier. She'd experienced an almost painful bout of shyness when he'd spoken to her parents. Josephine couldn't help but be captivated by his manner and- God, his looks…

She'd felt a stab of something that could be described with no other word except scandalous. She could almost feel that potent black stare focusing on her, but that was crazy. After all, what could a man like that want with a girl like her?

Josephine smirked off the obvious answer. Clearly he was getting those things and much more from her sisters. She would've known Marc Ramsey anywhere by just using her sister's descriptions to go on. Soft milk chocolate skin cascading over a toned 6'2" frame; a crop of thick curls covering his head in mounds of glossy black- and the eyes. That pitch stare that seemed to seer right into a person's soul.

Josephine shook herself back into the present when she overheard Ross and Clea giggling. Rolling her eyes, she acknowledged the sexy Ramsey clearly liked foolish women if her sisters were any examples.

Then again; judging from their conversation, they were giving him anything he wanted sexually so, why wouldn't he adore them? And why was *she* mourning the fact that *she* hadn't had him sexually? What would a virgin like her even know of seducing a man?

Apparently, seduction wasn't the path to securing a husband. Her sisters had opened their hearts; opened their legs actually, whenever the occasion suited them. Still, there were no suitors offering to make honest women of them. Josephine learned long ago that the way down the aisle was definitely not by way of the bedroom.

But God, he'd made her sizzle when she saw him. The promise of carnal delight practically hovered about him like a shroud. She knew a man like that would never want to be tied down with a wife, though. Not when he had his pick of any woman. Therefore, she'd be satisfied

Book of Scandal

overhearing her sister's exploits and pray that the chance to lose herself with Marcus Ramsey never presented itself.

***

Daphne rubbed her fingers through her mother's silken bed coverings and recalled the scene she'd just witnessed. Babydoll had ordered her to change the sheets by 4 p.m. - in time for her next *appointment*. Daphne was partly sickened by the fact that the woman could receive another man (or two) when she'd just had a lewd romp with a town councilman and church deacon.

The men's titles and the fact that both were married with children, wasn't half as stunning as seeing Babydoll take them both at once.

Still, there was something about it- something entrancing, hypotonic even. There had to be; Daphne thought. Why else would she be standing there trailing her fingers through linens soiled with the secretions of three adults?

There was power there, she told herself feeling her heart race beneath her pink and white halter. She recalled the scene through vivid flashes of the new memory. From the look on Babydoll's face, there was no doubt she was enjoying herself. Daphne had to wonder though how much of that *enjoyment* came from the power she had to feel. The things she did with those men got her damn near everything she wanted. Daphne wasn't so young she couldn't grasp the concept. Those men left paying not only Babydoll Monfrey's outrageous sex fees, but they left hefty tips in bulging envelopes on their way out the door. Their next *appointments* were already jotted in the woman's book.

Book of Scandal

It took power to train men that way- to get them to pay anything for your time and keep them coming back for more Daphne realized. She'd often heard her mother say what thrilled her most- beyond the money even- was hearing a client tell her he couldn't stay long due to business or family obligation and have him in her bed well past the time he swore he had to leave. Knowing a man had chosen *her* over a family obligation, gave Babydoll the biggest thrill. Daphne was dazed by the thought and still absently handling the sheets when her mother waltzed into the room.

"Girl, you ain't got that bed changed yet?" Babydoll scolded lightly, choosing a perfume from a litany of bottles on the dresser. Slowly she dabbed a bit of a fragrance behind her ears while observing her daughter. "You uh…never finished telling me about meeting Marcella at that party." She moved to the vanity re-checking the hairstyle for her next client.

"It was nothing much." Daphne's hands went weaker still on the sheets.

Babydoll smirked recognizing the intentional vagueness. "What'd you think of the great *lady*?"

"She *is* a great lady."

Babydoll's smile remained. Daphne's response was still vague but there was no mistaking that she was clearly smitten by the Ramsey matriarch.

"…she's got a lovely life." Daphne's voice sounded muted as she whipped the sheets off the bed.

"And you want that life." Babydoll selected new earrings. Her eyes were downcast, but she looked up in

Book of Scandal

time to spot her daughter whirl around to gape at her through the mirror.

"I didn't say that." Daphne resumed the bed changing. Secrecy was an ally she'd acquired at a young age. She didn't want anyone- her mother especially- knowing of any honorable aspirations. The two just wouldn't mix. She certainly didn't need the woman knowing of any aspirations that may or may not have involved the Ramseys.

It was too late for that now. Daphne knew it was when Babydoll looked up at her again through the mirror.

"If you want *that* life, you'll have to have that name." Babydoll smoothed a scented lotion across and under her ample bosom. "That means having one of those sons."

"Really Ma?" Daphne hoped her mother heard the haughtiness in her voice.

Babydoll took no offence. "Just how do you expect to get one of them with your reputation?"

"I don't have a reputation, Ma."

"Oh honey!" Babydoll laughed for a while, "You're Babydoll Monfrey's little girl. You had a rep before you could walk!"

Daphne rolled her eyes and went back to making the bed. "Can't you just let me have one thing?"

Babydoll left her vanity seat. "Lil' girl, having- *getting* a Ramsey won't be simple as batting lashes, speakin' soft and remembering what fork to use at the dinner table." She held her robe together and leaned across the unmade bed. "It'll take a lot more than that- *a lot*

Book of Scandal

more." Her plump lovely face brightened when Daphne
looked toward the bed. "Mmm hmm."

"I don't want a man that way." Daphne threw sheets
to the bed.

"And if you wanted any man besides a Ramsey, I'd
say 'good for you', but you can best believe them lil' stank
actin' society bitches at that cotillion are battin' lashes,
speakin' soft and probably fuckin' their way straight to the
Ramsey name. If you think holdin' out on a Ramsey will
get you one- think again."

Daphne felt the stiffness in her back ease as her
mother's words took root. Her house shoes slapped the
floor as she strolled to the window overlooking the sweet
innocent looking back lawn of Babydoll's Brothel- her own
personal name for her home. She suspected, it was known
by that name to a great many betrayed wives and girlfriends.

She wanted out- away from the stink of the place
camouflaged by the best French perfumes. She knew that
the stink of the place and the rep of the woman who bore
her would always be a chain she'd have to bear. But, oh
how easy it'd be to cover that chain by draping it in furs
and jewels, from her Ramsey husband.

In spite of a sweet tea party with Marcella Ramsey
she suspected the woman would have a fit if one of her
sons brought home a girl like her with intentions to marry.
She looked to her mother then. Babydoll Monfrey knew
what it took to get a man, keep him and keep him coming
back for more.

Daphne knew the answer was sex. How to wield it,
though? How to wield it into the tool of power the way
Babydoll had...she needed that knowledge. She craved that

Book of Scandal

almost as much as she craved the last name Ramsey and all the lavish beauty and grace the name carried.

~CHAPTER FIVE~

The low sound in Damon Ramsey's throat signaled frustration; when his confident stride brought him within sight of the library. He saw that his sister wasn't waiting there as they'd agreed.

The low sound in his throat was soon accompanied by muttered words of aggravation. The last thing he wanted was to step inside the building and have to play social butterfly to friends, associates and a slew of 'hopeful' girlfriends.

The frustration and aggravation; for that matter, began to wane when the library's front door opened and Catrina Jeffries emerged. She hurried down the wide steps that seemed to line the entire front side of the majestic white building.

Book of Scandal

Deep set eyes narrowed and Damon leaned against a tree trunk sheltered by the generous moss dangling around it. Catrina was almost frantically trying to stuff papers into a book. She kept glancing back at the big clock above the library entrance. The smirk curving his mouth then sparked one of his dimples. He wondered what chore she was late for at Jeffries Catering.

He thought back to the cotillion; faintly grimacing at whomever invented such a phenomenal waste of time in his opinion. Still, the thing had been worth attending just for a chance to meet her. He bowed his head then focusing on his sneakers one crossed over the other and wondered why he'd been so caught up over her. There'd been tons of girls traipsing around his family's home that day.

Catrina Jeffries was a looker no doubt- tall, almond brown skin, clearly athletic though that look probably came from lifting tubs of fish and chicken grease. He smiled. Even still, many of the girls at the party were pretty too- what was it about this one?

Had he developed a sudden liking to grease splattered clothes and haphazard ponytails? He must've. The way she looked at him that day...his heart had gone right to the soles of his Converse and she had him. He could barely recall his own name when she'd asked him.

He sighed then, blanking out the memory. He'd given her his first name only on purpose. She liked him that was clear. She liked him and she didn't even know he was a Ramsey. Course that never made a difference before. Girls had always been attracted, though they grew a tad giddier when they discovered who he was.

Book of Scandal

He didn't tell her because he feared she'd morph into some Ramsey-crazed scream box. Instead, it was the easiness of just being a boy meeting a girl and striking up a friendship. There was none of the usual drama- more accurately- the usual crap that came into play when the Ramsey heirs set their sights on a girl. Is it serious? Will they marry? Who's her family? Those were but a few of the blizzard-like barrage of questions sure to mount in due time.

Damon didn't know what future- if any- was in store for he and this girl he couldn't look away from or stop thinking of even after she was gone from his sight for several hours. He did know that he planned to enjoy a longer time as an ordinary boy striking up a friendship with an ordinary girl.

And if she asked his last name? Heavy brows rose as he quickly chose the answer. Why he'd do what so many Ramseys did best. He'd lie.

Catrina cast one last look at the clock and gave up stuffing the last book into her bag. She was ten minutes outside of being late and; even though her mother's bark was often worse than its bite, she didn't want to suffer Rosa Jeffries barking unless she really had to.

Catrina raced down the last of the steps and was on her way to the restaurant when she heard him asking if she needed help. Seeing Damon, everything she held fell to the sidewalk.

'*No*' she cleared her throat with noticeable effort upon realizing that the word hadn't even carried on her voice. "No." She managed after clearing her throat a second time.

Book of Scandal

Damon however, had already knelt to collect her things. Catrina knew what a sight she made standing there staring down at the boy's head, but she couldn't help it. His hair was cut close and black as his eyes but amass with waves. She wondered if they were natural or processed. She was banking on natural and her fingers ached to test her accuracy.

Damon lifted his head- his eyes took a slow journey along the length of Catrina's legs bared by the cutoffs she wore with a polka dot halter. Grinding on his jaw then, he commanded his hormones and thoughts to cool before he stood to hand her the bag.

"Thanks," she whispered, liking the way his solid black T-shirt and jeans complimented his body.

Damon nodded toward the bag. "Lot of books there for summer reading."

*Catrina Marie...*she called silently to herself in the manner her mother would. She commanded herself to pull out of the hypnotic spell this boy cast by doing little more than speaking.

"I um, it's just for fun."

He smirked and her mahogany gaze was drawn to his right dimple when it flashed.

"Fun?" Damon reached for the book she'd managed to hold onto when the others had fallen. *"Entrepreneurial Enterprise Made Simple.* Fun." He passed the book back to her.

Catrina immediately launched an explanation of helping her dad's business run more efficiently.

As he listened, Damon was infatuated by every physical attribute the girl possessed. Then he added

Book of Scandal

something more. The girl had a brain- one obsessed with business at that. His obsidian stare raked her with renewed interest then.

Catrina stopped herself short, realizing she'd once again let her tongue run away with her as it often did when the subject of business was in the air. She had so little time or opportunity to discuss the subject at home. Her dad wasn't as yet taking all her economic suggestions seriously. As a result, she'd taken to sharing her insights with anyone who would listen- including her fellow fish grease dumpers.

She made a point however, of catching herself before she bored a boy with it. She wasn't sure what to make of the look Damon was giving her then. She wasn't about to question it though.

"I have to get home." She cast another look toward the clock without really seeing it. "Thanks for your help." She sprinted off.

Catrina was turning the block when Damon found his voice and told her she was welcome.

***

"Jas!" Felix called before the boy headed into Sybil's Seams. "What's up, man?"

Jasper grinned, hearing the teasing tone in his brother's voice with regards to him headed into the local seamstress shop. "Mama sent me to pick up our laundry and stuff."

Playfully, Felix waved off the explanation.

"She ain't been wantin' to be seen much in public since the Ramsey thing."

Felix nodded, losing his taste for teasing. "Sorry man."

Book of Scandal

"Don't be." It was Jasper's turn to wave off Felix's words. "Nothin's gonna change. It shouldn't change. My mama shoulda never slept with your pop."

"*Our* Pop," Felix scratched the back of his head. "If that hadn't happened, I wouldn't have a brother."

"That's enough mushy stuff." Jasper drawled when they drew out of a hug. "I gotta get home 'fore Ma starts worrying 'bout her laundry." He made the joke while eyeing the wad of dollar bills he carried.

"You got enough, man?" Felix read through the slow nod. "You and Miss Belle okay for money, Jas?"

"Yeah, yeah we're good big spender!" Jasper laughed.

"Not a big spender, just a concerned brother." Felix folded arms across his gray shirt and shrugged. "Workin' at the factory with Pop. I can spare a little if you need it."

"We're alright, man. Plus I added four more lawns to my list of jobs- it's goin' good."

"Does he give y'all anything?" Felix stepped closer. "Pop? Does he help out any?"

"He used to." Jasper kept his eyes downcast. "I overheard him tellin' Ma. Miss Harry's keepin' a close eye on the dollars so..."

Felix accepted that as truth yet silently noted that his mother keeping a close eye on the money hadn't stopped Joe Cade's daily stops to Gordon's Liquor and Smokes for his favorite brew and cigars.

"You tell your Mama to keep askin' about the money."

Book of Scandal

Jasper was about to smile at Felix's advice but the gesture froze on his mouth mid-stream. "You better get goin'" He was looking off into the distance.

"Felix! Felix?! Boy get away from that filth!"

Harriet Cade's enraged voice carried clearly along the street and succeeded in drawing onlookers in a matter of seconds. Even folks inside Sybil's Seams either pressed their faces to the window or stepped outside the shop to view the budding scene.

"Ma-"

"Hush Felix!" Harriett was too far gone to be calmed. Though Joe Cade was known for his dalliances, having to see proof of the man's infidelity was just too much. Especially when that proof bore such a striking resemblance to her own son.

"See ya, Felix." Admirably in control of his temper, Jasper would've walked away had it not been for Harriett calling to him.

"Don't you walk away from me, filth!" Harriett turned to Felix once she had Jasper's attention. "What were y'all talkin' about? Lemme guess, that tramp, that trick?!" She turned back to Jasper. "That whore sendin' her bastard out to pass messages to my son to give to his sorry excuse for a daddy?"

"Ma please," Felix tried to embrace his mother only to be pushed away.

Harriett tucked her glossy black purse beneath her arm and went to wave a gloved fist before Jasper's face.

"You ain't nothin', 'cause your Mama ain't nothin'." She smiled nastily, seeing the boy's gaze flicker as her words cut deep. "Mmm hmm, used to be one of

Book of Scandal

Babydoll's girls before she decided she could make more cash on her back fuckin' other women's husbands and holdin' onto everything she made instead of sharin'."

Sybil Deas left her shop then, having caught wind of what was happening just past her door. She caught Harriett's shaking shoulders and tried to turn her toward the shop's steps.

"You keep away from my son! My *legitimate* son! You and your stank ass Mama!"

"Harriett! That's enough!" Sybil jerked the woman into silence and forcibly turned her toward the steps. She turned a soft motherly smile toward Jasper. "You go on home, baby. I'll send your things by delivery and you keep your money in your pocket. There's no charge."

An enraged Harriett Cade was shown inside the shop. Felix tried to catch up to Jasper but the boy was running down the street like he was trying to outrun the devil.

Jasper took refuge down the end of a block. He ducked down an alley, stood leaning against a brick wall and tried to catch his breath. He wanted to scream, but dared not call anymore attention to himself than he already had. He clenched fists, slamming them against the bricks and then clenching them even more tightly.

He winced, feeling his short nails piercing his palms. He savored the agony for minutes it seemed, then uncurled his hands and stared fixedly at the blood oozing from the cuts. In an almost awed fashion, he touched a finger to the blood; rubbing it between his thumb and index finger as though trying to solve the mystery of it.

***

Book of Scandal

"Why not in the corporate division, managing accounts, bringing in new deals for Ramsey?"

Quentin massaged his nose and managed a smile while inwardly trying to keep a strangle hold on his temper. "Age and experience are a part of this too, you know?" He tried to make light reference to the fact in a teasing style.

Marcus didn't get the joke. "Pop I haven't been a youth in years."

Quentin's expression sharpened toward Marc sitting across his desk. He wondered if the child had ever experienced the innocence of youth. The boy seemed to have come from the womb with an agenda. "Son understand this: no one, not even my head V.P.s started at the top. Everyone has to earn their way from the ground up. Everyone."

"You didn't." Marcus sneered.

Quentin almost laughed. "*I* started the company."

"Company'll be mine one day."

"You're sure?"

"Very."

"Then you shouldn't mind relaxing in the youth division 'til that day arrives."

"That's bullshit!" Effectively bested and not liking it one bit, Marc pounded a fist to his father's neat pine desk. "The youth division is small potatoes. I'll be done with college soon and what good is a fuckin' degree with no experience."

Quent's entire body stiffened. "You're goin' too far, boy."

"Screw it! I'll tell you what good that degree is-about as good as a condom without a hard dick inside it!"

Book of Scandal

Quent stood so suddenly, the heavy desk chair he'd occupied teetered back on the verge of crashing to the floor.

"Damn it to hell I've tried. God knows I've tried and now I'm done with it."

The soft, dangerous undercurrent in his father's tone, gave Marc pause for the first time.

"I swear if it weren't for your mother-"

"Mama's the only one who-!" Marcus stopped himself and backed away when Quentin shoved aside the chair and stormed around the desk.

"You get the hell out of my sight." The man practically growled, no love then only despise for the boy in his presence. "You get the hell out of here or that chair of mine that you want so badly will be up your ass."

Angry tears sprouted in Marc's dark eyes but he refused to let them fall. Bolting across the room, he threw open the cracked door which thundered when it slammed at the wall. Marc left the office seeing blood and never spotting Damon who waited in the hallway.

***

Carmen finished a final entry to her diary before setting the lock and returning the velvet bound book to its tin box. She placed the small box beneath a stone that rested at the base of the tree she leaned against.

Something popped or snapped in the distance and she turned in the direction of the sound. She glanced back at the stone and debated. The last thing she needed was for anyone to find and read her most private thoughts…desires. She shook her head then, warding off unseemly images filling her mind.

Book of Scandal

Deciding the book was safe; she pushed up and began her trek towards home. There was but the lightest nip in the air and she prayed summer wouldn't end too soon. The warmth made her feel alive, free and safe. The chill and eventual cold of winter kept her thoughts focused too closely on the always present air of eerie uncertainty lurking amidst her home and family.

As if on cue, the pop and snap sound broke through the more engaging sounds of nature and gave Carmen pause. Veering off the path toward home, she chose to investigate. She pressed her lips together and kept a grip on her fears then for sure.

Eerie uncertainty was almost tangible surrounding the area she headed towards. Since before her parents (and quite possibly *their* parents) had existed, all Ramseys were buried on the family property. Much of that was due to the fact that blacks and whites didn't share the same burial lands. Some long ago white Ramsey ancestor believed having the family take their eternal sleep together would ensure its strength in the afterlife. Carmen twisted her lips as if finding humor in that opinion- as if strength in the afterlife was necessary or even realistic. At least humor gave her the courage to continue her steps toward the burial area where she'd heard the weird sounds.

Nothing prepared her to find Jasper Stone seated at the base of one of the massive moss trees that encircled the cemetery. There he sat and Carmen felt her courage- give way to curiosity. She observed him before daring to intrude. Her eyes narrowed when she discovered the source of the pop and snapping. He'd been breaking sticks that littered the ground. She noticed that quite a few of those sticks were thick and dangerously ragged. Jasper broke them like they were twigs and she could see him wince when it caused him pain.

He appeared to stiffen then- straightening slightly from the tree like an animal that sensed its solitude had been threatened. Carmen moved in when he turned his head in her direction. She apologized for disturbing him before he could apologize for being on her property and she dropped down next to him before he could stand.

"Jasper!" Horrified, she'd spotted the true extent of the damage done by the sticks he'd been breaking in half.

"What are you doing?" She tucked the longer edge of her bang behind an ear and took a closer look at his hands. "You could pick up all kinds of germs from these rotting sticks."

"Doesn't matter," he grimaced when she touched one of the cuts.

"Your Mama would be worried sick if she saw your hands."

"Would she?"

"Sure she would."

He hadn't phrased the words like he'd expected a response. When Carmen glimpsed his face she knew there was more going on.

"What are you doing out here Jasper?"

"What's it feel like to come from greatness, Carm?" He watched the cemetery.

"Jasper?" Carmen shook her head. "What-?"

"Must be somethin' else to know the blood of good people, powerful and...respected people flows through your veins?"

"Jasper why-?"

"Do you know why I'm here, Carm?" He continued to watch the grave. "Because my Mama screwed some other woman's husband."

Carmen drew her knees up to her chin. She knew the story well. It was still a great scandal in Savannah's black community through it'd occurred some six or seven years before she was born.

She rubbed a hand across the knee of his faded denims. "Jasper don't-"

"I heard she was pregnant other times before me. She...got rid of 'em. She thought she had a catch in Joe Cade- figured I was the leverage she'd need to get him to leave his wife."

"Jasper don't. It doesn't matter." She perched on her bare knees and smoothed a hand along his forearm. "You had nothing to do with it- any of it."

He was already shaking his head. "Doesn't matter. I'll be paying for it for the rest of my life."

"That's true only if you allow it to rule you."

"But don't you see Carm?" He turned to her then. "It *does* rule me." His light eyes faltered to the cuts inflicted by the sticks and his own short nails. "The blood always rules. I'll be nothing because my Mama before me was-"

"Stop it." Carmen scooted closer and tugged the front of his shirt. "You're a great guy." She linked arms about his neck, pressing her cheek to his. "I won't let you do this to yourself. I can't stand to watch it, not when..." Instead of finishing the statement in words, she finished in action and kissed him.

Book of Scandal

Jasper's surprise quickly gave way to need. The kiss took on an intensity that overruled any innocent uncertainties that may have existed. Carmen behaved in the manner of a woman far beyond thirteen years. Her soft whimpers and rubbings against him, stoked a familiar tightening below Jasper's waist. She fully straddled his lap, losing her fingers in his silky hair.

Jasper made a move to steady Carmen and drew her closer. The pain in his hands; when they flexed, brought him back to reality.

"Jesus Carmen what the hell are you doin'?" The words came out in a hiss.

Again, Carmen chose action over words and simply stared her answer.

Jasper managed a chuckle in spite of all that had happened that day. "You're crazy."

"Why?" She challenged, quickly tossing hair from her eyes.

Jasper massaged his neck. "I don't have enough time to list all the reasons. Let's leave it at the fact that you're thirteen and a Ramsey."

Lashes fluttered when she rolled her eyes. "My name means nothing as for my age..." she shrugged a shoulder. "That's only a matter of time. It'll change."

"Your name is everything." He fisted a hand about her upper arm. "Don't forget that Carmen. You're good inside. Don't taint it...with filth."

"Jasper-"

"Stop." He stood, looked around the expanse of the cemetery then back at her. "Forget this happened."

Book of Scandal

Carmen looked away but not before Jasper spied her wide eyes glistened by tears. His expression softened but he wouldn't give in and stomped away from her.

R
~CHAPTER SIX~

A single knock on his office door, brought Westin's head up out of the thick folder he frowned over. Seeing his little brother at the threshold quickly removed the frown. Laughing then, Westin moved from behind the desk to greet Damon with a hug.

"Good to see you! Real good!" West drew the boy into another hug. His glee was genuine as both he and Quentin had their concerns that the boy might break from the family and not work for Ramsey when his time came.

"I stopped by to speak the other day." Damon explained while they hugged. "Kollette told me you were in a meeting."

"Ah," West's smile deepened at the news of a previous visit. It was like pulling teeth to get the boy to come into the office when he was home from school.

"Yeah I'd stopped by for lunch with Pop. He was um...too busy to see me when I got here."

West tilted his head. "Come on in, man." With a wave he ushered his brother toward the office living area.

Book of Scandal

While Damon took a seat, West headed for the bar and
withdrew two Pepsi Colas from the refrigerated under chest.
For a time, the brothers sat silently enjoying sips from their
respective bottles.

"You need to talk about somethin' man?" West
crossed ankle over knee while leaning back in the square
leather chair he occupied.

"Pop was with Marc."

"Were they talkin' or fightin'?" West's hand
tightened on the Pepsi bottle. Damon's answering look
roused a low curse in his throat. "What about?" He left the
chair.

"Somethin' about Marc heading a youth project."

West perched the bottle on the corner of his desk
and braced his fists atop the pine surface. "Ma's been
pushin' Pop to give Marc more responsibility in the
business." He turned and folded arms across the front of his
cream dress shirt. "We felt he couldn't do much damage in
the youth division since it's just gearing up. It'd be a good
first project for Marc to get his feet wet in." Again, West
cursed, massaging the area where soft hair tapered at his
neck. I should've known the jackass would throw it back in
Pop's face. I'd hoped I was wrong..." West blinked
suddenly, realizing he'd been rambling off his worries to
his little brother.

"Sorry man."

Damon waved off the apology. "You think Pop'll
try again or just forget it?"

"Probably try again." West stroked the square angle
of his jaw. "Ma really wants Marc to have a place here."

Book of Scandal

"Maybe he's not meant to have a place here."
Damon saw the look his brother flashed and assumed it was
because West didn't approve. Immediately, Damon stood
to defend his opinion.

"He's wrong West." Damon eased both hands into
the back pockets of his beige trousers and walked over to
peer out the window overlooking the Ramsey back lot.
"Somethin's not right about him. Never has been. Then
there's that weird hold he's got over Houston…"

"Hell you sound like Pop." Westin smiled in spite
of the seriousness of the conversation. "What's that fancy
private school teachin' you?"

Damon turned from the window. His pitch stare
relayed that he was in no mood to be teased.

"If goin' to that school's taught me one thing, it's to
see people for what they are not what just their words or
just their actions say- but a combination of both." Tugging
agitatedly at the collar of his black and beige striped top, he
thought of the private boarding school he'd attended for the
past three years.

The place had been established as something of an
experiment to test the waters of black and white co-
education. While Damon had made many new friends
outside his race, the experience away from home hadn't
been all roses. Over the years, it had become easier to read
between the lines of certain well-meaning remarks voiced
by his white acquaintances. In spite of their open-minded
upbringings by progressive parents, many weren't a step
above the blatant racists dwelling right there in Savannah.
They just knew how to mask it better, so to speak.

Book of Scandal

"There's something…wrong with Marcus." Damon reiterated, once more staring past the window. "I'm just asking you to keep an eye out."

West nodded when Damon gave him the benefit of his gaze. Silently, West admired his brother-acknowledging the man he was becoming. Their father had gotten it right. Damon would be the future of Ramsey, bypassing Marc and Houston without really having to try.

"Thanks for stopping by, man." West extended a hand to shake before drawing his brother into another hug.

***

"Hey man, get away from them shades!" Charlton blared at Houston. "You want everybody to know we in here and just ripped off a Chem lab?"

Houston's face tightened in the wake of an outburst. He chose to keep his mouth shut and let the tattered shade fall back in place across the window.

They'd selected the main storeroom for the Corner Market Grocer as their 'safe house' following the robbery. Located at the far end of an alley; the storeroom was equipped with a private phone and the building was mostly visited late night every two Sundays.

Charlton rolled his eyes away from Houston and back to Marcus who sat talking to their contacts about the success of the job. Like Houston had before, Charlton now looked as if *he* wanted to say something but saw the prudence in keeping his mouth shut.

To himself, he could admit how it stung when the contact asked to speak to the Ramsey- preferring to talk with Marc regarding the payoff for the stash of strange chemicals they'd lifted from the lab. If it hadn't been for

Book of Scandal

him making contact in the first place Marcus Ramsey
would've had nothing to hold his high powered discussion
over Charlt thought.

Of course, Charlton knew it had nothing to do with
Marc personally. It was the Ramsey name that had
mesmerized the Atlanta cigar man who was their front for
the goods. They could've probably made out with a fraction
of what they'd managed to lift from that lab and the man
would've still been salivating over the chance to talk
business with one of *the* Ramseys.

Marcus laughed over the phone just then. Charlton
pulled a cigarette from behind his ear, rolled his eyes and
swiveled the chair away from his friend.

Only one person in the storeroom could've been
happier than Marc. Jasper had felt like a kid on Christmas
when they broke the lock to Dr. Manford Pressley's lab.
The never ending rows of shelving carried bottles of all
shapes, sizes and colors. Jasper was in awe and could
barely remain focused on his real reason for being there.

Jasper had often dreamed of asking the doctor for a
job just to be close to the science. Whether he was a student
or not- the opportunity seemed like heaven. He'd cast off
the idea more times than he could count-figuring the doc
would never allow a black kid close to his prized
possessions and certainly not a black kid with *his*
background.

But there he was and he certainly planned to savor
the opportunity. In the meeting place at the grocer's
storeroom, Jasper relished the items he'd taken for his own
personal use.

Book of Scandal

What could he learn from the vials of unassuming liquids? What could he discover by studying them? Science-chemistry especially had always fascinated him. Had he been able to continue his education with college, chemistry would have been his course of study. Chemicals. The wrong combination was poison. The right could produce a cure to save millions. It was the same with people Jasper thought and took a few moments to observe the healing cuts in his palms. A combination of the right people could create a masterpiece. The wrong people-abomination.

"Marc? You sure this place is safe?" Houston brushed past Charlton to question his brother once the call with the contact had ended.

"Man, won't you get off that shit-" Charlton's tirade silenced when he glimpsed Marc's deadly look.

"The place is fine Hous," Marc reassured his brother.

"And Jeff? You sure we can count on him not to say anything?"

Charlton even cooled to wait on Marc's response.

Marcus was already nodding. "Jeff's cool."

"He's goin' to study law in school." Charlton drew another cigarette from his pocket. "How loyal is your friend to his callin'?"

"Very. But he wouldn't rat on a friend. He's loyal there too."

"Crazy," Charlton murmured while turning away to light the cigarette. "I'll never get how you can be friends with a lil' punk like that."

Book of Scandal

"Charlt's right Marc," Houston stepped forward wringing his hands, "it could be dangerous with Jeff knowin' everything."

"Don't y'all know it's always good to have a friend who's beyond reproach?" Marc rolled his eyes when Houston and Charlton fixed him with blank stares. "A person like that in your corner makes folks second guess how much foul shit you could really be into." He hitched a thumb across his shoulder. "Get the stuff packed so we can get out of here. Jasper? Jasper? Hey Jas!" Marc hitched his thumb toward the boxes waiting to be packed.

"So what'd the buyer say?" Charlton asked, once Houston and Jasper were at work.

Marc winked. "We'll talk later."

***

Catrina's energy was focused on scrubbing the surface of the rear tables. Her thoughts though, were focused on her last conversation with Damon. God, she didn't even know the boy's last name and probably wouldn't have the chance to find out now.

She could almost feel him zoning out when she launched her sermon on business. Boys always got that look in their eyes when she started to discuss her veritable obsession with it.

Boys usually grew bored with airheads but a girl with a brain didn't even stand half a chance. Oh well, she sighed and launched into scrubbing a greasy corner with renewed vigor. At least she'd have a few fond memories of the very fine chocolate-skinned enigma. She'd just settled the fact in her mind when he walked by the café's bay window.

Book of Scandal

Damon had planned to have a late lunch with Westin and continue their conversation from the week before. A last minute meeting pushed West to cancel though. As Damon would be heading back to school for fall term in a few more days, the chances of them having another time to talk seriously would probably not be possible.

Head bowed and hands pushed deep in his gray trouser pockets, Damon looked up in time to realize where he was. Without hesitating, he walked into Jeffries and locked gazes with her the moment he turned his head.

Catrina twisted the dishcloth she held and watched him approach. Her sparkling mahoganies were wide with expectancy.

"The section's closed." She blurted when only a table separated them. Closing her eyes then, she cursed herself. Airhead indeed...perhaps there was hope after all.

Damon smirked. "It's okay. I'm not hungry."

Catrina's expectant stare flushed with concern when he took a seat at the table she'd just cleaned. "Are you okay?" She sat as well.

"I'm good." His burgundy shirt crinkled at the shoulders when he shrugged. "Not looking forward to the end of summer is all."

"What school do you go to?" Catrina asked once she'd bit her lip on the question long enough. She'd never recalled seeing him around the halls of Booker T. Washington High.

Damon bristled inwardly, hoping the question wouldn't lead to more concerning his background. "I'm away at school."

Book of Scandal

"Away?" Catrina sighed, her gaze brightening in a dreamy manner as she fidgeted with the neck line of her striped blouse. "That must be out of sight."

Damon had to smile. "It's got its moments."

"Gosh," she flopped back in the chair. "I wouldn't know how to act if I went at least two whole days without bein' told to scrub somethin' or toss out somethin'."

His laughter came through full and genuine then. "My dad would say startin' at the bottom builds a strong leader." Damon broke his own rule against background information before he'd even realized it.

Catrina simply shook her head. "I should be Hercules by now then."

"You must miss your family a lot being away at school?" She noted once silence returned after more laughter had ended.

"I miss *some* of them."

"Ah! An aggravating little brother?"

"Hmph. Try aggravating *older* brothers."

Catrina laughed, but silenced when he slanted her a look. "Sorry."

Shamefully long lashes shielded his stare when he shook his head. "Don't be. I wish it was as funny to me."

"I'm sorry anyway. If it's not funny to you, I shouldn't have laughed."

Damon reached over to fidget with a glass pepper shaker. "You got any brothers or sisters?"

"No," she propped a fist to her cheek. "Lots of cousins, though. *Lots.*"

He chuckled. "Guess it's easier when they don't come home with you, huh?"

Book of Scandal

"If you say so," Catrina drawled and they dissolved into another round of laughter.

***

Daphne and Babydoll had debated tirelessly on the most provocative hairstyle for her *meeting* with Marcus Ramsey. In the end of course, Babydoll's word won out.

"Loose and tousled is more alluring." Babydoll was saying while taking in the results of her styling skills.

Seated at the vanity, Daphne stared at the mass of heavily teased blondish brown curls framing her face. Her mother was right.

The next debate involved attire.

"It's dumb to dress in anything too fancy…it won't be on long." Daphne reasoned.

"Oh no girl," Babydoll had disappeared into her walk in closet. "A woman can never spend too much time on appearance regardless of what's in store."

Daphne ceased further argument when she spotted the creation her mother whipped from the closet. Slowly, she ventured toward the bed, looking down on the empire-wasted chiffon lounging gown Babydoll had placed there.

In a daze, Daphne leaned in to rub the fine material between her fingers. Nothing she owned was as lovely. "This night could be the beginning of the rest of my life," she whispered.

Babydoll winked. "Let's get you ready."

Marcus was ready for a night of celebration and; in his opinion there was no better way to celebrate than with a vigorous round of sex. There was nothing better than sex-

Book of Scandal

period. He'd held fast to that opinion since losing his virginity at the sweet age of eleven.

Following the very generous payoff from the lab job, he was ready to throw a bit of his earnings around town. Calling Babydoll Monfrey was tops on his list. Marc smoothed the pad of his thumb across his brows and checked the crisp white ascot at his neck. He wondered who she'd set him up with that night.

Obviously not herself, though a night with the madam was in his budget and would certainly be money well spent given the woman's extensive talents. Babydoll had told him she had a special girl in mind-new and untouched. As he'd sampled many of Babydoll's other treasures; having the newest on the row, was as impressive as it was ego-stroking.

***

Babydoll arranged for a quiet evening at the house. She'd sent her other girls away for client weekends or simply given them the night off with specific instructions not to return before lunchtime the next day. She herself would remain down in her private parlor and be first-*second* to see the look of immense satisfaction on Marcus Ramsey's face when he strolled down her front stairs.

He'd be nothing but pleased. She was certain. Daphne was a vision and; while having the girl opt for a lifestyle similar to her own was not her intention; Babydoll knew sex had its rewards. If the girl snagged a Ramsey… oh the life she'd lead! The same would be true for her mother, Babydoll imagined.

Book of Scandal

"Marcus baby, what a pleasure to see you again!" Babydoll answered with a flourish when the bell rang promptly at 9:20 p.m.

Marc greeted the striking, older beauty with a kiss to the cheek and then passed her an envelope from an inside pocket on his black dinner jacket.

"Perfect." She thumbed through the wad of fifties in the envelope. "Come in love." She said, still counting the cash. Satisfied with the financial arrangements, Babydoll nodded toward the emerald green carpeted stairway.

"Third room on the left."

New, was the first word that sprang to Marc's mind when he saw the treat reclining upon the pillow and lace trimmed canopy bed. Like an adornment for a cake, she sat waiting for him and he felt his fingertips itch to touch.

"Marcus Ramsey." He introduced himself, feeling the flames stoke his ego when he witnessed the brightening of her gaze at the sound of his name.

"Daphne Monfrey," she countered, witnessing the same brightening of his gaze at the sound of *her* name.

"Your mother said you were new." He removed the suit jacket and ascot not caring where they fell. "I can see that you are." His shirt was unbuttoned and his hands went to his belt. "She also said you were untouched- that true too?"

Her lips curved and she settled back a bit more. "You'll have to find that out for yourself."

Marc wasted no time with more pleasantries and was on her a second later.

"How old are you Daphne?"

Book of Scandal

"Fourteen."

His gaze narrowed. "You mind being a whore like your mother?"

She arched her breasts deeper into his chest. "That would depend on how good at it I am."

He laughed shortly and took a moment to more closely observe her. "You're not an ordinary fourteen year old. I don't intend to treat you like one." He looked up, allowing her to see the intent in his dark stare.

Daphne's smile was knowing and approving when Marc tore the sleeve of the gown in his attempt to drag down the bodice. She'd tried to tell her mother it wouldn't last long.

His mouth was on her then, suckling surprisingly ample breasts. Feverishly, he pushed at the gown until his hand contacted with her bare thighs. She wore no undergarments and he shuddered over the discovery. His fingers skirted the folds of her sex, his ego flaring at the tiny sounds of desire rising from her throat.

Not wanting to deflower her too soon-not with his fingers anyway. He gently explored her there emitting his own grunt when her need slicked his fingers. Marc wanted to savor the treat, but decided that would have to come later. The young, eager confection in his arms was too provocative for her own good.

Quickly, he freed himself, parted her thighs to suit him and drove into her.

"You're no virgin," he groaned while moving in and out then rotating to draw moans from her mouth.

"Disappointed?"

"Hell no."

Book of Scandal

"So you…enjoyed our time together?" Daphne felt mildly agitated that it was happening so quickly.

Marcus however, was grinning as he continued to take her. "I'll tell you in the morning."

ℛ
~CHAPTER SEVEN~

Harriett Cade knew her attitude regarding Belleina Stone had the desired affect on her husband. Joe had been pretty obedient in the weeks and months following the Ramsey event. Still, Harriett wasn't naïve enough to believe her rages over the other woman would keep Joe's leash tight for long.

When his visits to Gordon's Liquor and Smokes (the ones he didn't think she knew about) went from one visit a week, to three, Harriett knew it wouldn't be long until he'd be hankering to revisit other vices.

She'd been following him for the last two weeks. Easy enough, since Felix had been sticking closer to home while waiting on a call about a new job. Harriett flexed her fingers around the steering wheel and grimaced. She'd have to find out more about this possible job as well. Could her baby really be contemplating leaving home? The idea made her shiver and draw the black shawl more tightly about her

Book of Scandal

round shoulders. Felix would never return to Savannah once he left.

Just then however, she had other matters to see to. In her son's old inconspicuous Chevy truck, Harriett kept tabs on her husband. Following at a reasonable distance was tough work. By the end of the first week, she was tired of sitting on the truck's tough leather seat until her ass went numb. She began to count all the chores and errands being neglected while she played detective. She had to at least give it one more week though. Then she'd admit to paranoia and let it go. If anything happened between Joe and his tramp after that, then so be it.

Fate intervened on the night marking 3 ½ weeks of surveillance. Harriett sat waiting outside Gordon's; toying between staying and just heading home. Just as well, she thought tightening the scarf about her French waves. Felix was already growing suspicious. She didn't think he was buying her church revival or choir rehearsal excuses much anymore. At any rate, she'd already decided to let it all go that night. This was crazy. She was better than this. *She* deserved better than this. She damn well deserved better than a sorry nigga like Joe Cade.

Laughter and heavy talking filled the night air. Harriett sat up to see Pilfrey Gordon leaning on the doorjamb of his establishment while seeing off his last customer- Joe Cade.

Harriett bit down on her bottom lip feeling the faint metallic taste of blood on the tip of her tongue. She felt that flutter in her stomach as her heart took a swim there and knew it was the sight of Joe that had done it. God, would

Book of Scandal

she always be a fool for that man? He'd made her love him, desire him, bear his child and practically raise the boy on her own while he'd given next to nothing in return.

"Well…he had given *some* things in return. He'd given betrayal, money thrown away on liquor, cigars and the occasional gamble- not to mention the many, many women he'd tossed in her face and the excuses/apologies that followed. In that regard, yes Joe Cade had given her much.

Pilfrey was waving off Joe who had settled in his truck and soon brought the engine to roaring life. Harriett waited until he'd driven off before she started the Chevy. With an expertise she'd acquired over the last few weeks, she followed undetected. Judging from the way Joe had floated into the truck earlier, she figured he was probably too mellow to notice a thing.

They were some five minutes from home when Harriett gave into the yawn she'd been trying to stifle. She prepared to take the turn which would lead to their street when she noticed Joe was heading straight. Either he was going a different route or too drunk to realize he'd missed the turn- or he had another stop to make.

The desire to yawn was gone. Harriett's dark round face was a picture of alertness. She pressed a little harder on the gas. Only another minute and a half confirmed Joe's destination- Belleina Stone's. Harriett's hands felt cramped around the steering wheel. Her gaze was blurred with tears but she pressed on- anger echoed in her body and mind. She could hear hate-filled words hissing almost with a life of their own throughout the close confines of the truck's cabin. Several times she squeezed her eyes shut tight to

Book of Scandal

ward off the tears and the angry hissing. She ordered herself to return home and forget this madness, but she pressed on and never veered off the path.

When he arrived at Belleina's, Harriett held back and parked an ample distance with the lights doused. She waited- wanted to give them time for hugs and kisses of welcome, hushed words of bursting desire. She wanted to catch them in the midst of it. Perhaps then and only then she'd be purged of her love and need for him. Perhaps then, she could walk away with no desire to turn back.

***

Westin heard Briselle's heavy sigh and snuggled his head closer to her chest. He took comfort in the sound of her heart beating below her breast. Of course, it didn't take long though to realize her sighs had little to do with contentment.

"You're gonna miss this." He undid the button up bodice of her dark mini dress.

Briselle scanned the moonlit beauty of the flower laden field. It had become her favorite place in all of Savannah- the place where she met the man she'd marry.

"I'll miss it a little." She laughed when he tickled her. "A lot, a lot!" Another sigh followed once she sobered. "I'm scared West."

"Scared to come with me?" He raised his head.

"Scared you'll regret that I did."

The muscle flexed along his square jaw. He wouldn't reassure her there; not when he'd done that time and time again. She'd have to come to accept that on her own.

Book of Scandal

She seemed to read his mind. "I'm not looking for reassurance from you, but from myself." She rubbed her thumb across the face of his watch glinting in the moonlight. "I'm scared I'll fail West and I'd have no one to blame but myself."

"Honey," he brushed the back of his hand along her cheek. All the while he battled the frustration that she'd blame herself for what she had no control over. This would be an issue until they were blessed in the way she believed would be her redemption.

"Will you promise me somethin'?" He sat up on the pallet they shared and pulled her with him. "Would you put the disappointments and...losses away once we go to Seattle? It's supposed to represent change- a new life for all of us. Old pain has no place there. You think you could try- see if it might help?"

Briselle's eyes glossed with the love she had for him and the beauty of his words. Nodding, she tugged on the hem of his pin-striped top and drew him into a kiss.

***

Marcus and Daphne collapsed on the bed- naked and slick with sweat. Daphne giggled insanely when he gnawed at her neck. Seconds later, she turned the tables, rolling over to cover his body with hers.

"Have you been with any of my Mama's other girls since our first night together?

Marc resumed his gnawing. "Why would I want them with I've got the cream of the crop?"

"That'd be Mama."

"But the apple don't fall far, right? Besides," he clutched her bottom, "this apple's firmer."

Book of Scandal

Laughter resumed, then kissing which Daphne put her all into. She knew it'd take more than a few weeks of screwing Marcus Ramsey to get him to give her his name. But as Babydoll said, 'sex was power'. If Marc's hunger for her were any example, her power was growing.

As though he'd somehow captured a glimpse of her thoughts, Marc suddenly pulled away."You gonna start getting' mushy on me?" He asked.

She rolled her eyes. "Where's the fun in that?"

For a time, he searched her face before deciding she was telling the truth. He flipped her beneath him and resumed feasting upon her body. Softly, Daphne heaved a sigh of relief.

***

After ten minutes, Harriett accepted the fact that her husband and his whore weren't going to sidle off to bed like good little lovers. Imaging them having a chat over coffee in the kitchen chilled something deep inside her. The relationship was more than sex, there was intimacy and it had lasted almost as long as her marriage. That he could talk to this woman, share things and laugh over private jokes with her was yet another thorn that would burrow deeply in her side and fester.

When she threw open the screen door however; the phrase 'be careful what you wish for'; dashed in her face like water. She'd wanted to see them in the act of it, then cursed when she thought it was not to be and raged that something more meaningful might be amiss. Now, what she wanted was there blaring like a bugle horn. Harriett watched while her husband took another woman from behind.

Book of Scandal

Her grandmother had once said men looked outside the home for what they couldn't get inside it. Harriett knew that was a crock of shit. Men looked anywhere for whatever it was they wanted at the moment. She'd been an open partner in their marriage bed. Joe got what he wanted-the way he wanted it. She'd never had a complaint either. Yet he chose his whore to fulfill what could have just as easily been obtained from his wife.

There he was giving to another woman what she once foolishly thought; during the stupidity of youth, was meant for only her. Pants and boxers pooled around the work boots he still wore. Belleina's dress was bunched up at her waist. Their groans and words of desire filled the kitchen to such a volume, neither heard or noticed her entering and standing there to witness their lust vent itself.

Dishes clattered against the brush of their bodies next to the counter; some fell to the floor. Silverware clattered and then skidded across the linoleum. When the gleaming butcher's knife slid to a stop at her feet, Harriett considered it fate.

Joe shut his eyes tight, feeling his release at hand. He squeezed Belleina's generous bottom, spreading the cheeks wider apart while shuddering a curse at the increased penetration. Belleina reached back, pulling one of his hands to her breast-aching for him to fondle the tip. She tossed her head wildly and moaned his name. Her lashes fluttered, her eyes caught a glimpse of light flash against the stainless steel surface of the toaster. Then she heard Joe scream. It was not a scream of pleasure.

Joe's flaccid sex dangled pitifully before him when he withdrew from Belleina. Frantically, he clapped at his

Book of Scandal

shoulder and attempted to reach what had pierced his spine.
His fingers just grazed the handle protruding from his back.
The pain was wrenching- his brain had somehow deduced
it was a knife but where had it come from? His wild twists,
as he worked to reach the blade, eventually turned him
toward his wife.

"Harry?" He fell to his knees.

Belleina watched, horrified when her lover
collapsed. She turned a scathing look toward Harriett.
"Bitch." She moved close.

Harriett had lost her zeal for arguing or talk of any
kind. She held a medium sized iron skillet which had also
fallen to the floor during the love fest she'd witnessed.
Before Belleina Stone spoke another word, the skillet hit
her mouth. Harriett scarecely blinked while bringing down
the pan on the woman's face and body.

"Joe!" Faintly Belleina realized the man was in no
shape to help her. "Jas!" She remembered then that her son
had gone out to Jonas Gray's farm for a job. He wouldn't
be back 'til the morning.

An eerie crack sounded, the next blow from the pan
split Belleina's skull. Harriett continued flaying the black,
rough skillet as though it were a whip.

Belleina was losing consciousness, barely able to
lift her arms to ward off the blows. It was a useless move
anyway. Blood blurred her gaze as it streamed her face.

Joe managed to dislodge the knife. Rising to his feet
would be another challenge. Slowly, he extended a hand,
unable to make a sound while watching the woman he
loved being massacred by the other woman he loved.

Book of Scandal

Drawing strength from someplace deep, Joe was able to stagger to his feet using overturned chairs and the table for support.

"Harriett," he reached his wife just as Belleina surrendered to the attack. For his trouble, he received a blow to the cheek from the iron skillet.

In an almost robotic fashion, Harriett traded her attack on Belleina for one on Joe. The pan came down repeatedly- relentlessly. No emotion registered on her face. Beating down her husband took much less time as he was already wounded.

Not until Joe's head fell back on the floor with a lifeless thud, did Harriett blink. Her eyes narrowed and she realized the extent of what she'd done. Still, there was no burst of tears or words of regret. She simply eased down to the blood smeared floor, pulled Joe into a loving embrace, fixed his clothes and rocked him slow.

ℛ
~CHAPTER EIGHT~

Savannah's black community was shocked by the savage double murder of Belleina Stone and Joe Cade. As the quiet street on which the late Ms. Stone resided rarely had any excitement, but for the annual Williams' Family Reunion, a savage murder was indeed cause for uproar, gossip and scandal.

Young Jasper Stone arrived home shortly after dawn on the morning after the murders. He'd returned from his landscaping job out at Gray's Farm to find the back screen door flapping against an unusually brisk morning breeze. The kitchen was in shambles and his mother lay in a pool of thick burgundy ooze. The blood had already begun to congeal around her body.

Book of Scandal

Humming an eerie serene tune was Harriett Cade who leaned against the open refrigerator door. She rocked her dead husband as if the man were simply taking a nap.

Word spread like fire once Jasper got past his shock and phoned the police. Folks made no secret about wanting to know what was going on. They left their beds and breakfast tables to gain a prime spot close to the Stone house.

There was no place for whispered speculations. Conversation hummed like machinery. Voices gained volume when the bodies were brought out and placed in the County Examiner's station wagon. Harriett Cade was brought out in handcuffs.

The aftermath was the only thing more shocking than the crime; which was perhaps only shocking to an outsider with a different sense of logic.

The town's women (and the men who were too unsettled to go against them) sided almost unanimously with Harriett Cade. There were already predictions that the woman wouldn't spend a day in prison following the trial- if there was one. Most everyone knew of the Cade, Cade, Stone triangle and the fact that Harriett Cade had been forced to look in the face of her husband's betrayal every day for the last 19 years.

***

In the days that followed, talk over the scandal was the highlight of dinner conversation in homes all over town. Conversations at the Ramsey home were no different. Even

Marcella; who rarely engaged in gossip, was vocal about the horror.

"Marcus how is Jasper? I bet the poor thing doesn't even know which way is up."

Marc shrugged, cutting savagely into the steak nestled beneath steamed vegetables. "Guess he's alright. I haven't seen him around."

"Isn't he your friend?" Carmen blurted at his careless response.

Forgetting the steak, Marc sent his sister a sly look across the table. "I got lots of friends, Carm." He winked.

Carmen immediately turned her head.

Marc's lurid dark gaze clashed with Damon who watched him with unmasked disapproval from his place next to Carmen.

Suddenly Damon chuckled. The gesture was not humor-induced. "Glad we aren't friends."

"Damon…" Marcella warned, knowing all too well that an argument was in the air. "Anyway Marcus, the boy's all alone in that house and I'll bet he's not eating worth a cuss with mostly everyone siding with Harriett." She shook her head. "No one's probably done the Christian thing and taken food to the boy, either."

Damon smirked over the whine in his brother's voice when Marcella told Marcus she was going to have him take some things out to Jasper.

"You hush; I don't want to hear it." Marcella waved off Marc's arguments with barely a wave of her hand. "Everyone's always talkin' about being like the Ramseys." She smiled and sent a saucy wink toward Quentin who watched the scene quietly from his end of the table. "Now it's time to see if they really mean it- see if they'll follow my example."

Of course, not everyone wanted to be like the Ramseys. Still, a great number did follow Marcella's example when word spread of the feast she'd had prepared and sent out to Jasper Stone.

Even Marcus shed some of his aggravation over being the bearer of the goods, when he noted the admiration on everyone's faces as they remarked on Ramsey style and graciousness. However, Belleina Stone's funeral was even sadder given the obviously poor attendance. The Ramseys and a few others attended, but given the extent of Savannah's black community the numbers were pithy indeed.

***

Winter 1961~

For lack of better phrasing; the final nail in Belleina Stone's coffin, came months later in the form of an acquittal for Harriett Cade. In spite of the support she'd garnered, more than a few were stunned by the outcome of the case.

Georgia law wasn't known for letting go of its chance to put a black face behind bars for the smallest infraction. To support Harriett Cade seemed to be an expectation of every married woman to stand up and speak out against adultery. There were some who felt Belleina and Joe; for that matter, received a raw deal. Few though were willing to voice it very loudly.

In spite of Marcella Ramsey's glowing gesture of food and supplies for Jasper Stone, no one else reached out

Book of Scandal

to the boy except those who'd hopped on the bandwagon in the beginning. Once the newness of that wore off, Jasper barely received eye contact. Marcella at least, maintained her interest in the boy. She sent out food and supplies via one of the town's markets when she felt he was due.

Marcus was pretty much useless in regards to passing along information on his *friend*. Carmen though, was a veritable fount of knowledge on the subject of Jasper Stone. Marcella's concern over the young man's overall well-being superseded whatever concerns she may have had involving her youngest daughter's interest in him.

Indeed, Carmen had grown very interested. She was deeply intrigued by Jasper's quiet, self-absorbed manner. In spite of that, she believed he appreciated the conversations they shared- brief as they were. Carmen wouldn't have been surprised to learn that; aside from the groceries sent by her mother, Jasper had no other human contact. He made no attempt to seek her out, but that mattered very little to Carmen.

***

Jasper cut his sentence short when he heard the crunch of brush underfoot. He saw Carmen approaching from a cluster of trees.

"Sorry," she winced over the fact that she was always apologizing. It was to be expected though, since she was always the one intruding upon the quiet shelter he'd constructed about himself.

"I'm done," he smirked and turned back to the tombstone.

"Gosh Jasper, I'm sorry." Carmen realized the true extent of her intrusion.

Book of Scandal

"Don't be," he eased a handkerchief in the back pocket of his brown trousers. "I've been able to talk to my mother more now than I ever have." He turned to face Carmen. "Sick, huh?"

"Sad."

"She never gave up hopin' that *Daddy Joe* would leave his wife." He started walking away from his mother's grave. "All those years and she still thought she was the only one. 'Cheat' was Joe Cade's middle name."

Carmen sat next to him when he eased down before the base of a tree. "I'm sorry about Mrs. Cade. She should've gone away for what she did."

Jasper was shaking his head. "Mama slept with her husband, got pregnant."

"What she did was still wrong." Carmen knocked a stick against the sole of her boot. "People should pay when they hurt others."

"Some would say my mother paid for hurting Miss Harriett...and Felix."

"Please," Carmen rolled her eyes and smiled. "Felix loves you- I can tell. When I overhear him talking to Georgie he says he's lucky to have you for a brother."

Despite his mood, Jasper's light gaze softened. "You know, you're pretty smart for a thirteen year old."

Fourteen as of February eighth."

They laughed a while, but as expected, the solemn aura crept up around them again. Carmen used her stick to trace idle designs into the hard ground. Jasper was again staring toward his mother's grave.

"I'm thinkin' about joining the army."

Book of Scandal

"What?" Carmen's stick broke beneath the force of her hold.

"I'm suffocating here, Carm. Guess I didn't realize how much 'til now."

"But that's crazy." She clutched the sleeve of his dark green turtleneck. "Savannah may be suffocating but to trade it for boot camp...?"

He managed to flash an adorable smile. "Guess it depends on one's point of view, right?"

"Jasper..." The idea sickened her and she inched closer throwing her arms about his neck.

Jasper didn't shrink from the contact, but welcomed it.

***

While Jasper Stone sat contemplating his future, Charlton Browning literally held the ticket to his own.

"You sure 'bout this, man?" Marcus was eyeing his friend's train ticket to Chicago, Illinois.

"This shit's small potatoes," Charlton eyed the station and the people milling around with a mixture of spite and pity. "I want bigger- *better*." He turned to face Marc. "I want the respect you get just by sayin' your name."

Anger outweighed whatever pride Marcus felt from Charlton's words. "The name belongs to my father," he sneered, spite sneaking into his dark gaze then. "People have respect for my father's name, but I'll have it too- you can count on that. People will hear the name Marc Ramsey and they'll sit up and take notice." He saw that Charlton was studying him rather closely and he set a sly smile in

Book of Scandal

place of his sneer. "Least you can glide into Chicago in style with the killin' we made."

"Right on," Charlton grinned as they slapped hands. "Houston and Jas complain when they got their cuts?"

"Hell nah," Marc slipped his hand into the deep pockets of his pea-coat. "Them fools was just happy to see them greenbacks."

"Surprised you ain't slide more Jasper's way with his mama gettin' killed and all."

Marc shrugged. "My own Mama done spent enough on the nigga to keep the two of us in the finest threads for three years easy." He muttered a curse over the fact. "I ain't got time for sympathy- aint' profitable."

"Amen," Charlt breathed, slapping hands with Marc again.

***

Houston accepted defeat once he'd realized his numerous excuses had no affect on his mother who; because of Damon being away at school, had saddled him with the task of collecting Carmen from the library. The days were shorter and Marcella didn't want the girl trudging home in the dark.

Houston parked the gray Ford, checked his watch and sighed. He was about to search the radio dial for a change of music, when he noticed the girl strolling the opposite side of the street. She looked familiar and; after a few moments, he'd recalled seeing her at his family's cotillion cook out last summer.

Settling back against the glossy leather seat, he watched her sashaying the tiny black purse she carried. He wondered how old she was- way younger than him that's

Book of Scandal

for sure. Of course, it could've been the blondish brown
spiral curls that lent to her youthful look. Whatever it was,
she was most definitely good to look at. He found himself
wondering if the hair color was real and felt a tightening at
his groin over the thought. Then, he saw Carmen leaving
the library. The girl his sister spoke with on her way down
the steps drove everything/everyone else from Houston's
head.

As dark as the little blonde nymphet was light, this
one had Houston sitting up for a closer look. Another
familiar face, he thought. She was fine in a way that was
both polished and mysterious. His gaze narrowed while he
studied her and then it hit him. The cotillion and fish grease.
He recalled the T-shirt she wore: Jeffries Catering. It fell
into place then. He recalled how easy and interesting she'd
been to talk with. He saw Carmen look toward the car then
and he bowed his head to shield his face.

"Yeah that's him," Carmen recognized Houston's
Ford across the street. "Are we gonna study together any
more this week?"

"I'd like to." Catrina didn't appear hopeful. "My
folks have a catering job for some hospital thing and you
know they're gonna want their best grunt worker for the
event."

"Sorry girl." Carmen laughed.

"Don't worry about it." Catrina hefted the strap of
her book bag across her shoulder. "Aside from studying at
our fantastic library here, I've certainly got no better
plans."

Book of Scandal

"Everything okay?" Carmen noted a twinge of something unsettled in her friend's voice.

Catrina bit her lip while debating on whether to share and then shrugged. "It's Damon- the boy I told you about? The whole thing's crazy. I miss seeing him in spite of the fact that we hardly know each other and our conversations rarely last longer than ten minutes."

"Aw girl…" Carmen squeezed Catrina's arm. "I'm sure he misses you too, being back at school and all. Didn't you tell me he's away?" She watched Catrina nod while silently marveling that her brother had told the girl so much about his school when he hadn't even told her his last name. She could only chalk it up to the fact that he didn't want his time with her ruined by all that being a Ramsey entailed. "It'll work out." She predicted.

"Thanks Carm." Catrina pulled her into a hug before they parted ways.

"Wasn't she at the cotillion?" Houston asked when Carmen settled into the passenger side of the car.

She pretended to be focused on one of her books. "Yeah, Jeffries is hosting some big thing for the hospital."

"Oh." Houston said.

The drive passed in silence.

***

At 23, Georgia Ramsey was well past the age when many of her peers were married and rearing their third or fourth child. Georgia didn't care what that made her. Being tied down with a houseful of crumb crooks wasn't her idea of a well-lived life.

Book of Scandal

Still, like any young woman, she had her dreams of the perfect home and husband. If only she could have the kind of *home* with the *husband* she'd choose.

Georgia gathered her hair into a loose mound and threw back her head while savoring the length of steel she rode upon.

"Damn G!"

"Shh!" Her hazel stare glinted sharp when Felix's bellowing voice filled her bedroom. Her hissed orders for him to quiet down were only met with louder grunts and she wound up tossing a pillow over his handsome face.

Felix retaliated with a slap to his girlfriend's bouncing bottom. "What's the point of havin' your own crib if you can't let loose?"

"This crib is still attached to my folk's house." Her grinding slowed. "They got a lot of nosy maids who love to gossip about what I do in here."

Felix folded a hand behind his head and let the other fondle one of Georgia's firm breasts. "You think they don't know anyway?" He grabbed her hips suddenly and thrust deep before she could reply. His mouth tilted in an arrogant smirk when *her* sounds of delight filled the room. She didn't care who overheard.

"I'm leavin' G," he told her later when they relaxed across tangled sheets.

"Mmm hmm…" she was more interested in the tangled triangle of curls above his soft penis.

Grimacing, Felix sat up. "I'm leavin' for good, Georgia."

"Why now?" She took heed of his words and flopped back on the bed. "With everything goin' on, why now?"

"That's exactly why- everything goin' on."

"Baby don't you think your Mama's gonna need you?" She braced her weight on one elbow and trailed her fingers across his sweat-slicked chest. "Your Daddy bein' gone and all?"

"Mama's got the whole town on her side. She's revelin' in that shit." He raked fingers through his hair and cursed again. "Harriett Cade's the representative for all women who been done wrong by their man."

The couple had to smile when Jerry Butler's *"He Will Break Your Heart"* wafted softly through the radio on the nightstand.

"Just like a man to take issue with that." Georgia tensed and sat up to face Felix across the bed. "Just how much was she supposed to take off Mr. Joe and Belle Stone? Bad enough the wench had his kid, but then he's still out there screwin' her like that?" Georgia sucked her teeth. "I can very well understand what your Mama was feelin'."

Felix had to chuckle, knowing Georgia definitely understood. Hadn't she told him on more than one occasion; and in explicit terms, what she'd do to him if she ever caught him with another girl? Strange as it was, he wondered if he'd ever even feel what he felt for Georgia Ramsey with any other woman.

"I want you with me G. When I leave I want you to come with me."

"Well-" her hazel stare faltered to the linens. Uncharacteristically, speechless, Georgia sat clearing her throat for a time.

"G?" He stroked the long, toned line of her calf.

"Felix I- I can't. *You* can't."

"Jesus Georgia. Trust me, my Mama's gonna be just fine."

"But you can't leave under a cloud of shame like that. What would people think?"

"Fuck 'em."

"Felix!"

He watched her close, not buying the outrage for a second. No, he didn't buy it not from a girl who once begged him to have sex with her in the grimy flat bed of his truck. She plain told him it was the rush of being discovered that made her want to do it.

"Come off it G," he brought his face close to hers. "Daddy's money is why you won't leave."

"That too," she smarted as if he'd slapped her. Her sharply lovely features took on a hard sheen.

He reached for her hand. "Baby I know the money part scares you, but we'll make it."

Georgia bristled and tugged her hand free of his. "How Felix? With the two of us workin' 'til our backs break and we come home too tired and weary to do anything?" She waved her hands. "I've seen enough people who live that way. Lots of 'em work for my parents and it's the *last* kind of life I want."

"I've heard your Pop talk about how hard he and your Mama worked and sacrificed to get what they have now. Your father didn't take a dime from his family to start Ramsey."

"They worked so their children wouldn't have to." Georgia threw back.

Felix threw his legs over the side of the bed and clutched his hands. His jaw muscles flexed as anger set in yet he tried his best to stifle it before asking the question he already had the answer to. "Does that mean you won't come with me?"

"If it means givin' up a pretty cool lifestyle to struggle everyday… then no, no I won't come Felix."

His expression harbored no anger then. She'd been honest and he'd expected nothing less of her.

Georgia's nails curved deep enough to draw blood from her palms as she watched him. Her eyes were wide, following his every move. He turned to drop a kiss to the corner of her mouth and then left the bed to collect his clothes.

Georgia felt her heart plummeting then scrambling back up to her throat before it plummeted again. She watched him moving around the room. She wanted to stop him, but couldn't make herself speak the words.

As he dressed, she memorized the range and power of his dark muscular frame. Desperately, she tried and failed to shut down the voice that told her it'd be a very long time before she enjoyed the sight of him again.

Fully clothed, Felix turned studying her sitting crossed-legged and beautifully naked in the middle of the bed. The intensity in his dark stare spoke volumes-it was saying good bye.

"I love you G."

Book of Scandal

Georgia waited until she heard the front door close before burrowing beneath the covers and indulging in a long cry.

~CHAPTER NINE~

Jasper couldn't have looked more stunned than when he opened his front door and found Carmen Ramsey on his step.

"Jeez," he hissed, tugging her in while checking for any onlookers. "What the hell are you doin' out here?" He slammed the door shut.

"I was concerned." Unfazed, she locked her hands behind her back and took a cool survey of the room. "My mother was concerned," she clarified with a shrug, "wants to know how you're getting along out here."

"And she sent you to check on me?" He couldn't believe it.

"No. I came out here on my own." She folded arms across her gold sweater and fixed him with a sour look. "I'll bet my brother hasn't been out here to see you, since

Book of Scandal

Mama sent him with that food. Hmph." The look on his face told her she was right.

Nervously, Jasper edged fingers along his sideburns. "You can't stay Carm."

"I only wanted to come see how you are. If you need anything, to talk..." She moved closer, the swish of her skirt sounded loud in the room.

"I'm okay." He said, though he'd appeared to consider her offer for a moment.

Carmen appeared crestfallen. She'd hoped with all the talks they'd shared, he was perhaps feeling a little more at ease with her. She could tell he was nowhere near okay. It didn't take much more than observing the dark surroundings to tell that was a lie.

No one could be *okay* in such a sorrowful environment. Her expression said as much when she turned to fix him with a knowing look.

"Shit." Dropping the act, Jasper took refuge on a newspaper-littered sofa.

"Can't we get out of here?" She tucked a leg beneath her after joining him on the couch. "How many times have you been out since..."

She didn't quite know how to continue and took another scan of the dim, musty room. In a far corner, stood a table lined with trays, plates, cups- she saw one of her mother's worn casserole dishes and gasped. The table held all the dishes of food people had been sending. None of it made it beyond that room.

Carmen jumped when something big crawled from one of the overturned cups. She jumped again at the sound of Jasper's voice.

"I been rinsing out most of the stuff from the spicket on the side of the house." Newspaper rustled when he slid down the sofa. "Can't make myself go in- go in there."

"Jasper," Carmen went back to join him, "why won't you let anyone help you?"

"Fuck that." He stood, fists clenched. "No body wants to help me- the few that have only did it because of Miss Marcella. Please thank her for me." His voice softened.

Carmen took his hand and pulled him back to the sofa. "You can thank her yourself. She'd love it if you came over for dinner." *Several dinners, actually,* Carmen thought knowing her mother would be horrified by Jasper's haggard appearance.

"Her concern isn't phony." She curled a hand about the collar of his shirt. "Neither is mine." Boldly, she leaned in and kissed him.

Frustrated by anger towards the town he called home, misery over his mother and anguish over his status in life, Jasper was too unsettled to do what he should. He couldn't resist Carmen's advances.

Growling something indecipherable, he met her kiss with a fire that should have stunned her, yet she was meeting it with a formidable heat of her own. They fell back to the sofa kissing, grinding against one another. Carmen arched closer, silently offering herself to him. She bit her lip on a trembling moan when he opened the front of her dress. She was almost afraid to move for fear that he'd stop circling his thumb about a nipple firming through the

Book of Scandal

delicate lace of her bra. When he suckled the nub through the fabric, she ground against him more feverishly.

Jasper tugged her legs apart, opening her to him. A renewed sense of desire exploded within him once his arousal was settled snug against her.

"Jas," she pleaded, easing aside one cup of her bra.

His mouth was on her breast an instant later but when she locked her legs behind his back he withdrew and cursed himself.

"What?"

"You've got to go Carm."

She tilted her head trying to make eye contact. He wouldn't look her way. "Why Jasper?"

Jasper kept his gaze averted and smirked. "Let's start with how old you are Carmen. Hell, we can start with how old *I* am."

"That doesn't matter." She tugged his sleeve when he laughed and started to move away. "My folks were teenagers when they got married."

"I'm twenty and you're fourteen Carm."

"Six years, so?"

"Dammit girl, your family'd kill me if they even suspected this from me." He finally gave her the benefit of a shocked stare.

"Don't make me ask you again Carmen." He groaned when she remained silent and motionless. A minute later she was leaving.

***

The scene with Carmen acted as some sort of catalyst for Jasper. He suspected it was nothing more than unsatisfied 'horniness' that filled him with a wealth of

Book of Scandal

energy needing to be spent. Whatever the explanation, he managed to get the house in order- scrubbing the food crusted pots and casserole dishes with a gusto that could have worked off the mightiest frustration. Jasper even ventured into the kitchen where he scrubbed away remnants of the murder until the area gleamed. He made an effort to pack away some of his mother's things. That task however, proved to be a bit too emotional and he called an end to the housework there.

In a freshly sanitized bathroom he showered and changed. Then, he settled back with his favorite Ray Charles' album and was reading when his next visitor arrived.

Praying it wasn't Carmen again (he wouldn't have the strength to resist her twice in one day) Jasper pulled open the front door and grinned at Felix who stood on the other side.

"How you doin'?" Felix asked when they drew out of a long embrace.

Jasper shrugged. "Alright, I guess."

"I'll say." Felix smiled while taking in the pristine state of the living room. His brows rose a tad when he spotted the book on genetics lying over the arm of the sofa. "What the hell?" He waved the hefty book toward his brother.

Again, Jasper's shoulders rose beneath his blue V-neck sweater. "What brings you by?" He asked.

"You know me well." Felix muttered not surprised that Jasper wouldn't buy him stopping over for an idle chat. He sat in the armchair flanking the sofa and braced elbows to knees.

Book of Scandal

    "I'm leavin' town Jas. I asked Georgia to come with me, she turned me down. Guess that's all over." He slammed a fist to his palm. "Hmph, you'd think with all the years together she'd trust me to take care of her."

    "She's a Ramsey. They're…different."

    "That's crap." Felix waved off the words. "I'll never buy that 'people with money are different', mess."

    Jasper's mind was on Carmen. "Different *and* better."

    "Bullshit." Felix waited to make eye contact with Jasper. "Bull*shit*," he repeated, "'Cause money or no money, your boy Marcus is still a phony jackass. You're a thousand times better than that scumbag nigga."

    Jasper had to laugh. "Glad you approve of me, brotha."

    Felix only joined in on the laughter for a second or three. "It stings Jas. The way she turned me down like that- at least she was honest about why…but, hell I love her."

    "Maybe it'll do you good to go." Jasper took his place on the arm of the chair Felix occupied. "Maybe she'll see what a mistake she made and when you come back, she'll beg you to take her with you."

    Felix was already shaking his head. "I don't plan on comin' back. Don't gimme that look." He said, feeling Jasper's glare. "You've said the same thing more times than I can count."

    "It's different for you. You got Georgia and respect." Jasper turned his head. "Besides that, you love her too much to stay gone forever. I could leave and never be missed."

Book of Scandal

Felix forgot his woes for the moment. "Man, when you gonna get over that worthless feelin' you always carry 'round?"

Jasper walked over to the sofa and collected the book he'd been studying. "When I've earned respect by creating it." He turned the book over in his hands.

***

Summer, 1961~

Nestled below the fold in the Wednesday Business section of the Savannah Chronicle, was a brief yet important article featuring the eldest Ramsey son. Quentin Ramsey had made good on his promise to push Westin to the forefront of the family. The article announced the Ramsey patriarch's plans to expand the lucrative family-owned business to the other side of the country with West leading the way.

The small article generated a real buzz around conference tables and breakfast tables as well. Whites and blacks alike speculated on the future of the Ramseys. No doubt the next article on Ramsey business moves would be far lengthier and definitely above the fold.

"So that's what you and Pop's father/son trip was about back in fifty-eight?" Marc slapped the newspaper to the breakfast table that morning.

Westin cast a blank look toward his brother. Eventually memory set in and he couldn't believe the boy's memory as he recalled the Seattle trip in 1958. To quell the other kid's pleas to come along, Quent told them it was a special getaway for West as he was the oldest.

Book of Scandal

Marcus was fit to be tied and turned his anger on his father. "So when's my announcement comin' Pop?" He folded arms across his pin-striped shirt and hooked his hands beneath the suspenders he wore. Confrontation eked out of the stance like a tangible thing. "With West on his way out, guess it won't be long, right?"

"West isn't on his way out." Quentin didn't bother making eye contact with Marc. Instead, he calmly continued eating his grapefruit half. "West'll be leading the establishment of Ramsey in Washington State but he'll also start having more of a say here at the headquarters as well."

"All that?!"

"Marcus."

Quieted for a moment at the sound of his mother's warning call, Marc smoothed a hand across his jaw while beginning a pace of the dining room.

"This ain't right, Pop. It's time I had a place."

"I offered you a job last year remember?" Quentin added more sugar to his fruit.

"That shit?!"

Marcella stood and landed a powerful slap to the back of Marc's head. The suddenness of the blow stunned her sons and her husband. "You sit your lanky ass down," she seemed to hiss.

"No respect is why you got no job." Damon smirked, but sobered instantly and was prepared to do battle when Marc stood again.

Quentin dropped a heavy fist to the table and silenced everyone effectively. "If you crave a place at Ramsey, there's one waitin' in the youth department." There was no trace of love or even like in the depths of his dark eyes. "Prove yourself there, you might move up. Otherwise, shut the fuck up."

Houston; seated next to Marcus, knew his brother all too well and laid a hand across his knee urging him to keep quiet.

The girls arrived in the dining room just then and quickly sensed the tension in the air.

Georgia leaned close to Carmen. "Damn, what the hell did we miss?"

***

Much later, Houston found his brother in the most unlikely place- the rec room the boys had begged their father to construct. Houston was sure Marc would have driven off somewhere, but there he was pounding away at one of the boxing bags in the center of the room.

Houston paused on the steps leading down into the room. "You alright Marc?"

"Does it look like it?!" Marcus landed several rapid blows to the worn bag.

Houston turned to leave.

"Hous?! Sorry man."

Houston made a reluctant decision to turn back toward the room. Marc's moods changed as often as the wind. Still, he met his brother at the base of the stairway and worked to unlace the gloves when Marcus raised his hands.

"We gotta stick together Hous. It's obvious sides already been chosen."

"I don't know why you're surprised. West *is* the oldest."

Book of Scandal

"It's about more than that," Marc used his teeth to tug away the loosened gloves. "Pop hates me."

"Marcus-" Houston silenced himself at the brief hurt he glimpsed on his brother's face.

"I always knew it. If it wasn't for Ma... he'd have probably sent me away long time ago."

Houston fidgeted with the neckline of his T-shirt. He dared not say that much of the reason for Marc's unrest lay at Marc's own feet.

It wasn't necessary for Houston to speak his mind. As usual, Marc read his younger brother easily. Angry; but knowing he'd need loyalty within the family- especially family who could be controlled, Marcus clapped Houston's shoulder.

"It's my own fault. I could've been a better son." He groaned, massaging his neck while faking acceptance of responsibility for his actions. "No wonder everybody hates me." He added for good measure.

"I don't hate you Marc. You always got me."

"Thanks man, thanks...I didn't mean to go on, but there's no one else I can talk to."

"That go both ways, Marc?"

"Sure." Just then however, Marcus appeared more interested in selecting which bench-press he wanted to work on.

"'Cause there's a girl...I like her, but...well..."

Marcus chose a bench and finally gave Houston the benefit of his attention. "Have you talked to her?"

"Not really," Houston kicked the toe of his sneaker against the wall. "She doesn't even know my name-doubt I'd have the guts to tell her let alone do anything else."

"Ah…" Marc's expression turned sly as if he understood what the issue was. "So you're afraid you won't be able to um…*rise* to the occasion?" He rolled his eyes when Houston's stare was blank. "Don't sweat it. By the time I'm done you'll be oozin' confidence 'round any chick you meet."

"Well I-"

"Gimme time to work out the details, then we'll go from there." He waved toward the weights. "Gimme a spot."

***

Winter 1962~

"She can vomit all over herself for all I care."

"Hell Ross, she's your sister. You can't do her like that over some society Negro."

Rosselle Simon's sneer rumbled from her voice, through her eyes to the stiffness in her back. "You think I don't know *you've* had him between your legs, too?"

"And what about you?" Clea Simon didn't deny the accusation. "Have you made out any better because of it?"

A creak outside the bedroom door caught their ears then. Rosselle rushed over on tip toes and whipped the door open to their baby sister in the act of eavesdropping.

Josephine dared not scream when Rosselle's nails dug into her skin.

"How much did you hear lil' bitch?" Rosselle whispered once she'd dragged her sister into the room and slammed her against the door. Josephine was sputtering and gasping for breath too much to answer. Ross balled a fist to coax a response.

Book of Scandal

Josephine prepared herself for the blow while thinking of an excuse to give her parents. Abuse from her two eldest sisters had become almost as natural for her as breathing.

Fernelle Simon ambled from the bathroom just then. "Y'all leave Josie alone," she groaned clutching her head and stomach simultaneously.

Clea forgot about Josephine and went to stare down at Fernelle who'd taken refuge on one of the dainty pink and white striped armchairs that surrounded a round white coffee table- a handmade gift from their father. The arrangement was set before the windows in Fern's bedroom.

"Well? Are you?" Clea blurted.

Ross left Josephine by the door and went to hear the answer as well.

"I think so." Fernelle's response could barely be heard.

It was enough for Ross who let out a curse only to have Clea shush her.

"What are you gonna do?"

Fern tugged her robe together. "I'll have to go see him."

"Idiot!" Clea raged.

"What do you expect him to do, Fern?" Rosselle knelt before her sister. "Hmm? You think he's gonna give you a ring and a room in the Ramsey mansion?"

Josephine moved closer then. She clenched her fists in the folds of her robe and waited for more info.

"I'm not counting on fairy tales." Fernelle sniffed. "I think he'll do the right thing though."

Book of Scandal

"Girl, *the right thing* and Marcus Ramsey don't even belong in the same sentence."

"Amen." Ross muttered in response to Clea's observation.

Fernelle pursed her lips and drew a tuft of her reddish-brown hair behind an ear. "Would either of you be sayin' that if you were in my place?"

Ross stood. "Don't go sittin' up on some high horse just 'cause you screwed Marc Ramsey and managed to get pregnant."

Josephine gasped her captivating gaze wide and awe-filled as she watched her sister's stomach. "You're gonna have a baby?"

Clea turned, blocking Fernelle's smiling face. She took Josephine's arm and dragged her out of the bed room.

"You speak a word of it and we'll beat you black and blue- leave you for dead in the woods behind the house, tell Ma some animals must've gotten to you."

"Clea!" Fernelle called her disapproval while Ross laughed.

Clea shoved her baby sister into the hall and slammed the door in her face.

***

Briselle feared her already large gaze would overtake her face if it widened any more. But this had to be some kind of mistake; she thought when the host behind the podium at Frederique's Chalet told her she was in the right place. And he said it with a bow, besides- Briselle marveled silently when the man asked her to follow him.

Book of Scandal

Westin called the day before and told her to meet him there for dinner. She was sure he'd been mistaken. The only thing black people went to Frederique's for was to wash the dishes once the white folks were done eating.

The new Savannah restaurant was the personification of 'uppity'. There were some whites who hadn't even been there for a meal. Perhaps Westin had arranged for them to get leftovers to eat in his car, she mused while her lips curved into the beginnings of a smile.

Wrong again. The host led her to an intimate round table set for two. Westin stood and sent her a wink.

"Thanks Reese," he grinned toward the host.

The man bowed once more and left the job of seating Briselle to Westin.

"What are you doing?" The flirty flip of her hair slapped her cheeks when she looked back across her shoulder.

"Helping you into your chair," his reply sounded innocent enough.

"West-"

His mouth was on hers before she could continue. "Sit." He ordered.

Briselle tucked the hem of the peppermint green and white trimmed wool dress beneath her and obeyed. For several minutes afterward she stared unseeingly at the menu West placed in her hands.

"You okay?"

"No."

"How about a dance?"

"No!" She looked around quickly to see if she'd been overheard. "We shouldn't be here West."

Book of Scandal

"Why not?"

Briselle flopped back on the burgundy cushioned chair. "When have you ever seen colored people come in here to eat?"

"I was hoping it'd be right about now if you'd tell me what you want to order."

Briselle was drained of any desire for further conversation as she watched the man she loved.

At last, Westin showed mercy. "It's alright, B."

The look she shot him was an utter statement of disbelief.

"We're gonna dance."

Her eyes widened so much then, she had to squeeze them closed against the ache. She felt West's hand at her shoulder blades. "West please-"

"Uh-uh," he patted her back and drew her from the chair in one seamless motion.

Briselle could've torn the worsted fabric of West's black suit coat as she gripped his sleeve and fought the urge to hide her face against it. Mustering dignity from someplace deep, she kept her head high as they strolled the short distance to the dance floor. Between being a black customer in a whites only establishment and the desire Westin always roused when he drew her close, Bri felt on the verge of a dead faint.

"You don't look relaxed enough to suit me," he murmured, the playful frown on his face adding something adorable to his striking features.

The next thing Briselle knew, West was plying her with a vigorous kiss. She didn't think to resist- she never did. Soon she was responding with an equal passion until the tiny stirrings of memory kicked in. She remembered where they were and strained for him to stop.

"What's the problem, B?"

She tugged his lapels. "What is going on? Are you trying to give me a heart attack-kissing me senseless at a place where we could be shot just for looking inside?"

"Jeez, I never knew you were so paranoid." He laughed softly when she bristled. "Baby pretty much everybody eating in here works at Ramsey. Or they're clients- including the owners. There is no reason to be afraid." He kissed the tip of her nose. "Sorry I upset you. I'd never put you in harm's way- not when I want you in my life forever."

"Well why are we here, then?" She loosened her grip on his jacket but continued to hold. "I'd have been happy going to any of our regular places."

Silently West acknowledged that. His alluring gaze was ever so flattering as it caressed her delicate honey-kissed features. God, there were so many reasons why he loved her.

"We've been together a long time, you know? I read in one of Georgia's magazines that men should do things for their women to keep the flames burning."

Briselle laughed, her ease slowly yet surely returning. "So that's what all this is about?"

"Not exactly." He felt around in his trouser pocket and retrieved a small box.

When the gray velvet box opened, Briselle's gaze returned to its earlier widened state. "But you already gave me a ring." She said.

Book of Scandal

Nodding slow West reached for her hand and kissed the modest piece of jewelry on her finger. "This one says you're my girl." He shook the velvet box. "*This* one says you're about to be my wife. Marry me, B."

She bit a trembling lip to stifle emotion, but of course failed as happy tears filled her eyes.

"Yes, yes..." she chanted while he eased the sparkling diamond on in front of the first ring.

The engaged couple kissed. They drew a round of cheer and applause from the rest of the patrons inside Frederique's Chalet.

Book of Scandal

𝓡
~CHAPTER TEN~
Late Spring 1962~

Damon had already wasted three of his precious Spring Break days simply watching Catrina Jeffries. How could he blame himself though? He could watch her all day. He smiled, resting his head against one of the leafy mosses lining the street across from her father's business.

She'd probably be pretty pissed off to know her dreaded duties of grease dumping and pan scrubbing were things he'd come to love watching her do. But what of talking to her? He wondered. Since that day when they'd talked more about his family than he intended, he'd backed off. He feared that conversation would spark others that would have her guessing he was a Ramsey. Sure he knew she'd find out sooner or later. As always though, he preferred later- much later.

Book of Scandal

His head raised a tad from where he leaned against the tree trunk. Curiosity sparked a frown at his brow. Catrina Jeffries' chore for the day wasn't one he'd seen her perform before. Pushing off the shady tree, Damon eased both hands into his jean pockets and walked slowly toward the curb. He watched her drag two large suitcases from the back screened porch and down the brick steps. She hoisted one and then another atop identical tree stumps. She pulled open the tops and went about spraying them with one hand while covering her nose and mouth with the other.

Curiosity won out and he had to know what the hell was going on.

Catrina's scream was muffled due to the hand still covering her mouth as she disinfected the rarely used cases. As usual, seeing Damon filled her with twin emotions of awe and embarrassment.

"Takin' a trip?" He tried to sound more playful than curious.

"You scared me." She swallowed and managed a smile. "Yeah, yeah I am."

The phony playful expression turned sharp with surprise and scant agitation.

"I go every summer to see cousins in Atlanta."

He nodded at the explanation. Unfortunately his scant agitation mounted slightly over the thought of her not being around. "Sounds like fun." He noted when she quieted.

Catrina's excitement barreled through then. "Oh I always have the best time. Most of my other cousins are either too old or too young- these are just my age."

Book of Scandal

Damon had to laugh then. Her excitement was truly contagious. "At least you'll get away from dumping fish grease for while."

Catrina rolled her eyes even as she laughed. "This trip can't come soon enough. I'm surprised my Mama didn't call it off once Daddy got the Ramsey wedding."

"Ramsey...wedding?" Damon blinked. This was the first he'd heard of Jeffries Catering handling the affair.

"So um...how long will you be gone?" More intrigued by her trip then, he hoped she wouldn't make it back in time for the event.

"Well that wedding is something I wouldn't mind seeing." Catrina knocked the spray can against the thigh of her denim pedal pushers. "But I'm still glad to be away two weeks before it and three weeks after."

Damon's relief then was short-lived. The reality of her being gone hit him like a sack of rocks in the face.

"I'll come see you when you get back."

She smiled at his soft promise. "That'd be nice."

Staring took hold for several long moments. When Catrina bit her lip, Damon lost whatever restraint that helped him maintain distance. He bounded over to her, cupping the back of her neck while his other hand folded over her hip and kept her close.

Catrina wasn't quite so agile. She was limp, stunned by his nearness and the feel of him touching her. The sound creeping past her throat collided with a shudder as his head tilted and he kissed her.

As though he'd been doing it all his life, Damon's kiss began slowly- teasing and gently stroking. His tongue caressed the ridge of her teeth and the roof of her mouth

Book of Scandal

before engaging her tongue in a dance that went from sweet to seductive in seconds.

Her chest heaving against his almost made him forget where they were. He couldn't push away though-not yet, not just yet. He indulged in a few more seemingly endless seconds of the enjoyable kiss.

When at last he pulled away, Damon nudged her nose and helped himself to another peck from her lips. "Enjoy yourself." He spoke against the corner of her mouth.

Catrina could barely nod. When he walked away, the strength that left returned to her index finger. She pressed down on the spray tab of the can she still held and Damon's departing figure was soon hidden behind a cloud of disinfectant.

***

Carmen bit down on her lip and looked down at the invitation she worried between her fingers. She knew he'd refuse, but she had to try.

Why? She blinked when the question flashed on like a bulb in her head.

Jasper Stone had told her time and time again that it'd never happen between them. Could she even blame him for saying that- it was crazy to say the very least. Sure there was the age difference, but that was easy to overcome. What she couldn't battle; didn't stand a chance of winning against, were his feelings of worthlessness. Years of contempt-blatant from Harriett Cade and more subtle by the rest of the community had done its damage. She wondered how much.

The back door creaked and Carmen gave a start realizing she hadn't even knocked. Jasper's expression was

Book of Scandal

a cross between surprise and helplessness as though he'd expected her there and was rattled just the same by her actual presence.

"Carmen," he greeted in the usual agitated manner while cupping a hand behind her elbow and pulling her inside. All the while, he studied the backyard to see if anyone had noticed his guest arriving.

"Why're you here?" He folded his arms across a worn black shirt.

"Jasper this is lovely…" she breathed, inspecting the transformed kitchen.

"Thanks," the agitation gave way to a fleeting sense of pride over her approval. "Hope it'll get someone willing to stay on or at least make an offer on the place before I leave."

The last caught Carmen's full attention. The soles of her shoes clattered on the gleaming linoleum when she turned to him.

"Can't stay 'round here any more Carm." He didn't give her the benefit of eye contact.

He had a list of reasons for leaving, but Carmen wouldn't cry as he ran them down. No she wouldn't cry. That'd make her seem like even more of a little girl. "When are you…going? I um, I wanted to invite you to my brother's wedding."

"West?" Jasper guessed, watching her nod. "I always liked him."

"So you'll come?" Her dark eyes were bright then.

"I hope to be gone by then." He turned to the sink and made a pretense of wiping down the counter.

Book of Scandal

To hell with being a little girl, Carmen thought tossing the invite to the table. She flung herself against his back and wrapped her arms tight about him.

"Wait, please wait. Do this one thing, please Jasper. Come with me to my brother's wedding, please. If you feel anything for me could you just give me that little bit of time?"

Her shudders tore at his heart. He turned quickly keeping her close; watching her as if stunned that she'd think he felt nothing for her.

"Carmen right now you're everything to me," he confessed, clenching his hands about her arms knowing her skin was far softer than the silky blouse covering it. His heart gave a little jerk below his ribs when he saw the light come back to her face.

"Jasper-"

"You're everything to me, but you know why this can't happen now." A wince marred his striking features then. "I won't ask or expect you to put you life on hold until mine is the way I'd have it."

Carmen was curious to know what that meant, but more interested then in the discovery that he had feelings for her.

When she interrupted his words with a kiss, Jasper didn't think of resisting. The moment in the kitchen was sweetness laced with steam and moved to the hallway, then on to Jasper's bedroom. There, he treated her to caresses Carmen had only heard about when Georgia cackled with her friends.

The talk was nothing on the reality of it. She didn't even feel Jasper unbutton her blouse. Not until she felt his

Book of Scandal

mouth on the lace covering her nipples did she realize. Moaning shamelessly, she arched softly eager for him to add more insistence to the maddeningly gentle swirls of his tongue. Knowing there was more, she boldly tugged aside the fabric, baring herself to the expertise of his lips. His hand had ventured between her thighs and his thumb rubbing the crotch of the cotton slacks, had Carmen grinding down for more.

Jasper would take it no farther than the intense petting he'd subjected her to.

"No don't, I want to…"

Jasper closed his eyes, calling himself a fool twice over for pulling away when she was so willing. Pulling away was just what he did.

Her gaze was questioning. "Did I do something wrong? Say something-"

"No, no Carm you did everything right." *Too right,* he said ordering himself to…soften before he left the bed. "I'm not worthy of you Carm-"

"Jasper…"

"And I won't dirty you more than I already have." He wouldn't tell her that he intended to come back. He wouldn't stop until he'd found her again and made her his in every way.

Carmen saw that nothing she could say would change his mind. She didn't argue when he helped her from the bed and to the door. She didn't allow herself to cry until she was well on the path back home.

***

Felix gnawed his jaw while debating, even as he turned the hanging moss tree-lined walk way leading to

Book of Scandal

Lula Mae's Dress Shop. He'd gone out to the Ramseys
looking for Georgia and was told she'd gone to be fitted for
her dress for Westin's wedding.

Felix massaged the area between his brows and
called himself a fool for trying. Georgia had always been
up front regarding her feelings for money and his lack of it.
The girl would never give up the security of wealth for the
comfort of love unless there were significant dollars
attached.

He questioned why he loved her so and knew it was
because he did, that he was walking straight into the face of
denial again.

Georgia had been fitted for her dress and was
selecting a few additional things for herself. She was trying
to decide between two sheath dresses before realizing the
only decision was to buy them both. She was laughing over
a comment made by one of the sales girls, when her
mahogany gaze widened at the sight of Felix walking into
the shop.

The girls; mostly friends of Georgia's, began to
whisper while making themselves scarce. Georgia kept
quiet, clutching one of the dresses as she waited.

"How you doin' G?"

The sound of his voice forced her to acknowledge
just how much she'd missed him in the months they'd been
apart.

"Are you just getting back?"

He smiled at her question. "About to go, actually.
Had a lot to handle-Mama and all…"

Book of Scandal

"How is she?" Georgia's head tilted at a curious angle when she noticed the grimace curling his mouth.

"Mama's gonna be fine. God knows she's got tons of friends and supporters who'll see to it."

"Felix I'm so sorry," her voice and stare reflected her love for him, "the way things turned out, I know-"

"Come with me."

Georgia turned away leaving the dress on the corner and going to browse the blouse rack.

He followed. "Come with me." He brought a hand down on hers to stop the browsing.

"I already told you I couldn't."

"Because of money."

It was Georgia's turn to grimace. "It's an unfortunate necessity."

"We won't be flat broke when we set out, you know?"

"And we won't be rollin' in it either, will we?"

"We don't need to be when it's just the two of us." He spoke through clenched teeth.

Georgia rolled her eyes. "I will not have this same argument with you again. Go on," she waved a hand, "do what you have to do and leave me be. I'll be just fine."

Felix's gorgeous dark features tightened into a sneer. "Rich and alone. That sound *just fine* to you, Georgie?"

She bristled and continued her browsing. "I could live with it."

Felix eased a hand into his trouser pockets and observed her closely then. "You know what? I believe you could." He moved in close, brushing the back of his hand

Book of Scandal

down her arm before leaning in to kiss her cheek. "Take care of yourself." He whispered.

Georgia browsed the rack until she heard the bell dangle above the glass door to signal that it had just opened and closed behind the man she loved.

***

"What the fuck you expect me to do about it?"

Damon's steps halted soon after he passed Marc's closed bedroom door. A closed door however wasn't quite enough to completely mute the rage in his voice. Damon assumed it was a phone call as he heard no other voices save his brother's.

The one-sided conversation continued. Damon was able to determine that Marcus was speaking to someone called Fern who wanted him to do something he clearly had no intention to do. He winced, realizing 'Fern' was a girl when Marcus called her several unsavory names.

"Shut the fuck up with all your cryin' and why'd you wait so long to tell me anyway? We ain't screwed in months...can your parents tell?...you didn't mention my name, did you?...Get rid of it...Shut up Fernelle. Get rid of it or else."

Damon heard the phone slam. After a second or two he continued on down the hall.

***

July 1962~

Westin Monroe Ramsey and Briselle Gabriella Deas were married on a pleasant starry evening. Thankfully the sultriness of the day hadn't lingered over into the night. A breeze filled the air and the crickets in the distance seemed

Book of Scandal

to keep their natural music in time to the jazz quartet that provided the alluring melodies which colored the event.

The ceremony was attended by much of the town. Many speculated on how many business deals had been brokered with such a high powered array of guests in attendance.

Still, no one could outshine the bride and groom. The couples' natural charisma, loveliness and intelligence flashed like a beacon. In truth, much of the real talk focused on the heights the Ramseys would climb with such an impressive, young couple leading the new regime.

Following the exchange of vows, the newest Mr. and Mrs. Ramsey were led by the elder Mr. and Mrs. Ramsey along with the guests on a trek deep into the estate. There, Quentin and Marcella revealed their gift to the newlyweds. As West and Briselle would be leaving soon for Seattle, the couple had decided not to head off for some lengthy honeymoon. Quent had the already exquisite cottage on the grounds newly remodeled. While it would be used by others in time, the newlyweds would enjoy it for the duration of their time in Savannah.

Josephine thought she'd never had a more incredible time than on the night of the Ramsey wedding. While her evenings were usually spent tucked away in the security of her home, this was the first 'night out' she'd ever really experienced in spite of the fact that she was already 19.

One other thing she had to thank her sisters for- her smile was faint and rueful. Their parents weren't as clueless

Book of Scandal

as Ross, Clea and Fern thought. Daniel and Martha Simon were clearly aware of their daughters' reputations and planned to do all in their power to ensure their youngest didn't follow the same path.

But tonight…tonight she was there. She was there enjoying the stars overhead, the candlelit paths and scent of fragrant flowers, music, delectable foods…this was living and oh how she wished it were her reality.

The remodeled cottage had been left open so that the guests could take a peek inside and marvel. Josephine oohed and ahhed as much as anyone had and reveled in the fact that she'd happened upon the place when it was empty. For a time, she sauntered around the cozy elegant space and fantasized. When she finally talked herself into leaving, she found her way out was blocked by Marcus Ramsey.

Josephine ordered herself to keep all wits about her. Swooning would not be tolerated. She was sure this Ramsey prince was well used to having that affect on women. She didn't know why it was important that she not be like the others.

Marc's enveloping obsidian stare was more probing as it set fixed and provocative upon her.

"I think I know your parents." He leaned against the doorway and continued his leisurely scan of her face and form.

Josephine waited for his gaze to lift from the chiffon netting across the bodice of her peach satin column dress. She was grateful for the matching stilettos which added several inches to her stature.

"I think you know my sisters better." She said once their gazes connected.

Book of Scandal

Something flickered in Marc's eyes- not anger, but more along the lines of intrigue. He stepped closer and the intrigue deepened when Josephine didn't cower.

"I know them all quite well. Intimately- you could say." A corner of his mouth tilted in anticipation of her reaction. Only the cool, assessing stare and faint smile remained.

He nodded toward the room behind her then. "Have you checked it out? My father spared no expense. The bed's probably like sleepin' on feathers."

Josephine didn't bother to look back and didn't seem overly impressed. "Your brother and his wife should enjoy being here."

Again his stare slid back to its preferred task of observing her. "And what would you know of how much they'll 'enjoy' it?"

Swooning is not allowed. Josephine saw fit to remind herself then. She understood why the man was so successful with women. While his looks were to die for many times over, she wagered that it was his seductive charm that both shocked women and drew them in like moths to flame. What made him dangerous was that he was all too aware of the power.

"How about testing it with me? Make sure my brother and sister-in-law are getting the best." He was asking, pulling a hand from his black trouser pocket to brush her bare forearm.

Josephine wondered how much more successful he'd be with women if he were clueless of his magnetism. She smiled and; with confidence, reached out to stroke the length of his silky white tie.

"I'm afraid I'll have to pass on that, but I'm sure you'll have no trouble finding someone to take that test drive with you." Lowering her gaze, she angled around him and strolled off the cottage porch.

Briselle had already exchanged her dazzling gown for something a little more conventional. Though they'd spend their time at the gorgeous, secluded cottage, West wanted to whisk her away for a night far away from everyone. A tiny black owned inn just past Marietta, Georgia would serve as the perfect escape.

Satisfied with the lavender shift dress and matching pumps she'd chosen for the trip, Bri decided her high chignon could use a few more Bobbie pins. She recalled seeing some in the bathroom which connected to two rear bedroom suites and went to check there. She found Georgia instead.

"Girl what-" Briselle switched on the light. "What are you doin' here in the dark?"

"Didn't feel like getting back up to turn the damn thing on after I sat down." She shrugged.

Briselle leaned against the counter. "Girl what's wrong?" Briefly she cupped her sister-in-law's chin observing her tear-streaked makeup. Nothing prepared her to see the hard-nosed young woman break into tears.

"You let Felix walk out of your life because you've got another love waging war on your affections." Briselle noted, once Georgia confided all that had happened. "What are you gonna do?"

Book of Scandal

"Too depressed to think about it," Georgia reached for a tissue but broke into tears before she could put it to good use.

"Ah honey," Bri pulled her into another embrace.

"I think I made a mistake letting him go, Bri." Georgia's voice was a shudder. "But what happiness could I bring him feeling the way I do?" She sniffled and shook her head finally bringing the tissue to her nose. "Love me or hate me, but I have to be true to myself."

"Honey why don't you come with West and me when we leave in a few weeks?"

"Come with- what? Bri what-?"

"It'd be perfect for you and me." Briselle almost laughed.

Georgia rolled her eyes and cursed something fowl. "Dammit Bri, I'm sorry. Here I am goin' on and on about my shit and it's *your* wedding day."

"Stop it and listen." Briselle shook Georgia until she stopped rambling. "I'm already on edge here, not as much as I *have* been, but enough to still make all this really scary for me. West is gonna be so busy with work. I know he'd feel a lot better if I had someone- family to be with." She winked. "Besides, doesn't Mr. Q want you all out there eventually, anyway?"

"But Bri, this is you and West's time. I just wouldn't feel right about-"

"You'd have your own apartment- a real one not something tied to your parent's house. More freedom, a new city, new people, experiences…"

"Gosh Bri," Georgia bit her thumbnail. "Are you sure-"

Book of Scandal

    "If you ask me that again, I withdraw the offer."
The new sisters-in-law laughed and hugged again.

Book of Scandal

~CHAPTER ELEVEN~

"Are you crazy? Mama would skin us if she knew we were here."

Marc tugged his arm free of Houston's grip and smoothed the wrinkles from his jacket sleeve. "We're grown Hous- act your age. Every man in the county's been to Babydoll Monfrey's more than once."

"Not Pop."

"That's 'cause he's the only man in the county afraid of Mama."

"Marc, man what are we doin' here?"

Grinning, Marcus turned to fix the crooked white ascot at Houston's neck. "You need more help than I thought," he teased.

Book of Scandal

"I've never...you know? Done it." Houston grimaced while massaging his neck. "I don't even have the dough to put down in a place like this."

"Don't worry 'bout it. This is on me."

The gesture touched Houston, but it was no big deal for his brother who'd made off like a bandit following the job at the chemistry lab. As he and Charlton Browning had cheated their two partners out of their fair share, Marc figured the least he could do was spring for his brother at Babydoll's.

Besides, as great a lay as Daphne Monfrey was, she was starting to grate on his nerves. He enjoyed the sex too much to worry that she was becoming possessive and a tad expectant. He'd already suspected that she was having more and more visions of Ramsey sugarplums dancing in her head. Dumping her off on Houston seemed like the perfect plan- one last taste of her and that'd be enough for him.

"Marc...I don't know about this..." Houston's edginess was gaining momentum once more. His attractive features were tight with apprehension as he focused on the house they headed toward. "I've never done it..."

Marcus finally took pity and clapped his brother's back. "Remember the girl you told me about? The one you can't talk to? After tonight, you'll have confidence out the ass. Literally." He waved a hand, urging his brother down the path to Babydoll's.

Daphne kept the house intentionally dark. Her mother was away on a weekend trip (work related). She didn't need any interested passerby noticing that clients

Book of Scandal

were visiting during the woman's absence. Not that her mother would mind, she'd welcome business continuing.

Still, Daphne wondered if she'd feel betrayed knowing her daughter was about to entertain not one, but two Ramseys. Babydoll couldn't even boast that. When Marcus contacted her about the tryst (which she'd discovered had a truly erotic sounding name- ménage a trois) she was at first rather disappointed. After all she'd hoped Marc might be developing some deeper feelings having been her first trick and all… Then, she began to see the better picture. With two Ramseys instead of one, her chances of securing a promising hold improved by far.

The room she'd chosen for the occasion was set for seduction. In truth, it was the only one befitting such an event. Her mother and the other girls often used the area for group sessions which they all took part in for an equal share of the profits.

The floor was carpeted by Oriental rugs and draping linens. The walls were decorated by erotic scenes from the *"Karma Sutra"*. Aside from a round glass table and chairs, the bed was the only other furnishing- and the only one needed. Decadent to say the very least, the round, king-sized creation sat atop a platform and was draped with silky dark coverings. Candles flicked from large oval vases set around the room and appropriately distanced from the bed in case things grew too intense…

The bell rang and Daphne gave herself an unorthodox once over in the mirrors covering the ceiling. Satisfied with the skin-tight see through chiffon gown and her curls piled high into two ponytails, she sashayed from the room.

Book of Scandal

Marc reconsidered his decision to treat himself to one last taste of Daphne when she answered the door looking like a cross between innocent girl and experienced love-slave.

Daphne's smile brightened for Marcus but she blinked and something more filtered her eyes when she spotted Houston. Instantly, she recalled him from the Ramsey party over a year ago. He'd barely looked her way then, perhaps after this night she'd receive a more pleasing reaction.

Houston couldn't believe his good fortune, recalling that this was the girl/woman he'd watched outside the library when he'd gone to pick up his sister. The little blondish/brown nymphet was even more unreal up close. His heart thudded inside his throat as he recalled wondering if her hair color was real. He'd know after tonight.

"Daphne Monfrey, my brother Houston." Marc had noticed the look between the two and was grinning wickedly while he made the intros.

Daphne waved them into the parlor where drinks waited. Marc indulged, while Houston held back. Daphne enjoyed the awe in his gaze when she drew him close and urged him to take part.

"Babydoll around?" Marc was asking.

"Out of town for the weekend," she shared, giggling at the wink Marcus flashed toward Houston. She spread her arms wide. "We have the place all to ourselves and can do whatever, wherever…"

Marc drained his glass. "Let's get to it, then."

Book of Scandal

The room carried a light, inviting scent that accentuated the soft appeal of the exotic music filling the room. Daphne took both brothers by the hand and led them over to the two chairs flanking the squat square glass table. She supplied them with more drinks, and then began a sultry dance routine to the tempo of the music.

She straddled Houston on the chair and continued the dance until Marc waved her over for his turn. That dance turned far more intimate, as Marc kissed and fondled Daphne boldly before loosening his pants and having her ride him. Houston began to stroke himself as he watched. Marc reached his climax, pushing Daphne away before she reached hers.

"See to my brother. It's his first time- ever."

Daphne's gaze sparkled more brilliantly as she understood. Eager to please, but carefully and slowly she treated Houston to an oral job before taking him to the bed. Marc didn't follow, but helped himself to more drink and enjoyed the scene from afar.

The moment between Houston and Daphne was lusty yet there was an undeniable tenderness present. With her words and touch, she coaxed him to relax. She rode him, and then guided him when he was on top. Finally feeling more confident, Houston took control and had her from behind.

When his brother had his fill, Marc was back for another round. Daphne pleasured Houston with yet another oral treat. For hours, the house was filled with three distinct voices of desire.

***

Book of Scandal

For hours, Fernelle Simon had sat along the waters off Tybee Island. The passing of each hour brought her closer to the frequent rolling waves of the Atlantic. At first, the water beckoned her attention and then her touch. By dusk, she was trailing her fingers tentatively along the waves when they rolled up to meet her.

For years, her father had been after them to learn to swim. She, Ross and Clea hadn't listened. Josephine dived in- literally and with a passion. Fernelle smirked, thinking of her baby sister.

It was ironic that the thing Ross and Clea hated Josie most for was the thing that made it impossible for her to feel anything but adoration. There was a mix of fierceness and an impossible sadness behind her sister's light eyes. Fernelle often meant to question it. She knew however, that whatever thoughts, fears, hatred her baby sister harbored were perhaps the girl's only real source of control- of strength in her world.

The waves came rolling in to cover her bare feet then. Fernelle cast a resigned look towards the water and stood. She'd miss her little sister, she'd miss lots of things. She curved both hands over her belly. No time for regrets then, she decided and tossed back her head. She focused only on the waves which appeared more raging in the distance.

Stepping forward, she strolled into the waters as if she were taking a walk through her favorite flower field. Even when the ocean floor dipped noticeably beneath her feet, she continued to walk, to stroll until the waves smothered her and stifled her breath.

***

Book of Scandal

Daphne knew there had to have been a time when her mother made her breakfast. Unfortunately, it had probably been so long ago, she was now too old to remember it.

That all changed when Babydoll arrived home a few hours earlier than expected and found not one, but two Ramsey males leaving by her back door in the pre-dawn hours. She waited until they'd driven off before heading inside where she found her daughter snuggled and content in bed.

Instead of indulging in the rest Babydoll was sure she must've needed, Daphne was counting 20s and 50s. Several lay in two neat stacks atop the bed.

Now, seated at the breakfast table with a platter of French toast and crunchy bacon before her, Daphne asked her mother if she was pleased.

"Way more than that, baby. *Way* more." Babydoll rested her plump arms across the table. "How'd you manage it?"

"Well…Marc called," Daphne didn't want to appear overly confident. "He called and I accepted. Mama, did I do right?" She added for good measure.

"Whoo!" Babydoll broke out the holler while leaping from her chair. "Honey! Honey, Honey, Honey!" She pranced and shimmied around the kitchen while twirling a dishcloth above her head. "Shit!" She cried in the most approving manner and flopped back into her chair. "Dammit girl, depending on Marc Ramsey to make a… honest woman out of you was a long shot but not impossible. Now his brother…I've never met but he's not as…savvy as Marcus. Am I right?"

Book of Scandal

Daphne replied with a tentative nod. She didn't dare let on how wonderful it felt to have her mother seeking her opinion and about men no less. Keeping her wits about her; Daphne talked about Houston's sweetness, and felt her value increase ten-fold when she told her mother she'd taken his virginity. Daphne continued to dine happily while Babydoll broke into another dance.

***

Daphne Monfrey may have been Houston's first, but his mind was still on Catrina Jeffries. Almost two weeks had passed since the romp at Babydoll's and; in that time, Houston's confidence blossomed. He hadn't returned for another helping of Daphne but; instead, spent most of his free time at Jeffries' hoping for a glimpse of Catrina. After three visits to the café, he'd learned she was out of town. Disappointed, but not discouraged, Houston decided he'd simply have to wait.

Patience was definitely a thing one learned as Marc Ramsey's younger brother. If one were coming after him, one would have to wait one's turn.

Waiting was not a thing Rosa Jeffries liked to do. When word reached her ears of the Ramsey asking about Catrina, the woman wasted no time phoning Atlanta to tell her daughter. Unfortunately, Catrina's reaction to the news was far below Rosa's preferred level of excitement.

"I swear you are just like your father. Do you know how many girls would kill for the chance to be noticed by one of them boys?"

"And he's probably out with one of those girls right now, Mama."

"You just hush your lil' smart mouth, say your
goodbyes and get back home."

"But Mama! Shell and me were gonna see the
Isleys-"

"Forget the concerts and play time with your
cousins. I want you back home now- I don't know what
your Daddy was thinkin' letting you go off when we had
that big wedding anyway."

"Baby?"

Catrina and Rosa ceased their arguing when the
baritone voice came through the line.

"Daddy?" Catrina smiled.

"King I was just telling-"

"I know what you were tellin' the child, Row. I'm
tellin' her to keep herself right where she is."

Rosa huffed. "Do you know one of the Ramseys has
been asking-"

"I know all about that boy snoopin' around." King
Jeffries interrupted his wife once more. "I won't have my
baby girl jumpin' through hoops for them uppity Negroes.
One of 'em wants her, he'll damn sure have to work for
her."

On the other end of the line, Catrina held the phone
to her ear and thought she'd never loved her father more.

***

Anything that cast even a shred of positive attention
Josephine's way was often cause for physical ridicule as far
as Clea and Rosselle were concerned. When Josephine
came across a letter written to her from Fernelle, however,
even Ross's and Clea's minds were more absorbed by
worry over their missing sister.

Book of Scandal

Fernelle had been gone over a week and; while the Simons refused to speak it, they knew the worst was camped right outside their door. That morning, another visit from the Sheriff brought no new developments in the case. The fact was as much a relief as it was another frustration.

The letter in Josephine's room however only increased the Sheriff's; as of yet, unspoken suspicions. It read like a goodbye, like a suicide note.

"No!" Martha Simon cried, while holding onto Josephine.

Daniel Simon moved closer to the Sheriff. "How long will you keep lookin' for my baby, Paul?"

"We've got no leads Danny," Sheriff Paul Reginald kept his voice low, his expression clearly troubled. "None of the places we've searched have turned up….and with this letter…"

"No…" Martha's voice was more of a shuddering moan then. "Paul," she sighed as though trying to gather strength. "You can't stop looking for her. Y'all are trained lawmen. Surely you have ideas on where a young girl might go…"

"Martha," Sheriff Reginald had stepped over to squeeze the woman's shoulder. "Did Fernelle have any friends? Any you haven't told me about already?"

"She had-*has* many friends." Daniel shared proudly.

The Sheriff smiled, realizing how the concerned father had misread his question. "Does she have a boyfriend, is what I meant Danny." He smiled softly. "Is there anyone she may have run off with?"

Ross and Clea exchanged stares then looked over at Josephine who quickly broke eye contact with her sisters.

Book of Scandal

The suave, gorgeous Ramsey couldn't have had anything to do with Fern's disappearance, Josephine thought. Still; in light of the current situation and Marc Ramsey's probable denial of Fernelle's baby being his, it was most likely the girl had done just what she'd alluded to in her letter.

The Sheriff took the silence in the room as his answer and decided he'd put enough on the worried family's mind.

"Let me know if anyone or anything comes to mind that might shed some light." He walked over to shake Daniel's hand. "I'll be in touch."

$\mathscr{R}$

~CHAPTER TWELVE~

Westin didn't hide the frustration from his face or voice when his younger brothers told him they were still conducting interviews to fill spots in the youth department.

"I wanted this stuff set in motion before I leave for Seattle in two weeks." He said.

"But West, you of all people know how important it is to have good people working beneath you, right?" Marc reasoned.

Westin bowed his head to make notes on his pad. He missed his younger brothers pass grins and winks to one another.

"So how much longer will this take?" West asked, still working on the pad.

Book of Scandal

"We're conducting the last of the interviews this week." Marc shrugged and studied something on the end of his tie. "I'm confident we'll be ready to implement the proposed youth activities before you leave town."

"I want all this mapped out, so these folk can go forward the minute they're hired." West gestured with his pen. "There should be no confusion on what employees will handle which tasks."

West was giving his brothers tips on how best to handle the duty he'd charged them with, when a knock sounded on his office door. The knob turned and an older gentleman stuck his head inside the room. The younger men stood at once recognizing Justin Somes one of their father's business associates and oldest friends.

"Sorry guys, Westin I bullied Kollette into letting me interrupt."

"It's no interruption at all." West said as he and his brothers shook hands with the stout, gray-haired gentleman.

"I only wanted a minute to congratulate you on the wedding and to apologize for not being there." Justin said when West took his hand.

"Thanks Mr. J. I think Pop said you and Miss Celia were on an extended trip?" West referred to Justin Somes' wife.

The man winked. "Always head off somewhere for our anniversary. Neither of us are party people so it takes the matter out of the hands of friends."

Male laughter rumbled in the room for several moments.

"Anyway West, just wanted to congratulate you again." Justin reached out for another handshake. "You're on the right path and with all the right tools- name, job, work ethic, respect and now the wife." He clapped West's arm. "And she's quite a beauty, but not only that. Briselle's got a sweetness and a strength about her. She'll make you a good wife in business and in pleasure."

Laughter rumbled again.

"You two take notes from your brother on how to do it right." Justin advised the younger Ramseys when he shook their hands again.

The meeting eventually resumed yet Marcus studied Westin with renewed interest.

***

Catrina returned from her fun-filled Atlanta trip to find her mother still harping on Houston Ramsey's visits to the restaurant. She knew in time her mother's ranting would blow over, but what unsettled her most was Carmen. Houston was her brother and Catrina only hoped her disinterest wouldn't put a cloud over their friendship.

She recalled meeting him at the Ramsey cotillion her family had catered. After all the descriptions from the waitresses about the cute Ramsey who'd been asking about her, it didn't take much for her to remember him. He'd seemed nice enough. She smiled, thinking of the fit her mother would have to know she'd actually had a conversation with him.

Still, the conversation and time spent with the Ramsey prince hadn't sparked a smidge of the emotion that Damon had.

Catrina cursed then and switched off the pink radio that played Brook Benton's *"Kiddio"*. She kicked a pillow across her bedroom and stewed.

Book of Scandal

It had been well over a year (actually two) and she had no idea who he was. Their encounters had been so few and so brief she was beginning to wonder if she hadn't dreamed the entire thing. She shook her head then. She hadn't been dreaming. If anything, she'd been pining-pining over a boy who didn't even have the decency to tell her his name.

Catrina smiled. As fine as he was, he probably had scores of girls *pining* after him. What made her different? He obviously came from money and she obviously didn't. He'd kissed her once; but probably figured correctly that she wasn't a girl who'd go any farther and decided to stop wasting his time while he was ahead.

Meanwhile, she was wasting *her* time moping over their lack of time together and letting all sorts of opportunities pass her by. Lord, how many dates did she turn down in Atlanta? She fiddled with the lace hem of her yellow gown and drew her knees up to her chin.

Now she was turning her back on another just because no 'Damon spark' emerged from a 5-10 minute conversation with Houston. Slowly, she left her bed and retrieved the pillow where it'd landed near the leg of her desk chair. Nodding, she made a silent decision.

***

Rosselle and Clea almost knocked each other down to get to the door once they'd spotted the shiny black Cadillac convertible and Marcus Ramsey leaving the driver's side. A slight shoving match ensued, which was called to a halt by Martha Simon.

"Hush up and get in that sittin' room. Both of you." She scolded while wiping her hands on the apron protecting her gray checkered dress. Quickly, she removed her apron and stashed it in the hall closet before opening the front door.

"Why Marcus Ramsey, what a surprise!"

"Ms. Martha, how are you today?" Marc smiled, watching his charm turn the older woman to mush.

Martha was already curling a hand around his arm. "Do come in and excuse the mess." She urged, leading him into her pristine home. "Girls...?"

Clea and Ross had already taken their places in the front room. They made a phony show of reading magazines and kept their expressions cool.

"Girls? Look who's here..."

Eagerly, the girls popped out of the twin mauve armchairs. Wearing sun-bright smiles; and posting up and down on their toes they resembled rockets about to blast off.

"Ms. Martha is Josephine here by any chance?" Marcus was asking before Ross or Clea could move forward or speak a word.

Silence hung heavy for countless moments. The sisters passed slow looks between one another.

"Uh..." Martha was even stunned but began a slow shuffle toward the foot of the stairway. "Yes she... Josephine?! Josephine!" She sang, and then patted a hand to her chest struggling to maintain her smile. "Oh dear, where are my manners? Are you thirsty, baby?"

"Uh no, no ma'am." Marc seemed just as flustered as the lady of the house. He seemed to give a start at the sound of footsteps on the stairway.

Clea and Ross noticed and were making their move to inquire.

Book of Scandal

"Yes Mama?" Josephine's hazel eyes widened at the tall, darkly gorgeous guest standing near her mother. She frowned then, noticing her sisters in the distance. "Yes Mama?" She queried more carefully then. Her face was void of emotion as she took uncertain steps into the room.

Martha laughed nervously. "Marcus Ramsey to see you, baby."

"Hey Josephine," sweetness echoed in Marc's voice and gaze when he moved past Martha. "How are you?"

Josephine told herself to blink and break out of his spell. "Preparing for school in the fall."

"I see." He gave a nod and glanced down at the shiny wingtips he wore. "Will that leave you time to be my wife?" He asked the second he looked up again.

Josephine stood speechless while Clea and Ross screamed their agony. Martha clapped her hands and offered up a prayer. Ross's and Clea's agonizing moans continued as Marc got down on one knee and produced a ring.

"You don't know me." Somehow Josephine was calm.

"I know enough." He offered the older Simon girls the benefit of a quick glance then. "From the few talks we've had, I know that you're sweet and strong."

Josephine didn't remind him that they'd only spoken once.

"You're the type of woman a man makes his wife."

Beneath the fabric of her rose blush mini dress, Josephine felt a fizzle of pride zip down her spine. She could almost feel her sisters bristling in the distance.

Book of Scandal

"Please Josephine." He squeezed her hands.

She indulged a glance toward Ross and Clea then. Streams of memory filled her conscience as she thought of all the nastiness, meanness and the way they'd thrown themselves at Marcus Ramsey's feet. He'd offered her the prize, though.

A vision of Fernelle emerged then and her smugness faded. She wouldn't- couldn't let herself believe Marc had something to do with her sister's disappearance. The Ramseys lived like royalty and she wanted a part of that. As Josephine *Ramsey*, she'd make sure her new husband never forgot the shabby way he'd treated her beloved sister.

She extended her hand for his ring, giving into laughter when her mother clapped.

Marc kissed Josephine's hand and then her cheek when he stood. He turned to Martha Simon then.

"I don't want to be disrespectful, ma'am. I should talk with Mr. Simon about this."

"Well Daniel-" Martha was interrupted by a key scratching the front door lock. She practically tripped over herself getting to the door to greet her husband.

Daniel Simon's stoic expression merged into a grimace when he spotted Marcus Ramsey in the room.

"Daniel," Martha drew her husband toward their guest. "The boy wants to speak with you...about Josephine." She nodded when Daniel flashed her a questioning look.

"I'd like to ask for your daughter's hand in marriage, sir."

Book of Scandal

Daniel was as speechless as Josephine had been. Looking over at his youngest child, the man stunned everyone when he crumpled into a sob.

"Oh, oh sweetheart," Martha hugged her husband and whispered softer words to soothe. "It's alright. Josephine seems very happy."

Before Daniel could speak, there was a knock at the front door. He squeezed his wife's hands and rubbed at the moisture in his eyes.

"Dan?" Martha's expression had taken on an air of suspicion.

Daniel was already on his way to the front door. He opened it to Sheriff Paul Reginald.

Martha was backing away as if the man brought with him a stench.

Paul Reginald removed his hat. "Martha I'm sorry-"

"Nooooo!"

Clea and Ross held onto each other as their mother wailed. Josephine reached out blindly, blinking when Marcus caught her hand.

"She was found along Tybee Island. The tide... brought her in...two days ago." Paul waited for Daniel to pull his wife close. "The Sheriff's office there saw our bulletin on Fernelle's disappearance and contacted us this afternoon."

Martha was mewling then, hanging limp in her husband's arms.

"Sheriff?" Marcus stepped a tad closer with Josephine by his side. "Are you sure it's her? Maybe-"

"Her father already made the i.d. son."

Book of Scandal

Daniel Simon broke into another bout of sobs. Martha finally clutched the back of his shirt, melding her grief with his.

Marcus pressed Josephine's hand to his mouth and brushed away the tears streaking her cheeks. "I'm so sorry. I- I shouldn't be here-"

"Damn right you shouldn't!"

"Clea!" Rosselle tried to shush her sister.

"No! No Ross!" Clea jerked away. "It's his fault! He got what he wanted and then the bastard turned his back on her. Now she's dead!" Clea's round dark face shined with tears and hate. "What now, Marc? Here to make it four for four?!" She sent a quick sneer toward Josephine.

Marcus ignored Clea as though she hadn't spoken. Instead, he closed the distance between himself and the elder Simons. "Sir, I *am* sorry," he bowed toward Daniel. "I've been very disrespectful with your daughters and I can never make up for that. But sir, I promise you'll not be sorry for giving me a chance with Josephine." He smiled when she moved close to her parents. "I knew she was the one from the first time I saw her. I knew she was more than a quick...I wanted more from her. She'll be treated like a queen, sir. You have my word on that." Marc extended his hand. "You've just lost a daughter, sir. I would be honored if you'd accept me as a son."

Daniel Simon sniffled and straightened. From his towering height he eyed Marc closely before nodding and accepting the hand the younger man offered.

Josephine stood on her toes and kissed her father's jaw. She took Marc's arm and led him out of the foyer.

"I'm going."

Book of Scandal

"Marcus-"

"Shh…" He kissed her cheek, lingering there to inhale her scent. "You need this time with your family."

"Your proposal," Josephine's lashes fluttered down to shield her gaze. "the timing, maybe it's a sign that we shouldn't-"

"Hey?" He cupped her face. "You wanna know what really made me come down here today? A visit from a friend of my dad's." He grinned at the confusion on her face. "He told West how lucky he was to have Briselle-what a catch she was and how the right woman was his greatest asset." Marc's thumbs caressed her cheeks and he nuzzled her nose with his own. "You're everything I could want in a wife, Josie."

She ignored her heart thudding in her ears. "You don't even know me."

Marc's smile was slyness and seduction in one. "You can be sure I intend to change all that."

***

Carmen peeked past the opened door and bit her lip before knocking. She heard Damon's ever-deepening voice when he granted entrance. She hesitated a second longer before crossing the threshold.

"Hey!" Damon laughed while reaching over to silence Chubby Checker's *"Party Time"* blaring from the radio on his desk. "What's goin' on?" He met his sister in the middle of his room for hugs and kisses.

"I've been by your room four times this week and you're never here." Carmen smiled and savored the hug. "Everyone's so busy…"

Book of Scandal

"Very." Damon's dark eyes grew close as they were filled with curiosity. "What's wrong Carm?"

"What are your intentions for Catrina Jeffries?" Carmen moved on and took a seat on the edge of the bed. "She's a friend of mine and I-um...I don't like the way you've been treating her."

Damon twisted his sneaker to one side and looked like the picture of uncertainty. "How do you know I-"

"Catrina let it slip one day about this boy." Carmen braced elbows on the thighs of her jeans and shrugged. "She said his name was Damon."

"Does she know I'm a Ramsey?" He settled slowly onto his desk chair.

Carmen shook her head, smirking when her brother sighed his relief.

"Carm I can explain why-"

"You don't have to. I get it. I just don't see why you won't...make your presence more known."

"'Cause sooner or later someone's gonna tell her who I am." His expression darkened. "I'm not ready to do it myself yet."

"And have you thought about Catrina? What's *she's* ready for?"

Damon was silent but his eyes sparkled then with curiosity.

"She's a pretty girl. Very pretty. Lots of boys drop by her dad's restaurant for a glass of water just so they can see her. She's not gonna ignore all that attention for long." Carmen watched him walk over to stare out the windows and decided to finish her say. "Especially not when one of those boys is Houston Ramsey."

Book of Scandal

The curtains billowed when Damon whirled around to gawk at his sister.

"He's been visiting Jeffries- a lot. Catrina was in Atlanta at the time, but she says her mother's drivin' her crazy trying to get her to call him."

Damon shrugged and leaned back on the window sill. "Well if her mother's drivin' her crazy to call, she must not be interested."

"And how long do you think that's gonna last? Especially when *you're* so distant? It's not fair to her Damon." Carmen stood.

"You should ask yourself if hiding who you are is more important than losing her to some other boy- Houston."

The door closed behind Carmen and Damon considered her parting words. It didn't take long for a confident smile to strike his double dimples. Thinking of his awkward older brother was reason enough to be amused. Houston would never pull a girl like Catrina. She was intelligent, ambitious, sexy as…

He eased one hand inside the back pocket of his jeans and clenched a fist with the other to beat his desk. No, Houston would never manage that.

***

"…And you can enjoy it all in the privacy of our bedroom."

"Mmmm…after my day that sounds like heaven," Quentin smiled at the sound of his wife's voice through the phone line. Marcella had been in the midst of sharing her plans for their evening.

Book of Scandal

"And all this because I gave them a second chance," Quent raved once Marcella told him his favorite meal was hot and ready.

Marcella's laughter was soft through the line. "Not only because of that. I can't even begin to list all the reasons why I love you so."

"And I love you Marcy."

"Hurry home, Quen."

Quentin tapped the receiver to his chin once the connection broke. Satisfaction lent a more dashing element to his already handsome features. Leaning back in his gray leather desk chair, he prayed the makings of a successful and respectable Ramsey future were in store.

He was on his way out the door when his wife's call came through. Once again, he reached for his briefcase, but detoured outside the office and decided to drop in on his sons. He'd felt a stab of pride when one of his executive staff told him the boys had been working late hours to ready some of the youth division.

Quentin knew Marcus felt it was a slap in the face being saddled with working there instead of something more integral to Ramsey. In spite of Marc's hard work as of late; Quent wanted no doubts when he finally gave him more responsibility. The youth division was a smaller portion of a greater place. The way Marcus handled himself there would determine much about his business future.

He'd just taken the quiet corridor leading to the youth wing, when a scream and dull thud met his ears. The sound rose from beyond the office at the end of the hall. Immediately, Quentin cursed his own stupidity, for he

Book of Scandal

knew that what he was about to walk in on would not be good.

The scream had undoubtedly come from one of the young women currently engaged in sex with his sons. Quentin wagered that it was the one Houston took against the far wall of the outer office. The young woman with Marcus had her mouth too full to scream as she pleasured him orally.

Quentin ignored the blood rushing to his head. He hurtled his briefcase against the door, effectively startling the four other people in the room.

"Get out. You girls get home." Quentin's voice was a rough grate.

The girls were fixing their clothes while rushing out with their heads bowed in shame. Quentin slammed the office door shut behind them. Houston quickly set his clothes right. Marcus though, took his time zipping slacks before rising slowly to tuck in his shirt.

"Tried to tell you this wasn't for me." Marc shrugged.

"Clearly you found a way to make it your own."

The surprising calm in his father's voice tempered Marc's anger with sudden regret. To have the man catch him with his pants down- literally, after all he'd done to maneuver a respectable profile like Westin…he'd never trust him again. If he ever had. In that moment, Marc acknowledged that Ramsey would never truly be his as long as his father had a say.

"Well Pop? Let me have it. It's what you live for, right? Right?!"

Book of Scandal

Quentin grimaced. "I'm starting to believe it's what *you* live for."

"You've never loved me." Marc stepped closer purposefully taunting. "You never loved me like the others. You only tolerate Houston- barely. I wonder…" His pitch stare turned into a squint as he pretended to concentrate. "Maybe Mama got tired of it all and went looking for outside pleasure while you were so busy building Ramsey. Are me and Hous even your sons, *Pop*?"

"Marcus!"

"Shut the fuck up, Houston!"

Marc had scarcely finished issuing the order when Quentin lunged for him. Suddenly however, he stiffened. His eyes bulged wildly.

"Poppa!" Houston cried, running to his father while his brother smirked.

Quent jerked eerily before crumpling to the floor.

Houston crouched next to the man. "Poppa! Poppa please, please stop! Marc? Marcus do something!"

"Alright," Marc made the promise but didn't move for several seconds. When he finally walked forward, it was to tug Houston to his feet, step over his convulsing father and leave the room.

***

Word of Quentin Ramsey's stroke spread rapidly throughout the Savannah community. Doctors still feared the worst was yet to come. In fact, the man may *have* died if the cleaning crew hadn't found him when they arrived for their nightly rotation.

Marcella remained by her husband's side. She only slept or ate when she allowed one of her children to bully her into it. It was on one of those rare days when his mother was away, that Damon had the chance to visit his father alone.

Quentin had not regained consciousness since he'd arrived at the hospital days earlier. The diagnoses weren't promising in that regard, but Damon knew his father was alert inside his ravaged body. He spoke as if the man were awake and avidly listening.

Houston and Marc's visits were non-existent, not to mention the fact that he'd been found in the youth division office- a thing no one else seemed to want to discuss. It didn't take much to put together that something had happened there resulting in Quent Ramsey's condition.

Damon spoke on all this while he held his father's hand to his bowed head. "I'll see to it that they don't ruin the family, Poppa. I promise you that." He sniffled and gave into the tears which had been pressuring his eyes. "Whatever it takes, whatever it takes Pop, I'll protect us. You can focus on getting better. Me and West can handle the rest." Damon pressed a lingering kiss to Quent's head and watched him closely for a long while before leaving.

***

Daphne worked to mask her relieved smile when she spotted Houston alone in a remote waiting room at the hospital where his father was being treated. She'd taken a huge chance coming there to risk being spotted by other Ramseys or worse, nosy townspeople whose tongues would surely wag if they saw the daughter of the town whore talking with a Ramsey son.

There he was though, looking adorable and oh so lonely. Her smile deepened. She'd known after their second time together that Marcus wouldn't be the one to give her what she most wanted- a room inside the Ramsey mansion.

But Houston...there was an edginess yet a sweetness to him that stirred something beyond sexual attraction. He seemed needy and lonely. She believed he'd cling to the first person who could make him forget those feelings. She would be that person.

Houston looked up when he heard the soft knock. A range of expressions from surprise to shyness to suspicion crossed his handsome dark caramel toned face. He made no effort to speak.

Daphne didn't mind. She'd come prepared with explanations. "I was sorry to hear about your father." Smoothing hands over tight white capris, she took a seat next to him. "Is there anything I can do?"

Houston couldn't help but find an appeal to her little girl looks and womanly prowess. She'd only been in the room a minute yet those aspects of her personality were as vivid as the emerald green of her sleeveless top. As on edge as he was about the circumstances regarding his father's stroke; having the blonde nymphet in his presence, was having a definite improvement on his dismal mood. So much in fact; for the first time, he finally felt up to visiting his father instead of hiding out in whatever deserted waiting room he could find.

When Daphne extended her hand, he accepted it slowly and returned her smile when she squeezed.

***

"Get out." Marc wasted no time with pleasantries when he saw that it was Damon knocking on his bedroom door.

Book of Scandal

"I won't be here long." Damon slammed the door shut and leaned against it. "I don't feel like spendin' anymore time around you than I have to."

The comment got Marc's attention for he raised his head, his dark gaze narrowing as he closely observed his little brother. "There was a time you looked up to me D."

"You're mistaken, I was lookin' at West."

The smirk froze on Marc's face. "Get out or I throw you out and I'd much rather throw you out."

"I'm leaving." Damon promised idly while surveying the framed picture of the Empire State Building on the wall. "Just wanted to make sure you were gonna do right by the Simons."

Marc tilted his head, surprised once again since no one as yet knew of his proposal to Josephine- unless her nosy sisters had spilled the beans.

"I hope you're arranging for them to get money."

"Money." Marc set aside the *Ebony* magazine he'd been reading.

"For Fernelle. You remember her, don't you?"

"What about her?" Marc kept his voice calm enough but the tight curl to his lip was the give away to his anger.

"Come off it." Damon pushed off the door and walked to the middle of Marc's spotless room. "I know. Aside from Pop goin' to the hospital, most of the town's talkin' about Fern Simon found washed up on shore at Tybee Island."

"So?"

Damon's pitch stare raked his brother's face with unmasked dislike and disgust. He possessed the calm of a

Book of Scandal

man beyond eighteen years. The affect was stunning. "*So,* she was pregnant by you when she died and in spite of the fact that you got out of it-so to speak- you still need to do what's right."

"How the fuck did you-"

"Need to make sure your door's closed good n' tight 'round here before you curse out some girl you screwed and dumped when she told you a baby was on the way."

Marc made a sudden move for Damon, but stopped himself before following through with the attack. Yes, the affect of the boy's calm was indeed stunning.

"I want that family taken care of." Damon folded arms across the beige short-sleeved shirt he wore and closed a bit more distance between he and his outraged brother. "Fernelle's sisters shouldn't want for anything. Finding a halfway decent husband will be hard enough since their reps are trash. And this marriage between you and the youngest one better work."

Marcus swallowed. "How do you-?"

"Oh yeah, that's another thing being whispered around town." Damon turned for the door but left his brother with parting words. "Pop worked hard for what he's done and he's too good of a man to have been saddled with a son like you." He opened the door and then looked back at Marcus. "I won't let you ruin us. I'll see you dead first. Take care of this." Damon left as quickly as he'd arrived.

***

The two young nurses in Quentin Ramsey's room gushed and practically fell over themselves when the door opened to the man's son. Each gave personalized reports on

Book of Scandal

Quentin. The news wasn't all good, but it wasn't all bad
either. During the early morning hours, the patient had
awakened. The doctors had yet to contact the man's family
and were delighted when Marcus dropped by. Like the
dutiful son, Marc said he'd handle contacting his family to
let them in on the news.

The nurses tending his father offered Marcus their
sympathies. They were also bold enough to offer any other
assistance he might need. Marc threw on all the charm for
the doting women and simply asked for time alone. Once
the nurses were gone, so was Marc's charming façade.

Quentin was indeed awake when his son arrived.
His speech hadn't returned- his gaze however spoke
volumes as he stared down his son and the nurses.

Alone together then, no remorse or hint of upset
glinted in Marc's dark stare. He coolly observed. The
focused intent of his gaze was enough to raise anger in
Quent's own eyes.

"It must be eating you alive to have missed out on
the chance to get rid of me and Hous over what you walked
in on." Marc braced his hands to the edge of the bed and
grinned. "Gotta hand it to ya, Pop. Your lil' baby boy came
callin' figuring he could do the deed." Moving from the
bed, Marc stroked his jaw while contemplating. "God to
have that kid on my side…" he said to himself before the
grin returned. "He's got confidence and balls for
days…told me my marriage to Josephine Simon *better*
work. Oh yeah," he winked at his father, "we're engaged.
She's a sweet lil' thing, respectable, fine and trusting-
you'd like her. 'Course D didn't come to wish me luck.
Wants to make sure I do right by the Simons with Fernelle

Book of Scandal

Simon washin' up on Tybee knocked up with my kid and all." Marc laughed at the horror he saw in Quent's eyes.

"I didn't kill her Pop if that's what you're thinking. That *is* what you're thinking?" He sat in the chair next to Quent's bed and toyed with the bouquet of flowers on the nightstand. "Pop, Pop always thinkin' the worst of me. Was there ever a time when you thought the best?" Marc let the silence hang for a while before he shook his head.

"No, I didn't kill her but D's still got me over a barrel. But understand this, Pop, none of you should sit back and think I'll never go after what's rightfully mine at Ramsey. Your golden boy West has all the right stuff- all the ethics but it'll take more than that. It'll take a hell of a lot more than that to make Ramsey what we want it to be." Smiling then, Marc rested back in the chair and crossed his ankle over his knee.

"Sometimes you have to go through the back door to get to the front. All your money and respect made you forget that, Pop. It's how you made Ramsey what it is for Christ's sake." He grimaced, focusing on the crease in his trouser leg while allowing himself to calm. "Your time is passed and Westin is definitely not what Ramsey needs to usher it into a new time." He moved close to his father's bed then. "*I'm* gonna see to it that my place is secured and there's not a damn thing you can do about it."

Quent bristled, veins outstretched when Marc brushed the back of his hand across his hair.

"Do you really think you're gonna recover, Pop? Hmph. I've heard it takes some folks years to even re-learn how to hold a pencil." He leaned back in the chair again. "By then, I'll be top nigga at Ramsey. I'll take it so far, no

Book of Scandal

body would believe a thing you had to say against me. They'd just feel sorry for you. 'Poor Quent. Ain't been the same since that stroke turned him into a feeble ole man.'"

Marc watched his father closely. He was trembling hard then and; any minute; the nurses would be there to administer sedation drugs. He stood and leaned close.

"Thanks Pop," he whispered near the man's ear. "Had I known this would be the result, I'd have arranged it so you could've walked in on me and Hous screwing all those other young department candidates." He kissed his father's cheek and left the room.

As Quentin Ramsey's doctors feared and expected, the man didn't last much longer. He died on one of those rare days when his children didn't drop in for visits and his wife had allowed herself to be bullied into a day of rest.

What the doctor's hadn't expected though, was that Quentin wouldn't die of the stroke which had taken his speech. Instead, it was a heart attack brought on by that final visit from his second eldest son.

PART TWO
1965-1970

$\mathcal{R}$
~CHAPTER THIRTEEN~

Quentin Ramsey's death threw the family, the company and the community into a tailspin. Marcella Ramsey's anguish over her husband's sudden demise made everyone wonder whether the woman's despair would cause her to sell off the company and leave Savannah. As Quentin's trust in his wife was well known, no one was surprised that he'd left her in charge of it all with their eldest son at his mother's side.

Marcella took it one step further and gave over the entire kit and caboodle to Westin; who had assumed his responsibilities in Seattle with an ease that stunned and impressed everyone. The Savannah headquarters was ripe for picking with Houston and Marcus putting themselves in line for the top spots. As Westin had always championed

Book of Scandal

for them to have more power in the business, the young men made very successful attempts in impressing their brother.

The same could be said for Damon. Now on the brink of his senior year in college, he was working doggedly to secure a place at Ramsey before graduation. Damon knew Marc's and Houston's…endeavors wouldn't wait for him to become a more permanent fixture of the place. Nothing was more important to him, than keeping the promise he made to his father before the man did.

Like her brothers, Carmen was working towards security as well- her own. She pleaded with her mother to be sent off to school. With her father dead, West and Damon involved in their own interests and her best friend Catrina Jeffries, away at college as well, Carmen had no desire to remain under the same roof as Marcus and Houston.

Catrina Jeffries thrived being away at school. Realizing her ideas to streamline her father's business weren't as far-fetched as she thought; Catrina often returned home to make her dad's head spin. Despite his daughter's dazzling advice, King Jeffries was pleased that his money to put her through school was being well spent.

It was no surprise that Catrina's head was filled with figures and facts. In an on going effort to forget the mystery boy; who fizzled out of her life as smoothly as he'd entered, Catrina accepted more than a few dates while away at school and when she returned home. Young men who came courting were disappointed that the outings never went beyond a kiss on the cheek or worse; a handshake. Still, they were pleased just the same to have Catrina Jeffries on their arm.

Catrina even saw Houston Ramsey on several occasions. Of course the time spent seemed less like a date and more like an excursion with a cousin. That suited Catrina just fine. In spite of her best efforts to forget Damon, she was far from accomplishing that feat.

As hopeful as he was to push things to a more intimate level, Houston remained patient. That wasn't difficult, considering he had Daphne Monfrey still tending his sexual needs.

While Daphne's hopes spanned far beyond the bedroom, she'd not make the same mistake with Houston that she had with his brother. She'd be satisfied with sex…for a while, confident it would get her what she wanted in time.

Marcus married Josephine Simon two weeks after his father's death. If anyone was shocked or disapproved of the timing, nothing was said. Marc of course had a ready excuse and simply reasoned that after all the unhappiness it was time for the Ramseys to cast off old sorrows and look forward to new joys.

Following a whirlwind courtship; that she felt extremely guilty over in light of Quentin Ramsey's death, Josephine Simon was introduced to a world she would have never imagined for herself.

Marcus Ramsey liked to impress and; being the object of his 'impression' Josephine could scarcely catch her breath amidst all the incredible experiences Marc lavished. The same was to be said for the bedroom and Josephine could see why her sisters fought like cats and dogs over the man. He had a skill that was a mix of sin, seduction, danger and attentiveness that brought her to orgasm even before the act was consummated. Knowing that she'd benefit from such exquisite service each night, she couldn't help but feel a mite smug.

For her smugness however, Josephine couldn't drown out the hollow persistent voice that warned her not to be fooled by the act.

***

"Sorry." She apologized from her spot just inside the doorway of the study when Marcus looked up and saw her there.

He used the papers he'd been reading to wave her over. "Everything alright?" He asked once she was seated on his lap.

"I shouldn't complain." Josephine kept her eyes trained on the silver belt buckle which gleamed from his waist.

Marc nibbled along her jaw until she giggled. "What's wrong?" He encouraged once she was more at ease.

"I…" Josephine stared up and around the study. The paneled walls and leather furnishings made her shiver. "I honestly don't know what to do with myself in this big house of ours."

"Well haven't you enjoyed the things we've done so far?"

The tease brought heat to her cheeks and a darker tinge to her honey complexion.

"I bought this house for you. It's your decision to do whatever you like to make it a home." Again, he began to nibble her skin infrequently grazing his nose along her jaw and neck. "You should be done with it by the time our sons arrive, right?"

Talk of such things moved a shiver of anticipation along Josephine's spine. No seeds of that nature had yet been planted, still she found herself praying for the day.

She kissed him. "Are you so sure they'll be sons?"

"Without a doubt," Marc's expression was razor sharp and provocative in its intensity. "You're perfect. I picked you because you'd be the perfect wife to the man I intend to become- a great man. A great man needs sons. Beautiful sons." He nuzzled her cheek while stroking the line of her thigh covered by the silk of her lounging robe.

During the hug they shared, Josephine dismissed the shiver of unease mingling with her desire.

***

The saying 'be careful what you wish for' rang true in Carmen's mind more often since the bulk of her family seemed to have been scattered to the winds. As a result, she rarely made trips back to visit unless her mother made an issue of it.

That day; as she lounged in her favorite room overlooking the rear of the property, was one of those times. Carmen counted the days until she had to catch the train back to school. At least she and her mother had nice visits- rather prophetic visits in her opinion.

It seemed as if Marcella were schooling her, preparing her, telling her things she'd need to know as she matured. Carmen recalled teasing her mother that it sounded like she wouldn't want to tell her those things later.

Book of Scandal

While Marcella's smile was easy, she'd offer no response to the observation.

Shaking off the thoughts, Carmen rolled her eyes to the magazines and mail one of the housemaids handed her on the way into the sunroom. Her mother had lost interest in seeing to the mail- the task fell to Houston or to herself or Damon when they arrived home from school.

Shuffling through the glossy *Ebony*, *Vogue* and *Gentleman's Quarterly* along with the usual litany of bills and special offers she came across a worn envelope riddled with stamps. Her name was on the front along with Jasper's.

Carmen shrieked, scooting up in her chair as it dawned that Jasper had written to her from Vietnam. Turning her back on the overcast day beyond with windows, she ripped into the envelope.

A foreign scent rose from the pages and; for a time, she inhaled the aroma imagining herself actually taking in the same air with Jasper. She began to read; loving his descriptions of the beauty, chilled by his descriptions of the horrors and intrigued by his awe with it all. It was as if he were a student researching instead of a soldier on tour.

Whatever the case, he sounded more content than ever and Carmen told herself that had to be a good thing. Her heart flipped when at the end of the letter, he wrote that he was curious to see the woman she'd become. He hoped she'd write to him although he planned to be home soon and she was the only one he hoped to see.

'*Jasper*' he signed.

Carmen's eyes closed as she pressed the pages to her face and inhaled.

***

Book of Scandal

Damon raised the volume just a tad beneath the Duke Ellington/John Coltrane arrangement in an effort to drown his brother's usually welcomed voice. As Westin was presently warning him of how busy a college senior year was, Damon rolled his eyes in no mood for a lecture.

"...you won't have time for poking around Ramsey with all that going on, D."

"I'm fine with it, I swear. And anyway, what better time to come to learn at Ramsey than while I'm literally still a student?"

From his home office in Seattle, Washington Westin relaxed behind his desk and nodded at the young man's reasoning. His mouth curved down in the tell-tale sign of being impressed. "You sure I can't talk you out of this?" He tried again.

"Not a chance."

"D, isn't there a girl or three who wouldn't be wanting a bit of your time?"

Damon's fist clenched on impulse, his thoughts going to Catrina Jeffries which was where they usually were when he wasn't obsessing over getting into Ramsey to keep an eye on his brothers.

"It won't be a problem." Damon said before his silence grew too telling.

"So have you thought about what department you'd like to be in?"

"I don't think that department's been invented yet, West."

Westin turned his suede swivel toward the windows lining the rear of his office and listened while Damon spoke on what was called troubleshooting.

"Lots of companies are putting the area in place." Damon leaned over to turn down the Ellington/Coltrane arrangement. "The idea is to have a department that pretty much keeps watch over the business dealings and ensure things run...above board and by the numbers."

"Sounds like a company police."

"More or less."

Westin shifted uncomfortably in his chair. "Why would you think we'd need somethin' like that?"

"I think it's important we put this in place now- as a safeguard while there isn't a reason for it." Damon relayed the explanation he'd already rehearsed, knowing West would ask and knowing *he* wasn't prepared to give the man his true opinion.

"West, with all the changes taking place at Ramsey- more people are gonna be coming to work for us." Damon shrugged and slid down in the hardback chair before his desk at home. "It won't be the same as working exclusively around family and friends who're from where we're from. They'll be different people with different ways of doing things. Ways that; while productive, may not be in Ramsey's best interest."

The explanation gave Westin pause and he began to consider the validity in his brother's argument. Suddenly, he laughed. "Man, you sure you haven't already gotten that degree and runnin' your own biz someplace?"

Damon joined in the laughter, propping sneaker-clad feet against the desk. "When I first heard of the concept, I knew it'd fit in well at Ramsey."

"And you want in on the ground floor?"

Book of Scandal

That he'd mentioned *any* floor told Damon the man was surely warming to the idea.

"I can make it work, West."

"I don't doubt that. But you know some won't look too favorably on this new addition." West stroked his jaw while concern filtered his black stare. "Many may be offended or plain mad as hell to have their shoulders looked over and worse, by the founder's youngest son."

Damon straightened. "It wouldn't be like that West. But *if* there was a problem, it'd be my duty to seek out the source and investigate it. I'm not out to tell people how to do their jobs. I promise you that."

"I'll need something in writing, D. Something I can review before I make a final decision."

"Not a problem. You'll have it." Damon ordered himself to calm even though his heart was in his throat. "Thanks West."

"Makin' no promises, D."

"I know, thanks West."

"Get to work on that proposal."

***

Daphne's blondish curls bounced wildly and she let out a triumphant laugh when Houston cursed viciously as he came inside her. She knew to expect the reaction whenever he'd been pleasured most exquisitely. She delighted over being the one to bring about the sensation.

"I wish I could put you on a shelf somewhere." Houston panted while squeezing her hips. "I could have you whenever I wanted you."

Book of Scandal

"You could have that." Daphne managed to keep her voice calm despite the familiar lilt of her heart beneath her breast.

"You'd really do that? Take no other clients, but me?"

Daphne's lashes fluttered in the wake of tears and wave of shame that clutched at her. Of course Houston Ramsey's thoughts weren't even running along the same hemisphere as hers. "Silly," she pushed playfully at his chest. "What else would you think considering... Besides, my only clients have been you and Marc and not even Marc since that first night after the three of us..."

"So you're serious?" Houston scooted up in bed, his dark caramel face brightened by expectancy.

"Well our time together means a lot to me, Houston." She shrugged, needing to remain calm to take full advantage of the moment. "I want to be at my best for you and that means not letting myself get tired out by taking on more clients." She bit her lip when his gaze faltered as though the depth of her confession had unsettled him.

"Actually I'm glad you brought this up." She folded her legs beneath her and toyed with the tangled covers. "I *had* thought about maybe branching out with other clients. I could learn so much more if I broadened my horizons- new experiences-"

He caught her so suddenly, she'd scarecely seen him move. His grip was painful. She welcomed it.

"Don't even think about that." He kissed her hard. "Ever."

Book of Scandal

They fell into another round of sexual exploration. That time, Daphne's orgasm surged not from arousal but from power.

***

Seattle, WA

"Are you sure he's just a college kid?" Briselle Ramsey was asking while she prepared dinner one evening. West had just told her about Damon's call and the review he'd sent per their conversation. Briselle was surprised and very impressed by the young man's ambition as well as his ideas for the company.

"Especially with Marc and Houston posting up to be the top dogs back there."

Westin pushed aside the salt shaker he toyed with and fixed his wife with surprised eyes. "What do you think of that?" His wife had never shared any of her opinions regarding Ramsey goings on.

Briselle checked the macaroni casserole in the oven and shrugged. "Daddy said it wasn't a secret that Mr. Quent had...concerns about Marc being in charge."

West leaned back on the kitchen counter and watched his wife go merrily about her cooking. "Did he say why?"

"I don't think he ever went into detail." She added sugar to a pitcher of tea. "I guess it was the way he was so overjoyed- maybe relieved that you were ready to take over. Daddy said Mr. Quent always bragged about Damon too, talking about his quick brain and how you two were gonna take Ramsey to great heights. He never mentioned Houston or Marc." Briselle was checking her greens then and noticed her husband's silence.

Book of Scandal

"Did I say something wrong?" She smiled knowingly while wiping her hands on the apron protecting her gray mini-dress. "I know the wife's place is in the kitchen and out of the business but you *did* ask."

West braced off the counter and pulled Bri close. "The wife's place is in the kitchen, in the business and in the bedroom."

"Well...we can't go to the bedroom yet." Her lashes fluttered when he gnawed her neck.

"Mmm hmm, didn't I also say 'in the kitchen'?"

The couple was engaged in a heated kiss when Georgia found them.

"Shit!" She gasped before bursting into a nervous laugh. "Sorry y'all," she whipped off a checkered jacket and found her key inside. "I really need to give this back to y'all."

"Hush girl." Briselle was headed back to the stove.

"Seriously," Georgia set the house key to the dinette table. "Y'all just got married, don't need me droppin' in unannounced when you want to be alone."

"Didn't I say 'hush'?" Bri waved a dipping fork in the air. "Go sit your butt in the dining room, I'm about to bring out dinner."

"Thanks Bri, but I don't really have much of an appetite. That's what I stopped by to tell you." Georgia's tired expression was mirrored in her movements when she shrugged back into her jacket. "I'll probably grab some soup and call it a night."

"Georgia-"

"Good night."

Book of Scandal

"Georgia?" Bri moved from the stove, but gave up when her sister-in-law rushed out of the kitchen and toward the front of the house. She turned to find Westin sampling a corner of the macaroni. "Aren't you worried about her?"

"What?" West's handsome dark face registered pure innocence. "She said she was gonna eat some soup."

Briselle shook her head.

"Georgia's gonna be fine." West blew across the chunk of casserole on the spoon. "She's just kickin' herself in the ass 'cause she knows she made a mistake with Felix." He savored the macaroni and cheese.

Bri slapped her hands to her sides. "Well what the hell am I gonna do with all this dinner?"

"Trust me, it'll get eaten." West turned and wiped his hands on her apron. "Right now you can just forget about it."

"Why?"

Westin tugged her close again. "I think we were sayin' somethin' about the bedroom."

***

"Cotillions and birthday parties are what's puttin' you through school lil' girl."

"Daddy…" Catrina closed her eyes and struggled to find the additional swell of humbleness she knew she had stored somewhere. "Daddy I'm sorry and I don't mean to make it sound like I'm looking down on those things only…" she worried the tassel of her robe fastening and spoke carefully. "Business could quadruple if you were only willing to add just a few other services to the client

Book of Scandal

list." She bit her bottom lip watching as her father massaged his jaw-a telling sign that he was deeply concentrating.

"All the time I'm seeing businessmen at the café holding their business meetings." She continued, "Maybe you'd consider catering business lunches and a few hospital functions. People would pay well for something like that."

"Girl, stop aggravating your Daddy with all this talk." Rosa Jeffries had walked in wiping her hand on a dish towel.

"My talk could make us rich, Mama."

The natural arch of Rosa's brows raised a notch when she heard her favorite word.

"You tellin' me this stuff off the top of your head, Cat?"

"No Daddy," Catrina shuffled through the notebooks beside her. "I've got it all written down." A smile brightened her lovely face when she proudly pushed a folder across the table.

"I've been working on it all summer." Catrina's mahogany stare shifted from her father to her mother who hovered over his shoulder and studied the proposal as well. "Talking to you about this is all I've been able to think of."

Rosa pursed her lips and cocked a brow towards her daughter. "You'd do better to think about returning some of Houston Ramsey's phone calls."

Leaning back in the dining chair, Catrina tried not to appear smug. "I have returned his calls, Mama. We've been out several times when I've been home during my semester breaks."

"Well..." Rosa was obviously impressed.

Book of Scandal

"Don't get too involved with them people, Cat." King warned.

Catrina straightened and nodded fast. "I won't Daddy and I only see Houston as a friend anyway."

Rosa brought her hands together in a quick clap. "That's what me and your Daddy started out as."

Catrina smiled and watched as her father eased an arm about her mother's waist. "Sorry Mama, but if I ever marry into a family with money I'll definitely be bringing in some of my own."

***

"And this stairway takes us back to the parlor," Josephine's tone was airy with a touch of regality as she led her mother and sisters through her home.

Of course Martha Simon had visited several times since her daughter became Mrs. Marcus Ramsey. Clea and Rosselle had yet to accept any of their sister's offers to visit, until that day. It was obvious that Martha wasn't all together pleased by the gathering. She knew Ross and Clea well and could only hope their decision to visit their younger sister wasn't part of an ugly plan. Well…she could always hope.

Josephine was discussing the furnishings and their origins, when the phone rang. She was pleased to hear her husband's voice on the other end of the line even though he barely responded to her greeting.

"I'm bringing some people home for dinner tonight."

Josephine managed to keep her smile from wavering. "Tonight?" She inquired softly, well aware that her sisters were watching like hawks.

Book of Scandal

"Gerald Scales, William Green and Horace Monroe- along with their wives. And one of 'em's allergic to seafood, so none of that Etoufee you like to make."

She ignored the rumblings of frustration in her stomach. "Thanks for letting me know, Honey. You've um, thought of every detail." *Except how long it'll take to prepare a meal for eight people and what in the world to serve.* She tacked on a sweet laugh for her family's benefit.

"We'll be there by seven." He hung up without as much as a thank you.

"Alright then, no no you don't have to do that, I'll be fine." She carried on the phony conversation with Marcus and then tacked on another laugh for her sisters. "I love you too. Bye bye."

"Two guesses who that was Clea."

"Rosselle hush." Martha ordered with a scowl. "It's sweet to have a husband call in the middle of the day. Your Daddy does it and we've been married almost forty years."

"Yeah it is sweet, Ma." Clea sauntered around the beautifully furnished white brick parlor. "But some men act that way just to cover up things they've done that are *less* sweet."

"And Marc's just full of sweet gestures." Rosselle said once Clea's words had hung heavy in the air for the better part of a minute. "Like all that money he's sending to Daddy for the family."

Josephine's light eyes widened briefly but long enough that the girls took note of her surprise.

"Hmph, I'd say he's buying redemption. Wouldn't you, Clee?"

"You two stop it!" Martha hissed.

Book of Scandal

Josephine wouldn't give them the satisfaction of seeing her crumble. "Isn't it time for y'all to get past the jealousy?"

"Talk to me about jealousy when all the women your husband's still fuckin' start to come out of the woodwork."

"Clea!"

"It's alright, Ma." Josephine ignored the pricks stabbing her heart and held her head a smidge higher. "Are you upset Clee because you're no longer one of those women?"

Rosselle came to her sister's defense. "You may be livin' high and fancy now but Marc's still the same nasty muthafucka he's always been." She tucked her purse securely beneath her arm. "You have no idea what he is and that's probably good. Better to be shown than told. I'm sure that'll be soon. Ma, we'll see you at home."

Josephine waited for the door to slam before giving in to the desire to break down.

"Oh baby," Martha rushed to soothe and drew her daughter into a rocking embrace. "Don't pay no mind to that talk."

Josephine shook her head against her mother's bosom. "I never dreamed of living this way. I never *cared* about living this way." She sobbed.

"I know baby, I know…"

"Daddy gave us a good life." Josephine sniffed using the lace sleeve of her cream smock to wipe at the tears. "That life would've been good enough for me and to have a man who'd love me as much as Daddy loves you."

Book of Scandal

"Honey…" Martha stroked the braid crowning Josephine's head and kissed her temple. "Marcus loves you."

"Now that I've tasted this life, nothing else will do." Still resting against her mother's breast, Josephine studied the elegance of the room. "I have to make this work…"

"You listen to me. I don't want you talking this way." Martha jerked her daughter slightly as if trying to bring sense back to her head. "Remember the day he came to propose? How handsome and gentlemanly he was? Clee and Ross are just jealous." She used the hem of her sweater to dab a tear from Josephine's cheek. "Men come courtin' 'em all the time in spite of their reputations but those two still got high hopes of livin' like you are." She nudged Josephine's chin. "What's eatin' away at them is that you got all this beauty 'round you and you didn't have to open your legs first to get it."

Josephine cherished the embrace and the patented mother cooing that was a sure path to contentment. While the words and comfort should have eased her mind, Josephine couldn't silence the nagging voice that chanted Marcus Ramsey was a mistake she'd live to regret.

Book of Scandal

R

~CHAPTER FOURTEEN~

"I like it. I like it a lot." Roland Bray was a boisterous heavy set light-complexioned man with a quick humor and slow yet formidable temper. Damon had known the man all his life and knew he couldn't have asked for a more suitable partner to help run his department.

"Obviously your brother's got a lot of confidence in you." Roland noted, referring to Westin who'd gained his own share of confidence and respect in the wake of his father's death.

"The last year and a half has seen lots of changes at Ramsey." Roland braced thick fingers against one another as he reared back in his seat at the table. "I believe Quentin would be proud."

Book of Scandal

"Thanks Mr. Bray-Roland." Damon corrected himself, remembering the man's insistence that he call him by his first name. "I hope this means you're interested in my proposal?"

Roland Bray had been with Ramsey for years. The forty-something businessman held not only experience but a tremendous measure of loyalty and respect from the employees.

"Having you for an ally would allow this thing to run far easier." Damon added.

Roland nodded once again leafing through the bound proposal Damon had provided. "I have been wanting to get involved with a new project."

Perceptive as ever, Damon smirked. "But...?"

Absently, Roland brushed his fingers across the neat mustache he sported. "It's nothing you don't already know, kid. Lotta folks will be suspicious about what this new branch will be doing. They'll be wary, afraid- suspicious may be a better way to put it. Have you thought about that?"

"It's the one dark spot I can't shake since coming up with the idea." Damon admitted, scanning the crowded dining room at Bowman's Delicatessen. "It's the reason I want to bring you in first. With your approval, I'm hoping it'll assure everyone else that we aren't spies or cops tryin' to take anybody down. But if there *are* concerns, strange or even unscrupulous matters in the wind this department could be the place to air those concerns and have them looked into."

Roland was impressed, his brows raised as he nodded. "Overseeing something like this, for a company

Book of Scandal

like this could have huge possibilities. It'd become the heart of the company so to speak. How do your two older brothers feel about you having that kind of power?"

"They don't know yet." Damon grimaced thinking of Marc and Houston. "Westin's gonna meet with them to discuss it."

"And what happens if they don't like it?"

"They'll have to get over it." Damon pushed aside his unfinished turkey sandwich. "Westin's for it and he's in charge."

Roland's laughter started as a chuckle that erupted into a roaring bellow. "You got a shit load of confidence, boy!" He extended a hand. "I like it. Count me in."

The new partners were shaking hands when a waitress stopped over to ask if they needed anything else. The girl's eyes were all but glued to Damon who requested another soda and graced her with his heart-stopping dimpled smile. Roland grinned and asked for more coffee when the young woman finally gave him her attention. When she'd gone, Roland headed off for the bathroom.

Damon opened his portfolio and put a check next to Roland Bray's name. He was feeling confident and rather happy until he saw Houston walking into the deli with Catrina Jeffries on his arm.

No one aside from family or close friends recognized the tell-tale signs of Damon Ramsey's temper heating. That was pretty much because Damon had such excellent control over his emotions. Also, because little happened to truly rile him. Goings on with his brothers was to be expected, so no emotional upsets there. Now however, there was the telling clench of his jaw, the erratic dance of

Book of Scandal

the muscles there and the narrowing of his black stare as he rested his cheek on his fist.

He watched the couple looking around to choose a seat in the crowded room. Damon was so preoccupied by the way Houston cupped Catrina's elbow- the way his hand pressed to the small of her back to guide her to an unoccupied table in a far corner. He didn't think of what he'd have said if they'd seen him.

He thought back to his talk with Carmen when she told him of Houston's interest in Catrina Jeffries. He'd cast it off then with little more than a shrug. Actually seeing them together now...his brother was infatuated.

Hell, how could he not be? Damon slid his gaze back to Catrina. He accepted that his earlier reaction to what Carmen had said had been a lie. This didn't sit well with him. He didn't like this. He didn't like this at all.

"This place has the best Chicken fried steak." Houston idly commented once the waitress had walked off with their drink orders.

Catrina crossed her arms over the emerald linen jacket she sported. "Thanks a lot." She retorted and smiled when her pointed remark drew Houston's head up from the menu he studied.

Laughter sounded at the table when Houston caught the joke. He reached over to take her hand as their chuckles settled.

"You know, makin' me laugh is not an easy thing to do." He said.

A playful frown tugged at Catrina's lovely face and she settled back in her chair. "That's terrible. Laughter should never be so hard to come by."

"Well it is for me." He shrugged. "Guess it all depends on who's responsible for it."

Catrina bristled minutely and tried to tug her hand free when Houston's expression intensified.

"I want you to meet my family."

"Houston no," she blurted, shaking her head while his hold on her hand tightened consistently. "I- it's too soon I…" Meeting his family would put a far too serious mood on this- this…acquaintance than she'd like.

"I'm just not ready Houston and besides," she reached over to pat his hand. "I'm more interested in getting to know you better first."

He appeared to understand, focusing on her hand resting across his. "I've never done anything *all* right Catrina. Not one thing and that's unheard of for a Ramsey- especially a Ramsey son."

The waitress returned with their Pepsi-Colas and Houston quieted until they were alone again.

"I've got three brothers- one who's smart as hell in business, another who can charm the pants or panties off anyone and then one who's got it all wrapped into one with looks that can actually stop a woman from talking." He grinned. "You know what sort of looks it takes to do something like that?"

Catrina toyed with the straw in her glass while her thoughts settled on Damon for a brief moment.

Houston was shaking his head. "My great ability is being awkward. Nothing I say or do ever comes out right."

Book of Scandal

"Houston…" Catrina brushed her fingers across the back of his hand.

He turned the tables, clutching both her hands in his. "You're the best thing. The *only* thing I've gotten completely right and I want my family to see that. Seeing you would change everything they think they know about me."

Silently, Catrina berated herself for not taking pity on the man. At the same time she berated herself *for* taking pity. Smiling, she nodded. "Alright Houston. Alright."

***

"Mr. King is gonna be one happy man in a few weeks." Marcus predicted while preparing for bed.

The impromptu dinner party had been a complete success and everyone had to know how Josephine had managed it. Her admission of relying on Jeffries Catering had her high brow guests whispering about the well known black restaurant few of them had frequented for anything more than a quick lunch or a bite to eat after a day at the office.

"I'll bet Mr. Jeffries will be pretty shocked to have a whole list of white folks calling his line." Josephine smirked while removing her earrings. "Guess I'll believe *that* when I see it- or hear of it." She mused softly, believing her husband's assurance in his guests was only them saying anything to butter up a potential Ramsey client.

"Candace Scales swears she's gonna call him for her dinner party in two weeks." Marc shared while removing his cuff links.

"Scales?" Josephine inquired absently, unclasping the pins that secured her chignon.

Book of Scandal

"Gerald Scales' wife. The old guy?"

"Right," Josephine had to laugh silently recalling one of their guests referring to the 30ish Mrs. Scales as Mr. Scales nurse.

Josephine's amusement didn't last long though once Marc's voice filtered in as he continued to rave over the evening. He'd never once really come out and told her she'd done a good job. He'd certainly never apologized for putting her on the spot for planning the dinner in the first place.

"Oh well, I sure was grateful when Mr. Jeffries took the order. Dinner parties aren't things they do, but he's looking to expand so..." She selected a lotion from the array of bottles on the vanity. "I was so hysterical when I called thankful someone had taken pity on me."

"Well everybody sure was impressed. I think they'll give me anything to sign Ramsey." He began to whistle while unbuttoning his shirt.

"Did I tell you my family came to visit yesterday?" Josephine's wicked juices were flowing hot and heavy by then. "They couldn't stop talking about all that money you're sending them."

Marc turned from the floor length mirror.

Josephine bowed her head to hide her smile. Her husband's good mood had vanished.

"What the hell did they bring that up for?"

She shrugged, feigning interest in lotioning her elbows. "Actually they were talking about how sweet you were to call me in the middle of the day." The words made her gag. "Ross or... maybe it was Clea said you were doing lots of sweet things and mentioned the money." Her sigh was dramatic when she set the lotion back to the vanity. "They did say they weren't sure if it was really sweetness or for redemption."

Marc crossed the room. "Redemption?"

"For Fernelle," Josephine spoke without hesitation. She looked right at him through the mirror and loved the spooked expression that shadowed his face when he heard her sister's name. "Guess it makes sense they'd think that. She was pregnant with your child when she...died."

The brass backed vanity chair hit the carpet with a thud when Marc pulled Josephine out of it.

"Never mention that. Ever." His hold was tight on her arms even as his voice was whisper soft. "I never want to hear her name again. Do you understand me?"

Josephine nodded, her light eyes raking his face expectantly.

Smiling then, his expression turned light and he brushed the back of his hand across her cheek. "Sorry for bullying you into that party tonight." His lips followed the trail his hand had taken over her cheek. "Talking to you about people you don't know and all the while you were here having to deal with your jealous sisters." His lips blazed a sultry path along her jaw and neck. His hands massaged her form pliant beneath the satin nightgown she wore.

As livid as she felt toward him, Josephine felt herself reacting- anticipating more of his touch. She hadn't even realized he'd undressed her until he gathered her close and carried her to their bed.

***

Book of Scandal

Briselle was sprinting towards the front door after the bell rang. She laughed, finding Georgia out in the hall and quickly waved her inside the house.

Clearly suspicious, Georgia scrunched her nose and glanced around. "What's going on? Did West make another genius move at Ramsey?" She yawned, pretending to be bored.

Briselle slapped her sister-in-law's arm. "Y'all need to stop actin' like you don't care about each other. Come on and have dinner with us."

"Bri..."

"At least stay for drinks." Briselle didn't wait for an answer but tugged Georgia into the living room where Westin sat laughing and talking with Felix Cade.

Georgia was hardly one to burst into tears (unless it was from laughter). She certainly never gasped, shrieked or committed any of the purely feminine reactions she found so stupid. Gasp was exactly what she did when she saw Felix enjoying drinks with her brother.

"Hey Georgie," West casually greeted from the relaxed position in his favorite armchair.

Felix rose quickly from his relaxed position. His ebony gaze was unguarded, revealing all the desire and need coursing through him.

That look was mirrored in Georgia's stare.

"Well then," Bri smoothed hands across her burgundy checkered skirt, "I'm gonna go and check on things in the kitchen. Help me West? West?"

"Right," he tuned in having been momentarily fascinated by the staring session between his sister and Felix.

Book of Scandal

"What are you doing out here?" Georgia was first to break the silence when they were gone.

Felix was shortening the distance between them. He rounded the sofa and cupped her face when she was close enough to touch.

"You look so good," his voice was a whisper before he kissed her.

Her mind was blank when he finally let her up for air. "What are you doing here?" She managed after quite some time.

"Had a meeting." His hand remained about her neck, his thumb stroked her cheek and he studied her as though he were fascinated. "The car drove by Ramsey. I took a chance on seeing if I'd recognize anyone inside. Got to see the big boss himself."

"Meeting?"

Georgia listened intently, greedy for the information he shared about what he'd been doing since leaving Savannah. He told her about making it to California where he was getting a couple of garages off the ground. He was working to get a deal in place for parts, hence the meeting in Seattle.

"You've done so much." Disbelief was evident in her wide stare.

"Tried to tell you I was serious, G."

The remark stung no matter how softly it'd been delivered.

"I was sorry to hear about Mr. Quent." Felix said following another bout of silence. "He was a good man."

Georgia smoothed hands over her arms chilled beneath the aqua blue of her snug sweater. "I hoped you'd

Book of Scandal

come back for the funeral but seeing as how you were in California..." she blinked at the feel of tears behind her eyes.

"It was way after the fact when I heard." He started to touch her but changed his mind and eased a hand into his trouser pocket. "I don't really keep Ma aware of my every move."

"Right I- I understand." She gave a quick toss of her hair and smiled. "I was so sorry about what happened to your father but...I really didn't understand what you were going through 'til I lost mine." She gave in to the tears then. "It feels like nothing will ever be right again."

"Shh..." Felix moved close brushing her tears away with his thumbs. "You know that's not true and Mr. Quent wouldn't want you thinkin' that way."

"Damn," Georgia cursed when his soothing deep tone only triggered more tears. "My life's such a mess." She sniffled and looked around at the cozy elegance of the living room. "West and Bri have it so together while I feel like a sheet twistin' in the wind."

Felix bit his lip. He wouldn't ask if she was regretting not coming with him. He already knew that she was, but she'd never admit it. Still, he was intent on having her. The challenge would be in having her believe that she was fully in charge of the situation when it was her heart that was truly in command.

"Hey y'all, come on and eat!" West called when he and Bri brought steaming dishes into the dining room.

***

"What's the world comin' to when a fool like you manages to dodge the draft?" Marcus laughed full and long

Book of Scandal

for what had to be the tenth time since him and his old friend Charlton Browning sat down for drinks.

"Hell, when you got no place to call home, them fools got no place to come knockin' or send their bullshit letters."

"Right..." Until then, Marcus figured only those with money found creative ways to dodge the dreaded draft. Though Charlton found the humor in his genius, Marc was concerned by his friend's living situation and said so.

"All's well, man. Shit...I need to be able to pick up roots quick with all I got goin' on."

"You mind elaborating...if you can." Marc waited until the waitress set fresh drinks to their table.

Charlton winked, feeling a surge of confidence and something a tad darker coursing through him. He was older and a great deal wiser-this wouldn't be another instance of Marc Ramsey's name and charm overshadowing him. He'd spent the last several years bumming and looking for his next meal. He'd been making connections and acquaintances that hadn't presented themselves easily. There had been too much hard work and sacrifice put in to not have those seeds of effort sprout into benefits. Benefits for himself; and others as well. But for him first and foremost.

"If you're interested, I do have a proposition to discuss."

Marcus felt the familiar stirrings of excitement in his stomach. In spite of his standing at Ramsey, he knew all too well how impressively Charlt's...propositions paid off. The possibilities made it all too good to not at least hear out.

Book of Scandal

"I've got a connection to a supplier of industrial equipment." Charlton tugged a pack of cigarettes from his brown suede suit coat. "The shit is top notch though it has seen its share of use."

"Shoddy." Marc guessed.

"Inexpensive." Charlt corrected with a cool smile and lit his cigarette. "Cheap as far as you, me and my supplier know. For your accounting department at Ramsey however..."

Marcus grinned narrowing his striking stare. "Hmph, *cheap* becomes top dollar."

Charlton raised his glass. "And we pocket the difference."

Chuckling deviously, the old friends shared a toast.

"I like it. When do I meet the supplier?"

Charlton's cool vanished. "You deal with me only." He shrugged at the faint suspicion lurking in Marc's expression. "Keeps things simpler that way."

"Do I at least get to take a look at the equipment?" Marc signaled the waitress for a refill. "The money folks at Ramsey are squares but even they know junk when they see it."

"Next week sound good?"

A handshake across the table confirmed the date.

***

Daphne rang the bell to the Ramsey's majestic hilltop home before she lost her nerve. She'd debated on the visit for so long- since Quentin Ramsey's death actually. She prayed that all the talks to keep herself motivated enough to see it through would keep her from backing out now.

Book of Scandal

The door opened and it was clear from the look on the young maid's face that she did not approve of the visitor.

"Yes?"

"Yes, yes Daphne Monfrey to see Mrs. Ramsey."

The maid eased a hand into the pocket on her uniform. "I doubt anyone here is interested in whatever you're...selling."

Daphne bristled, feeling a definite chill through the long sweater covering her pantsuit. She leaned in on motivation to keep her feet planted on the porch. It didn't work. When she would have cowered and backed away, she heard the voice as cool and regal as it'd been the first time she heard it.

"Who is it, Tammy?"

Before Tammy Burnett could respond, Daphne inched forward.

"Hello Mrs. Ramsey." She watched in awe as the lady of the house arrived at the front door.

Recognition filtered Marcella's expression. "Babydoll Monfrey's girl."

"Hmph," Tammy grunted.

"Daphne Monfrey ma'am. I-I'm sorry to just drop by like this-"

"Nonsense child. It's been years since my party on a summer's day." Marcella's alluring gaze misted over with memory as though she were recalling the happy occasion. "Where are my manners?" She gave a start, turning back to her guest. "Come in child. It's been way too long since you've visited me, you know?"

Book of Scandal

"Yes ma'am," Daphne's voice was hushed as she crossed the threshold. "I didn't know if it'd be appropriate." She looked over at the maid who still hovered.

"Tammy go get us some hot tea and cookies." Marcella bustled the girl off, then took Daphne by the arm and led her deeper into the house. "I could certainly use the company."

"You?" Daphne blurted. "But you have so many friends."

"Right. Friends *my* age- who make me *feel* my age." Marcella followed the words with a saucy wink. "My kids are practically gone. Having some young life in the house is just what I need."

"I was sorry to hear about Mr. Ramsey." Daphne said when they entered the living room. "It was a real loss to the town. He was a great man."

"Yes...yes he was." Marcella tapped her fingers along the fireplace mantle. The area teemed with family photos. Her gaze was riveted on pictures of her late husband.

"The two of you must've had a beautiful marriage." Daphne strolled the room, trailing her fingers across the glossy carved wood framing the sofa and armchairs. "Beautiful children, beautiful things, beautiful people..."

Marcella turned from the mantle. "Beautiful marriage and children are all that matter."

Daphne hid her grimace. "Anyone can be married and have kids. It takes special people and respect to have the rest."

"Honey all people are special in their own way." Marcella's silver linen duster swished lightly as she

Book of Scandal

approached Daphne. "As for respect, well…respect is something earned."

Daphne's smile held a politeness. "I'm sorry, but everybody knows anyone with the Ramsey name is respected at birth."

"Ah yes," Marcella tapped her fingers to the silver chain at her neck. "The 'respect by birthright' crowd…" her voice was light but her expression was anything but. "Those folk work twice as hard to keep their respect as others do to earn it." Marcella focused full on Daphne then. "It's not an easy thing to keep honey and if one isn't careful, it can slip away without being noticed until it's far too late."

***

"How'd he talk you into this shit?" Marcus' temper was thoroughly stoked over Westin's news of Damon's approved proposal for an in-house troubleshooting department.

"Just what the hell is it?" Houston didn't bother to hide his edginess over the idea or his confusion over what the idea actually entailed.

Marcus propped his wingtips on the black lacquer coffee table in the office. "It's a way for baby brother to get his foot in the door and get past havin' to answer to anybody in the process."

A heavy thud sounded drawing Marcus' and Houston's attention to the speaker box where Westin's voice transmitted from his Seattle office. The brothers knew West had just slammed his fist to the desk as a command for silence.

Book of Scandal

"The proposal's a good one. Look it over so you'll know what to expect."

"Oh we know what to expect." Marc's upper lip curled. "We can expect our shoulders bein' looked over every damn day by our nosy little brother."

"Well I guess you'll just have to get used to it." Westin's low voice brooked no argument and was followed by the sound of papers shuffling across his desk. "As for the business, the two of you will be overseeing day to day operations with the assistance of key people. They're experienced and were hand-picked by Dad. Your respect for them and attentiveness to their input is expected."

Marcus flashed his middle finger toward the speaker box.

"As for Damon's troubleshooting department, he won't be running it single-handed but with a similar group of experienced and hand-picked folk as well. How the three of you work together will determine whether any of you ever get any *real* control."

Houston felt a chill and slanted a quick glance toward Marcus to see if he'd noticed his reaction. In that moment, Westin had sounded exactly like their father.

"I'll be in touch."

When the speak box line buzzed it was Marc's turn to slam *his* fist to the table.

"What's D up to?" Houston rested elbows to knees when he leaned forward in the armchair.

Marcus left the sofa shoving his hands into the deep pockets of his trousers. "Tryin' to live up to some promise he made to Pop about keepin' the family squeaky clean."

Book of Scandal

Houston stilled. "What? Does he? Does D suspect somethin' about his stroke? We were there and-"

"Stop. Houston? Stop." Marc raised a hand and shook his head to soothe his brother's paranoia. "No one knows that for sure. *No one* and it'd better stay that way." He waited for his brother's nod and began a stroll of the office.

"No, this will all come down to a case of loyalty from the Ramsey execs picked by Pop." Stroking his jaw, Marc spoke more to himself than Houston. "When they see how much richer I intend to make them... well we'll just see how long it'll take before Westin's *real* control comes our way."

$\mathscr{R}$

~CHAPTER FIFTEEN~

Briselle and Georgia were folding shopping bags following a day in town. Briselle would be heading home, but dropped Georgia off first and helped her cart her wares inside.

"Seems like old times with Felix around, doesn't it?" Briselle asked while propping three shopping bags against the side of the love seat.

"What's that supposed to mean?" Georgia let the bags she held; fall to the floor in a clutter.

Briselle shrugged. "Nothing at all, it's just nice seeing him again and he's looking so well. Very well." She went to collect the bags Georgia let fall. "I'm betting I'm not the only woman who thinks that."

Book of Scandal

"Jeez Bri, how many times are you gonna talk about this?"

"Sorry," Briselle smiled at the sour look Georgia shot her in response to the phony apology. "So have you two been alone since he's been back?"

Georgia removed her gloves and tossed them to the message desk in the living room. During the past week, she and Felix had spent most of their time out with Westin and Briselle. It was just as well, Georgia decided.

"He's going back to California soon- no sense in getting all riled up over him again."

Briselle studied the buckle on the side of her black go-go boots. "So you're regretting not going with him, huh?"

"Shit Bri, gimme a break, would you?"

Briselle threw up her hands. "Alright, alright. Guess I'll be saying goodnight." She tugged Georgia into a tight hug, grabbed her purse and breezed down the hallway.

Briselle was heading out just in time for Felix who stood outside and was just about to ring the bell to the apartment.

The uncertainty on his dark handsome face appeared to deepen. "Sorry Bri, I didn't know you and Georgie had plans-"

"No such thing." Briselle was already tugging him inside by the sleeve of his trench coat. "We're done." She pointed down the hall. "Bedroom's that way."

Leslie Gore's *"You Don't Own Me"*, wafted from the bedroom radio. Georgia had already headed off to start trying on dresses once Briselle walked out. Just then she wore only a lacy peach bra and panty set while deciding on which frock to try on first. She held up one dress and was viewing herself in the floor length mirror when she saw Felix. Embarrassed, she gasped and whirled around to make certain he was really standing there.

"How...?"

"Briselle," was his only explanation as he walked toward her.

Georgia didn't realize she was backing away until her hip brushed the armchair near the bed. She swallowed, watching him with a mixture of expectancy and awe as he removed his coat and went to work on the shirt tucked inside his trousers.

"I um, what can I do for you?" She grimaced at how weak that sounded.

Felix barely smiled. "You know damn well," he said kissing her then as he backed her to the wall.

Georgia's moan rose instantly, hungrily she absorbed the kiss. Her response was eager and fiery. Every part of her shivered in the wake of his fingertips skirting her flesh as he removed the scant under things covering her body.

"Felix," she whimpered when his fingers plundered her sex. "Felix, I can't go with you."

He smiled then. "I know. That's why I came to get something for the road."

An impressively long, impressively wide shaft claimed her then. Georgia could have slid down the wall were it not for Felix holding her there and taking her with a zeal that lasted well into the night.

***

Book of Scandal

    Josephine stood before the floor length mirror pulling her hair up into a ponytail as she often did before heading down each morning to make breakfast for Marcus. She bit her lip, freezing when he emerged behind her.
    "You'll be late." She warned when his hands covered her breasts and he began to lavish her neck and shoulders with kisses.
    "I think apologizing to you is more important than being late."
    "Apologizing?" She faced him then.
    The probing dark gaze was soft as he watched her.
    "I was wrong to put that kind of pressure on you with that dinner party especially when you'd never given one before."
    Josephine would've smiled at his words, but he was kissing her before she could make a move.
    "That's why I'm giving you two months to plan the next one." He said when he finally let his wife up for air.
    "The next one?" Josephine went cold beneath her gown.
    "I'm striking while the iron's hot." He headed into the closet to select a tie. "West just put me and Hous in key positions at Ramsey. I want to celebrate and make connections while I'm doin' it."
    Josephine eased down to the arm of the chair next to the closet. "But isn't being in key positions connection enough?" She asked when he emerged from the walk-in area. Giving another party was not on her wish list.
    Leaning against the doorjamb, Marc lifted a brow at Josephine's intelligent and candid query. "West also gave Damon a key position." He said.

Book of Scandal

"Damon? But isn't he still in college?"

"Damn right and makin' good use of his education."
He held out two ties silently asking Josephine to choose.
"He already convinced West to go ahead with some
oversight department with him in charge."

Josephine nodded, hiding her smile as she moved
close to assist him with the tie. She was beginning to
understand the importance of this next party. Her husband
was trying to buy loyalty, to ensure confidence and that
secrets would be kept over whatever shady scenarios he
had in mind for Ramsey's future. Though she felt it best to
keep quiet on that particular observation, she was too
curious not to ask about the rest.

"Marcus, why did you marry me?" She asked once
he turned toward the mirror and observed her work on his
tie. He turned quickly to face her and Josephine couldn't
tell if he was surprised or angry.

"Obviously you intend to be in the spotlight with
lavish parties, high profile meetings." She took the tie
they'd decided against and went to replace it on the rack
inside the closet. "I'm neither lavish nor high profile. I
think you're going to be terribly disappointed."

She felt him behind her in the closet and breathed
deep before turning. She easily deciphered the look on his
face then as pity. She would have preferred anger.

He kissed her forehead. "So innocent," he muttered
into her skin. "So perfect," he leaned back to study her
more intently.

Marcus didn't elaborate on the phrases. Silently, he
thought how delicate she was. Non-abrasive. She was the
kind who knew her place. The kind who would allow him

Book of Scandal

to do what he needed without question, right by his side all the while. She'd be lovely, elusive, giving him respect and admiration in all the right areas.

He kissed her again. "I married you because you're the kind of wife a man like me needs."

Josephine watched her husband in complete bewilderment as he left the room whistling a happy tune.

***

Houston arrived at work that morning feeling as though he were visiting a dream where he was completely invisible. This wasn't the case of course, but he may as well have been invisible for when he arrived in the front office of Ramsey's Youth Division his *hand*-selected assistants didn't even register his arrival.

Most were either seated around the big desk in the corner or draped over it while laughing over something his younger brother had said. More livid than he could ever recall being, Houston opened and closed the door with more force that time.

Silence registered.

Damon thanked the young women for their help and they all scurried off whispering hushed good mornings Houston's way.

"Morning Houston," Damon greeted, slowly rising from his brother's chair.

"Why're you here, D?"

"Just interested," Damon spanned the room coolly. "Lots of women here. Just wondering why no men made the cut."

"Does it matter to the troubleshooting department?" Houston's top lip curled into a hateful smirk.

Book of Scandal

Damon shrugged and stepped around Houston to further observe the office. "There are many more young black men on the street with too much time on their hands."

Houston rolled his eyes. "I'm sure they're hiring in the manual labor division." He turned to perch on the edge of his desk. "We need women who are used to the day to day grinds of office work. Most men would go crazy in a second with this sort of shit."

"Women, huh?" Damon eased a hand into his burgundy trouser pocket. "But these are girls, Hous. Barely out of high school."

Houston folded his arms over his salt and pepper suit coat. "That's why it's called the *youth* division."

"They only report to you?"

"Why the hell are you here, D?" Houston's voice was softer, more dangerous then.

Damon's calm was almost tangible. "West told you about my assignment."

"And just what do you think's goin' on here?"

In truth, Damon had no reason to suspect his brother of anything...yet. The devil in him however, made him want to rile Houston to no end.

"It's just interesting that you'd take an interest in the...youth department. Doesn't seem like your style." His smile was playfully taunting.

"You get the hell out!" The fact that Houston hissed the phrase did nothing to diminish its fire. He caught hold of his temper, but had already grabbed the attention of the assistant who was only making a pretense at work nearby to oogle Damon.

Book of Scandal

"You got no business here," he stepped close to whisper. "I don't care what Westin or anyone else has to say."

"Did the same go for Pop? He collapsed right here in these very offices, didn't he?"

Houston stepped back, his face taking on an ashen quality. "What are you gettin' at?"

"Just curious." Damon's smile held no humor. His dark gaze relayed his suspicion. "I've always been curious. You and Marc hardly visited him in the hospital. I think you were only there once, right? Marc too."

Forgetting his unease, Houston moved close. Damon's smile was more genuine then. The possibility of a physical encounter with his brother was exactly what he wanted.

"This is mine, D. I'll damn well have the respect that goes with it. Go sniff around for your own toy." He left his brother with a disgusted look before walking off.

Gaze narrowing, Damon nodded accepting the challenge more fully than Houston realized.

***

August 11, 1967

Dear Carmen,

They took the bullet out of my arm. I lost feeling in it for a while but I don't think they'll have to amputate. I was sort of down about that. It could've been cool to have a robotic arm- I'd feel like some villain in a movie.

Anyway, they're gonna let me out of here just the same-honorable discharge and all. Everybody's so jealous, but in a good way. They're all real happy for me. I've made some good friends here. The guys are even giving me a huge send off when I finally get my walking papers. I've really made good friends

Book of Scandal

here Carm, some of the best I've ever known. I pray I'll have the chance to see them again.

I've actually already been in touch with a friend back in the world (back in the States). He's a doctor I met over here in Nam. He's a good man. I've learned so much from him. He was highly decorated before he left. His life was his work; but he's an old man and I was lucky enough to meet him before he left. Doc was eager to have a student to pass on his teachings so I did some work for him here and made a grip (a lot of money).

Anyway, I won't say more. I don't want to jinx a good thing. I hope to see you soon, Carm. I miss you.

Jasper

***

Westin's laughter was soft when he felt Briselle's death grip clench on his arm. It was a third time it'd happened since they'd arrived at the annual gathering to welcome new businessmen to the area.

"You know you've already charmed everyone you've met here tonight." He spoke close to her ear while smoothing his hands reassuringly across her bare arms. "If anyone should be on edge it's me. I doubt they'd spare me the time of day if it wasn't for you."

"Stop." She slapped his arm. "I know you're just trying to make me feel better."

"Is it working?" He smoothed a hand across her skin where the V of the black dress dipped low in the back.

Briselle stood on the tips of her pumps and kissed his jaw. "It's working very nicely, thank you."

West nuzzled his nose against hers. "Anytime."

Briselle shook her head; for now was definitely not the time for him to be reassuring her. This was his time to shine and dazzle. She'd begun to realize over the time

Book of Scandal

they'd been in Seattle that Westin Ramsey shined and dazzled without doing much more than simply walking into a room. The event that night was proof of that. The gathering was by invitation only and Briselle couldn't help but notice she and her husband were two of the only two black people in the room.

    She'd stepped past the entrance doors that evening with suspicion clouding her brain. She couldn't imagine why the Seattle Business Group would want Westin there- unless it was to gawk or make the white folks there feel charitable. Slowly, she began to realize that they wanted West there because he'd impressed them. The man was quickly growing a respected rep in the town. As a result, Ramsey's rep grew just as quickly. Briselle could see it in the way everyone listened intently when her husband spoke. She heard it in their questions- everyone eager to pick his brain and even seek his advice on ventures they were thinking of starting.

    Of course, Westin Ramsey wasn't the only pretty new face in the room that vibrated with conversation, the clink of glasses and the rhythm of jazz. The Seattle Business Group reached out to up and coming business people throughout the Northwest Territory; partly to lure them to Seattle which was still a growing city.

    In spite of all that, Briselle still wasn't sure what to make of the group of seven olive-skinned males who drew boisterous laughter from everyone they spoke with. Aside from her husband and his brothers, *beautiful* was a word she'd never associate with men. Dammit all, if the seven charmers in her line of sight weren't just as beautiful and just as dangerous looking as the Ramsey brood. What's

Book of Scandal

more, the seven olive-tones were headed right towards her and her husband which accounted for her death grip on West's dark suit coat.

"Natural resources," Stone Tesano rounded out the list of his family's interests which spanned throughout the States as far as Italy- the home of their ancestors.

The seven were in Oregon then scoping out the area they'd often dreamed of exploring and cultivating once they were old enough.

"Though some of us still aren't quite there yet," Gabriel Tesano teased Roman and Vale the youngest two of the seven.

"Still, we're all here because of our father's insight." Humphrey Tesano remarked while taking a swallow of the scotch he held.

Pitch Tesano nodded in agreement with his older brother. "We owe it to the man to take our family as far and as high as it can go."

"Sounds familiar," West grinned, "I tell myself the same thing almost everyday."

"That's pretty clear Westin," Aaron Tesano commended. "Ramsey's name is all over the place. Your dad would be proud."

"We hope to follow your example, Westin." Roman added. "Hopefully our generation can be the one that does it right."

"Hmph, just so it doesn't take too long." Vale cautioned, his dark eyes sparkling as he watched Briselle move up to kiss her husband's cheek.

"Fine business, fine wife, damn right your dad would be proud." Vale added.

Aaron joined in on the chuckling but his gaze held a dangerous glint. "Our little brother often speaks out of turn," he clapped a hand none too gently upon Vale's shoulder, "this time is no exception but I have to agree that she is a beauty, Westin."

The seven raised their glasses in a show of agreement. That time, it was Westin who leaned down to bestow the kisses Briselle's way.

***

"I can't believe a fool like you is 'bout to be an attorney!" Marc's words were beginning to slur just a tad at the onset of a third round of drinks.

Jeff Carnes raised his shot glass for what had to be the eighth toast of the night. "I gotta pass the bar first, man."

"Ha! Fool I hate to tell you, but we passed the bar a long, long time ago!"

More laughter rumbled between the two friends and was interrupted only by the waitress who approached the table.

"Get you or your friend anything else, Marc?"

"I'll let you know." Marc's sly wink was accompanied by a slap to the woman's barely covered bottom.

"So how's married life treatin' you?" Jeff watched the woman saunter off into the smoke-filled room.

Marc shrugged, tapping his fingers to a few bars of Eddie Jefferson's *"Yardbird Suite"* while his mood turned

a tad somber. "'Bout what I expected, man. Rather boring."
He burst into another swell of laughter.

"Lies," Jeff shook his head. "I've seen Josephine.
Life with her should be anything but boring."

"Oh don't get me wrong, she's damn good in the
sack. Besides, I need her."

"Well there you go!" Jeff raised his shot glass in
another toast. "Never thought I'd ever hear you admit to
needing anybody."

Marc rolled his eyes. "Fuck that. I need her for the
respect it's gonna take to rise like cream the way West
did."

"Man," Jeff grimaced, reaching for the second glass
of gin he'd ordered. "Don't take the girl for granted. I seen
that shit too many times at the firm. The attorneys I intern
for make a fortune in divorces stemmin' from all kinds of
reasons. They all say the one thing that sparks all the drama
is that the wives feel taken for granted." He tipped the glass
in Marc's direction. "Just be sure that she knows you
appreciate her."

Marc chuckled and reached for his suit coat hanging
across the back of a chair. "I think every time she walks
'round that big ass house or goes shoppin' she knows how
much she's appreciated." He pulled a handkerchief from
the jacket pocket and mopped his brow. "All that
'appreciatin' takes loot. Lucky Charlt's back in town with
his money-makin' ass."

Jeff groaned and signaled the waitress for a refill.
"Be careful, man. That nigga's no good- don't want you
goin' down with him."

"Be cool Jeff. Ain't nothin' like that in the wind. Charlt just likes to share the wealth- literally."

Jeff sighed. "Just lookin' out for you, brotha."

"Good." Marc slipped a twenty inside the waistband of the waitresses' shorts when she brought a refill to his bourbon in addition to Jeff's gin. "So I guess when you pass the bar, you'll be bringin' me on as a client?"

Jeff laughed. "Like you'd give a shit about any advice I'd have."

Despite the haze of a few drinks too many, Marcus sobered. "I'd definitely give a shit. I plan on goin' all the way here and I'll need someone like you in my corner." He extended a hand. "Can I count on you, man?"

Jeff observed Marcus for a while before nodding and leaning over to accept the shake.

***

Catrina had just finished up a meeting with Dawson's Printing. Her intentions were to get a bit of advertising for Jeffries Catering- reasonably priced of course. While most of the town knew her father's business, she wanted them to know Jeffries could handle the more elaborate business type affairs in addition to family gatherings and luncheons.

The unexpected dinner party for Josephine Ramsey had already generated quite a surge in business for more elegant affairs. Catrina was certain that was just the tip of the iceberg.

She was making a few notations on her pad while leaning against the hood of her cousin Steven's Olds. The soft clearing of a throat, gradually tugged at her interest.

Book of Scandal

Her lips parted and she suddenly felt a chill that had nothing to do with the black and white mini-dress she sported. "Damon," she swallowed seeing him an arm's length away.

"It's been a while." His gaze raked her several times before he spoke.

She smiled. "A *long* while," she took in the subtle more striking changes in his features.

"I wasn't sure you were even in Savannah." He moved closer.

Catrina's brows arched. "Have you been looking for me?"

"Jeffries isn't the same without you." He leaned against the car.

"I've been away at school."

"Georgia?"

"North Carolina." She tossed her pad through the open passenger side window. "A girl's college in Greensboro. I'll be heading back soon for fall term."

A muscle flexed in Damon's jaw when he bowed his head and absorbed the news. "How's your mother coping with her top grease dumper gone?"

Catrina had to laugh. "Actually I've been promoted." She shrugged. "Promoted myself, anyway. I hope to diversify my dad's business."

"So you're working for your dad's business too?" Damon bit his lip the instant the question slipped past.

Catrina caught the slip and tilted her head. The guy never talked about his family business. He never talked about his family at all.

Book of Scandal

Damon offered no further insights and was pleased that Catrina didn't request any. Their eyes did the speaking for the better part of the next minute.

"I better go." She headed for the driver's side. He caught her arm when she brushed past him.

She didn't dare look his way but could all but feel his onyx stare peering through her.

"Can I take you out sometime?"

Her eyes snapped to his and she almost gasped.

"I um…I don't think that's a good idea." Catrina almost didn't recognize her voice and tugged free of his hold.

"It was good to see you Damon." She settled into the car and drove away.

Book of Scandal

~CHAPTER SIXTEEN~

Steel mill safety was the topic of that morning's executive committee meeting. Virtually everyone agreed that the topic was of utmost importance and deserving of being discussed at length. The possibility of costly accidents, repairs, loss of life…meant many more involved discussions would be warranted.

"It's good that we're all in agreement on how high a priority this is." Preston Schaefer spoke over the mix of voices in the room then. "But during these discussions, it'd also be important for us to constantly be mindful of the expense of the plans we're wanting to outlay. If we want top-notch safety, cost will be a factor."

"A huge one," Rusty Xavier added. "We're gonna have to pay top dollar if we expect the best."

"We're aware of all this guys." Someone chimed in.

Book of Scandal

Marcus waved from his seat at the table. "I suppose another question that bears asking is whether you all are pleased with your current suppliers. Equipment's the bottom line in a discussion about safety."

"And right now we're scattered with suppliers." Rusty mopped his brow with the handkerchief from his front pocket. "I've always been an advocate for consolidation- one supplier for all our needs."

"I may have some thoughts on that." Marc reclined in his seat when everyone looked on in interest. "If you all approve I'd like to lend my support- it'd be the best way for me to learn about who supplies Ramsey with what it needs. Mr. Xavier's idea could save us a ton of money and perhaps offer greater efficiency by dealing with one equipment supplier."

A murmur of conversation filled the room again. Marc hid his smile when he noticed the number of heads beginning to nod.

"I'd like to move that we let Marc run with this."

"Second."

Preston Schaefer stood. "All those in favor?"

Rusty Xavier clapped Marc's shoulder when the motion passed. "Congrats, son. But don't think we've just done you a favor- no one wants all the extra work you're in for."

Finance V.P. George Farris stood then. "Before we get out of here everyone- I'd like us to recognize another young Ramsey at the table."

Marcus smiled over at Houston.

"Damon." George Farris was waving toward the young man. "Your insight and the inception of Ramsey's

Book of Scandal

new trouble shooting department showed a lot of guts and intelligence. Your interest in the well-being of your family's business deserves a round of applause."

The applause broke out seconds later. It was several more minutes however before the group left the room. Everyone wanted the chance to shake hands with Damon.

Marcus also garnered his fair share of handshakes. He was laughing with the last of the meeting attendants, when Houston ambled over.

"Don't sweat it, man." Marcus said already knowing what fueled the sour look his brother wore.

"The little jackass isn't even done with school and he's already getting nods from the top. Headin' his own division..." Houston slammed a fist to his palm.

"Houston? Hous? Calm down." Marc brought his hands down over his brother's shoulders. "I've got irons in the fire that'll pay off big for both of us- putting us in charge of it all. Even West's know it all ass." He gave Houston's tie a tug. "Just play it cool."

Houston told himself he could do that after Marc slapped his arm and walked off. He was making headway until he was five steps out of the meeting room door and overheard two secretaries.

"...Gorgeous and take charge. It's a shame Marc's already off the market." One of the young women complained.

"But Damon's still unattached." The other said and rested a hand over the front of her blouse as her eyes rolled in a dreamy fashion. "Could you imagine going to bed with *that* every night?"

Book of Scandal

The ladies giggled and walked on. Taking advantage of an empty desk, Houston picked up the phone and dialed Daphne Monfrey.

***

"You have surpassed every one of my former students." Owen Dowd stirred his green tea while complimenting his young apprentice. "They'd studied the field for years and never have I seen such dedication. I'll admit that I'm curious to know what fuels it."

Jasper smirked, but humbly accepted the doctor's commendation. Owen Dowd was already a legend in the field of genetics well before volunteering to lend his medical expertise in war-torn Vietnam.

Jasper had met the man when an attack on the base sent almost half the soldiers there dead or infirmed. Most of the doctor's own staff had been killed and the man enlisted the help of any man who was still standing. Jasper's work ethic and observant nature intrigued the doctor from the start.

"I've always been interested in learning new things, sir." Jasper took a sip of his tea only grimacing slightly as he was slowly becoming fonder of the taste.

The doctor laughed. "That sort of dedication goes way past curiosity, son. Try again." He urged.

Jasper sighed while silently asking himself if he couldn't trust Owen Dowd, who could he trust? The man had shown him a compassion he'd never known- not even from his own mother. He thought of Carmen, but told himself that was different.

Book of Scandal

Dr. Dowd had seen him at his worst, at his most terrified. He'd already confided things to the man that he hadn't to another soul. Why not this?

"I've always been intrigued by it." He set aside the delicate cup and saucer. "Chemistry. How the right or wrong mix could make the difference between beauty and abomination." He shrugged and looked around the coziness of the doctor's living room. "Wasn't until I learned of genetics that I realized how much more...involved it all was."

The doctor leaned forward. "What got you interested in all this?" Owen Dowd felt all other questions leave his tongue when Jasper finally shared the story of his mother's death and the circumstances of his birth.

"I know I can't remake myself, Doc." Jasper shook his head as though trying to make sense of it all. "Just being educated on how certain genetic patterns could intersect, collide to form greatness or catastrophe...it'd be enough for me."

"Son," the doctor grimaced as if realizing what Jasper's concern was. "You aren't catastrophe or abomination. If that were the case, you certainly wouldn't care about the why of it all." The man focused on the cuffs of his sweater then. "You'd be...hell son; you'd be out to wreak havoc and devastation instead of using your mind for the good of research."

Jasper rolled his eyes, prepared to argue but straightened when the doctor clutched his knee.

"I want you to hold onto that interest, dedication and confidence son." Owen Dowd's wrinkled, weather-beaten face brightened with a smile. "You're embarking

Book of Scandal

upon a magical path. The field of genetics is still so untouched, so undiscovered. The future will tap into those discoveries. New paths will be forged. The sky will be the limit and we scientists," he winked at Jasper. "My boy, we scientists will be gods." He clinked tea cups with Jasper and they laughed.

***

In spite of all the accolades thrown his way earlier that day, Damon Ramsey was in a fierce mood. He'd left the meeting straight away, returned to his office and slammed the door in a none too subtle warning that it was best he not be disturbed. With the lights dimmed, he thought about Catrina Jeffries.

He couldn't help but wonder if things were more serious between her and Houston than he thought they'd go. She was a great girl and could probably find something to love in anyone. Obviously she knew Houston was a Ramsey. Hiding it was something his brother would never consider.

Damon smirked over his own *plan* and how it'd backfired. His intention was to court Catrina and have her come to him without knowing he was a Ramsey. She wanted nothing to do with him- that was clear the other day outside Dawson's. She didn't even know who he was and if he were to tell her, she'd shut him out for good. She'd figure any interest on her part then would have him thinking she was a gold digger.

The smirk deepened. Did he just say his intentions had been to court her? What a laugh. The idle conversations they'd had were just that. Sure there'd been enough substance there to tell him Catrina Jeffries was a compassionate, intelligent girl with an intelligent spirit and even more beautiful...everything else. Still he was kept at bay by his preoccupation with the family he didn't want her to know he was a part of.

Damon left the corner of his desk and traded it for the comfort of the sofa in his office. He'd been obsessed with finding a way into Ramsey since he'd first gone away to school. Living under Marc's and Houston's thumbs; having a clear view of their cunning, stoked a determination deep within. The vow he made to his father was a constant memory. The promise not to let his brothers ruin the family weren't just words spoken amidst the anger and fear of losing his dad too soon.

Westin was too busy to really see it, but the matter beamed clear as day to Damon. Trouble was in the wind. Marcus and Houston were setting a stage that could lead to the Ramsey name being synonymous with scandal.

***

"Yeah, this'll convince 'em. The fools are obsessed with this safety crap." Marc nodded fully satisfied by the papers he scanned. The documents detailed the history of the equipment he was in the market to purchase. "Lucky for us they'll pay through the nose to get it." His ease merged into a mood more serious. "I don't want this comin' back to bite me in the ass Charlt."

"That's what the papers are for." Charlt reached for the cigarette he kept perched atop his ear. "You flash that shit," he gestured to the papers with the matches he held. "You'll see what I mean when you show 'em to your folks at Ramsey."

Marcus observed the papers again.

Book of Scandal

"Not only did my client provide us with this top notch, *second-hand* equipment but they also secured the inspection paperwork that went along with it when it was all fresh off the assembly line."

The rise of his brows proved that Marc was impressed. He scanned the papers a third time. "Won't they question the date? The equipment's got some years on it."

"There's been some doctoring there." Charlton took a few drags of the cigarette. "The signatures are authentic."

"As far as *you* know."

"As far as *everyone* will know."

"And if this goes to hell and this inspector," Marcus paused to find the name on the papers, "Shayne, decides to cry foul?"

Charlton was already shaking his head. "You ain't got nothin' to worry 'bout there."

Marc simply folded arms over the brown suede jacket he wore and waited.

"The cat hit rock bottom when his wife left him-citing neglect." Charlton grinned. "The idiot was obsessed with his job but when the wife left and took the kids, he lost the job and took up the bottle." Charlton took a couple more drags. "The cash he's been paid to keep his trap shut, is our insurance and *his* ticket to enjoying his favorite pastime- drinking."

"Shit Charlt," Marcus whistled. "Done your homework, nigga." He commended.

"So we got a deal?"

Laughter roared as handshakes were exchanged.

***

Book of Scandal

There was a more confident swagger in Daphne's step when she arrived for tea with Marcella Ramsey that afternoon. An unexpected call from Houston several days earlier followed by a mid-day rendezvous at his office, had been just what she needed to instill her mood.

Houston had been both gentle and possessive. She was gradually; albeit still a tad slowly, reeling him in. Daphne pushed the bell and braced herself when she heard the buzz echo faintly inside. She'd be prepared for the snooty greetings the maids reserved for her. That day, she was determined not to cower under their disapproving stares. She'd walk into the Ramsey mansion with her head held high and a fair amount of disapproval directed *their* way.

Nothing prepared her for the possibility that sometimes the Ramseys answered their own door. The young woman who met the doorbell's ring was so lovely, she gave Daphne pause. The girl also greeted Daphne and none of the contempt she'd grown so accustomed to.

"Hello, you must be Daphne. I'm Carmen Ramsey. My mother's expecting you." Carmen stepped away from the door, pulling it further back while she waved Daphne inside. "I hope you won't mind me hoarding in. I don't get to spend a lot of time with Mama being away at school and all. I really do miss our tea parties."

Daphne managed a bright enough smile and an energetic enough nod. She wasn't the least bit happy about having to share her special time with Carmen Ramsey *hoarding* in- daughter or not.

Carmen led the way to the parlor where her mother waited. Marcella was already seated in her favorite and

Book of Scandal

chair and knitting what looked like caps-tiny ones that could only fit a baby.

"Well look who's here," Marcella's bright smile mirrored the delight in her hazy gray stare.

Carmen stepped aside and waved Daphne close.

Uncertain how her familiar manner with the woman would be perceived by her daughter, Daphne held back. Marcella was already outstretching her hands for the hug which was Daphne's usual greeting. Carmen seemed to be waiting on the embrace as well and laughed when Daphne leaned down and kissed her mother's cheek.

Daphne didn't notice any disapproval on the maid's face when the woman walked in with a tray of tea, sandwiches and cookies. At any rate, Daphne was far too preoccupied by what was in store for her during the present get together. Surely Carmen Ramsey knew what her mother did for a living. Daphne silently admitted she was more than a little curious to know what she thought of it.

Carmen however was resuming the conversation with her mother and was kind enough to draw their guest into it. "So Daphne what do you think of us having a birthday luncheon for my mother?"

The idea was such a delight, Daphne couldn't suppress her gasp. "It's a wonderful idea. With all your friends and the house would be so incredible-more incredible than it already is. It'd be such a glamorous time. I'd love to go to something like that."

"Well it looks like we've got at least one supporter of this idea, Carm." Marcella's voice lilted with a hint of laughter.

Book of Scandal

Carmen poured tea and made no comment. Daphne's excitement began to wane as her unease returned in response to Carmen's pleasant yet coolly observant manner.

It could have been because Carmen was waiting to ask what sort of sandwich she preferred, but Daphne wasn't quite so trusting. What's more, she felt simple in the outfit she wore. Carmen was dressed in similar fashion- a nice burgundy cotton blouse and skirt set. Still, she exuded a grace, a poise and intelligence which made Daphne feel grossly inadequate.

"I don't need any parties. At my age no one wants to be reminded of birthdays."

Carmen slapped her mother's knee. "Stop it. You're a young woman still. Quit talkin' like you're Grandma Lil."

"Lord what a character!" Marcella burst into laughter at the comparison to her husband's mother Lillian Ramsey. "I think she started complaining of arthritis when she was sixteen."

Daphne even laughed then. "What about *your* mother, Ms. Marcella?"

More laughter rose between the Ramsey women.

"Talk about a free spirit," Marcella shook her head. "Dena Croix Whitman took nothin' off no man- not even my daddy." She boasted. "But Lord he loved her...the more he raged over her antics, the more in love he fell I think."

Carmen was nodding. "Grandma De always told me and my sister Georgia that the test of a man's love was in how much of your craziness he was willin' to put up with before he turned you over his knee."

All three women burst into laughter.

"She said that's when the *real* fun began!" Carmen added.

Marcella's eyes grew misty with tears once the laughter began to soften. "No party, girls." She sighed and resumed her knitting. "That's for you young beauties with all the men hanging on your every word." She pretended not to notice both girls looking away shyly.

"Have you heard from Jasper lately, baby?"

"He's been working a lot. Says he may be home soon."

"And what of *your* young man, Daphne? Surely you must have one." Marcella inquired with a flirty wink.

Daphne slanted a quick glance toward Carmen prepared for any *funny* remarks that might trip past her lips. There was nothing but a cool, regal smile illuminating her lovely features. Daphne hated her.

"There *is* someone, Ms. Marcella but…I don't think he has a clue about how deeply I feel for him."

"Thank you baby," Marcella accepted the hot tea from her daughter, "well my my Daphne, I'd say our conversation is about to become much more interesting."

***

'Exquisite' was virtually the only word Martha Simon uttered while surveying the transformation of her daughter's home. If anything, the change only made the place more incredible.

"I can't believe how hard you worked to put this together, baby."

Book of Scandal

Josephine eased her hands into the pea green smock she wore and shrugged. "It's an important event- my duty is to make it a special one."

"And you're right on track with that, honey." Martha brushed her daughter's arm when she moved past. "Not everyone's got the knack for putting together a party."

Silently, Josephine acknowledged how doggedly she'd worked and why. She was dead tired at the end of the day and usually didn't get to bed until well after Marc had fallen asleep- which was pretty late considering when he chose to arrive at home.

The party planning had also given her the excuse to resist her husband's advances. As the event was for his glorification, he didn't seem to mind letting her pass on 'bedroom duties'. There were nights when it was all she could do not to vomit when he came near her. Most times, he didn't even bother to wash away the stench of the other women. She often wondered if it would have been easier to bear if he did...

Martha was watching her strangely and Josephine realized she must have said something.

"I guess you chose them because they were Fern's favorite."

The flowers. She'd forgotten the florist had left a few baskets to give her time to be sure the scent was to her liking. Carnations. A somber mood set in as both women mourned and remembered.

"I won't let Marc forget her, Ma." Josephine's voice sounded hoarse.

"Honey," Martha cupped her daughter's elbows and gave her a shake. "Marcus married *you*, remember that. He

Book of Scandal

loves you, wants to take care of you and is worthy of your respect. Why! Just look around at what he's already given you!" Martha swung out her arms and practically swooned over the room.

Josephine didn't bother arguing. Anyone would be overwhelmed by her lifestyle. Her mother was certainly no exception.

"You're right, Mama." She patted Martha's hand and took one of the Carnations from the basket. "Marc's shown me- given me so much and yes he's very worthy." She inhaled the flower's scent. "I pray one day I can be wife enough, mother enough to... repay him in the manner he deserves."

$\mathscr{R}$

~CHAPTER SEVENTEEN~

Damon focused on work and pushed aside agitation over his relationship or rather, his lack of a relationship with Catrina Jeffries. It pained him to say he was concerned by Marc's and Houston's quietness. Things had been running rather perfectly within the youth division. Outreach programs to needy children in Savannah and surrounding counties; as well as assistance to infirmed seniors and nursing homes, were tops on the division's list. There seemed to be great successes at every turn.

Marcus was insinuating himself in practically every area of Ramsey. Clearly, he was working diligently to learn all there was to know about his father's company. Damon had even heard some teasing that Westin should watch out that his younger brother didn't take his job.

Book of Scandal

Still, in light of all those successes, Damon was uneasy for he'd known Marcus and Houston Ramsey long enough to know quietness on their end usually equaled trouble brewing.

"Can't you give your big brothers a little benefit of the doubt, son?" Roland Bray chuckled over his young colleague's suspicions.

"No." Damon's response came without hesitation.

Roland sobered then. "What do you suspect Damon? Seriously."

"Can't put a hand on it," Damon stood from his desk and moved toward the windows behind it. "I only want to put a few safeguards in place before I head out for fall term."

Again, Roland's mood eased. "Senior year of college- Congratulations, D. Your professors will be proud of all you've accomplished here."

"Thanks Ro." Damon's smile didn't brighten the darkness of his eyes though. "I didn't do any of it for the compliments. I made my dad a promise- I plan to keep it."

Nodding, Roland decided it was best not to question the remark.

"I want Marcus watched. I don't want him aware of it." Damon turned back to the desk. "Put your best people in place for it, Ro. I want every decision- every scrap of paper he pushes- reviewed."

"What about Houston?" Roland asked.

"I want a ringer in that youth department." Damon's features tightened noticeably when he dropped into his desk chair. "Houston may be an idiot, but he's just as dangerous when Marcus pulls the strings."

Book of Scandal

***

Carmen took time out from reading her hefty novel and inhaled the fragrance of the flowers surrounding her. The area had been her preferred spot for relaxation, reading and writing to Jasper since she'd been home for the summer. Reading Jasper's letters there had allowed her to focus on the words, on him writing the words and imaging herself wherever he was. Content with the thought, Carmen returned to her reading.

She almost jumped from her skin when she thought she heard his voice behind her. Turning on the bench, she blinked at the figure standing a few feet in the distance. At first, she believed she'd been caught up in some daydream. When the figure moved forward, she gasped and pushed herself from the bench.

Jasper moved as though he were dazed. Repeatedly, his warm browns raked Carmen's still petite; yet more womanly form. God she'd changed. He could scarcely grasp the concept that she could grow any more beautiful than she'd been when he left. Yet there she was- standing there with a mix of elation and expectancy in her provocative stare.

And wonder. Carmen thought as her gaze traveled over Jasper in the same fashion that his had wandered over her. Other than speaking her name when he'd arrived earlier, he'd said nothing more. No matter, for Carmen could almost sense the self confidence surrounding him like something tangible. He'd always been gorgeous but those looks now combined with a subtle pride and assurance. He was beautiful. She felt her mouth curve to say his name but heard no sound pass her lips. She wanted to move close but

Book of Scandal

feared she'd break into a run and knock him down when
she flung herself into his arms.

Carmen didn't need to run. Jasper had lessened the
distance between them. For a time, he only stood there
trailing his fingertips across her face. She closed her eyes
and relished the touch, believing it was all she needed.

"I missed you Carm."

Losing her restraint then, she arched into him
suddenly and kissed him deeply.

Their hands were as seeking as their mouths. Soft
moans filtered in and out between them. Carmen didn't
want it to end but Jasper couldn't forget where they were.
Gently, he eased back.

"We can't do this here."

"Where then?"

Her bold response caused him to laugh. "I've
missed you," he confessed again.

"How long have you been back?" Carmen asked
when they returned to the bench where she'd been reading.

"Five months."

Carmen's expression changed a tad. "Five months?"
She wanted him to hear the hurt in her voice.

"I'm sorry," he leaned close to kiss her temple, "Dr.
Owen keeps me busy."

"Dr. Owen?"

"Owen Dowd," Jasper grinned, thinking of the man
then. "I told you about him. We met in 'Nam."

Carmen began to nod as her memory freshened.

"Anyway, I've been so busy I don't think I even
realized how long it'd really been."

Book of Scandal

"You must be enjoying your work." Her eyes began to sparkle again as she watched him.

"It's important, could make a lot of difference. Anyway..." he shrugged, preferring not to go into all the boring scientific details then.

"I can tell it means a lot to you and...you look great."

"So how's school?" He asked, though her compliment pleased him greatly. "I was surprised to know your mama let her baby go."

"She seemed content with it." Carmen fidgeted with the hem of her sweater and smiled. "She even said it was time for me to make my own way in the world. That the time would come when she wouldn't be around to guide me." Her expression shadowed then. "I think she's still missing Daddy more than she's letting on. The things she says sometime...I think she's ready to be with him."

"They had a great marriage- great people." Jasper quietly raved.

The easiness returned to Carmen's light eyes and she grazed Jasper's thigh. "Mama's gonna be so thrilled to see you looking so...incredible. She um, she's always asking about you."

"Miss Marcella was always good to me. 'Specially after my mother died...'" He brushed Carmen's hand where it rested on his thigh. "They don't make good people like your parents very often. Wish I could figure out the combination that produces such phenomenal beings."

"Jasper please," Carmen laughed. "Trust me, there is *no* magic combination. Folks make a choice to be decent or criminal." She rolled her eyes toward her family's home in the distance. "People think it's got so much to do with blood, background and fancy trappings…there's always a choice to be made, Jasper."

"People in town never would've treated me the way they did if my mama hadn't been thought of as the slut who got herself pregnant by a married man with a kid."

"*Choices* Jasper. Those people made a choice to shun you. They weren't worth your time."

"Those people who shunned me, Carm," he smirked then, "one day they'll be in awe of me."

***

After an extensive bout of planning, Josephine Ramsey was ready to introduce her husband to the best of Savannah society. What she didn't realize was that she was introducing herself and that everyone was most impressed. Making an impression wasn't difficult to achieve considering the surroundings. The event began late evening with the setting sun competing with the glow of candles set in various areas of the house and expansive back patio.

Evidence of Josephine's green thumb was everywhere. Hanging baskets of vibrant roses, tulips and carnations filled every room with splashes of color and fragrance.

Josephine had expected to be by her husband's side for the better part of the night. There'd been no time for that, however. There were as many guests clamoring for Josephine's time as there were for her husband's. In fact, Josephine had such a fantastic time mingling with her guests; who invited her to join various clubs and committees, she didn't give her husband a passing thought.

Book of Scandal

Catrina had been receiving just as many accolades for her work on the Ramsey party. No one could argue that Catrina's determination to broaden her father's business had been a sterling achievement. Jeffries Catering's first formal business gala, boasted an almost equal number of black and white clientele.

Catrina had been so overwhelmed by the beauty of the event and her part in it. She'd been a lot like her mother that day, seeing to every detail far more diligently than necessary. Eventually though, nature called and she excused herself to use the facilities and take a moment to catch her breath.

She gave herself another pep talk before heading out of the downstairs powder room. When she opened the door, she found her way blocked by Damon's tall frame. Twice, Catrina tried to form words but met with no success. It mattered little, since the question was clearly reflected on her face.

Damon merely smiled. He advanced, forcing her back into the dainty half bath.

"What are you doing here?" She blurted, the click of the lock behind him having reignited her speaking abilities.

He leaned on the door. "I was invited."

"Why?"

"Why not?" He pressed off the door and began to advance again until her back was flush against the wall.

"Who are you?" She managed despite the fact that her heart was in her throat. Her lashes fluttered when her gaze lowered to his mouth. The last things she saw were the

Book of Scandal

striking dimples bracketing an incredible mouth. Then her lashes fluttered close and she prepared herself for his kiss.

Catrina whimpered something incoherent before his lips melded with hers. His cologne was fantastic and she clenched her fist to resist the urge to draw him closer. Damon wasted no time plying her with a *sweet* kiss. The act went to full blown torrid in the span of two seconds. His tongue thrust so deep and lusty that Catrina felt the back of her head bumping the wall beneath the force of the kiss.

She moaned, hardly noticing that he'd undone the buttons of her blazer until both his hands cupped her breasts. Then, she was kissing him back with her own brand of lust. She could have sworn she'd heard him chuckle during the kiss- she didn't care. She didn't care if he was used to having girls so easily give into him. He was kissing *her* then and she intended to enjoy every second.

Catrina knew she could have kissed him for hours. He had a way of tilting his head this way and that as if taking advantage of every angle possible to deliver his kiss. She arched in closer to rake her fingers through the silky crop of his close cut. It was only then that she felt the smooth fabric of his suit coat against her skin and realized he'd taken her out of her blazer *and* blouse.

"Wait...Damon..." He had to wait. She had to tell him to wait, didn't she? That's what proper young women did, right? They certainly didn't allow themselves to be cornered in powder rooms by virtual strangers who kissed and fondled them half out of their clothes.

"Damon stop," her voice was firm that time. "I don't know...who you are. You- you don't want me to know..."

Book of Scandal

In response, he cupped her chin keeping her in place for another kiss. Catrina indulged for another several glorious seconds before she somehow found the willpower to push him away.

No words were spoken. She grabbed her clothes, shrugging quickly into the garments.

Damon leaned against the wall. Hands hidden in his trouser pockets, his dark eyes followed her every move as she focused on dressing and making herself presentable.

It was no use, Catrina discovered when she looked into the mirror. A quick toss of her head put her glossy tresses back in place. Her lips were another matter- way fuller than normal. Not to mention her eyes. No matter how much she blinked, she couldn't get the mellow, sleep-sexy look out of her gaze. She looked thoroughly kissed and exquisitely aroused. Damn him. Giving up the battle with her appearance, she left the room without another glance toward him.

Catrina managed to immerse herself in work for the next hour. Everything was running smoothly and she actually spent the bulk of her time answering questions about her father's business. She set up meetings with various guests who wanted to hire Jeffries for their next big gathering. She wouldn't allow herself to think of Damon and the scene in the powder room. His name in her head was enough to send her hands shaking and a dull throb someplace best left unmentioned.

She was scribbling away on her notepad and thinking of how proud her parents would be when they heard of all the interest in their business. Her thoughts were never far from Damon though. It was no surprise that when she heard her name and felt a hand squeeze her arm, she responded accordingly.

"Damon..." she moaned.

"Catrina?"

She looked around realizing it had been Houston Ramsey standing near and not Damon. Thankfully, she'd spoken the name softly enough so there was no need to explain her misspeak to Houston.

"Hi." She smiled brightly and cleared her throat to dispel any nervous twinges in her voice.

"Cool party." Houston's light brown eyes scanned the living room filled with guests and servers with platters of delectables. "I um," he turned with obvious uncertainty in his gaze then. "I wanted to know if you'd go to another event with me next week. Nothin' as lavish as this," he waved in the general direction of the crowd.

His uncommon attempt at humor set Catrina at ease and she laughed.

"What do you have in mind, Houston?"

"Dinner with my family."

Her remaining laughter faded quickly.

"I'm sorry- sorry for taking so long to make it happen." He shoved his hands into his cream trouser pockets and glanced down. "So much goin' on... everybody's been real busy... including you, so..."

Catrina knew he was waiting on her acceptance, but speaking then was a feat impossible for her to achieve then. She'd already agreed to meet his family at some point, but hadn't counted on it actually happening. Silly. Meeting his family was sure to put their relationship on a level she'd

Book of Scandal

never intended for it to reach. She knew where Houston's feelings were heading. All the while *she* was caught up over some sexy idiot whose last name she didn't know and whom she'd probably spent all of thirty minutes talking to over the entire time she'd known him.

What's more, she'd made a promise to herself to stop turning down the multitude of dates she'd been offered. Houston Ramsey was a perfect place to begin.

"I'd love to go." Once more, she flashed him a dazzling smile.

So elated, Houston let out a yell and drew Catrina into a hug.

***

"You're only here because Mama asked you to come."

"Well, what can I say? Ms. Marcella's got something a man just can't say no to."

Carmen laughed and prodded Jasper's ribs with her elbow. She'd been teasing him about attending Marc and Josephine's party at the woman's request.

"I'm gonna have to ask her about that." Carmen was still laughing while she and Jasper strolled arm in arm. They'd been chatting and chuckling all during a lengthy walk around the grounds.

The party was still going strong after over three hours. Carmen; who wasn't much for parties, couldn't recall when she'd had such fun. If only the gathering weren't in her brother's honor. She spotted Marcus across the courtyard as she and Jasper headed for the house. She began tugging his arm, the second she spotted her brother.

Book of Scandal

Changing directions was out of the question though once Jasper caught sight of his old friend. He wanted to show off a bit of what he'd become during his time away.

Carmen smothered a curse when she saw Marc wave in their direction.

"Marc." Jasper's voice was as robust as the handshake he offered once the distance closed between them.

"Good to see you man!" Marc looked truly pleased and shook Jasper's hand in both of his. "How's it feel to be back in the world?"

"Can't complain," Jasper looked down at Carmen on his arm. "Can't complain at all."

Carmen read her brother easily and smiled to herself. She wondered if Marc was aware of the awed expression on his face. She could see him sizing up Jasper- his manner, speech and knowledge of his subject matter was clear as they spoke on the war, its future and even how business was at Ramsey.

"Jasper Stone, the big man. With his own little temptress on top of everything else." Marc's pitch stare eased toward his sister then.

Jasper felt Carmen's grip tighten on his arm. He had to admit he liked it. She'd held his arm on countless occasions. This time though, her grip made him feel like her protector. From what, he had no idea...

***

Josephine felt literally like the queen of her castle. The house was fabulous and decorated even more fabulously for the party, everyone raved over the music- the live jazz was exquisite mingled with classical arrangements;

Book of Scandal

when the group took five. Every selection was
extraordinary. The food and service was unparalleled. Even
the weather was cooperating and guests had their choice of
enjoying in or outdoor luxury.

Josephine smiled as she wound up her trek through
the maze at the edge of the property. She recalled one of
the VP's wives saying as long as the guests were laughing
count it all success.

That opinion was emphasized when Josephine
overheard two women somewhere in the maze laughing
boisterously. They were nearby from the clarity of the
laughter and speech. *Count it all success*, Josephine told
herself. Slowing her steps, she decided to take in a few
more compliments about her party.

"...Word is the live band travels with Gillespie. I'm
having the best time, but I knew I had to come for that!"

"I've been having the best time too and you're
right- the band is cool, but I just came for Marc Ramsey."
The woman giggled. "I mean that in the literal sense, girl."

"Scandalous!" The other woman told her friend.
"You are bad!"

"And *he* is good- *very* good."

Josephine could've laughed over the phrase
'eavesdroppers never hear anything good'. She could've
damn well laughed if she weren't seething with anger.
Surprisingly, she felt no emotion towards the woman, the
anger was all for her loving husband. She tore out of the
maze, through the garden and into the house. She scarecely
wasted time sparing glances to her adoring guests as she
flew past them with the short train from her gown floating
in an elegant blur. She found Marc who appeared to be in

Book of Scandal

deep conversation with about four or five executive types. They looked intense and not to be disturbed.

Too damn bad, Josephine decided.

"We need to talk." She told him without waiting for a lull in the conversation before she cut in.

Marc simply raised a hand in a silent request for quiet. He didn't bother with looking in his wife's direction.

"This won't take long dear," Josephine stepped closer, intentionally clipping her words as she spoke. "Just a little matter about someone *coming* to see you."

Taking heed then, Marc turned. His onyx stare narrowed when he noted the wildness in his wife's light eyes. Something warned him not to trifle with her and coolly, he excused himself from the gentleman he conversed with.

"In our own damn house?! During this fucking party I slaved over for your lying ass?!"

"You shut your mouth," Marc's hiss was almost drowned when he slammed the bedroom door behind them.

"All the things I've heard..." Josephine was beyond listening as she paced the room frantically. "I never believed it. No matter how strongly everything warned me that it was true," the train of the gown whipped about her as she ranted, "I never believed it 'cause I hadn't seen it- it was all hearsay. But this time," her gaze narrowed and she angled her head, "this time I heard the shit directly from one of your sluts!"

Marcus closed the distance between he and his wife in the span of two seconds. He grabbed her arm and gave her a firm jerk. "I won't ask again."

Book of Scandal

"Or what?!" She spat, taunting him with her words and; unconsciously, her body. "What? Are you trying to tell me I'm mistaken you son of a bitch? That you didn't just screw some bimbo right here in our-" Her argument was silenced by his kiss then.

Affectively aroused, Josephine melted into him. For a time, she indulged in the coaxing kiss, but she wouldn't allow herself to be subdued by want. She began to struggle then, wrenching against Marc, pummeling his chest with her fists. Marc however, only appeared to grow more aroused.

"I don't want it," she seethed.

"You will."

Her struggles renewed and she prayed for the ability to vomit right there in his face. She'd already dry heaved over the scent of sex and perfume from his earlier conquest. The aroma clung faintly to his clothes and added fuel to her anger. She clawed at his neck and may have tasted victory had he not turned her to face the wall. In moments, he had the chiffon folds of the elegant gown bunched about her waist. He freed himself in one smooth motion and took her from behind.

Josephine lost her will to fight. She went limp over the reality of what had just happened. She had been raped by her husband. She closed her eyes, turning away when his chin rested on her shoulder.

"Remember your place," he breathed heavily into her neck. Dipping a finger inside her then; he trailed the tell-tale moisture along her cheek, fixed his trousers and left the room.

Book of Scandal

~CHAPTER EIGHTEEN~

Josephine maintained her position near the wall some three minutes after Marc's departure. Slowly, she pushed away from the lavender painted surface. Her steps and manner gained energy on the way to the bath room. She stripped off the dazzling gown, stepped into the shower and tried to scrub herself raw. After twenty minutes, she slid down the tiles and curled herself into a ball in the tub. Water pelted down on her and she prayed the drops beating her head would clear images of the scene that had just taken place between she and her husband.

Martha Simon found her daughter still curled in the tub some fifteen minutes later.

"Girl what in the world are you doing in here?! You got a houseful of people to see to." Martha shut off the water and frowned.

Book of Scandal

"Party's almost over, Ma."

"But aren't you going to see it through?" Martha
fiddled with the black fringe along the hem of her sequined
blouse. Gradually, she took stock of the disheveled bed
room. "Honey what in the world...? What happened in
here?" She was turning to pick up the discarded gown when
she heard her daughter's wail.

"Baby..." Martha knelt beside the tub and pulled
Josephine into a rocking embrace.

"I hate him Mama. I hate him. I think I've always
hated him."

"You're talking about Marc?" Martha pulled back
with a look of disbelief shadowing her lovely round face.
"But honey, why? When he's given you-"

"Oh Mama please! He raped me." Josephine shook
her head as fresh tears spewed. "He raped me." She
whispered that time.

"Baby," Martha shook her head, "but that's not
possible."

"I want out. I want out of this hell." Josephine
rapped her fist to the porcelain. "I'm gonna get out of it. I-"

"Stop this! You hush and think. *Think* Josie."
Martha held her shoulders in a vice grip and shook until
Josephine's gaze connected with her own.

"You think about your life now." Martha gave
Josephine another jerk to usher the words home. "Think
about your life if you walk away now- what skills do you
have, Josie? You forgot about your schooling when your
last name changed to Ramsey. Marc would turn you into an
outcast if he's as ruthless as you say." She shook her head

Book of Scandal

defiantly. "I won't see you wind up old, broke and alone like Clea and Ross or dead like…"

"Mama…" Josephine perched on her knees to draw Martha close when she burst into tears over the thought of Fernelle.

"I have to see at least one of my girls do it up right." She'd accept no more of Josephine's comforting embrace and pulled back. "In the end girl, you have to ask yourself if it's worth going back to the life of Josephine Simon after living the dream as Josephine Ramsey."

***

Full bodied laughter rambled from the table of devastating, well-dressed men in the far corner of Pete's Tavern and Spirits. The sound drew dozens of female stares and those of several males who wished such charisma and allure were theirs to enjoy if only for a moment.

Since their first meeting, Westin Ramsey and the Tesano brothers had developed something of a kinship. The men saw eye to eye on several topics from business to sports. Still, it was their opinions on business that fueled the interaction. West had become especially close to Roman, Aaron and Pitch Tesano. The foursome met for drinks at least once a month. The business topic that evening centered around Las Vegas and its awesome appeal.

"So what do you think West?" Roman asked once Aaron had shared their plans to purchase property there.

Westin grinned while shaking his head and reaching for the cognac he'd ordered. "Never made you cats for the casino business."

Again, laughter rumbled.

"Not quite exactly what we had in mind." Pitch said, laughter still coloring his voice. "We definitely want to grab some property while we can." He shrugged. "Thought we'd extend you an opportunity to come in with us."

"Mmm…" Grimacing then, West contemplated his response. He wanted to be clear without stepping on the toes of his new friends.

"I'd need time to think on it." He winced, knowing the rest of the statement couldn't be said any plainer. "My family's never really had those…sorts of interests." He watched the brothers exchange knowing looks and believed the new friendship was surely reaching its end. No matter how subtly spoken, a stereotype was a stereotype.

"Guys, I think he means mafia interest." Aaron's deep voice held a humorous undertone.

"Sorry West, you made friends with the least glamorous side of the Tesano family." Pitch spoke with true apology lacing his words. "Land development's our game. Condos, neighborhoods, business complexes…"

"Yeah, pretty boring stuff," Roman added.

Aaron shrugged. "Sorry."

Seconds later, yet another round of laughter was rumbling around the table.

"I'm sorry fellas." West practically chuckled the words.

"No need," Aaron waved a hand. "Our own father thought we were idiots trying to craft some new business interest when we had a gold mine waiting for us if we chose a place in the family business." He threw back the rest of his gin tonic. "We care about our family too much to

Book of Scandal

have folks always thinkin' we're gonna take a hit out on 'em because our last name ends in a vowel."

The laughter then was a bit less boisterous.

Westin realized then how his friends had had to combat their own share of racism. "You guys sound like my little brother Damon. He's obsessed with keeping the family name pristine."

Aaron nodded while tapping his fingers to the Muddy Waters groove filling the air. "Your little brother sounds like a good man."

"So? What do you think now about coming in with us on Vegas?" Pitch was asking.

"Still need to think on it," West raised his glass, "but the possibilities are looking good to me."

The foursome touched their glasses in toast.

***

Josephine pulled herself together, put on her gown and headed downstairs twenty minutes after her chat with her mother. She was halfway down the hall when she turned her face toward the wall and gave into another sob.

What had she gotten herself into? She recalled her pride when Marcus asked for her hand right there before her horrible sisters. He'd seemed so... in love with her but in hindsight and; probably more in her right mind, she realized he wasn't in love. For whatever reason he'd *needed* more than wanted to marry her. Wasn't that what he kept saying?

She was the type of wife he needed to make himself look like something other than the slime he was. She was his shroud of decency. In reality she was no more to him than the trash he betrayed her with.

Book of Scandal

The reality of it threatened to send her into another fit of crying. Hearing her name being called forced her to act accordingly.

Jeff Carnes had already grown concerned though and was pulling her around to face him.

"What is this, Jo? What's wrong?"

Her tears returned a split second later.

Jeff moved in close offering her the expanse of a considerably broad chest to cry into.

"Is it Marc?" He asked, already knowing that it was. He rocked her a bit when she nodded against his chest. "Can you get past it?"

"Do I have a choice?"

"You always have a choice, Jo." Jeff pulled back to watch her closely.

She rolled her eyes. "Right. Choose to go back to my non-glamorous and non-affluent life."

"Sugar that's not important."

"Hmph. Spoken like a man whose always had money."

"Josephine money at the expense of one's dignity and self esteem just ain't worth it."

"Hmph. Spoken like a man." That time Josephine had a smile in place.

Jeff mimicked the gesture, but gave her a quick shake for good measure. "You promise me you'll keep in touch if you ever need to talk in confidence."

"Thank J," she sighed and brushed away the lone tear clinging to a lash, "but I can't afford your fee."

"But your husband can. He made me a job offer." Jeff explained when Josephine tilted her head. "I just decided to take it. Keep watch over things- including you. That'll be true whether I'm working for Marc or not."

"Jeff," Josephine fell against him again. "Thank you."

He patted her shoulder. "You're gonna have to be strong if you choose this life."

***

"Sorry about that guys," Marc was already back out at the party. He made a bee-line to the group he'd been talking to before Josephine's interruption.

Of course, the five executives could've cared less. They had the ear of Marcus Ramsey and would utilize whatever time they were granted.

"I believe we were discussing insurance when I was called away."

"Right. Insurance and other employee benefits." Reese Bergins explained.

Marc's dark gaze shifted between the men. "Is there some problem?"

"Oh no, no Marcus just the opposite." Reese looked to his colleagues who all nodded their agreement. "In fact Ramsey boasts one of the most impressive employee packages in the nation- that's among white *and* black owned companies. We don't have to tell you how impressive that is in light of how few black owned companies there are."

"Well I've always believed being a stand-out is deserving of praise."

The execs chuckled over Marc's response, but were soon looking to Reese to continue. They couldn't be certain

Book of Scandal

how their opinions would be received by the second Ramsey son.

"Quentin Ramsey was diligent in his efforts to provide for his employees. He believed that employees who were content with their income and well being were more productive workers."

Despite the accolades, Marc sensed the underlying agenda residing amongst the group. Hooking thumbs about his suspenders, he smiled. "Does more productive equal more expensive?"

Again, the execs exchanged glances. Clearly, they'd regretted even considering voicing differing opinions regarding Quent Ramsey's ideas.

"My father and I rarely saw eye to eye, gentlemen. That became more evident once I expressed my interest in the business."

The men nodded, their ease slowly becoming more noticeable. George Crown stepped forward then, grimacing toward his co-workers before he spoke.

"Marcus we all had the greatest respect for your father."

"I'd never question that you felt otherwise George. But?"

"Well…it's been our feeling that Mr. Ramsey may've been a bit…overzealous in his planning for the employees. The benefits and allowances made for the workers-"

"Those in the industrial, manual labor level especially."

Book of Scandal

"Right," George nodded back toward Reese who had spoken. "We feel those packages may've been too lucrative- in other words, too expensive."

Drake Kratchins stepped up then. "If we were able to modify some of those allowances, we could perhaps increase the company's budget by as much as twenty or thirty percent. Maybe more."

"Are we in some sort of financial trouble that would make this necessary?"

"Oh no, no nothing like that Marcus." David Bookman waved a hand and grinned. "It's our job though to improve the company's financial outlook- this is but one suggestion- one that could be set into place rather smoothly."

"Do you all have anything in writing?"

"We've done the preliminary numbers." David said.

Marcus extended his hand for shaking. "Have them on my desk Monday morning."

***

Briselle's mouth thinned into a tight line when a teary, red-eyed Georgia answered the door.

"Girl why don't you stop bein' an idiot and go wherever Felix wants you to?" She pushed her sister-in-law from the door.

"It's not that easy."

"Why? Because he can't pamper you well enough yet?"

"Screw you Bri," Georgia shuffled off toward her living room. "I love him Bri. I'm in love with Felix- I've always been in love with him, but with him I feel weak. I don't feel like myself."

Book of Scandal

"But honey what's wrong with that?" Briselle smoothed her black mini dress beneath her and perched on the end of the stout coffee table. "If it's over the man you love?"

"Please Bri," Georgia's lashes fluttered as she rolled her eyes. "Everybody's love story isn't the fairytale you and my brother have."

Briselle stiffened. "That's no fairytale. West and me have our share of heartache, trust me."

"I'm sorry Bri," Georgia scooted close to squeeze Briselle's hand. "I'm sorry for sounding cold, but weakness- it just ain't in my vocabulary."

"Really?" Briselle smirked, brushing a tear from Georgia's cheek.

"Shit." Georgia flattened both hands to her face and smeared away the remaining moisture. "When a woman's weak in love she's about as much good as a used trash bag."

"Georgia!"

"Hell, it's true." Georgia left the sofa. "It's dangerous for a woman to be so far gone over any man. I grew up in a family of four boys and I watched every one of 'em including your Westin, treat girls like they were dirt." She shrugged. "I admit West's made a lot of improvement but I give you all the credit for that." She waved toward Bri. "Damon's a sneaky devil too, but he's good at the core. I think the right one'll whip him into shape when he meets her." She smoothed hands across her robe's sleeves as if chilled. "Marcus and Houston are destined to be monsters in love and life. I pity Josephine and whoever claims Houston as her lawful wedded."

Book of Scandal

"But honey, Felix's not like either of them."
Briselle turned on the table to watch Georgia pace the small elegantly furnished room.

"It's not about Felix. It's about me and feeling like I'm not in control." She smirked. "Trust me, I feel like that enough when I'm in bed with the Negro."

"Are you saying you're afraid he'll hurt you if you lose control with him?"

"There's a place somewhere inside me that doesn't feel that way." Georgia puffed out her cheeks and mulled over the statement as she paced. "I *know* that place is somewhere inside me, but I've got no idea where it is. Dammit Bri," she bowed her head as the pressure of tears returned. "Why can't I just trust it? Why can't I trust *him*? What's wrong with me that I can't trust the man I love?"

"Oh honey," Briselle left the coffee table and went to pull Georgia close.

***

Carmen's light eyes were wide when she stepped into Jasper's Decatur apartment. The place was far nicer than he'd led her to believe.

Jasper was quiet, lingering behind while Carmen strolled the apartment. Whether Jasper was aware of it or not, the place was a compliment to his personality and all he'd become over the years removed from Georgia. Though sparsely furnished, there was a warmth stemming from the artwork and masks he'd collected. Carmen spent more than a few moments observing the handcrafted wooden shelving that held several pictures of friends and scenery from Vietnam.

Book of Scandal

She could feel his warm browns on her then and straightened from the shelf. "So are we still gonna see '*To Sir With Love*'?"

"Um," Jasper changed his mind about lingering behind then and slowly crossed the distance separating him from Carmen. "I was thinking we could stay in." He left only a few inches between them and shrugged. "If you don't mind?"

Something in his voice and swagger sent Carmen's heart to thudding a bit harder. "I um…no, no I don't mind." She pressed her lips together and glanced around the small room. "Are we gonna watch television?"

"No."

The thud became a throb in her throat. "What um…" she tried to swallow around the lump there when his body nudged hers. "What are we gonna do?"

His deep stare narrowed when he smiled. "May I show you?"

There were no words to be spoken then. She could barely nod and hoped that was enough of an answer. Adorably, Jasper bit his lip and his gaze lowered to the neckline of the snug mushroom colored sweater Carmen wore. For several seconds, he simply brushed his thumb across her collarbone as though he were mesmerized by the look and feel of her there. The simple touch was potent enough though to render Carmen impatient for more.

Posting up on the toes of her wedge-heeled Hushpuppies, she nudged his jaw with the end of her nose loving the faint but incredible scent of his aftershave. Gradually, Jasper's fingers drifted from her collarbone to the buttons securing the sweater.

Book of Scandal

Carmen forbid herself to ask that he hurry. She'd waited so long and knew the important moment shouldn't be rushed. Unfortunately, that was difficult to take heed of just then. To hell with not rushing, she told herself. She at least had to kiss him.

Jasper moaned his surprise when her tongue thrust heavily against his. His fingers weakened on the buttons of her sweater- this kiss had his total attention. He became thoroughly absorbed in it and took command of the act then probing his tongue deep and lustily.

It was Carmen who removed her sweater and tugged Jasper's hands from her face to cup them on her breasts. She almost slid down the length of his body when his thumbs worked the nipples into firm peaks. The floor disappeared from beneath her feet then and she realized he was carrying her further into the apartment.

She felt softness cushion her back and her body trembled at the realization of being in his bed. Her thighs began an uncontrollable quiver when he tugged at the waistband of the brown plaid skirt she wore. In seconds, the garment along with her tights and panties were gone- she was nude beneath him.

"Jasper I…"

It took him sometime to drag his eyes away from her body. How long had he fantasized over what she'd look like? Finally he brought his gaze to hers.

"What?" His mouth smoothed across her heaving bosom.

Book of Scandal

"I haven't," her lashes fluttered and she cried out once his lips closed over a nipple as his fingers manipulated the other. "I've never…"

He smiled and moved up to kiss her earlobe. "I know," he whispered before resuming his task at her breasts.

Content and powerfully aroused, Carmen settled deep into the now tangled bed coverings and let him take charge. She raked her nails through his short, soft hair and arched instinctively when he suckled her ever firming nipples. She hardly noticed he'd removed his shirt and trousers until his hard chiseled form rested flush against her.

Jasper worshipped the rich creamy caramel length of her voluptuous frame. His mouth was everywhere kissing, stroking…there was so much he wanted to introduce her to. Just then though, he could think of nothing other than taking her and being taken in return.

"Look at me Carm," he waited for her lashes to flutter open and then he kissed the corner of her mouth. "You may not enjoy this part."

Before she could question the comment, Jasper hooked her thigh across his hip and lunged forward to bury his sex to the hilt inside her. Carmen cried out once, her nails curving into the taunt skin of his shoulders. Before her mind could fully settle on the pain, the most awesome sensation filtered through it. The cries on her tongue mellowed into moans. She cupped Jasper's butt which rotated in a sultry, lust driven fashion. Moments later, Carmen was mimicking the rhythm instinctively.

"I thought you said I wouldn't like this part?" She gasped, squeezing his rear to drive him deeper.

Book of Scandal

Jasper's laughter rumbled softly and mingled with his groans of satisfaction.

***

Houston dropped Catrina's hand otherwise he would have crushed it when they arrived for dinner to meet his family. It was then, that Houston discovered his mother had also invited another of his...close friends.

Daphne had always held a keen interest in keeping up appearances and in what others thought of her. That night, those *interests* took a backseat along with everything else as she stood there being introduced to her man, his family and *his* girlfriend. Her mind teemed with questions which were answered in a few sentences: Catrina Jeffries was the daughter of two respected entrepreneurs. She was educated. She was beautiful and everything a Ramsey bride should be.

To make matters worse, Carmen Ramsey arrived soon after along with the man in her life- Jasper Stone. When Daphne discovered Carmen and Catrina were dear friends- could the evening get any worse? In a word, yes. She'd never felt more like trash when she resumed eye contact with Houston.

Well...*she'd* resumed eye contact. Houston, on the other hand, tried to do everything but look her way. At any rate, there wasn't much time left for mingling once introductions were made. The group sat down to a feast. Daphne ate with gusto to douse the sob in her throat.

A lively conversation enhanced the meal. Jasper held the diners entranced by his stories of being a soldier on tour in Vietnam. Even Marcus seemed enthralled by the

Book of Scandal

stories, though he stayed true to form when he thanked God that the government hadn't honed in on any of the Ramseys to serve.

Laughter continued and then it was time for an array of sinful desserts. Catrina was thrilled that the evening was almost at its end, but happier still that it'd been a good evening. Things only got better when she saw her favorite chocolate cream pie on the dessert cart.

"Houston told me it was your favorite, honey." Marcella told Catrina having noticed the awed expression on her face.

No one other than Houston and Carmen noticed the deadly look Daphne flashed Houston's way.

Catrina didn't notice a thing. Her lashes fluttered close on her first bite of the decadent pie. She savored the taste and quickly prepared for more.

"Sorry I'm late everybody." Damon was unbuttoning his hunter green suit coat while pulling out the only vacant chair at the table. "Good to see you Jas." He reached across the table to shake hands with Jasper and locked gaze with Catrina. "Hello." He said.

Catrina felt the chocolate sour on her tongue. She pulled her stare away from Damon's striking dimpled smile and fixed Carmen with a drowning look.

"Thought you were always on time, D?" Houston made the snide remark once introductions were made.

Damon shrugged and pulled the pie plate down the table. "I'll just have some of this." Again, he captured Catrina in his bottomless stare. "Is it as good as it looks?"

Book of Scandal

Catrina's hand weakened and she felt every bit the uncertain little girl, barely capable of a nod. "It's very good." She managed.

"Well let's get out of here and have dessert in the living room." Marc suggested, and was soon standing with his plate in hand.

Marcella was already waving toward the two maids who were entering the dining room then. "We'll finish dessert in the living room and bring out some hot tea and coffee."

Thankful for the commotion of everyone heading for another part of the house, Catrina made her escape. She hurried in the opposite direction searching for the first dark room she could locate.

She found one a brief distance from the dining room, leaned against the door when she pushed it shut behind her and prayed for the strength to breathe. She doubled over instead, hair falling into her face while she wrapped her arms about her waist.

All sorts of questions raced her mind- all sorts of criticisms. First, she called herself a fool for not suspecting- never suspecting. But how could she? He'd been so slick about it all... damn him. She thought she was too smart to be made a fool of and all along he'd been playing her for the biggest fool of all.

Damon found her some five minutes later. The second he touched her shoulder, she turned and slapped him full across his face.

He barely flinched. "I'm sorry."

"What for exactly?" She shook hair from her face and let him view the full extent of fury in her eyes. "Well?

Book of Scandal

What? For lying to me? Playing me for an idiot? Thinking I
was a gold digger?" She tilted her head and took a step
closer. "I mean, that *is* why you didn't want me to know
your last name, isn't it? I might've done something to trick
you into marrying me- that's how it works, isn't it?"

"Catr-"

She slapped him again. "Lying sack of horseshit!"
She hissed and shoved him. "Get the hell out of my way!"

Damon wouldn't budge. Instead, he grabbed her
tight, yet massaged her upper arms through the cottony
fabric of her mauve dress. She tried to wrench free and he
tightened his hold.

"It wasn't like that," he whispered against her cheek.

"Let go of me."

His mouth was on hers then and he was backing her
against the closest wall. The kiss was deep, hard and she
responded. She had no choice. Her body wanted this and
her body was telling her mind to go to hell. She could've
broken loose when his hold eased and his hand lightly
trailed her back. She moaned, eagerly dueling with his
tongue and adoring the helpless whimpers he uttered in
response.

"I love you," he groaned during the kiss and then he
was burying his face into her neck. "I think I loved you
almost from the first time I saw you." He looked at her then.
"I had my reasons for not telling you but they had nothing
to do with what you're thinking."

"I don't want to hear it," the explanation only
stoked more of her anger.

Damon bowed his head feeling his jaw clench as his
temper heated as well. He had no one to blame for the mess

Book of Scandal

but himself. She didn't trust him now and there was nothing he could think of to change that.

"Come with me," he didn't mind begging when she twisted to get away from him again. "Please just let me talk to you." He nuzzled her ear, kissed her cheek and could feel her melting.

They were both so absorbed in one another, neither noticed they were being watched.

Daphne's light eyes narrowed in a mix of surprise and confusion. What was going on? They'd acted like strangers earlier and clearly they were anything but. They were playing Houston for a fool and part of her was angry enough with him to let them get away with it. He deserved it for the way he'd misled her.

A small voice mentioned that he'd not really done that. After all, their relationship had started off as sexual and had continued that way. In spite of the things he'd confessed when they lounged during the afterglow of lovemaking; he saw her as nothing more than his slut. Babydoll Monfrey's best pupil. This was something her mother hadn't prepared her for- the possibility that sex might not pave the way to a man's heart.

Then what was the answer? Wait for Catrina's and Damon's playing around to be revealed? Or reveal it for them?

There was no time to mull over the answer. Carmen stood down the hall and Daphne made a dash in the opposite direction. She hadn't moved so quickly that Carmen hadn't spotted her though.

Everyone was wondering where Catrina and Damon were. Under the circumstances, Carmen felt it best if she

Book of Scandal

were the one to track them down. Her steps slowed when
she saw Daphne peering around into the smoking room.
Her steps quickened at Daphne's mad dash and a fist
clenched when Carmen saw what held the girl's fascination.
She cleared her throat and the scene dispersed.

"Everyone's waiting in the living room." Carmen
said.

Unusually subdued, Damon only nodded in the
general direction of his sister's voice. "I'll call you." He
told Catrina and suppressed a sigh when she rolled her eyes
and turned away.

Carmen waited when her brother had left the room.
"Catrina...I'm so sorry-"

"I thought we were friends, Carmen?" Catrina's
voice sounded hollow in the dark room.

It chilled Carmen and she smoothed hands across
the sleeves of her crimson sweater vest. "We are friends."

Catrina shook her head. "Did you really think I'd do
your brother foul once I discovered he was a Ramsey?"

"No Catrina no." Carmen rushed to her friend and
forced her to turn. "It was never like that. You don't know
the half of it."

"You're so right." Catrina punched a cushion when
she walked past the sofa. "Even when I saw him at Marcus
and Josephine's party I didn't think- never put it
together..."

"Honey why would you?" Carmen moved close
again and caught Catrina's waist to stop her from moving
farther. She smiled and shook her head. "This won't make
you feel any better, but where Damon's concerned things
always have a way of working out in his favor- it's why

Book of Scandal

Houston hates him so. In this family, everything's a call for congress especially regarding intimate relationships." She pulled Catrina to sit with her on the sofa.

"My brothers have been burned a lot and it's turned them hard, guarded...they'll do most anything to protect themselves from that. Damon liked you from the first- all those years ago, girl. That's the truth, I swear it. I think he just wanted to enjoy being with you without all the drama being a Ramsey brings into everything. I'm so sorry for the part I played in it," the ponytail curls slapped her cheeks when she shook her head. "I pray you can forgive me Catrina. I don't have any girlfriends and I truly don't want to lose you over this."

"Carmen..." Catrina blinked tears from her lashes and pulled her friend close.

The young women were still hugging when Houston knocked on the doorjamb.

"I should be getting home Houston." Catrina wouldn't look his way as she stood.

"But everybody's still in the living room. I don't think they're done trying to find out everything about you." He tried to tease.

"Houston..."

"There was a call from her folks when I left the living room to find her." Carmen squeezed Catrina's shoulder. "They need her back home."

"Everything okay?" Houston came over to squeeze Catrina's hands.

She nodded, still unable to maintain eye contact with him. "I just need to get back," she whispered.

Book of Scandal

"Sure thing," he pulled her hand through the crook of his arm.

Catrina looked back at Carmen just before rounding the corner with Houston. "I'll call," she promised.

***

Arriving at work on Monday morning to an office full of problems was the last thing Damon felt like dealing with. As he'd had the grand idea to begin Ramsey's troubleshooting department, he supposed he had no room to complain.

It took less than ten minutes for him to realize the problems were pretty much related. They'd come from varying departments but the problem was along the same general line. Employees all over Ramsey wanted to know why the benefits they depending on to supplement their family's health care needs or their own retirement expectations had suddenly been cut.

"Alright everybody let's settle down here. This is gonna be one hell of a morning." Damon spoke to his team while frowning over the folder one of the assistants had passed him.

"How do you want to start this, Damon?" Barry Reynolds asked.

"We can start with somebody tellin' me what the hell's goin' on here?" Damon slapped the folder to the conference table causing the contents to spill down the length.

"All we've learned is that the cuts started gradually a few weeks ago." Barry said.

Book of Scandal

"Started with the elimination of a few minor perks," Roland Bray shrugged, "nothing big but now these *cuts* are dipping into more pertinent employee benefits."

"Bobbie, I want you and your staff to record every name and specific complaint from the employees."

"We're on it Damon," Roberta Lowery nodded while making notes on her pad.

"Meanwhile, I'll make a call to the employee services division, see who authorized this…"

"Good luck with that, D." Roland grimaced. "Maybe you'll have more luck that I did. No body seems to know where the authorization for the cuts originated."

Damon braced his fists to the table, feeling his temper growing darker than it'd been over the last three and a half weeks. A sinking feeling was brewing in the pit of his stomach. He'd need to do more digging before any fingers were pointed.

"Let's get to work y'all." He said then, waving a hand to adjourn the meeting.

Bobbie walked by with the folder Damon had tossed and patted his back when she handed it to him on the way out.

Damon only took a moment to wallow in despair then focused on the folder's contents again. In addition to the general summary of complaints and departments affected, there was the vast list of management staff. Settling behind his desk, he hoped there was at least one manager, supervisor or team leader who might have a clue about what was going on. He reached for the phone and started dialing.

***

Book of Scandal

Catrina's Monday morning wasn't getting off to a better start. She'd returned from the library Sunday evening to over ten messages from Houston Ramsey. Her roommate- also from Savannah- couldn't believe Catrina was spacey enough to give a Ramsey the run around.

Catrina regretted what she was about to do, but it had to be done. She'd known since leaving the Ramsey dinner over three weeks ago. Her parents were stunned that she'd wanted to return before the new semester began. Her acclaimed work for the business had kept her so busy, but the Jeffries decided not question their daughter heavily.

At school, Catrina spent the bulk of her time cursing the day her family got the job to cater the Ramsey cotillion. That's where all the mess began after all.

Nevertheless, she couldn't dismiss how incredible Damon...*Ramsey* had been. She should've known he was one of them. Lord, was there an average looking one in the bunch? She'd constantly asked herself. Did they all have to be uncommonly gorgeous? Gorgeous, hmph. Where Damon was concerned, looks were only the beginning.

There was a quiet power he exuded without saying or doing a thing. The intensity of the affect only made him more appealing. Then, there was that dangerous element lurking in the dark depths of his eyes which promised he could be lethal if provoked.

Thinking of him, his touch on her skin sent Catrina into a slight tremble. The messages from Houston rustled nosily between her fingers. With a curse, she checked her jean pockets for change. She had a call to make.

***

Book of Scandal

"What's he done this time?" Westin groaned when he took Damon's call and asked how the troubleshooting biz was going. The obscenity Damon uttered in response to the light hearted question was a clear indicator that the call related to Marcus.

"With some prime figures on his side in the employment division he helped to arrange the dissolving of several key employee benefits." Damon shared the news coolly, his mood was anything but cool.

Westin uttered the obscenity that time. "What *prime* figures?"

"No names yet, but this move increases Ramsey's bottom line by an impressive percentage. I've got accounting working on the actual numbers" Damon leaned back in his swivel and massaged his eyes. "Looks like the money saved was dispersed among these *prime* figures in employment so don't bank on getting your hands back on those funds."

"That fuckin' snake." Westin whispered the curse but it sounded just as fierce. "Stupid," he swiped a stash of papers from his desk. "How the hell did he figure on getting away with this?"

Damon's jaw muscle clenched over the dread of sharing more foul news. "Various managers and supervisors of the affected departments were *met* with, given a proposal with the new cuts and told to share the news with their employees. The supervisors had nothing actually in writing, but it spread through the grapevine that it'd all come from the top and that Marcus Ramsey would reward those supervisors who made the transitions smooth." Damon leaned over his desk and resumed

Book of Scandal

massaging his eyes. "I've got shit on this end, West. No names on what management was rewarded, what that reward was or when it'd be received."

Silence filtered through the line and Damon though his brother may've hung up on him. Finally, he heard the rustle of papers on the other end of the phone.

"Thanks D," Westin said and then slammed down the phone.

Damon stared at the dead instrument for a second or two and then clenched a fist. "To hell with it," he seethed, tossing down the receiver and leaving the desk.

***

Catrina was shoving a book into her bag; while making her way up the steps leading to her building, when two of her dorm mates walked outside.

"Lucky wench," Rachel Brown grinned.

"*Smart* wench," Tamara Anderson corrected. "He's *way* sexier than his brother." She said and bumped hips with Catrina.

Catrina spared a minute to watch the girl's saunter down the gray steps and then she shook her head and went inside. She understood Rachel's and Tamara's remarks the minute she cleared the dorm foyer. Her gaze clashed with Damon Ramsey's. He was waiting for her in the vacant waiting room.

"I wouldn't leave him alone any longer, baby." Dorm mother Hattie Leer advised from her post just inside the office. "Your dorm mates been eyein' him like the last piece of sweet potato pie at a church picnic."

Catrina squeezed the strap of her bag where it rested on her shoulder. "Thanks Miss Hattie." Slowly, she moved

Book of Scandal

toward the waiting room but stopped just inside the doorway.

"Since it didn't look like you were going to return any of my calls…" he shrugged.

She rolled her eyes and pulled the strap of her bag from her shoulder. "What do you want?"

"To talk to you, that's all."

"I don't have anything to say to you."

"Good, then you won't interrupt me while I explain."

"Explain." Her gaze sharpened.

Damon took a chance on moving closer. "I didn't mean to hurt you Catrina. Never. I never set out to do that."

"Right. You just didn't tell me your last name because you wanted to be sure I was refined enough to handle it."

He bowed his head, jingling keys in his trouser pockets then. "I thought you didn't want to talk?" He quietly reminded her.

Again, Catrina rolled her eyes.

"You don't know how things change when I include Ramsey after my first name." He shrugged and began to walk the room. "Girls have gone from interested to insane in the span of a second. I've seen it." He gave her a look as if to confirm it was all true. "It's like they're almost worshipping because of a name I had nothing to do with. It's like all they see is the name- I'm just what it's attached to."

The explanation was so sincere, so sad. Catrina couldn't believe it. How could a man so intelligent and incredibly fine be so unsure of himself? To think it was all about a name when a girl talked to him was beyond idiotic. She didn't realize she'd uttered the thought aloud until she noticed his grin.

"Trust me, it's happened more than I care to admit- not always, but more than enough." He leaned on the back of the sofa, hands still hidden in the pockets of his navy trousers.

"I don't doubt that the girls I've known have been very interested but once they hear the name..." His dark eyes rose to her face. "When I met you, Catrina I-I actually forgot how to talk. Just knowing you was the most fun I'd ever had in my life and I was selfish- too selfish to share my name and risk ruining that."

Catrina wasn't moved by that part of the conversation. Her lips thinned and she kicked the toe of her pump against her bag. "The talks we had...and at *no* time did you trust me even a little to talk about who you are."

"I guess, I didn't." It was Damon's turn to look down at his shoes. "For that I'm sorry especially since my not trusting you damaged whatever trust you may've had in me."

"I called Houston. Broke things off." She said when silence had hovered between them longer than a minute. "I didn't tell him...about us." She read his expression and then smirked. "Guess I can't be trusted after all."

"Catrina." He left the sofa and moved toward her, halting his steps when she backed away. "May I call you?"

Again, she smirked. "Guess you can do whatever you like. You're a Ramsey."

A lost look clouded Damon's bottomless gaze as he watched her leave the room and take the stairs up.

Book of Scandal

    "Don't fret over it, honey." Hattie Leer advised. "Give her a bit of time, but don't give up."

    Damon's eyes remained on the staircase. "Never," he vowed.

$\mathscr{R}$

~CHAPTER NINETEEN~

Tuesday nights at the Haven Clinic were usually pretty quiet. Founder Dr. Wayne Potts considered 'quiet' sometimes a blessing and other times a curse. Of course, *no* business was a good thing given his line of work and given the area where his line of work was located.

When he'd decided to do something about the lack of decent healthcare in the poorer parts of Savannah, the area had a true need. Dr. Potts felt his work would never end. After 4 ½ years in existence, the health of his patients had so improved that he'd been repeatedly commended by the city and state for his phenomenal work.

Many of the patients; he'd began seeing at the start of the clinic, were children. He'd watched them grow, head off to school or start their own families. Parents often

Book of Scandal

thanked him and said he was the reason their kids had a chance at a real life.

Dr. Potts was so close to his patients, he knew them all on a first name basis. Yet he couldn't recall speaking any name with half the horror that he did on that quiet Tuesday evening when seventeen year old Connie Williamson was rushed into the clinic. She was convulsing, beaten and raped.

Dr. Potts' frantic questions to the staff or the people who brought her in were met with blank looks or panicky shakes of the head. No one could tell the doctor anything other than the girl had been found naked in a field behind the town grocers.

The clinic was soon alive with the sounds of staff being summoned. They rushed to and fro doing the doctor's bidding for his young patient.

"I want you to contact the police and then her parents." Doctor Potts told his head nurse once he'd administered meds to cease the girl's convulsions.

RN Betty Sheridan nodded quickly and cast one last terrified look toward the battered young woman, before heading out to make the calls.

"Who did this to you child?" Wayne Potts buried his face in his hands, expecting no response to the question.

It was sometime before he discovered Connie was trying to speak. He put his ear close to her swollen lips and strained to listen.

"Houston Ramsey."

***

"Damn straight he has every right to kick you out over this."

Book of Scandal

Marcus shuddered. "Can he really do that?" Though livid, he didn't mind showing fear before his friend.

"Yes, he can really do that." Jeff Carnes replied without hesitation, and then rolled his eyes. "What the hell were you thinkin', man? Aside from how much dirty money you could pocket at your family's expense?"

Marc hiked up his trouser legs and took a seat on the sofa in Jeff's office. "What are my options?"

"Own up to it. Own up to it all. Even the shit they haven't found out about yet." Jeff leaned back in his desk chair, taking mild delight in the fact that he'd caught his client off guard. "Knowing you the way I do, I assume there *is* more shit. My morning's clear so why don't you tell me about it?"

***

Catrina experienced a feeling of déjà vu when she walked into her dorm that evening and found Damon waiting in the lobby.

"Have you eaten?" He asked when they were in earshot of one another.

She shrugged. "Just going to the cafeteria after I change."

"May I take you out?"

"Damon, I don't-"

"I won't stop asking until you say yes."

Expecting as much, Catrina bowed her head and silently admitted she was tiring of the cold act. She remembered how unsettled she'd been when she left him down in the lobby three days earlier. She was sure she'd never see him again.

Book of Scandal

Damon strolled toward her with both hands hidden in the pockets of his salt and pepper trousers. He thrust out his elbow and Catrina followed the silent order to take his arm.

Her eyes were wide when she surveyed the plush dining room in the hotel restaurant. The Sherry Hotel was a place she and her friends had only dreamed of being taken to.
"Will you be putting the meal on your room, Mr. Ramsey?"
"Yeah, thanks Calvin." Damon signed the pad the maitre'd offered when they stopped at the podium.
"How long have you been here?" Catrina asked.
"I never left."
It took some time before Catrina was able to swallow around the ball that had lodged in her throat. "Look, if it helps you to know it, I accept your explanation. I can understand where you were coming from."
Damon halted his steps and looked down at her. "Do you trust me?"
She bristled. "I don't really know you well enough, do I?"
He didn't take offense. "Guess we'll have to do something about that."

Catrina merely wanted to satisfy her curiosity over what the rooms looked like at The Sherry. At least, that was the excuse she made herself believe. Of course the suite was to die for, but too soon the familiar feeling of simmering arousal was rendering her weak.

Book of Scandal

"I um, I should get back." She whispered, her mouth going dry when Damon tossed his suit coat to a chair. He stalked her then until she was between him and the dresser. His fingers trailed her cheek, her neck and collarbone-bare thanks to the scooping line of her gold sweater.

"I didn't think I'd see you again." She felt as desperate for conversation as she was for his touch.

"Why?" His onyx stare was focused on the path of his fingers along her skin.

Catrina bit her lip and didn't care if he felt her trembling. "For someone like you... someone like me would be easy to forget, replace..."

"Shut up." He told her seconds before his tongue filled her mouth.

The moment turned steamy in a second. His hand cupped her neck loosely, his thumb tilting her chin and keeping her in place for his kiss. Catrina melted as expected, arching eagerly when he hoisted her against his tall, leanly muscular form.

Something fluttered beneath her ribs when she wound her arms about his neck and buried her fingers in his silky dark hair. Her nails raked the close cut waves which tapered at his neck and; shamelessly, she nudged her breasts against his chest.

Damon took the silent cue, carrying Catrina up the steps leading to the canopied bed in the farthest corner of the room. He broke the kiss to nuzzle her ear and the sensitive spot below it. With deft, expert fingers he undid the buttons lining the back of her sweater. The bra followed the sweater's disappearance.

Book of Scandal

Catrina knew she should resist, but what he was doing to her nipples then felt too incredible to deprive herself of. She let him have his way and tossed both hands above her head. Damon cupped both his hands about her breasts, molesting one nipple with rubs and squeezes while his tongue soothed and suckled the other. Instinctively, she began to rotate her hips in another silent plea.

The phone rang and continued to ring. Damon seemed content on ignoring it, understandable given his groans and whispers as he feasted on her nipples and every other bared area of Catrina's body. When the ringing ceased only to resume suddenly, he finally took heed and broke away from her.

"What....? How the hell did they find me here...no, no it's alright put it through...Colby what the hell-? What?...shit..."

The agitated exchange on the phone told Catrina the interlude was at its end. She'd slipped back into her bra and had her sweater across her chest by the time Damon slammed down the phone.

"Houston's in jail," he said.

***

"Is this for real?" Damon was asking the next morning while he and Colby Martin waited in the hallway outside the courtroom. Colby was the ringer Damon had requested be put in the youth department to keep an eye on Houston.

"I didn't witness the incident, thank God." Colby worried her chin with rapid taps from her fingernails. "Judging from what I *have* witnessed- including my own share of run ins with your brother- I don't have a doubt that he did this."

Damon was still in a state of disbelief. Colby's perky voice sounded muffled in his ears. He'd seen the girl Houston attacked. His first stop had been to the hospital...Such rage- the attack on that girl had been pure rage personified. He predicted the father would want blood. Damon knew *he* would.

"It's a pure mess," Colby's light green stare widened when the judge's chamber doors opened.

Houston walked out with Jeff Carnes and went right to Marcus, crying on his brother's shoulder like a child.

"'Scuse me, Damon," Colby whispered, nodding as Jeff approached.

"He confessed the minute he sat down in the chair." Jeff said.

"Fuck." Damon's fists clenched as he stared down his brother, "there gonna be a trial?"

"It's sticky- Houston being a Ramsey and all."

"What the hell's sticky about it? He did it. That girl's a mess and he needs to pay."

"Why don't you try remembering you're talkin' about your own brother?" Marc called.

"I don't give a damn about my own brother if it's at the expense of a raped and beaten girl." Damon slid his gaze toward Houston. "What the fuck were you thinkin'? That child's father has every right to want your head on a plate and I sure as hell wouldn't mind helpin' to serve it up."

"His head on a plate could be substituted."

Marc smiled. "You see a way out of this, J?"

Jeff massaged his neck and moved from Damon's side. "The father's willing to accept money for... his daughter's suffering."

"Jesus..." Damon breathed.

"See how nice it is to have money, D?" Marc chided, ignoring the foul look his brother shot him.

"I'm all for seein' this fool in jail, but it'll have to wait until after a trial I guess." Damon posed his words to Jeff. "In the meantime, this jackass is damn well out of Ramsey."

"You can't do that!" Houston cried.

"No, he can't," Marc folded his arms across his suit coat. "You got no authority to do that, D."

Damon shrugged. "No, I don't. But West does."

Marcus rushed after Damon, catching his arm before he cleared the arched doorway to the judge's corridor. "You know that's not a good idea. Have you thought about what kicking him out of the company would look like publicly?"

"Well I don't know Marc." Damon tugged his arm free of his brother's grasp. "I'm thinking raping and beating a girl already has him looking pretty fucked up- publicly." He spared Houston a sneer and continued on his way down the hall.

"Pop wouldn't want this to ruin the business, D."

Damon's broad shoulders stiffened. In seconds, his steps slowed and then halted all together.

Marc smiled and strolled over. "It was important for him to keep the family looking good. Let Hous pay off the girl's folks. Give him the same chance you gave me." He spoke the last softer in Damon's ear.

Book of Scandal

Grinding down hard on his jaw, Damon felt so incensed he could scarcely keep his eyes open. Long lashes settled down over his gaze which had impossibly turned a deeper shade of black.

The decision was made of course. After all, hadn't he promised his father to do whatever it took to keep the family above scandal?

"D?"

"He fires every last one of those *kids* and hires adults." Damon spat, keeping his back turned. "More men than women. A cash payment to that family out of his own pocket and in the high five figures. If they want more, he'll fuckin' well give it or he'll rot. I'll make it my mission to see that he does." He continued on down the hall then, leaving his brothers and Jeff Carnes staring open-mouthed in his wake.

***

Marcella Ramsey finally agreed to the birthday luncheon her family seemed obsessed with giving. Many of her friends attended and; to Marcella's own surprise, she had more fun than she'd expected.

Westin and Briselle even made a special trip out for the event. Georgia joined the festivities as well.

In addition to family and Marcella's older friends, Daphne and Jasper had also been invited. It was clear to most everyone there that the handsome soldier was thoroughly smitten by the youngest Ramsey. No surprise there; Carmen kept her hands wrapped around Jasper's arm and consistently gaze up adoringly at him.

Daphne Monfrey, on the other hand, wasn't quite so moonstruck. Her man had yet to make an appearance at his

Book of Scandal

mother's birthday party. She'd stolen a moment to ask Marcella about his absence and was told that he hadn't been feeling well for several days. She debated on going to see him. They hadn't spoken since the dinner where he'd arrived with another girl on his arm. Daphne was still weighing her options when she overheard Jasper Stone inquiring of Houston as well.

"Man's been workin' hard. Just takin' some time for himself." The explanation was fast and flimsy. Marc was far more interested in observing his sister and her beau.

He sported a wolfish grin and Carmen wondered if Jasper noticed. She prayed not, but couldn't stop squeezing Jasper's hand until Marc excused himself. She gave a start when he suddenly pulled himself free and leaned down to look directly into her eyes.

"Are you afraid of him, Carm?" His mouth thinned to a grim line. The answer was obvious. Her increased trembling and unsettled gaze confirmed it adequately.

All explanations and conversations were stifled between everyone when one of the housemaids burst past the screened back porch enclosure. Fredrina Scales rushed over to Westin and Damon. Whatever she said had both men hurriedly kissing their mother and then rounding up all guests who worked for Ramsey.

"Freddie?" Marcella waved over the maid and clutched her arm. "What is it?"

"An accident Miss Marcy. Somebody's dead."

***

Much of the farm machinery Ramsey produced came out of the South End yard. Foreman Boyd Henries stood with a grim look shadowing his usually kind face.

Book of Scandal

His back stiffened and the grim look took on a darker sheen when he spotted three of Quentin Ramsey's four sons headed his way.

"Give us a run down, Boyd." Westin asked while handshakes went round.

"Run down is 'zactly what it was, West. We make so much of our own machinery- maybe this'll get us to makin' *all* of it." Boyd mopped his neck with the handkerchief always perched in the back pocket of his wash worn work pants. "One of the cranes just- just snapped. Like a damn twig...dropped a bin of scrap metal on a group of workers below..." Boyd mopped his neck again. "Injured three and one- Garret Lucas was killed on impact."

"Is that normal, Boyd? For a crane to just snap like that? Do you think it could've been overloaded?" Damon asked.

Boyd was already shaking his head. "The thing was no where near capacity and no- it ain't normal."

"What about the crane operator? What's his story?" West's voice was dangerously hollow as he surveyed the wreckage in the distance.

"I've worked with Pat Thomlinson seven years. I'd vouch for him to anyone who asks. He's one of the best- if not *the* best." Boyd punched his fist to palm. "That's the reason why it was Pat workin' the crane. It bein' a new toy and all...only right Pat have first dibs operatin' our best equipment. The way that crane just snapped though..."

"Boyd?" Westin prompted.

"I don't want to speak out of my place, West." Boyd's grim look had mellowed into an uncertain one.

Book of Scandal

"That could never happen, Boyd." West stepped closer to squeeze the man's shoulder. "You been here since my dad started Ramsey. I'd be very disappointed if you didn't say exactly what was on your mind."

Boyd winced while stroking the salt and pepper stubble on his chin. "The way that thing snapped West...it was like the thing wasn't new at all. Pat said it himself."

While Westin pondered Boyd Henries' suspicions, Damon's gaze had already slid toward Marcus; who had been abnormally silent since they'd all left the party. Eventually, Marc felt the weight of his brother's glare and met it.

"What did you do?" Damon hissed.

"We're gonna have to get the investigators out here." West was saying, shoving hands into his jean pockets as he walked over to his brothers. "What a damn mess. What?" He quickly tuned into the sourness between the two men.

"Why don't you tell us where you got all our *new* equipment?" Damon almost growled.

Westin's confusion cleared. "Muthafucka," he whispered seconds before landing a blinding punch to Marc's jaw.

***

Word of the deadly accident spread fast throughout the Ramsey organization. There was no need for rumor embellishment since the truth was so much juicier. Damon put to work every resource in the oversight department. He wanted Marcus gone and was obsessed with finding the necessary information to make it happen. The fact that Marc purchased the shoddy equipment wasn't enough. He

Book of Scandal

could easily claim he had no idea it was defective. What Damon needed was to find someone to confirm that Marcus Ramsey knew all too well what he was buying.

***

Marcus waited outside the boardroom, hoping for a chance to speak with Damon. His younger brother's quiet mood had him on edge to say the least. When he'd learned that it was Damon who'd called a sudden meeting with Westin and Jeff Carnes, his paranoia went into overdrive. He kept expecting to see Charlton Browning pop up from somewhere. No way was Damon digging him up though. His globetrotting friend was probably not even in the country.

"Westin, Marcus Ramsey, Jeff Carnes, I'd like you all to meet Mr. Leland Shayne. Mr. Shayne's a former equipment inspector."

Marcus looked ill and didn't mind if it showed. Damon had produced someone better than Charlton. Leland Shayne's *coerced* signature was on every document for the shoddy property.

West had already taken note of Marcus' reaction. "Have a seat and talk to us, Mr. Shayne."

Like a bursting dam, Leland Shayne shared his entire story. Before all was said and done, the man even spoke of Charlton Browning's offer of cash in exchange for his signature. The testimony was thorough and damning. Jeff threw down his pen in a defeated manner. Westin thanked Shayne for his time and called in an assistant to make the man more comfortable. Damon waited to hear Westin give Marc his walking papers.

Book of Scandal

"Where do things stand with the widow and the injured men?" West asked Jeff.

"No one knows anything about the equipment being sub-par. If we can get them to take a settlement out of court before the investigations are done…we may have a shot at curbing this entire mess."

West leaned across the table and shook hands with Jeff. "I appreciate this, man. I know you hadn't counted on such an encompassing job when you took my brother's initial offer but you've proven to be a loyal and invaluable friend. I pray you'll remain with us for the foreseeable future." West slanted a glare toward Marcus. "I got a feelin' we're gonna need you."

Damon felt something nasty in the wind and stood to voice his complaint.

Westin's hand was waving before anything could be said. "Take a seat, D."

Marcus kept quiet, though his expression appeared more hopeful.

"Until I decide what to do, Marc is stripped of any decision making authority, so is Houston." He pointed a finger toward Marc. "I don't even wanna see your name on a purchase order for toilet paper. You've proven to be too volatile for Ramsey. Damon; with the guidance of his colleagues in the oversight department, will have full say over day to day ops in all areas."

Marcus worked hard to keep his mouth closed. He was angry and humiliated but knew better than to push it.

"Fuck that, West! I want this nigga out!"

"Damon. We're brothers."

"Screw that." Damon closed his eyes and tried to rein his temper before speaking again. "West, I promised Pop."

"I promised Pop too. Promised I'd see to the family," West shrugged. "That includes Marc and Houston."

"They're out of control, West. You don't know the half of it."

Marc's apprehension returned, but Damon didn't see fit to offer up more dirt just then.

"We need a better solution here, West. Not just a temporary state of play." He said.

"I agree with you, D but it'll take time to come up with something truly appropriate." West's dark stare shifted between his brothers. "Once all this is in place, I don't intend on changing protocol until we all retire."

R

~CHAPTER TWENTY~

After two weeks, Daphne worked up the courage to pay a visit to Houston's apartment in town. She'd actually worked up the courage days earlier but had hoped he'd make the first move. Call…apologize for hurting her…

When he answered her ring at the door, there was no apology in his eyes but there was desire. Daphne decided she approved of that way more.

Houston didn't waste time with greetings. He pulled her into a kiss that sent the tingles already coursing her body into a more rampant surge.

"What happened?" Daphne moaned during the kiss. "Why'd you disappear, why haven't you called…?"

Houston felt a rage rising in him at the mere mention of Catrina. Her call to dump him with no explanation was as unexpected as it was devastating.

"Houston…"

"I don't wanna talk about it." He squeezed her once before releasing her arms.

"So how's work?" Daphne bumped her fists to the sides of her brown checkered bellbottoms and tried a new approach.

Houston wanted to discuss work even less than he wanted to discuss Catrina Jeffries. "That place has been a waste of my time," he growled.

Daphne followed him across the newspaper strewn living room. "But you seemed to love it there."

"It was pushed on me, Daph." He kicked a beer can and watched it roll under the coffee table. "Pushed on me and Marc because our father didn't really want us involved with Ramsey. He just did it so our mother would stop buggin' him about it."

"Oh Houston I'm sure that wasn't all it. He had faith in you and Marc- he was your dad, after all."

"Hmph, he may've had faith in Marc," Houston stroked the stubble darkening his light caramel-toned face. "I've never been right at anything. Can't remember a time when I felt the old man was looking *at* me and not *through* me." He dropped down on the sofa. "West had the smarts, Marc the charm, guess we all lucked out on looks...that fuckin' Damon lucked on on a shit load of all that and then some. I don't know how I wound up in this family, Daph." He grinned and studied his hands. "I wouldn't be surprised if someone told me the Ramseys found me on their porch steps and took pity on me."

"Houston..." Daphne joined him on the sofa. "God... I can surely relate to that."

Book of Scandal

Houston appeared surprised by her admission. His own admission was one he'd never shared with another living soul. He took note of the emotions affecting her exquisite face and realized she *could* relate.

"One day, Daph. One day people will respect me the way they respect my brothers." He nodded as though seeing the future spread out before him. "I'll have it all-respectable life, wife, kids..." he laughed then and flounced back on the sofa. "Shit, who am I kiddin'? Who'd marry me, pathetic as I am?"

"Oh Houston stop it!" Daphne shook her head and balled a fist to her knee. "Damn that Catrina Jeffries."

"Daphne?"

"I was so hurt that night you showed up with her on your arm. When I saw them together, I was glad, glad that she was doing to you what you did to me." She swiped the tears dampening her cheeks. "I saw them together that night at the dinner. Damon and Catrina. It wasn't their first night meeting- they already knew each other. They knew each other quite well judging from what I saw happening between them." She pressed her lips together and took note of Houston's quiet and stillness. A voice warned she'd already said too much, but she took no heed and shared all that she'd overheard.

"Don't waste your time feeling unworthy of Miss Perfect Jeffries. She's not the woman you need." Daphne didn't care if he saw desperation in her eyes then. "I'd never disrespect you with another man. You're all I want. I love you."

Houston smiled, cupping Daphne's face and studying her angelic features with an intensity that had never been there before. He kissed her mouth, then stood and left the sofa to stare past the windows.

***

Marcus wouldn't allow the shame of Westin's decree to keep him out of Ramsey even if he did spend the majority of the day behind the closed doors of his office. Damon would've been surprised to know that Marc wasn't up to his usual plotting. Instead, he was learning- teaching himself what he hadn't learned in college regarding international business.

Marc's interest had moved far beyond petty equipment and human resource issues. He wanted Ramsey on the international stage- a presence to be reckoned with. That would require doing things above board-playing by the rules until power allotted him the ability to *make* those rules.

***

"Reggie?" Catrina's face was a picture of surprise and agitation when she saw the state of the main dining room. "Why's the place shut down on a Thursday night?"

"A gentleman rented it out for the evening." Reggie Jeffries explained while browsing albums from his place at the host's podium.

Catrina's agitation cleared. "Wow."

"Mmm hmm, said it was for him and his special lady."

Catrina laughed and set her purse and keys to the nearest table. Her amber swing coat flared a bit more gaily as she observed the atmosphere. She took a leisurely stroll around the soft lit area. Tiny lamps on the tables gave off a glow similar to candlelight. Just then, the sounds of Marvin

Book of Scandal

Gaye and Tammi Terrell's *"If I Could Build My Whole World Around You"* filled the air.

The hypnotic serenity was shattered much like the double front doors of Jeffries Café when they suddenly burst open. Glass and wood lay in Houston Ramsey's wake when he bolted inside.

"What the hell?" Reggie grabbed Houston's arm, but found himself knocked aside and into the host's podium.

"Houston!" Catrina cried, running over to help her cousin who was bleeding abundantly from the cuts on his neck and face. Boldly, she ran over and shoved Houston's chest. "What are you doing?!"

Houston's response was a backhand blow to Catrina's cheek which sent her to her knees.

***

Following the very meaningful discussion with Houston, Daphne felt a proposal would soon be at hand. His strange reaction; when she told him about his brother and Catrina Jeffries, wasn't exactly what she'd hoped for. Still, she had confessed her feelings and he seemed to understand and perhaps agree that their fates were intertwined.

Daphne was so certain of that future; she visited Marcella Ramsey to announce her interest in the woman's son and explain the *misunderstanding* with Houston and Catrina Jeffries when Marcella inquired. There in the elegant sitting room; with the usual tea and lemon cookies between them, Daphne waited for some outrage or disgust from the Ramsey matriarch.

Marcella leaned forward with her hands extended and smiled when Daphne obliged in taking them. "When my time came, I'd hoped to die in the peace of knowing all my children were settled down."

"Miss Marcella?" Daphne tilted her head; her light eyes reflected a surprise over the comment.

"This is wonderful news." Marcella reached for her tea cup and sighed. "Houston was the one I fretted most over. Always so uncertain of himself. You'll be good for him."

Daphne blinked, feeling happy tears behind her eyes. For the next fifteen or twenty minutes, the women talked of a possible wedding.

"Ma? Mama?!" Carmen rounded the sitting room door then. "Mama, phone."

"Thank you, baby." Marcella left her chair but gave Daphne a hug before seeing to the call. "You've made me very happy, child."

"I'll show you out Daphne," Carmen said when her mother had ventured off. She bounced away without bothering to ask if the visit was at its end.

Daphne didn't argue the matter. At the door, she crossed the threshold with an added lilt to her step. "Houston's not interested in your friend Catrina." She said, while pulling on her gloves. "It's me, it's always been me. I was just telling Miss Marcella. She's very happy for us."

Carmen leaned against the door and absently fiddled with a flipped lock of her hair.

Daphne smiled over the girl's obvious attempt at being bored. "I know you're disgusted by me, just like most of the phonies in this town are. You best get over it. I'm sure to be your sister-in-law one day."

Carmen's smile was barely there. "I don't actually care one way or another. My brother is an idiot and deserves exactly what he'll get- that includes you." She closed the door in Daphne's face.

***

A cut and bleeding Reggie had stumbled off to find help while Houston continued to rage at Catrina. Reggie didn't have long to look; for all the commotion soon brought the family on hand, rushing into the dining room.

"Daphne Monfrey's got a whore for a mother but she's got more decency that you and my whole fuckin' family!" Houston barked while Catrina attempted to stand.

"She told me 'bout you and D playin' me for a fool!" He followed the statement with another blow. "A daughter of a slut is more respectful than you'll ever be." He sneered.

King Jeffries let out a roar and was bounding to his daughter's defense. He never had the chance, for Damon arrived in time to witness his brother's actions.

Still on her knees, Catrina's ears were ringing but she heard someone scream. Then, everything happened in a blur. An instant later, it was Houston on the floor being ravaged by Damon. She felt someone's hand on her elbows and was led to a chair. The Jeffries' had a ringside seat for the vicious attack.

No one attempted to separate the Ramsey brothers. For several moments, the sounds in the room were a mix of thuds to Houston's face from Damon's fists. Houston's moans of pain mingled with the sounds of Aretha Franklin's *"Think"* vibrating through the speakers. He was

Book of Scandal

driven by frustration and anger over Houston's reckless and unforgiveable actions.

"Damon! Damon stop!" Catrina called, suddenly fearing he'd kill his brother.

Damon had Houston poised to receive another blow. Stopping to observe Catrina's bleeding lip and the darker shadow of a bruise on her cheek only threw his rage into overdrive.

"Daddy!" Catrina called when Damon continued the beating. "Daddy? Steve? Preston? Do something!"

"There baby, shh…" Rosa kissed the top of her daughter's head. "Let him give the jackass what he deserves."

"Daddy please!" Catrina burst into fresh tears.

Slowly, King urged Steve and Preston forward. Reluctantly, they obeyed. It took their combined efforts to pull Damon up but they managed a firm grip when each took hold of an arm. Damon got in a few good kicks to Houston's side before he was pulled completely clear of the man's writhing body. Reggie had recovered somewhat and did his part in shoving Houston out onto the sidewalk.

Damon jerked out of Steve and Preston's hold. Giving an indignant tug to his tattered suit coat, he ambled over to King Jeffries while reaching inside his pockets. Finding his wallet, Damon handed the man every bill inside.

"Sorry Mr. King." He managed a grim smirk when the man patted his shoulder.

Damon walked over to where Catrina sat cupping her mouth. Her alluring mahogany gaze was wide as she watched him with a mix of disbelief and awe. He knelt before her, brushing aside her hand in order to observe her

Book of Scandal

cheek and lip. Muttering a curse, he bowed his head and ordered his temper to cool.

"I had the place shut down for us." He sighed, grimacing at the wrecked dining room. "This was all for you."

Catrina gasped and looked around with renewed awe.

Damon stroked her swollen lip for a few seconds more, and then reached into the deep inner pocket of his coat. He withdrew a small box.

"Will you marry me?" He smirked adorably when Catrina's eyes pooled with happy years.

***

Winter 1970~

Marriages, births, death. Changes within and along the immediate edges of the Ramsey clan happened in rapid fashion following the night at Jeffries Café.

Josephine gave birth to Quentin and Marcella Ramsey's first grandchild in the winter of 1969. Moses Tahir Ramsey was adored by everyone who saw him. Marcus of course strutted around like the proudest of fathers while his wife lost herself in the love she had for her beautiful son. Hatred for her son's father however, continued to fester.

Moses' name in itself was a testament to how grateful Josephine was for the child's ability to bring sanity to her life. She cringed whenever Marcus boasted of the baby. She recalled the day she rushed home to tell him of the pregnancy only to discover him at home naked in his study with two busty young women from the secretarial pool.

Book of Scandal

Daphne Monfrey finally got her man when she and Houston married a month after Moses' birth. The ceremony surprised family, friends and associates alike especially once Houston's rape charge was effectively swept under the rug.

Needless to say the Ramsey/Monfrey wedding was the most heavily attended gathering of the year. No one wanted to miss the chance to witness one of the Ramsey princes tie the knot with the daughter of the town madam.

As always, it was Marcella Ramsey who set the stage on decorum. The woman was clearly elated by her son's choice for a wife. None of the hundreds of guests were about to say or do anything to upset the newest Ramsey bride.

In keeping with the new marriages, Damon and Catrina exchanged vows in late March 1970. The wedding was held in Atlanta- home to the majority of Catrina's family. Westin, Briselle and Georgia flew out for the event with Marcella and Carmen in attendance as well. The occasion was a tribute to the love, desire and commitment existing between the gorgeous couple.

With so many unions in the Ramsey world, everyone speculated on the future of the Ramsey daughters. Carmen spent an increasing amount of time with Jasper whenever he was in town. While no talk of marriage had been spoken, the love between the two was unmistakable.

As for Georgia, she was on a mission to claim her own identity with a vengeance. After editing a few press releases for Westin, she realized she had a knack for the job. As a result, she decided to lend her talents there. In

Book of Scandal

Georgia's own boisterous words, she'd 'ensure the family wasn't being *screwed* by the press.'

***

Marcella Ramsey was content that her children were settled or close to it. She no longer waged war against the sickness that no one could put a finger on. Marcella clearly recognized it as a broken heart. She went to join her beloved Quentin when she passed away on a stormy Sunday in August 1970.

R

~CHAPTER TWENTY-ONE~

Catrina Ramsey had emerged as the chief planner of events and advertising for Jeffries Catering. Her father was steadily losing his enthusiasm for the grind. Any day, Catrina expected her parents to announce their move back to Atlanta and retirement. Catrina didn't mind- her love for the position she'd crafted, hadn't waned.

Besides, the work helped to keep her mind off her husband. Something wasn't right with him and she knew it had to do with Ramsey. Doggedly as she tried, she couldn't persuade him to confide in her, but she knew he could desperately use the chance to discuss his concerns.

Book of Scandal

She was on the phone one evening settling a date for a Jeffries' event when Damon arrived home and threw his briefcase against the wall.

"Lonnette we'll talk more tomorrow, alright?... alright, good night. So how was your day?" She sweetly inquired of her husband once she'd ended the call.

Instead of answering, Damon went for a drink.

Catrina followed him to the bar. "Why won't you talk to me?" She curled her toes into the silver shag carpeting lest she scream her frustration at him.

Damon sloshed bourbon into a stout glass and drained it. In a smooth move, he tugged his wife close and plied her with a throaty kiss.

Instantly affected, Catrina curled her fingers about the lapel of his tanned double-breasted suit coat.

"I can think of better things to do with you," he began to tug at the button securing the bodice of her coral shirtwaist dress.

"Something's wrong and I'd really like you to tell me about it." She managed in spite of the maddening swirls of his tongue below her ear.

"I should take you on a honeymoon."

She laughed at his poor attempt for a conversation change. "We had one."

"Miami wasn't what I had in mind." Both his hands were at work then on the buttons. "I want to take you away. Away from Savannah, away from Ramsey."

"Baby why won't you talk to me?" Her hands closed over his.

"I told you why."

Book of Scandal

Catrina felt the sudden brush of air against her skin and knew; without looking that her dress was on the floor. "Damon, wait," she moaned when he kept her in his arms and moved them away from the bar. "Mmm...wait-" the request ended on a gasp when her bra followed the dress.

This was about more than lovemaking she knew. Damon was more interested in silencing her questions. Little did he know that only made her more determined to seek answers. Still, that could all wait. Just then, she was more preoccupied by her husband's touch.

Damon kept moving her back until she felt the unyielding edge of his desk bumping her thighs. One hand cupped her neck to keep her in place for his kiss- as though she'd even think of evading it. His tongue thrust hungrily, masterfully and she; in turn, ground herself shamelessly against him. In seconds, she was pleading.

"Thought you wanted to talk?" He grazed his fingers along the edge of her bikinis. His double dimples flashed when she gasped at the feel of his thumb stroking her to orgasm.

Eagerly, she wound her arms about his neck and stood on her toes to kiss him more comfortably. She draped a leg up over his hip offering more room for his seeking fingers. When Damon began to thrust them deep, she uttered a breathless cry and began to ride them. She heard him speak a low curse when he broke their kiss. Next, everything from the desk hit the floor at one swipe from his arm. Flat on her back then, Catrina heard her panties rip. His tongue plundered her mercilessly as he shrugged out of his clothes.

Book of Scandal

Feverishly aroused, Catrina rested her arms above her head and arched into the devastating kiss. She bit down on her lip when the lengthy stiffness of his arousal replaced his tongue. She would have locked her legs around his back, but Damon prevented that. Bracing a hand upon each thigh, he kept her open effectively deepening his lunges inside her.

"I'm ruining your desk," she moaned feeling a heavy stream of moisture oozing after each of his thrusts.

"Let me help," he never withdrew and covered her fully when he joined her on the desk. Tugging one of her legs across his shoulder, he trapped her wrists in his hand and took her with a wildness that had them both crying out into the room.

Sated, they only rested atop the desk for a moment. Then, Damon tugged his wife across his shoulder and carried her upstairs to continue what had only just begun.

***

Josephine returned from her shower to find Marcus lounging on the chaise in their bedroom. So much for flipping the lock before she'd gone into the bath, she thought. There were probably keys to room in that house she knew nothing of. She went about her nightly routine hoping Marc would grow bored and leave but he just continued to stare. That was almost as unsettling as his crass words and the feel of him touching her.

Marcus relaxed on the lounge wearing nothing but black sleep pants slung low on his lean hips that did little to hide his arousal. In spite of a very healthy sex life outside his marriage, he'd had enough excuses from his wife for not wanting to sleep with him. It'd been well past the time when the doctor said she could resume relations yet nothing

Book of Scandal

had happened in that area for months. She'd grown more curvaceous, beautiful and desirable. He'd be damned if she'd turn him away another night.

Accepting that he wouldn't be leaving, Josephine decided to make another unnecessary trip to check on Moses in his nursery. Looking down on the baby, she thought how perfect and peaceful he was.

God, was she doing the right thing in remaining there? Didn't her child deserve a better life than the one he'd have with a father like Marc? A voice seeped into her silent questions, reminding her that the child also deserved to eat. How did she expect to support him? That is, if Marc let her take him in the first place.

Josephine stiffened then, feeling his probing, unwavering gaze on her before she turned and actually saw him in the doorway of the nursery. He moved forward and she moved to leave. He caught her arm before she reached the threshold and pulled her into a kiss. He didn't seem to care that her moans were ones of disgust and not pleasure.

Josephine heard ripping and realized their struggling had caused a tear in her robe. No matter to Marc, who only continued to rip and tear, linking the shreds about her waist to secure her against his bare chest.

With strength of will, she shoved him and landed an echoing blow against his face. She made another attempt to leave the room, but tripped on the tangles of the robe. Seconds passed and then she was flipped over and trapped beneath Marc's weight. She didn't want to give him the satisfaction of making her struggle, but she felt compelled to fight. Then Moses began to whine in his sleep, and she ceased her attempts to break free. Marcus had no shame and took his wife against her will on the floor of their son's nursery.

∗∗∗

Houston got the call at the office and came rushing to see to his wife. He found her in the sitting room of her mother's house. In a place teeming with police, emergency workers and scantily clad women, Daphne appeared unfazed.

Babydoll Monfrey had been found dead in her bed that afternoon. The news buzzed all over town and had actually reached Houston at Ramsey before the call came through.

Slowly then, as if uncertain, Houston stepped into the room and joined his wife on the sofa. When Daphne saw that it was him emotion surged and she rested her head on his shoulder.

"They know anything?" He kissed her forehead.

Daphne fiddled with the clasp of her watch. "They won't say officially 'til the medical examiner sees her but the emergency workers think it was natural. However *natural* a heart attack is," she sniffled and shrugged. "Looks like she passed in her sleep."

Houston felt her shuddering against him and thought she was crying. He tried consoling her with back rubs until he realized she was laughing.

Sure enough, Daphne's light eyes were filled with happy tears. "Doesn't that just beat it all? I just know Mama's lookin' down on this crap pot of a town and laughin' at the bastards here who expected her to die some foul death of some whore's disease." She bumped her fist against his thigh. "A heart attack…how normal,

Book of Scandal

how…respectable…" she tossed her head back and blinked away tears. "It's all she ever wanted for me, you know? Respect. She regretted I'd never have it because of her- who she was…"

"Shh…" Houston kissed her temple and smoothed his hand along the amber cotton sleeve of her dress. "You've got respect. You're a Ramsey and respect is ours for keeps."

***

Carmen had been living at home since her mother's passing. She had every intention of returning to finish her schooling but decided to take a bit more time off. She wouldn't linger long and; to ensure it, she released the house staff. Only two or three would come in once a week to keep the place tidy.

Then, there was Jasper. They'd made the house their regular meeting place when his schedule permitted. Carmen's hands slowed over her hair. She'd been putting the finishing touches on the upswept style when her thoughts lingered on his *schedule*. Jasper; while far more confident and charismatic, was still as secretive as ever. How she longed to know how he spent his time away from her.

The bell rang and she sprinted to the windows, squealing at the sight of his Impala Coupe parked below.

"Coming!" She called out when the front bell rang again. She sprinted from her room and down the stairs. Whipping open the front door, she barreled against him and kissed him deep.

"Why don't you ever use the key I gave you?" She asked when they came up for air.

Book of Scandal

The uneasiness; that he rarely showed anymore, crossed his face then. "I don't feel right about it." He shrugged and scanned the yard beyond the porch. "Walkin' up into your parent's house that way…"

"Jasper…" she tugged at the front of his lightweight cardigan.

"It's not right for somebody like me, Carm." He smiled suddenly and reached inside the olive green slacks he wore. "Got somethin' for you."

The gold charm trimmed in silver and dangling from a solid gold chain rendered Carmen speechless. She bit her lip when he swirled his index finger, silently instructing her to turn and let him link the piece about her neck.

"Jasper…it's beautiful," the charm was small but weighty. "This must have cost you a fortune."

"What?" He inquired of her expression when she turned. His rich brown gaze was narrowed in suspicion.

"I've had money all my life, Jasper." She patted the charm. "I've been at my happiest doing the simplest things and being with people who have way less than me and still get the most from life."

Jasper leaned back on his long legs and watched her closely. "What are you tryin' to say Carm?"

"Just that…" She batted the side of her sunflower yellow slip dress. "You don't need money to be with me and I don't want you resorting to…underhanded things because you feel like you have to impress me."

Jasper's laughter seemed to echo throughout the foyer. "Is that what you think I'm doing? Something illegal? Couldn't be farther from the truth." He chuckled and shook

his head. "Remember me telling you a bout Doctor Dowd?
I'm still working for him, but it's all so outrageous and
complex and well…boring." He shrugged. "At least that's
what you'd think if I tried to explain it to you. I couldn't
bear to watch your eyes glaze over while I tried to explain
cell structure and molecular mass."

They both laughed then.

Jasper cupped Carmen's face and nudged her
forehead with his. "Just know that what we share and what
I'm learning and involved in with Doctor D… I've never
felt more complete or accepted."

Happy then because he was; at last, happy,
Carmen's dark eyes glistened. She stood on her toes and
kissed him.

Jasper kicked the front door shut and carried her
upstairs.

***

Marcus raised his hands in a playful show of
surrender. "I swear I'm totally clean!"

Jeff Carnes managed a grin that didn't quite reach
his eyes. "Take a seat," he waved toward the other side of
the table.

"You know how honored I am to have that position
at Ramsey?" Jeff asked once the waiter had left with
Marc's drink order.

Marc frowned. "Sounds like you're sayin' goodbye,
man."

"Not completely but in so many words- yes."

"What the hell does that mean, J?"

Jeff thanked the waiter who returned with Marc's
cognac and a refill on his Scotch. "Corporate law is cool,

Book of Scandal

but a lil more than I bargained for and not what I went to school for."

"No matter. You're doin' a hellified job."

"Thanks man, but I feel like I'll be burned out by the time I really get started." Jeff leaned back in his chair and fiddled with the end of his tie. "I've been offered an associate's position at Best and Monroe. They've never brought in a black associate and if I turn 'em down, they may never bring in another."

Marc sipped his drink and grimaced. "So what? You tryin' to be some activist muthafucka now?"

"No, no nothin' like that but it's a chance I don't wanna turn down. I can do a lot of good for families aside from the Ramseys." Jeff lowered his gaze to the table. "I already talked to West and the other counselors in the legal division."

"J..." Marc stiffened but the look in his pitch gaze was pure unease. "I need you, man."

Jeff grinned. "I'll offer you my services personally. I'm not abandoning you, Marc- just need a little variety, you know?"

Marcus reciprocated the grin. "I can relate," he drawled. He leaned forward and shook hands with his old friend. "Wish you the best, man."

***

"How much is it gonna cost to make this go away?" Damon rubbed his fingers across the dark waves of silk covering his head and tightened his grip on the receiver.

A man chuckled on the other end of the line. "It's not us, D. But you're damn lucky she got *me* when she

called. Anybody else on staff would've run with the story
lickety split."

"Shit. Sorry Carl thanks for the update."

"So how you gonna handle this, D?" Carlton
Wadkins asked.

"How long can you stall her?"

"Not sure. The girl's hell bent on getting paid for
what she claims your brother did to her."

"Oh he did it alright." Damon sighed and began to
pound his fist lightly against the side of his head. "I knew
this shit would come back to bite us."

"How'd y'all managed to keep this out of the courts
the first time?"

"Think Carl, how else? Money." Damon pushed
away from his desk and swiveled his chair around to face
the windows. "Guess we should've thrown a little the
daughter's way instead of shoveling it all to her sorry father
who swept her rape and beating under the rug for five
figures."

Carl grunted. "I think she wants a little more than
five figures, D."

"Damn right she does…listen Carl, thanks again. I
need to go figure a way to clean up another Ramsey fuck
up."

Damon dialed out to his assistant the second the call
with Carl ended. "Bobbie? Get Houston on the phone."
***

The greedy little bitch, Houston chanted the phrase
over and over in his head while slamming his way out of
the car and into the house. He should have never given her
the time of day when she came sniffin' around his desk for

Book of Scandal

a stroke of Ramsey dick. Greedy and conniving, she threatened to expose what had been going on between them after hours in the youth division. That's when she'd left him no choice but to teach her a lesson. Now she was back demanding more than they'd already given her shady father and boy wasn't Damon just eating it up?

Letting out a frustrated wail, Houston kicked one of the maple cabinets holding he and Daphne's combined record collection. He took a seat and massaged the bridge of his nose for a while. He raised his head slowly then as though sensing something wasn't quite right.

"Pris? Prissy?!" he called out to the housemaid who usually had a stiff drink waiting the minute he stepped through the door.

The drink arrived, but it was Daphne who delivered it and not the sweet housemaid he'd *handpicked*.

"Where's Prissy?" Houston took the drink and settled back to his favorite chair.

"Priscilla's gone. More accurately, I let her go."

Houston bolted from the chair, pushing it back against the carpet. "Daphne, what the hell?"

Daphne re-tied the tassels of her robe. "The girl had absolutely no idea how to keep a house. Wherever did you find her?" She asked coyly. "She probably never even swept a room in her life- looked way too young to even know what a vacuum was. Besides…" she crinkled her nose distastefully and punched a pillow on the sofa. "Our house is way too small for a maid- nothing like Josephine's mansion. *Definitely* nothing like your parents' place. I don't know what the hell you were thinking when you hired her Houston…"

Book of Scandal

> *I was thinkin' that she could give me a damn good*
> *blow job when you're tired or too naggy- which seems to*
> *be often lately.*

Houston dragged himself to the bar and poured another glass of vodka.

"Don't worry over it, baby. I'll hire the next one." Daphne hummed a little tune while she strolled from the living room.

"Shit." Houston downed his drink.

***

"What the fuck you know 'bout boatin' nigga?" Marcus chuckled while lounging on the chaise he'd grown accustomed to sitting in and watching his wife prepare for bed.

Charlton Browning's laughter rumbled with ease. "I don't know shit, man but I can sure as hell learn. You know how much opportunity would open up to me with a fuckin' ship at my beck and call?"

"Man, you crazy! You pull that off and I'll be the first to salute and call you captain."

"All about the money, man." Charlton raved. "What I need is backing- a helluva lot of backing. Investors I'd give a set cut to but who'd have no ownership in the thing."

"Well you-" Marc cut himself off when Josephine walked into the room. "Hey Charlt, lemme catch you later- this sounds like somethin' I wouldn't mind getting in on."

Marc left the lounge as Josephine slid beneath the covers. He watched her while undoing his PJ bottoms and letting them fall away to reveal his toned nude form. He joined his wife in bed. When he touched her, she didn't react in any way.

Book of Scandal

Josephine simply watched the ceiling while Marc trailed his mouth all over. He suckled and nibbled in a manner that never failed to have a woman moaning in no time.

"Dammit Josie," he hissed after nibbling her breasts for almost two minutes. "Is this your new thing or what? Actin' like you don't want it?" he cupped her jaw and made her face him. "I can make you want it, you know?" He smirked sinfully upon noticing the faintest flutter of her lashes. Smoothly, he slid a finger inside her and smiled broadly when he discovered she was damp.

"Let's see if we can get it a little wetter." He whispered against her ear and kissed his way down her body until his mouth replaced his fingers.

$\mathscr{R}$

~CHAPTER TWENTY-TWO~

Carmen's laughter turned many heads which was usually the custom whether she was laughing or not. The youngest of the Ramsey children had grown into a stunning beauty. Carmen's laughter then was simply in reference to the joke Jasper had just shared.

The reality of being out together like an ordinary couple, enjoying dinner and the presence of others had a lot to do with it. The fact that Jasper arranged it all to surprise her meant more than he could know. They'd even been blessed to have an especially nice waiter who stopped by their table just then to ask if they'd like more coffee.

Jasper waved it off, while Carmen patted her non-existent waistline beneath her peach slip dress.

Book of Scandal

"I couldn't eat or drink another thing." She said and playfully puffed out her cheeks.

"Guess we're done, man." Jasper reached into the small front pocket of his beige and black checkered vest. "We'll take the bill." He told the waiter while slapping another tip into the younger man's hand.

The easy grin Jasper sported faded when he noticed Carmen's expression. She was staring fixedly across the room. Jasper scanned the soft lit crowded dining area. Seeing Marc, he knew that was the cause for Carmen's sour look.

"Small world," he said while his warm brown eyes narrowed toward Marcus' table. "That Josephine?"

Carmen snorted. "My brother doesn't take his wife out unless he's trying to impress someone."

Jasper shrugged. "She must be a business associate." Jasper was already losing interest in Marc's presence.

Carmen's laughter lilted once more. "He's only interested in associating with women in the bedroom, Jas."

Before Jasper could comment, he saw Carmen look down quickly and knew Marc had spotted them. Moments later, he felt a hand on his shoulder.

"Good to see you Jasper." Marcus barely glanced his friend's way as they shook hands. His eyes were already locked on Carmen. "She's a beauty, huh Jas? You're a lucky guy."

"You're always workin' Marc." Jasper teased slyly to satisfy his own curiosity. "This business or pleasure?"

Book of Scandal

Marc chuckled and tugged on the charcoal suspenders beneath his suit coat. "For me, business *is* pleasure."

Carmen stood then, slammed down her napkin and walked away from the table.

"'Night Marc," Jasper's tone was absent as he took care of the check, the waiter had just delivered and left after Carmen.

She was already halfway across the parking lot when he caught her arm. Jasper pulled her the rest of the way with him. At his car, he pressed her against the passenger door of the Impala.

"Not tonight, do you hear me Carm?" He bent to glare directly into her eyes. "You tell me why he makes you act the way you do. I may be an only child but even I know when agitation goes beyond sibling shit. Start talkin'."

Carmen's lashes fluttered then in what appeared to be an attempt to control anger. "Yes, it goes beyond sibling shit." She curved her hands beneath his elbows. "It goes grotesquely beyond sibling shit and unless you want me to throw up all over your nice suit, you'll let me leave it at that."

***

"Dammit West," Briselle hissed and snatched the key from her husband's shaking hand.

"Georgia?!" Briselle was calling once the door was open and they were rushing into the apartment. "Georgia!"

"In here!"

"Jesus Georgia!" Westin cursed when the smell of vomit met them at the bathroom door.

Briselle pushed her husband out of the way while he groaned and covered his nose. Then, she went to see to Georgia who was crouched at the toilet she'd been heaving into. "Lemme guess," she said while searching for towels in the cabinet above the commode.

"Damn that Felix Cade." Georgia moaned seconds before another bout of nausea claimed her.

"Shut up, girl." Briselle went to wet a small cloth at the sink. "As I recall, the man requires a bit of assistance to make this happen."

"Never happened before…"

Briselle giggled. "Did you think you were immune, honey?"

"What the hell am I gonna do with a baby?" Georgia moaned when Briselle knelt to wipe her face with the cloth. "I never thought working was my cup of tea but I really like what West has me doing at Ramsey. Shit…" She pushed away the washcloth. "Now what am I gonna do?"

"Exactly what you've *been* doing. A baby doesn't need to change things." Briselle studied her fingers tapping the tights where they stretched across her knees. "A baby could actually make things even better."

Georgia only rolled her eyes.

"Did you tell Felix?"

"For what?"

"Georgia! Don't tell me you're thinkin' of not tellin' him?"

Georgia stood and walked barefoot to the sink. "I'm not bringin' him in on this 'til I know what I'm gonna do."

Book of Scandal

"What you're gonna do?" Tiny furrows lined Briselle's brow. Slowly, she stood. "Georgia?"

"I just haven't decided whether…"

"What? Whether you'll keep it?" Tears began to glisten in Briselle's wide stare. "How can you be stupid enough to even consider doing something like that when-when a baby…A baby's a blessing. Some people won't even know that kind of joy and for you to just throw it away…"

"Jesus…" Georgia closed her eyes, understanding then and cursing her own insensitivity. "Bri, Bri I didn't mean it." She tugged her sister-in-law close. "I didn't mean it."

"You shouldn't keep this from him, Georgia." Briselle advised once they'd hugged and cried a while.

The stubborn sheen returned to Georgia's lovely features. "I don't know where he is half the time." She smoothed hands across her slip and raised her chin defiantly. "I don't know what he's doin' or who he's doin' it to."

"Georgia-"

"I won't put myself out there like that." She shook her head. "That's the one thing I won't do, Bri." Coolly, she strolled from the bathroom.

***

Damon and Catrina were having a heated session on their kitchen counter. Like a dutiful wife, Catrina had gotten up to make her husband's breakfast before he went to work. Damon arrived in the kitchen dressed only in the sleep pants Catrina had tugged off him the night before.

Book of Scandal

Preparing breakfast was forgotten. Damon was nibbling her jaw while his thumbs manipulated her nipples.

"You're gonna be late," she moaned.

"Not gonna- *am*." He corrected and kissed her deeply.

"I'm trying...trying to be a good wife, mmm...fix your breakfast..."

"I prefer you be a good wife and let me take you back to bed."

"You know you're being too silly too early in the morning." She laughed.

Damon hugged Catrina then and it didn't take long for her to figure it was an act. His embrace had less to do with arousal and more to do with weariness.

"You don't want to go to work, do you?" She felt him shake his head on her shoulder. "Baby, why?"

"Just tired Trina, that's all."

"No, no that's not all." She leaned back to study him and could see more than weariness in the darkness of his eyes. She cupped his face. "I want you to tell me what's wrong."

Sultriness crept into his gaze. "Damn girl, what fool would want to go to work with this at home." He drew her robe further apart to reveal more of her breasts.

Catrina tugged the gauzy black fabric closed. "You can forget about seein' any more of this unless you tell me what the hell is going on?"

Damon braced a hand on either side of Catrina against the counter and bowed his head.

Again, Catrina cupped her husband's face and waited for his eyes to meet hers. "Doesn't being your wife at least grant me the privilege of knowing a *few* of your secrets?" Her heart melted at the sight of his double dimpled smirk. Unfortunately, the gesture disappeared as quickly as it'd flashed. "Damon do you trust me?" She asked.

He nodded almost frantically. "With my life. More than anyone or anything."

"Then why-?"

"Because I'm afraid."

"Baby...of what?"

"I can't lose you Trina. Ever," he swallowed, raking his dark stare across her face and body. "I couldn't handle that."

She smoothed her hands up over his chest. "Baby why would you think you'd lose me?"

He looked sick. "My family- things they've done, things *I've* done to keep the peace..."

"Is this about what Houston did?"

Damon laughed over the innocent query. "What he did is only the tip of a very nasty iceberg."

Catrina nodded as though settling the matter in her mind. "Guess you're about to get your wish then. No way are you going to work until you tell me everything." She pushed him away and slid off the counter. "Start talkin' D, while I start breakfast."

***

In a surprise move, Westin flew Marcus and Houston out to Seattle for a two week stay. The guys were of course thrilled and filled with plans on how best to spend their vacations. They weren't off the plane an hour before West informed them that it was no vacation. The trip was

Book of Scandal

work and observation- their observation of Ramsey and *his* observation of them. Afterwards, Marc and Houston would know if they still had places at Ramsey.

One of the highlights of the grueling work trip however, had to be the evening out for drinks and cigars at a local gentleman's club. It was quite a culture shock for Marc and Houston to see blacks, whites and even those of the Latin persuasion all mingling together with such ease. The Tyler Cove took their motto very seriously. On a plaque above the entrance, it read: *The Only Color We See Is Green.*

All were welcomed and the atmosphere was rich with male laughter, boisterous voices, cigar smoke and the clink of glasses. Still, what most impressed Houston and Marcus were the Tesanos who were thrilled to meet more of the Ramseys.

It was a very telling few hours. Roman, Pitch and Aaron gravitated toward Westin and had non-verbally claimed him as their own. The four had even ventured off to their own table away from the others. Humphrey, Stone, Grekka and Vale had sensed an immediate kinship with the younger Ramseys.

This was especially true of Vale who craved the ideals and conversation of those closer to his age. Of course Marc did more of the talking. Houston sat practically mute, though he did nod and laugh at all the right times.

"Tell us about some of your interests Marc, personally speaking." Grekka asked once Marcus was done talking on the challenge of being one of many men in a

Book of Scandal

powerful family. "Where do you see Ramsey in say, fifteen, twenty years?"

"I'd like to see us have a formidable presence on the international market." He responded with no hesitation, eager for the chance to make an impression. "Aside from that, I hope to make a name for myself beyond the Ramsey name and accomplishments."

"You have any plan in mind for making that happen?" Vale asked while his older brothers nodded their approval of Marc's words.

"A few ideas...I've got a friend who's looking to invest in a ship." Marc shared after brief hesitation that time. "Once he learns more about the industry, of course. It sounds like something I'd like to get in on."

Stone was lighting a fresh cigar. "Keep us posted on your progress there."

Marc's grin spread. "Will do. Will do."

***

Daphne would never admit to making a mistake in marrying Houston. After all, he was a Ramsey. Besides, admitting she made a mistake was acknowledging a colossal waste of time and that was something she'd never concede to.

No doubt he'd had his eye and probably his hands on that little maid of theirs. Daphne had always known he had a predilection for youth and as she was outgrowing her pigtails phase...She wouldn't think of that. Houston was her ticket to the life, the life*style* she wanted and damn well intended to have.

He could start by getting her Ramsey. She'd dreamed of living there since the first day she'd set foot inside it during the cotillion so many years ago. Now, there it was- empty, lifeless yet still pulsing with the elegance and mystique it held when its mistress Marcella Ramsey ruled it with her charm and grace.

Daphne knew she'd have to start impressing upon her husband a bit more strongly as to how badly she wanted that house. Her hints about the size of their home in comparison to Marc and Josephine's castle weren't getting through.

Perhaps a weekend stay would do the trick. The place was empty now. Her husband shared her desire for flawless appearances and respect. Putting down roots at Ramsey would achieve that in no time flat. She smiled while observing the house from her perch atop the hood of her car.

Daphne had taken to viewing the house in much the same manner one might go window shopping. The Ramsey family home was the only treat she wanted from the window. Yes, a weekend stay would be just the thing. She'd speak to Houston when he got back from-

Her thoughts curbed then and her mind blanked altogether when movement along the far side of the house caught her attention. Daphne remained still on the Cadillac's hood for hours it seemed. She'd convinced herself that it was an animal- or her eyes playing tricks on her-when out ran Carmen Ramsey and Jasper Stone. The couple was naked and frolicked across the rolling green of the lawn.

Daphne closed her eyes to the sound of Carmen's laughter and clenched her fists against the sides of her Levi's. The lovers collapsed on the ground and tumbled

Book of Scandal

down the hill in an erotic embrace. Once they'd
disappeared from view, Daphne summoned the ability to
move. She looked down into her palms, finding them
bloody from her nails.

R

~CHAPTER TWENTY-THREE~

Georgia had taken to having dinner in a local pub not far from her apartment since she'd started the PR work for Ramsey. The vitality of the eatery- of Seattle itself- rejuvenated her each day. She often took time to pat her back for making at least one good decision in her life so far. She wondered then if she was on the way to making one more and thought of the baby.

Felix's baby. God, Bri was right. She had to tell him. But then what? Would he expect her to come away with him? Sure he would. Would she? She had a life in Seattle- a life she was really enjoying. She felt like she was making it on her own, supporting *herself.* While it was never something she'd fancied, paying her own way felt surprisingly good.

Book of Scandal

"Would you like a stronger drink, Miss?"

The waiter's deep voice jerked her from her thoughts when he approached the table from behind.

"No um," Georgia cleared her throat and reached for her glass. "I'm fine," she gave a little shake of the iced ginger ale.

"What if I insisted?"

Georgia looked up with a frown, her mouth dropping open at the sight of Felix. She watched him angle his athletic frame into the chair across from her.

"What are you doing here?"

"Have a drink with me." He countered.

"I...no," she declined, taking note of his attire. "Nice suit," she nodded while trying to dismiss how incredible he looked in it.

Felix merely shrugged off the compliment. His gorgeous dark features were drawn into a harsh mask. "I didn't bother to go back to the hotel after my meeting."

"You've...been staying in town?"

"Been here a week."

Georgia smirked. "And you didn't bother to tell me."

"I'm telling you now."

She wasn't impressed. "What? On your way out?" She gave a toss of her glossy bobbed hair. "Thought you'd stop off for a little romp with old Georgie, huh?"

Felix's jaw muscle twitched but he never lost his cool. "I can get that anywhere, G. Very easily and without all the lip service and attitude...well maybe just a little lip service." He graced her with a sly wink.

"Why don't you go on then?" She rolled her eyes.

"Have a drink with me."

"Jesus what is it with you and drinks?" She kicked the toe of her wedge-heeled Socialites against the leg of the table. "I'm perfectly fine with my ginger ale."

"I see…is that because you're trying to be good to our baby?"

Georgia gasped. Her eyes were wide as moons then. "How?"

"Stopped by your apartment first and you weren't there- thought you might be with West and Bri." He tugged on the cuff of his dark jacket. "When I got to their place, West just assumed you'd already told me."

"Idiot!" Georgia almost knocked over her drink. "It's a wonder he hasn't pissed away Daddy's company as stupid as he is."

"Were you gonna tell me, G? Don't bother to answer, I think I can guess."

Rather than defend herself, Georgia gathered her things and rushed from the dining room leaving Felix to handle her bill.

It was a rainy Seattle night and she moaned that the conditions would seriously ruin her hair. She'd rather face a torrential downpour than Felix's wrath just then. Besides, it was only a few blocks to her building. She broke into a fast walk and barely made it half a block before she was grabbed.

Her scream sounded curdled amidst the rain. Felix backed her against a wall leading into an alleyway.

"I don't need to hear it," he said when she opened her mouth to talk. "Fool," he growled seconds before his tongue plundered her mouth.

Book of Scandal

The kiss rendered Georgia pliant against his frame. She was drained of any desire to argue.

"Felix-"

"Shut up, G." He gave her a little jerk and kissed her more savagely while squeezing her breast beneath the gold vest of her skirt suit. Once satisfied, he pulled back to glare at her. "I've been in town closing a deal on property for my third garage."

Third? Where has the time gone? She wondered.

"Headquarters is in San Diego but I suppose I'll be working from Seattle for the foreseeable future."

Georgia blinked rain and tears from her eyes. "What are you saying?"

His dark eyes glinted fiercely. "I'm saying Seattle is where I'll be for the foreseeable future and that I'll hound you to hell if you don't marry me and quick." He gave her a harder jerk then to drive his point home.

Georgia nodded, blinking more rapidly then. "Alright, alright Felix. Whenever you want. Whenever you want." She said and instigated the kiss that time.

***

"The Triumvirate?" Catrina turned the word over in her head.

Damon cut another slice from the monstrous T-bone he'd ordered. "Fancy way of sayin' the three of us- Marc, Houston and me will share equal power at Ramsey South.

Catrina toyed with a lock of her flipped hair. "How did *that* decision go over?"

"Marc was fit to be tied." Damon grinned, recalling the man's reaction, "West said he could leave anytime. Houston was the surprise though. He almost looked happy, but it was like he didn't want Marc to know." He shrugged. "Guess it makes sense for the fool to be happy- he's lucky to have a job and not be sittin' up in some prison like he deserves. That, and the fact that he won't have to make any *real* decisions about anything."

Catrina twisted creamy fettuccine noodles around her fork. "And how do *you* feel about all this?" She kept her gaze on her plate.

Damon chewed the steak while contemplating his answer. "It's important to keep the family together. Mama always wanted this but she never had a full idea of how difficult and different we all are. Pop knew," he grimaced and set down his fork, "he wanted Marc and Houston out before they ruined it all, but he knew how Ma felt about that. I made a promise to him to see that *Ramsey's* name never suffered regardless of what I had to do."

"And does that still mean hiding the dirt they pull no matter how gruesome it is?"

"Sometimes," Damon winced, but his response was honest. "It may very well mean that sometimes, Trina. But I know I can make this *triumvirate* work. Marcus knows he'll have to have *my* say if he expects to get anything done. Maybe it'll cause those two to think before they do somethin' stupid."

Catrina folded her arms across the long black wool duster she wore and frowned. "What if they decided to go *behind your back* and do somethin' stupid?"

Damon muttered a curse. "Then heaven help us." He grabbed his glass and drained it.

***

Book of Scandal

Briselle told herself that she'd talk to Westin later when she peeked into his study and found him working. She'd changed her mind about talking to him three times that week. When they spent time together, she told herself not to ruin a fun time with heavy talk. She was running out of excuses.

"Come over here," West didn't look up from his papers when he called out to his wife.

Bracing herself, Bri made quick work of closing the distance between she and her husband. Less than a second after she rounded the desk, he had her on his lap.

"Aren't you busy?" She asked when West's fingers disappeared between the folds of her robe.

"Never too busy for this…" he murmured against her jaw as softly as his fingers explored the sensitive inner flesh of her thigh.

Briselle shivered. "That's obvious…" she bit her lip when he pulled back to study her.

"You tryin' to attempt a joke?"

"No I-" She cleared her throat. "I'm trying to tell you you're gonna be a father." She felt him grow still beneath her and lowered her eyes. "Guess I should've said you-*may* be a father."

"How long have you known?" He asked, his dark gaze turning stormy when she said 'three months'.

Briselle quickly straightened on his lap. "The doctor said the first three months are the most important. If things progressed well…our chances could be better this time. The others… the others barely lasted beyond a month and a half." She shook her head then as her breathing grew labored. "I'm so scared West. I was gonna wait 'til after I felt it move or kick before I said anything and then Georgia..." She bit her lip and focused on wringing her hands. "I was so happy for her and then she said she wasn't gonna tell Felix. I didn't want to play that game with you. West, what if-"

He wouldn't let her finish. "It'll be different this time." He caught her chin and waited for her light eyes to meet his dark ones. "You'll have everything you need. I won't let you raise a finger even if I have to fly Miss Sybil out here to make you mind."

Briselle laughed through the tears that sprang to life. "Are you happy West?"

He squeezed her chin. "You always make me happy."

***

Carmen would be leaving for school in a couple of weeks. She decided to soak up as much time at home as she could. Jasper wouldn't be down for another visit until the following week and he'd already promised to see her back to school even though she told him that was completely unnecessary.

Besides, he had his own affairs to see to. Jasper's mentor Owen Dowd had passed away from heart disease and Carmen knew Jasper had been stunned by the loss.

In the meantime, Carmen contented herself with the serene beauty of her home and contemplated her future.

The air wasn't quite so brisk that afternoon and kept her on the front porch swing longer than she'd intended. The still of the late evening was beginning to lull her eyes close when gravel crunching alerted her to the car coming up the driveway.

Book of Scandal

Carmen squinted, not quite recognizing the battered Lincoln that jerked to a halt on squeaking brakes. She stood and moved to the edge of the porch. From the railing, she watched a faintly familiar young woman climb out from the driver's side. As the woman drew near, Carmen's confusion cleared.

"Tammy?"

Tammy Burnett offered a wavering smile and fought a battle with her gaze to keep it from faltering. She won the battle.

Carmen was elated to see one of the housemaids from her parents' employ. When she'd let the house staff go, she feared those who'd become like family would never be seen again. She ran down the porch steps to greet Tammy with hugs and kisses.

"It's so good to see you! How've you been? What are you doing with yourself? You talked about going to school- did you follow through with that? Well how are Mr. Vance and Miss Suzetta?"

Tammy laughed at the barrage of questions as Carmen pulled her into another hug. "They're fine." She said remarking on her parents. "Everything's going very well. Very well."

Carmen tiled her head slightly when she edged back from the embrace. Something told her 'very well' wasn't the complete truth.

"Why don't you come in?" She gave Tammy a tiny shake.

"Why don't we sit on the porch, Miss Carmen?"

Book of Scandal

"Okay," Carmen noticed the uneasy look Tammy cast toward the house. "Well I'm at least gonna bring us out some hot tea and sandwiches- it'll make our visit nicer."

"The house is so quiet now. I've been having regrets about letting the staff go but... I felt it was time, you know?"

Tammy nodded and set her tea cup to its saucer. "Everyone understood. With Mr. Quent and now Ms. Marcella gone and your sister and brothers... you were right." She tugged her sweater about slender shoulders and her round cocoa toned face took on a haunting quality as her eyes surveyed the front lawn. She smiled bashfully upon noticing Carmen watching her. "A lot of the older folks were nearing retiring age and then us younger ones were ready to go make our places in the world."

"Well you look fantastic," Carmen reached over to smooth a hand across the woman's denim clad knee. "I'm so glad all's well with you."

Tammy broke into sudden tears.

"Tammy?" Carmen's voice sounded hushed as she left her rocking chair to kneel before Tammy's. "Honey why'd you come here today?"

Several moments passed before Tammy raised her tear-streaked face. "I heard a rumor that Houston attacked a girl who worked for Ramsey. It was a while ago, shortly after me and my folks left..." she fidgeted with the tissue Carmen had pushed into her hands. "I don't know if it was true or not-rumor and all... Lotta people said the family was money hungry so..."

Confused by the story, Carmen shook her head.

Book of Scandal

"Regardless of the family's motives, I knew it was true. I knew it because Houston was the type of man to do something like that and because he learned everything he knew from his brother."

Carmen gasped. "This is about Marc."

"I had his baby, Carmen. A girl." Tammy's lip trembled. "He didn't want it- told me to get rid of it when I told him. He said he didn't care how."

Carmen squeezed Tammy's hands into hers.

"I gave it up at birth. I never looked back. No one knew." Tammy looked back at the house. "I had to work and I couldn't hurt my parents- or yours." She turned her hand over to take Carmen's. "Mr. Quent and Ms. Marcella been so good to my family and I couldn't say anything to scandalize my parents- they had to live and work here too."

"Tammy did you love him?" Carmen asked in a tender tone. She was stunned by the woman's reaction- a wild mix of tears and laughter.

"No..." Tammy wiped her sweater sleeve across her nose. "No Carmen I never loved him. I was...*prepared* for him."

Carmen's hands fell away from Tammy's and she straightened. "What did you say?"

"That's what he called it. Started when I was eleven- with him rubbing me on top of my clothes and then beneath them..." Tammy sniffled and tilted her head back. "He um, he'd take me out to the cottage and do other things, oral things. I never struggled, I...I think he thought I liked it."

Carmen stood, pushing her hands into the side pockets of her checkered swing dress. She walked over to

Book of Scandal

stare across the lawn. "He didn't care whether you liked it or not." She said.

Tammy sniffled again. "One day he took me to the cottage to 'give me what he'd been preparing me for' was sort of how he said it. He forced me...it wasn't the only time after that and- and..." she couldn't finish.

Carmen took pity and ran over to envelope Tammy in another hug. "What can I do for you?" She asked while they embraced.

"I don't want money." Tammy pushed away. "I've always thought that until I told someone- this would always haunt me, rule me." She smiled pitifully. "Now I'll have to see if my theory's right."

"Let me help you." Carmen asked.

Tammy's smile brightened. "You already have- just by listening. I didn't even know anyone would be here. It was a blessing that I found you."

Carmen stared unseeingly past Tammy's shoulder. "He should burn- he should burn in all manner of ways."

"He should do more than burn. But my Mama always say evil don't last always." Tammy's expression grew telling. "He'll be dealt with- one day."

Carmen nodded and pulled Tammy close again. "Damn right. One day."

Daphne had clenched the hem of her sweater vest until her hand had gone numb. She strained to hear more of the conversation she'd walked up on. Once the car had been parked out of sight, she set out on one of her treks across the Ramsey lands.

Book of Scandal

How she craved an hour or two inside the house- if only to pretend. She knew Carmen would be heading back to school and took a chance she'd be gone. There she was though on the front porch and with company- vaguely familiar company. Daphne couldn't place where she'd seen the other woman- then she heard them say something about someone burning and wanted more dirt.

Such was not to be. The vaguely familiar woman and Carmen began discussing their future plans, enjoyed a bit more tea and sat for a while in silence on the porch.

Daphne decided to leave before she was discovered. She cast one last look at the woman and set off with her mind racing.

***

"These cats are for real Charlt," Marcus was saying through the phone in his office at Ramsey.

"Who are they?" Charlton asked following a few silent moments.

"Hard to put a bead on 'em. First sight, I'd have said Mafia, but they talk like bonafide businessmen." He chuckled. "I still got the feelin' that a few of 'em walk on the ill side of legal."

Charlton laughed. "So how much they offerin'?"

Marc made a tsking sound. "See man, that's what you don't get about folks with money and stature. *We* don't discuss the dollars 'til we're ready to deal. It's gonna take a lot more than slick talk and petty ideas to get these dudes to come to the table."

Charlton had made his way out to Hawaii where he was bunking with a buddy from his days in the Navy once

Book of Scandal

the dodging caught up with him. The arm of the chair he occupied grew dented from the blows of his fist.

Marc's haughty attitude could still set him on edge. Charlton didn't know what angered him more, the power Marcus had to do it or the fact that he still let it set him on edge.

"I got a feelin' they're serious and ready to deal some serious dough. If you're serious about this shit, you need to take it slow and do it right."

"Don't worry," Charlton unfurled his fist. "I damn well plan to."

***

"That fucking maid!"

Houston looked up from his stew and cocked a brow toward his wife. "There a problem, dear?"

"I knew she looked familiar," Daphne hissed and flopped back upon the high backed chair at the dining table. "That snippy little maid I met the first time I went to visit your mother at the house."

"Who?" Houston frowned.

"Tammy, Tammy something…I can't recall the last name. It was her, alright."

Houston didn't need the last name. "When did you see her? Daphne?" He called when she still seemed dazed about the face from the past.

"Out there at the house- I went out to look around. Carmen was there- I couldn't get inside." She smoothed the back of her hand across her jaw. "She was on the porch with that Tammy- talking about somebody needing to burn."

Houston's spoon hit the floor with a clatter.

Book of Scandal

  "Houston…" Daphne scolded and went to clean up the spill. "You done with this?" She didn't wait for her husband to respond and went about clearing bowls from the table before she disappeared into the kitchen.

R

~CHAPTER TWENTY-FOUR~

"She was probably there to pick up a check." Marcus guessed when Houston told him about what Daphne saw.

Unlike his brother, Houston wasn't so quick to brush it all off. After all, he knew what had gone on between Marcus and the young maid. He knew what had gone on between Marc and *all* the maids. He also knew that someday somehow some of it would return to haunt his brother. What affected Marc generally tended to affect him, no matter how large or small a part he played.

"You ready for this meeting in our new roles?" Marcus was asking. He was in full business mode-gathering files, scanning them, making corrections.

Houston shrugged while massaging hair where it tapered at his neck. "What the hell does it matter to me?

Book of Scandal

You and Damon'll be butting heads over…whatever anyway."

"Fuck Damon," Marc growled and slapped a folder against the side of his burgundy slacks. "The fool thinks this decree of West's is gonna have me slinkin' off in the shadows or kissin' his boy scout ass. I ain't about to let that happen." He went back to scanning the files. "I waited too long to have a foothold in this place to lose out on any opportunities it might provide me."

Houston stood to leave, realizing Marc was thoroughly involved in prepping for the meeting. His hand paused on the doorknob. "Whatever Tammy was discussing with Carmen it ended with them talking about how someone should burn for what they'd done."

Marcus stopped and straightened behind the cluttered desk.

Houston left the office to the sound of papers spilling from the folder hanging limp in his brother's hand.

***

"I don't care how you spin this. These cuts against the employees won't happen."

Marcus brought his fist down on the conference room table. Houston flinched noticeably in response, while Damon smiled.

"You're tryin' to run this place in the same soft-hearted sappy way Pop did."

"And Ramsey's a multi-million dollar company now." Damon reminded his brother.

"Fuck multi-million." Marc spat, leaning forward to clench a fist to the close curls covering his head. "I'm gonna see Ramsey grow bigger and stronger than that. So strong, white companies won't have a choice but to step aside for us and we ain't gonna get there makin' concession after concession for these damn employees."

"The *damn* employees make it possible for you to live in that ridiculous ass castle of yours." Damon sneered, ignoring the warnings that he was losing his temper. "I say we ain't cuttin' a muthafuckin' thing."

Marc let loose an unexpected chuckle. "Who the hell you 'spose to be, nigga? From what I see, you sittin' alone on that side of the table. The majority," he waved toward himself and Houston, "that would be on our side."

"Marcus, Marcus you never listen to the entire show." Damon laughed then too. "Guess that's why you almost repeated ninth grade, huh? Did you ever hear West say our decisions hinged on votes? The shit's gotta be unanimous. One for all, all for one and all that crap."

Temper raging, Marcus' lashes fluttered close and he cursed himself silently. Preoccupied by Tammy Burnett and what she'd said to his sister, he'd let Damon swoop in and make him look like an idiot. This was definitely not the day for his little brother to try his hand at looking like a big dog. Without another word, Marc stood and decided to leave.

"Givin' up?" Damon couldn't resist one last barb. His teasing mode changed over to deadly when Marc lunged for him.

Houston proved quick on his feet then. He managed to grab Marc's arms, keeping his hands curved tight into the man's jacket's sleeves. Houston held him back, knowing full well the damage their younger brother could do to a face and body.

***

Jasper sat in a state of stunned awe and then shook his head. "Could there be some kind of mistake here, sir?" He asked of the man seated across from him.

Wesley Carroll Vining, Esquire smiled sympathetically at the young man who had yet to grasp the fact that he was a multi-millionaire.

"Doctor Dowd had no children, son." Wesley Vining sought to explain once more. "What family he had left him a good number of those millions you just inherited. The research facility you also inherited, made the doctor millions more besides. Now, it's all yours."

Jasper ran a finger inside his shirt collar and stood. "Why would he do this?" He whispered while pacing the dim, graceful office.

Wesley Vining chuckled. "I asked the good doctor that very thing. By the time he was done explaining, I understood perfectly. He said he'd sensed a kinship in you Jasper- something which came through in word, deed and personality. He said, in all his years of learning, teaching, researching, he'd never met anyone who measured up to the passion- the desire to obtain as much knowledge about the field of study he'd been mesmerized by his entire life."

"But Mr. Vining," Jasper shook his head yet again. "I'm a nobody. For Doctor Owen to waste-"

"Hold it right there, son." Wesley Vining clasped his beefy hands together atop a pristine desk. "I've known many people. I've met and counseled a great many educators, heads of state, even some royalty, but never, had I met true genius until I met Owen Baker Dowd." Wesley began cleaning spectacles he'd pulled from his vest pocket.

Book of Scandal

"A man that insightful that gifted didn't make errors in judgment."

Void of argument, Jasper eventually reclaimed the seat before the attorney's massive pine desk.

Nodding, Wesley Vining affixed the spectacles across a long, thin nose which seemed out of place in the middle of his round face. "Doctor Dowd called in a few favors and got you accepted to his Alma Mater- you're on your way to college, son." He smirked when Jasper appeared stunned anew. "Seems the good doctor intended for you to continue his work." The attorney laughed when Jasper slid down a bit in the chair. "Son? Are you up to doing this now?" Wesley removed his specs and tapped them to the thick folder he'd read from. "We're only at the tip of the iceberg here, you up for it?"

Jasper blinked, nodded and cleared his throat. He straightened in the chair. "Yes. Yes sir, for Doctor Owen, I sure as hell am."

***

Carmen was perched on the edge of Roberta Lowery's desk. The two young women were laughing and talking when Carmen heard her name. She turned to see Houston on his way toward her.

"Bobbie would you tell Damon I stopped by?" Carmen eased off the desk. "I really need to see him."

"Sure thing, girl." Bobbie stood from her chair to kiss Carmen's cheek.

"Why was Tammy Burnett at the house?" Houston approached just as Bobbie left the desk.

"Tammy? How-?"

"Daphne told me."

Book of Scandal

Carmen leaned on the desk again. "What was Daphne doing at the house?"

"Dammit Carm, why was Tammy there?"

"Why are *you* so interested in a maid?"

"Was she there to pick up a check?" Houston had never practiced the art of subtlety and he wasn't about to start.

"No, she wasn't there for a check." Carmen toyed with a bouncy lock of her hair and surveyed her brother with open suspicion. She wasn't about to give him a run down of her conversation with Tammy. Besides, part of her believed he already knew. The reality of it had anger roiling like sickness in her belly. She allowed the emotion to get the better of her.

"I'm here to see Damon about a story I just heard. Sick events that occurred right under our very roof." She pushed off the desk and stood face to face with her brother. "Since I can't see West right now, Damon'll do just fine."

Houston groped his pockets for a handkerchief and mopped sweat from his neck. He watched Carmen storm down the corridor, then he ambled over to Bobbie's desk and called Marcus.

***

Westin leaned against the doorway to the sitting room and rapped lightly against the jamb until he'd captured his wife's attention.

"When I told you to take it easy, I didn't mean to become a prisoner in this house."

Briselle's smile was there but wavering. Gently, she set down the book she'd been reading. "All during those first three months, I prepared myself to lose it." She looked

Book of Scandal

down at her hands smoothing across the wheat colored housecoat she wore. "I've never been pregnant longer than two months before. I'm into my fourth month now and back to being terrified." She swiped at an escaped tear. "I don't want anything to harm it."

Westin pushed his tall frame off the doorway, dropped his coat and briefcase to the sofa and came to sit at his wife's feet. "You couldn't harm it if you tried. You're the most careful person I know." He kissed her hand where it lay in her lap. "The others...the other babies- they weren't meant to be, darlin'. It wasn't our time."

"I think it kicked." She whispered. "At least that's what it felt like." She took West's hand and rested it against her belly. "I started to call Doc Seltzer but I didn't want to overreact. Isn't it too early for it to be kicking, West? What if-?"

"Hey?' He moved up to kiss her forehead, cheek and mouth. "It's a sign."

"A-a sign?" Briselle spoke the wore as if it were foreign to her.

"Look at how different things are for us now, girl." He toyed with the soft hair curling about her face. "We're married, got a new life, new connection to each other, new town in a whole new part of the country. Georgia's *working* and *pregnant?"*

Briselle burst into hearty laughter.

"Now if *that* ain't a sign, tell me what is?"

"Our child will be fine." He said once their laughter curbed. "It'll be a force to be reckoned with and time enough for all the so-called bad asses in this family and anybody else." West leaned close to brush away another of

Book of Scandal

Bri's escaped tears. "I can't ease your mind about all this. Only you have the power to accept what will be will be-good or bad. But Bri," he nuzzled his dark handsome face into her neck. "If you expect the baby to have a fighting chance, you gotta put these bad thoughts on the back burner, you know?" He kissed her mouth again and stood.

"West?" Briselle called when he was back at the doorway. "Thank you."

***

Romance was the order of the evening at the secluded Ramsey mansion. Following his meeting with Owen Dowd's attorney, Jasper snapped out of his daze, packed clothes and headed for Savannah.

He'd called ahead and told Carmen to expect him and she certainly was when he knocked on the door around four that afternoon. He had no chance to tell her his news, for she drew him into a kiss the moment he crossed the threshold. They made love in the midst of soft music and candlelight for hours it seemed.

The lion share of candlelight radiated from Carmen's bedroom. Jasper placed her gently upon crisp lavender sheets and made quick work of their clothes. He made quick work of *his* clothes. Carmen's dainty cream colored negligee hit the floor soon after he'd arrived at the house. Their movements on the bed were languid and tender. Though quite familiar with one another already; their mouths were seeking traveling every area of each other. When Jasper claimed her body, Carmen cried out that she loved him. Moments later, Jasper was murmuring his love for her while nibbling her earlobe.

Book of Scandal

"Jasper! Oh Jasper it's all so incredible. I'm so happy for you." Carmen rested across Jasper's chest later as they lounged on her tousled king-sized bed. He'd just told her of all the miraculous changes in his life.

"I still can't believe he did this, don't understand *why* he did this and for me." Jasper smirked at Carmen. "I can only admit that to you. Sayin' it to anybody else...I feel like I'm second-guessing Doctor Owen's decision."

Carmen nodded. "I understand." She raked her nails across the sleek expanse of his chocolate-toned chest. "Your background- what you suffered because of your mother...you never felt worthy." She pressed a sweet kiss to the center of his chest. "Maybe now you will and not because of the money. Doctor Dowd didn't know anything about you, he only knew *you, saw* you and what he saw was good. So good."

Jasper kissed her hard. "What's so good, is you. So good for me. I don't deserve you Carm."

She hugged him tight. "Yes you do."

Jasper glimpsed his wristwatch when their laughter quieted. "It'll be dark soon. I should get going."

"I wish you wouldn't."

"Carm..."

"Please Jas? Please stay?"

Uncertainty shadowed Jasper's attractive milk chocolate face and he bit his lower lip. Regardless of all the time they'd spent together at the Ramsey house, he'd yet to spend an entire night. He'd never assumed and Carmen had never pressed, until that night.

"My stuff is still at the motel."

Book of Scandal

She cupped his face. "So go get it. I want you to stay all night-*every* night until it's time for us to go."

They sealed the decision with a kiss.

***

Felix couldn't believe Georgia didn't want a lavish wedding and reception. If anyone would relish the moment as center of attention surrounded by hundreds of adoring guests and dressed in a gown to kill for it was Georgia Willette Ramsey.

"Hush." Georgia waved off her fiancé's summation and finished filing a folder of notes in the cabinet behind her desk. "Anyway, I'd feel too trashy walkin' down the aisle already knocked up."

"G..." Felix's features tightened. "Don't say it that way."

"Sorry, *pregnant.*" She whirled away from the cabinet and graced him with a bow. "But there's no glossing over the fact that it'd still be trashy."

Felix came round to perch on the edge of the desk. "I always thought people who went for all the frills felt stronger about holdin' it together."

"Hmph. That's because they know they'd have a pissed off family who went to all that expense so they could throw it away like yesterday's-"

"Trash?"

Georgia laughed and came to sit next to Felix. "It's just not for me- all that sappy stuff."

"That because you're a hard-nosed businesswoman now?" He nudged her shoulder.

She fiddled with the lacy cuff of her blouse. "I just became a businesswoman. I've always been hard and that's just it." She gave a quick toss of her elegant bob. "I don't regret being that way- I won't apologize for it. Trouble is, I don't know how being hard fits in with being a wife."

Felix turned slightly toward her. "What are you tryin' to tell me, G?"

She looked toward the windows outlining her office, but Felix took her chin and made her look his way.

"It's just…if we don't work out-"

"G…"

"Just let me say this, okay?" She pulled his hand from her chin and squeezed it. "If we don't work out, I want you to know I'm sorry."

His expression softened and he grasped the neckline of her blouse. "Shut up, G." He whispered before kissing her.

***

Carmen heard the faint sound of gravel crunching beneath car tires and she shivered in anticipation of Jasper's return. She wrapped herself in the bed sheet and went to meet him at the door in what she considered a far more enticing outfit than she'd worn when he'd visited earlier that afternoon.

She was halfway down the staircase when she realized a key was scratching the lock. A second later, Marcus stepped into the foyer.

Every part of her said to run, but she stood her ground refusing to be frightened by him… that time. He stopped near the archway leading toward the staircase.

"Why'd Tammy Burnett come to see you?"

"You know damn well *why*."

"Watch it little sister," Marcus smiled, but the gesture was danger personified.

Carmen though, was too angry then- angry over her brother's obvious evil and how he'd used it to belittle others. "Or what?" She spat, emboldened by her despise. "You can't threaten me with losing my job or with my family being tossed out on the streets." She sauntered down to the next stair and crossed her arms over her chest. "That *is* what you threatened Tammy with, isn't it? I wonder how many others?" She sneered, never really taking note of the way Marc advanced up the staircase.

"Between you and Houston, I wonder just how many maids there've been."

Marcus stopped his advance.

Carmen smiled. "Yeah, I know what he did to the girl in the youth division. I'm willing to bet he dallied with quite a few of them." She shrugged. "Guess this one just got out of hand, huh?"

"You shouldn't be talkin' about things you don't understand," he practically growled the words.

"Fuck you Marcus. You, Houston and that bitch Daphne with her nosy ass. The three of you will rot in hell one day."

Marc smiled then. "Not today."

Carmen found herself in her brother's vice grip before it even registered to her what had happened. She screamed, trying to wrench her arms from his grasp and succeeding. She scrambled back up the staircase, but the sheet twisted about her legs and hindered escape.

Marcus caught hold of her just as she reached the second floor landing. Carmen still fought wildly, biting,

Book of Scandal

scratching…She succeeded in drawing more than a few painful grunts from him. Soon though, he had her out of the sheet. Carmen slapped him hard once he'd rolled her to her back.

"Damn you!" Her face went ashen when she read the intention in his eyes. Fight rose up in her like a wave and she pit her fists against his chest and neck.

Marcus pulled her across his shoulder and carried her screaming into her bedroom.

Jasper had finished packing his things, but hadn't left the motel. He sat on the edge of the room's bed and studied the simple yet elegant silver band with its diamond setting. He intended to propose before taking Carmen back to school but he wouldn't press for an answer until they saw each other during their first breaks.

How many times since their first time together had he wanted to propose? Countless times. Finally, he felt worthy enough to do the deed. It'd be a lengthy engagement. He wouldn't marry her until they were both done with their educations and ready to move forward.

Satisfied that the plan was solid, Jasper grabbed his bags and pushed the ring into his jean pocket. He was ready to see the look on Carmen's incredible face when he got down on his knees and asked her to be his wife.

Carmen lay trembling and naked in the middle of the bed but it was Marc's face that held the look of true terror. He'd been so blind with rage he could hardly recall the events of the past few minutes. He recalled enough though-enough to know that he was a dead man. West and

Book of Scandal

Damon would tear him apart…He was a dead man…if his sister talked.

"Don't make me do this again, Carm." He forced himself to complete the sentence. "Don't say a word about tonight or what you *think* you know about that Burnett bitch." He buckled the belt around his slacks. "Don't make me do this again." He said one last time before leaving the room.

Jasper felt so elated by what was about to take place, that he almost drove head on into the car that raced toward him along the winding road leading to the Ramsey place. He straightened abruptly behind the wheel and tooted his horn at the wayward driver. Even that near miss, wasn't enough to sour his mood and he whistled along to the smooth crooning of the Delfonics hit from back in '68, *"La La Means I Love You"*.

The whistling continued well past him parking the Impala and shutting down the engine. He pranced up the wide porch steps and knocked only to discover the door already cracked open.

Jasper's guard heightened. "Carmen?" He whispered, his brown gaze alert as he observed. He made his way up the staircase as if drawn there. His heart lurched to his throat when he saw the sheet on the landing. He bolted for Carmen's room, stopping cold when he saw her curled upon the bed.

"Carm? Carmen?" His voice sounded more frantic the closer he came to her. He sat on the bed and placed his hand to her shoulder. She whimpered like a wounded animal and curled into an even tighter ball.

"Carmen...baby what is it?" His breathing was forced as he took in the sight of her- a mute, trembling mass. He bowed his head to stave off the fear claiming him.

Then, after a few more terrifying seconds, Jasper's gaze narrowed. He recalled the seemingly insignificant car that had passed him on the road moments earlier.

"Marcus was here." He stated rather than questioned. He had his answer though when she whimpered again and trembled with renewed vigor.

Jasper didn't dare touch her then. His rage was so peaked that he didn't trust himself to do so. Rising then, he pulled the bed spread across her body and secured the house before he left.

***

The sound of shattering glass had Josephine rushing down the staircase with a fireplace poker in hand. The elegant train of her coral house robe flew like a flame behind her and she held the look of a ravishing angel. Whoever threatened to awaken her sleeping baby was about to get the beating of his life.

"It's Mr. Marcus ma'am." Fritz, the houseman whispered the news while casting uneasy glances toward the study.

Josephine kept hold of the poker, but let it dangle at her side while she went to investigate.

In the study, Marc was attempting to pour whiskey into a glass. His hand shook so badly that he poured most of it on the floor where the previous whiskey bottle had shattered.

Josephine watched the scene in awe. Before she could question it however, a booming knock sounded at the

front. Fritz barely had time to pull open the door, when
Jasper Stone bulldozed inside.

Josephine ran out to see to the new commotion.
When she saw the rabid look on Jasper's face, she simply
pointed toward the study.

"Josie!" Marcus called when he spotted his old
friend. "Josephine call the cops! Now, dammit!" His voice
carried on a pitiful chord.

Fascinated by what she hoped was about to take
place, Josephine leaned against the study doorway. Fritz
was joined by many other house servants; who came to see
to the uproar. They all sent Josephine the strangest looks
when she told them everything was fine.

Meanwhile, Jasper was on the rampage, massacring
everything in his path. Marcus could barely get to his feet
when Jasper threw him across the desk. He made no
attempt to fight back.

Josephine felt her body jerk with every punch. She
imagined herself in Jasper Stone's place as the attacker
giving her jackass of a husband a mere slice of what he
deserved.

Jasper wore himself out punching. Inhaling deep
gulps of air, he gripped Marc's jaw and smiled when the
man squealed in pain.

"I don't know what you did to her, but I know it
was vile." He snarled, squeezing Marc's jaw tighter. "The
day she confesses it, is the day I come after you. God help
you then because no one else will and you sure as hell
won't survive what I'll have on tap for your pathetic ass."
He let Marc drop like a bag of rocks and kicked him away
when he landed at his boots.

"Josephine..." Jasper groaned when he snapped out of his rage and observed the affects of his wrath. "I'm so sorry."

Josephine's smile was broad and gleeful. "There's absolutely no need for you to apologize for this."

For an instant, Jasper's eyes softened with understanding.

***

Marcus and Houston walked such a fine line everyone questioned the sudden change in their demeanors. Josephine didn't breathe a word of what happened with Jasper Stone. Her silence was mostly due to the fact that she didn't completely understand what it was about. She knew her dearly beloved certainly wasn't going to confide.

Not that it mattered overmuch. It was enough fun watching Marcus; not only looking across his shoulder for Jasper, but wondering when or if Josephine would spill the beans about what she'd overheard. Of course, Jasper hadn't revealed much- what he did say was cryptic at best.

At any rate, Josephine kept waiting for Marc to threaten her with it. He hadn't made a peep, though. Josephine wouldn't let herself grow too confident however. The old Marc would resurface soon enough. She'd just enjoy the peace until then.

***

Daphne finally tuned into the fact that something she'd said about Tammy Burnett had set her husband and his brother on edge. It was clear that Houston was even more out of sorts than usual. She sensed his paranoia and couldn't resist letting the feeling penetrate her as well.

***

Book of Scandal

Briselle and Georgia had settled into the reality that they were about to become mothers. Briselle felt a sense of hope for the first time. Her doctor's appointments went splendidly, her health was at its peak and all looked fine with the baby. The sisters-in-law were so elated by all the changes in their lives, they formed their own mommy's club. Ignoring their husbands' amusement, the young women met every other Saturday for shopping, movies or simply tea and treats at home. On a particular tea and treats afternoon, the club gained an unexpected member.

"Cowardly son of a bitch."
"He didn't walk away Georgie."
"Right. He probably didn't even take time to tie his shoes after you told him you were pregnant." Georgia drawled.
"It wasn't like that Georgie." Carmen braced her elbows on her knees and puffed out her cheeks. "I was the one who broke things off with him."
"What?" Georgia moved closer to the armchair Briselle occupied. "What made you do a dumb thing like that?"
"Georgia…" Briselle scolded. Her gaze narrowed when she turned back to observe Carmen, taking note of her strange mood.
"I still say he's a son of a bitch," Georgia pushed her hands into the front pockets of her apron, "bet he didn't waste time heading out when you told him to hit the road. Men…"
Briselle closed her eyes, knowing where the conversation would lead. Felix would be lucky if he got

past the front door that evening. "Uh, Georgia let's get Carmen some more tea," she passed her sister-in-law the half empty ceramic pot. "And fix her a sandwich. I know that plane food leaves a lot to be desired."

Georgia did as Briselle asked. She left the room grumbling about the shortcomings of men while she switched out of the living room.

"Now why don't you tell me what happened?" Briselle left her chair to sit next to Carmen on the sofa. "What really happened?"

Carmen was undoubtedly emotional, but she didn't break into tears. In a manner that was nothing short of eerie, she told Briselle about her special last evening with Jasper and what happened after he left.

Briselle sat in shock for a full minute, and then scrambled to the end table for the phone.

"What are you doing?" Carmen gasped.

"Calling West."

"You can't!"

"Carmen!" Briselle tried to break free of the woman's grip on her wrist.

"No Bri, no!"

"Honey what-"

"You can't say a thing- nothing Bri, do you hear me? Not a word to my family- especially West and Damon."

Briselle took a moment to catch her breath. "Does Jasper know?"

"He...suspects. I wouldn't confirm it. He half killed Marcus just on the suspicion of it."

Book of Scandal

"He deserved it and more. Oh God Carmen how can you let him get away with this? Why can't you-" Her eyes lowered to Carmen's stomach. "Oh no..."

"Now you see why?"

"Honey..." Briselle squeezed her hands. "What will you do?"

Carmen hugged herself. "Have it. Love it."

"Honey," Briselle uttered a silent curse. "This won't be an easy pregnancy. Every day, you'll be reminded of it. You don't have to have-"

"No Bri. I won't do that." Carmen smiled and brushed her hand along Briselle's cheek. "I can pretend it's the baby Jasper and I should've had."

"It could be, you know? It could be Jasper's."

Carmen smiled over the romantic notion. "It'd never work out that beautifully and there's no way to tell...living the lie is the next best thing."

"Sweetie..."

"Promise me, Bri." Carmen held the flaring sleeve of Briselle's blouse. "You keep this. You take this to your grave."

It was the last thing Briselle wanted, but she'd do nothing to upset Carmen not when the woman already felt so alone. "To my grave."

"I wanna hug." Georgia whined playfully when she returned to the room and found Carmen and Bri embracing.

"It's gonna be fine, girl." Georgia whispered and kissed her sister's temple. "We're gonna be the best Mamas three kids ever had. Hell y'all, this shit has got to be some sort of sign."

Carmen and Briselle exchanged skeptical looks.

Book of Scandal

Georgia rolled her eyes. "Come on, the three of us in this situation- at the *same* time?"

Briselle took their hands. "It's a *good* sign then. We're gonna raise these three with all the love we can muster." She squeezed Carmen's hand tighter. "We're gonna teach 'em to respect themselves and others."

"We're gonna teach 'em to be strong." Georgia added with a pert nod. "They're gonna have the kind of strength this family's gonna need to face whatever's waiting down the road."

Carmen nodded and a genuine smile broke through on her face. "Strength," she repeated.

Laughter erupted between the three and another hug was in order.

Book of Scandal

~EPILOGUE~

Winter 1971~

"Come spring you'll be a mother of two Mrs. Ramsey. Two can make a wealth of noise, I know."

"I'm ready." Josephine's smile was hopeful. "My Moses is barely two, but I can already tell he's a little *too* curious. He needs a little brother or sister to lavish some of that curiosity on. Maybe having someone else to occupy his time will keep him from being such a busy body."

Dr. Benson Yontz bellowed a laugh. "You're in for quite a surprise then, Mrs. Ramsey. Have you settled on a name yet?"

Josephine's easy expression sharpened a tad. "If it's a girl, Fernelle- after my sister who... she passed away

Book of Scandal

unexpectedly many years ago." She sighed. "If it's a boy, Fernando- that's close enough too."

Dr. Yontz was a bit somber then. "I can tell you loved your sister a lot."

"Yes," Josephine nodded and gripped the strap of her purse tighter. "We were very close. My husband thought a lot of her too- this way he'll never forget her."

***

"Ouch!" Catrina gasped and placed a hand to her side. Without looking, she knew her husband had pushed himself to stand from the kitchen table.

"It's alright," she called, "one of 'em just kicked the hell out of me."

Slowly, Damon came round the table and joined his wife where she leaned against the counter. He and Catrina had been told to expect twins soon. The possibility of a double birth had the family on pins of excitement.

The mom-to-be however was more excited by the possibility of the babies making their debut and kicking something besides her insides.

"Quiet as lambs now," Catrina laughed when Damon put his hand on her stomach. "You must have some power over them."

Damon smirked. "They know who's in charge."

"Right…let's see you say that when they're out and using your head for a punching bag."

"Trina…" Damon seemed to grow serious then. "I just hope they're good and not…not monsters." He pulled his hand away from her stomach when he spoke the last word.

Book of Scandal

Catrina pulled it back. "You don't have to worry about that. They will be good- good through and through. With you for a father, they'll have no choice."

Damon looked down. "My father was a good man." She cupped his face and made him look up. "Yes. Yes he was."

Finally Damon nodded as though he'd decided to dwell on that fact alone. He gave a refreshing sigh and squeezed his wife's hands where they rested on his face.

"I predict this next generation will make the Ramseys the family my father wanted. It'll be tough- we've really made a mess of things."

"Amen." Catrina agreed with a smile. "But I've got faith in them too."

"You think they can handle it?" Damon asked and felt double kicks thud against his hand.

"Ouch!" Catrina laughed. She was still laughing when Damon pulled her into a kiss.

Greetings and Thank You for Reading This Latest Ramsey Effort,

Now you know where all the drama originated. You've also been given a peek into how this drama orchestrated much of what occurred in the original series and what's to come in the stories featuring the Ramsey cousins.

Authors often thank their readers for making what they do possible. When I say 'thank you readers', it goes far beyond simple gratification. At the onset of this series, I had no idea the 'Elders' would play such a key role in the progression of the book. Various readers have contacted me since the release of the first title in 2006. I've been asked whether a story on the Elders would be forthcoming. I'd never even thought of a story on Marcus, Houston, Damon and all the rest- so to complete this project has been an incredible experience for me. I treasure your encouragement.

Thank you just doesn't seem to cut it when I try to express how much I appreciate my reader base. Spending your hard earned money and your valuable time especially following these characters and situations from my imagination means the world to me. I love you guys.

See you in 2011 with "A Lover's Shame".

Blessings,
AlTonya
www.lovealtonya.com

AlTonya Washington began her writing career in 2004 with the publication of her first novel "Remember Love". Since then, the award-winning author has published works in the contemporary and historical romance genres. Her most recent projects have resulted in work from the erotica genre under the pen name T. Onyx. The Ramsey series is her most expansive literary effort. In addition to working on new twists and turns for her various writing endeavors; AlTonya spends her days in North Carolina as a Senior library assistant. She also wears the hat of Mom-which is her most rewarding endeavor.

46038110R00234

Made in the USA
Middletown, DE
20 July 2017